Praise for *The Well*

"Stephanie Landsem breathes fresh life and understanding into the story of the woman at the well. Under her skilled pen, the characters, the setting, the history of ancient Samaria spring to life. *The Well* is a debut to stir the soul."

—Elizabeth Ludwig, author of *No Safe Harbor*

"It's a rare story that you can't put down. Even rarer is a story that compels you to set it aside, reflect, and pray before you can go any further. Stephanie Landsem takes a tale you think you know and leaves you breathless with unexpected discoveries. I found myself stunned by *The Well* and humbled and inspired by the faith journey of her characters. This is a masterpiece."

—Regina Jennings, author of *Love in the Balance* and *Sixty Acres and a Bride*

"A captivating account based on a familiar biblical story. Stephanie Landsem brings clarity, hope, reflection, and plenty of enchantment to *The Well*."

—Alice J. Wisler, author of *Rain Song* (Christy Finalist) and other Southern fiction

"As you open the pages of Stephanie Landsem's *The Well*, get ready to embark on a journey through the places where Jesus traveled—breathe the scent of an olive grove, taste the barley bread and sweet melon, walk along the dusty road to Galilee. Most of all, get ready to have your own faith stretched as you read about those lives Jesus touched and how they were never the same again."

—Ruth Axtell, author of *Her Good Name* and *Moonlight Masquerade*

"Stephanie Landsem breaks into historical biblical fiction with an intriguing and compelling story. *The Well* is sure to win the hearts of readers, and Landsem is a welcomed new voice to the publishing world."

—Rachel Hauck, bestselling, award-winning author of
The Wedding Dress and *Once Upon a Prince*

"In *The Well* Stephanie Landsem has written a biblical novel that tells about a little-known woman's encounter with Jesus which will resonate with readers. I felt I was right there, struggling with Mara, aching with her in all her agonies, and cheering for her to struggle through them. Stephanie Landsem is a writer to watch."

—Lauraine Snelling, author of the Red River of the North series and *Reunion*

The
WELL

The
WELL

a novel

Stephanie Landsem

HOWARD BOOKS
A DIVISION OF SIMON & SCHUSTER, INC.

New York   Nashville   London   Toronto   Sydney   New Delhi

Howard Books
A Division of Simon & Schuster, Inc.
1230 Avenue of the Americas
New York, NY 10020

Scripture quotations taken from THE HOLY BIBLE, NEW INTERNATIONAL VERSION®, NIV®. Copyright © 1973, 1978, 1984 by Biblica US, Inc.®. Used by permission.

First Howard Books trade paperback edition June 2013

HOWARD and colophon are trademarks of Simon & Schuster, Inc.

For information about special discounts for bulk purchases, please contact Simon & Schuster Special Sales at 1-866-506-1949 or business@simonandschuster.com.

The Simon & Schuster Speakers Bureau can bring authors to your live event. For more information or to book an event contact the Simon & Schuster Speakers Bureau at 1-866-248-3049 or visit our website at www.simonspeakers.com.

Designed by Kyoko Watanabe

Manufactured in the United States of America

10   9   8   7   6   5   4   3   2   1

Library of Congress Cataloging-in-Publication Data
Landsem, Stephanie.
    The well : a novel / Stephanie Landsem.
        p. cm.
    1. Samaritan woman (Biblical figure)—Fiction. 2. Bible. N.T.—History of Biblical events—Fiction. 3. Women in the Bible—Fiction. I. Title.
    PS3612.A5493W45 2013
    813'.6—dc23
            2012023945

ISBN 978-1-4516-8885-6
ISBN 978-1-4516-8886-3 (ebook)

To my parents, Bill and Jeanette Wetzel,
who know and live sacrificial love

Chapter 1

Dread coiled like an asp in Mara's belly as the watery light of dawn seeped through the chinks in the roof of the clay house.

Only a short span of dirt floor stretched between her mother's corner of their one-room house to where Mara and her little brother lay pressed against its farthest wall. Mara's worn cloak, pulled over their heads like a shield, had failed to block out the carnal whispers that had drifted through the confines of the dark room during the long night. Shame and fear had twined with tormented dreams until she prayed for dawn.

Now, as the murky beams of weak light puddled on the floor, Mara raised her head and strained to see through the gloom. *Is Alexandros still here?*

Relief trickled through her stiff limbs. Her mother slept alone in the corner. When had Alexandros left? And where did he go? How could Mama be so foolish? *Please, Lord, let no one find out about him.*

Mara's bare arms, prickly with cold, were wrapped around Asher's small warm body.

She slipped from under her cloak and eased herself away from her little brother. As she kissed his smooth cheek and tucked the tattered wool around his shoulders, he opened his sleep-clouded eyes.

"Shh, my sweet, go back to your dreams," she whispered, rubbing his back. Asher garbled a few words, wedged his thumb in his mouth, and closed his eyes again. Mara stroked his back until his mouth went slack and his breath buzzed in a steady rhythm.

Silently, she crept past her sleeping mother. Nava lay crumpled in the corner like a pile of dirty rags. She would not stir until mid-morning. Then she would act as if nothing had happened, as if she'd done nothing wrong.

Alexandros, a pagan from Sebaste, had visited her mother before. He didn't seem concerned about Nava's reputation. He ate their food, little as there was, complimenting Nava more boldly and laughing more loudly after each cup of wine.

Each time, they had been lucky. No one in Sychar seemed to know of his visits. Not yet. But the Sychar Samaritans did not abide sinners in their midst. When they found out—and they would find out—the strict townspeople would turn on them. They would surely stop providing the barley and oil that Mara's family needed so desperately. They could, according to the law, march down the hill and drive them out of Sychar. No one in Samaria would take in a disgraced woman, a crippled boy, and a daughter old enough to be married.

Starvation or exile. Which was worse?

Mara stepped outside into the damp chill of dawn. The birds, chattering more loudly as crimson light stained the eastern sky, seemed to be scolding her. They should be scolding her mother. *What are you doing to us, Mama?*

Tall cedars and even taller mountains surrounded the little house, throwing dark shadows over the doorway and onto the front courtyard carved out of the scrubby bushes. A jumble of chipped clay pots and jars sat along the wall next to piles of straw and kindling. A few paces away, a whisper of smoke rose from the black remains of the cooking fire.

The familiar rumble of hunger twisted Mara's stomach. Asher would be hungry too. The good people of Sychar gave them almost enough barley to live on. She knew exactly how much they had left: two meals' worth—if they were careful. There would be no more if the town discovered Nava's shame. Mara bent toward the fire to add a handful of straw to the last glowing coal, but straightened with a breath of surprise as a looming form rustled out of the dark bushes.

"Good morning, Mara," Alexandros said, adjusting his short tunic.

She turned her head away, but not quickly enough to miss the smirk on Alexandros's lips.

"I'm thirsty, girl." He dangled a water skin in front of her averted face.

She glanced at him as she took it, careful not to touch his hand. His eyes were bleary and puffed—the result of the wine he had drunk last night—but his smirk of lingering satisfaction deepened. He didn't look ashamed of what he had done with her mother. But why should he be? A pagan from Sebaste need not submit to the strict laws of Sychar.

Mara ladled the last of their water into the skin as Alexandros leaned against the wall, watching her. He was a big man, solid and strong, with short brown hair and light eyes that she tried to avoid. His clothes were clean and well made, and gold rings flashed on his ears and fingers. She had heard whispers that some of the village women thought him handsome, but he reminded Mara of the wild dogs that prowled the hills, preying on lost lambs. She handed the water skin to him without a word and bent back to the fire.

He drained the water in several big gulps, then crouched down close beside her. "What do you have for food?" he asked.

Mara hunched her shoulders and inched away but didn't reach toward the cooking pot. If he ate their barley, she and Asher would go hungry today. She watched the tiny licks of flame devour the handful of straw. "Just some barley."

He grunted and waved his hand. "Don't bother. Barley's for animals." Alexandros heaved himself to his feet. "Time for me to go." He followed the worn path to the back of the house, where he had left his pack animal.

Mara fed a piece of kindling to the crackling fire. She couldn't let him leave without asking. She had to know. She stood, rubbed her damp hands down her dirty tunic, and followed Alexandros.

A rickety lean-to clung to the back of the house, and the garden stretched behind, tilled and planted. Alexandros unhobbled the huge, spotted donkey that had stripped the leaves from Mara's struggling fig tree while his master had defiled her mother. It bared its long, yellow teeth at her. Crossing her arms in front of her chest, she swallowed hard and blurted, "Are you going to Sychar? To the marketplace?"

If he showed up in Sychar, just over the hill to the east, at this time of morning, there would be questions. If they didn't know already, someone would surely discover where he had spent the night. She wouldn't be surprised if the bragging dog told them himself.

He stepped close enough for her to see his bloodshot eyes and the rough stubble on his jaw. She ducked her head and focused on his sandal-clad feet.

"Afraid that the pious Chosen Ones of God will disapprove of your mother's good fortune last night?" he asked.

Mara kept her gaze on his worn leather sandals, but her face burned like the rising sun. He knew what would happen if the strict villagers found out that her mother had entertained him overnight.

"What? Worried that the last of God's Chosen People won't give you and the boy any more barley if they find out that Nava shared her bed with a pagan?" He stepped even closer. She smelled his sour sweat and the stench of last night's wine on his breath.

Mara's legs weakened, and her heart pounded. Who would give charity to a woman who flouted the laws of Moses so shamelessly? Her mother had done more than lie with the pagan; she had put her family at his mercy. One word from him in the marketplace and . . . starvation or exile.

Alexandros ran a warm, moist hand over her hair and down her cheek. She squeezed her eyes shut. He cupped her chin and lifted her face. "Let me see those eyes of yours, girl." His hand tightened painfully on her jaw.

She opened her eyes. His face was close, his eyes narrow and rimmed with red.

A smile lifted his thin lips. "If you keep me happy, there won't be any reason for me to spill your secret, eh, girl?"

She wrenched her face away, fear drying her mouth. Alexandros laughed and jerked at his donkey, turning the big animal toward the path that ran west. "I'm low on merchandise. I'm heading to Sebaste this morning, then to Caesarea. Tell your mother I'll be back in a couple of weeks." He paused, and his gaze traveled from Mara's head to her dirty bare feet. He licked his pale lips. "I'll be looking forward to seeing you again." He started down the path, away from Sychar, but looked over his shoulder. "Don't worry, Mara. This will be our little secret . . . for now."

Mara's heart slowed its frantic pounding only when Alexandros and his donkey disappeared around a twist in the path.

She rubbed her face where the imprint of his fingers still burned, then picked up the empty water jar. A trip to the well, where women traded gossip like men traded grain in the marketplace, would surely tell her if anyone in the village already knew of her mother's shame. She threw a striped cloth over her long, tangled hair and started up the steep path.

Mara crested the ridge above her house and descended into a wide valley, her lips moving over her morning prayers. She prayed first for Asher and then for her mother as Gerizim, the mountain of blessings, rose on one side and Ebal, the mountain of curses, swelled on the other. She thanked the God of Abraham for the recent rains that had watered their garden and then asked for her grain jar somehow to be filled. She begged that her mother's secret shame would remain known only to her.

Lord, send the Taheb to your people. The ancient appeal eased her mind like a soothing balm. Someday the Taheb, the Restorer, would come.

She passed the outskirts of Sychar, just a cluster of clay houses and a marketplace. A few women stood in the shadowy doorways. She knew them all by name, had known them all her life. Some turned their backs to her as she passed. A few shook their heads, their mouths pinched in disapproval. If they found out what Nava had done last night—if just one had seen Alexandros this morning—their outrage would descend like a plague of locusts.

Just past the village, the path met a wider, deeply rutted road.

It came from Jerusalem and stretched north through Galilee, all the way to far-off Damascus. Her pace slowed as she walked past wide swaths of green barley and groves of silver-green olive trees. Around a sharp curve lay Jacob's well, the only source of water in Sychar. She dragged her feet around the bend, forcing her head up and straightening her shoulders. She had done nothing wrong.

Jacob's well, a hole in the ground ringed by a low wall of rock, was surrounded by half the women of Sychar. Facing the brood of women was never easy, but the covey of young mothers stung the most. They crowded together like a flock of sparrows, chirping and twittering, shutting her out. Mara had once been their friend, but none of them had spoken to her in years. Some were no older than her fifteen years but already married and proudly showing swollen bellies or babes in their arms.

The older women huddled in bunches, murmuring in low voices that stopped abruptly as Mara approached. Several heads jerked up. They looked at her with narrowed eyes and down-turned mouths. Mara's hands grew damp and slippery on the smooth clay jar, and her legs trembled. She stumbled, almost dropping the heavy jar. *They must know. What will they do to us now?*

Mara lowered the jar from her head and pressed it to her chest. A burning heat crept up her neck, but she refused to look down—that would be a sure sign of guilt. In the quiet, the bees droned in the lavender bushes and birds chirped their morning song.

She straightened her shoulders and met Tirzah's stare, then Adah's. The undeclared queens of the village, the two women made it their business to pass judgment on the less fortunate of Sychar. Usually, that meant Nava.

Adah's bulbous eyes flicked from Mara's wild, tangled hair to her dirty feet. Her head swiveled on her long neck, and she bent her tall, bony frame to whisper into Tirzah's ear. Adah was married to Shimon, a prosperous merchant in Sychar. She was his second wife, a fact that Mara could never forget.

Tirzah smirked and whispered back to Adah. Tirzah was married to Zevulun, the richest man in the village. She seemed to have more flesh than mere bones could support. Her face blended into her neck in cascading folds of skin, and her fine linen dress stretched over the wide expanse of her midsection.

At last, Adah and Tirzah turned back to the cluster of women. Mara let out the breath she had been holding. *Something is going on, but it isn't about Mama.* This time.

Mara hugged her jar and stepped in line for the well. The women's voices were somber, their faces grim. If they had been talking about Nava, she would hear the outraged gasps and titters that signaled scandal. No, this seemed to be another sort of bad news.

When the older women had filled their jars, Mara crouched close to the low rock wall. She lowered a dried gourd down the well, and a cool breeze stirred from its depths. From that first draw, she took a long drink, forcing the water down her tight throat. Then she sent the gourd back down again and again, filling her jar to the top. It would be heavy, but she could make the water last two days.

"Good morning, Mara," said a soft voice behind her.

Mara turned and smiled at Leah. At least she was always kind. Leah's long, silver hair fell down her back in a thick, shining braid that caught the sunlight. Although stooped and frail, Leah still fetched her own water; she had no servant or daughter to do it for her.

"Let me help you with that, Leah." Mara reached for the old woman's water jug and set it on the edge of the rocky opening. She sent the gourd back down into the well.

"And how's your mother today?" Leah asked, her quick eyes darting toward the other women and back.

Mara replied carefully, "Sleeping when I left." She tipped her head toward the women. "What is it?"

Leah bit her lip. "They found Dara this morning, dead, on the east side of Mount Ebal."

Mara dropped the rope, and the full gourd splashed back down into the well. "Dead? What happened?"

"She must have been gathering wood and fallen down a ravine. Jobab always said she was clumsy." Leah took the rope from Mara's still hands and began pulling.

Clumsy. She had heard Jobab—old enough to be Dara's grandfather—complaining in the marketplace about his young bride. Dara burned the stew and her hands as well. She broke her arm when she fell down a stony path.

A heavy ache filled her chest. Dara was her age and one of the few girls who still talked to her, although not since she'd married at the early age of thirteen. The girl had lived with Jobab on the far side of Mount Ebal and rarely came into the village. When she did, she rushed through her marketing, her head down and not a word for anyone. As though she was afraid.

Guilt brushed her spine like a cold hand. She should have made the climb to the shepherd's hut to find out why Dara had so many bruises and injuries.

Leah poured water into her jar with shaking hands. "She lost another baby last month. Jobab was so angry." Bright tears glittered on her wrinkled cheeks. "I should have told someone. I should have checked on her."

It wouldn't have mattered. A woman's word against a man's never did. Dara was Jobab's second wife. The first had died not long after giving birth to a stillborn boy—fell and hit her head on a stone. Poor Jobab, the men would say, his wives died before they could give him an heir. Poor wives.

Mara brushed her hand over Leah's stooped shoulders. She lifted the heavy jar to her head and turned to the road. A flurry of motion caught her eye, then her path was blocked.

Mara stepped around the girl who had once been her best friend. "Good morning, Rivkah."

"Mara." Rivkah's smile stopped Mara mid-stride. Her eyes swept over Mara's tattered tunic, her uncombed hair. She ran a hand over her own dark braids, twisted into an elaborate design and pinned with brass ornaments. "I wanted you to be the first to know. Jebus and I are to be betrothed. The ceremony is today."

Mara sucked in her breath. She steadied the jar on her head. She and Rivkah had been childhood friends before Adah, Rivkah's mother, had married Shimon and turned her back on Nava. Like all little girls, Mara and Rivkah had spent their days talking about their betrothal ceremonies, dreaming of husbands and families. A husband meant security and protection and, most of all, children—the ultimate sign of God's favor. They had always assumed that Mara would be the first to marry, but Rivkah, more than a year younger, was betrothed first.

"You are blessed," Mara said. She heard the tremble in her voice. "Jebus will be a good husband."

"Yes, he will. He begged for the betrothal to be shortened. You know how men are." Rivkah smirked. "But it will be a full year. My father insisted."

Mara looked down at her bare feet and ragged tunic. *Yes, I do know how men are.* She stepped around Rivkah and hurried toward the road.

As Leah fell into step beside her, Mara slowed but didn't speak. She couldn't.

The path forked—one way went to the village, the other to the valley. This was where they would part. Leah patted Mara's arm with her gnarled hand. "Your time will come, my dear."

Mara shook her head and swallowed hard. No, her time would not come. They all knew that. She nodded good-bye to the old woman.

The path blurred under Mara's feet, and the heavy water jar pressed down on her head. She should be mourning Dara— although she barely knew her—but she mourned for herself instead.

Rivkah was betrothed. And to one of the last unmarried men in Sychar. She couldn't even hope for a young, handsome husband like Jebus. Not anymore. Rivkah would be married in one year and probably with child soon after. *I'll still be struggling to feed Mama and Asher. No one will marry me.*

Today Rivkah's childhood dreams would come true. Her father and brothers would carry her in a litter to the house of her handsome groom. Her sisters and friends would scatter nuts and dance to the music of harps and tambourines. And Mara wasn't even invited.

I'd be content with any husband who treated me kindly and put food on the table. Anyone who provided clothes and a roof that didn't leak. Anyone who would take care of me and Asher.

No, there would be no betrothal for her. No man would make a marriage offer for Mara, daughter of Nava, the most disgraceful woman in Sychar.

"Mama, you can't let him come here again. You know that, don't you?"

Nava didn't answer. Mara knelt next to her mother's huddled body, hoping that she would listen to reason, but Nava just pulled her cloak closer around her shoulders and turned her face to the wall.

"Mama, if they find out . . . what will we do?" Mara's voice rose.

"What's the matter, Mara?" Asher piped up from the corner. "Mara, what is it?" He crawled to Mara and climbed into her arms. He was small for his age and too thin, but she had never seen a more beautiful child in all of Sychar. His almond-shaped eyes were deep green. Long, dark lashes brushed his high smooth cheeks. Asher snuggled up to her, and she pressed her cheek to his dark curls. She kissed the top of his head and breathed in his musty sweet scent.

Yes, Asher was a beautiful child. But he had been born lame. Not just lame—deformed. And in Sychar, deformity meant sin. Nava's sin.

He was in all other ways a perfect boy, but one leg, knotted and bent, hardly looked like a leg at all. The heel of his foot pointed sharply outward, like a misplaced elbow. The foot twisted so that the pink sole faced upward, and his deformed toes closed like a fist. But Asher's heart . . . his heart was as pure and sweet as the water from Jacob's well.

Mara pulled his thumb from his mouth. "Asher, no. You're almost eight."

Nava pushed herself up from her mat. "Let him be." She folded her legs and patted her lap. "Come sit on Mama's lap."

Mara pushed Asher into his mother's lap. "Stop treating him like a baby."

He snuggled up to his mother and stuck his thumb back in his mouth.

Nava didn't rebuke him. She pulled him closer and stroked his arm.

Even with dirty hair and a sleep-lined face, Nava was lovely. Her honey-toned skin was only slightly lined from thirty summers. Her teeth flashed white and straight behind dark, full lips. Long, black lashes and straight, black brows highlighted her perfect features. Even now, when other women showed signs of age, Nava's skin stretched smoothly over high cheeks, and her chin was a firm, straight line.

Mara dipped a worn wooden ladle into the water jug and gave it to Nava. She had heard the same words her whole life: she was the image of her mother. Except for their eyes. While Nava's wide eyes were as green as Egyptian jade, Mara's were a startling mix of green shot with gold. No one had ever said they were beautiful.

Nava drank, then passed the ladle to Asher. "My poor baby boy. Why must God punish you for the sins of your mother?"

Blood rose in Mara's face. "Mama, you act as though you have no choice." Mara carried the heavy jar to the coolest corner of the house. "I didn't see you asking Alexandros to leave last night."

Even as Nava buried her face in Asher's skinny neck and wept, Mara didn't regret her words. Why couldn't she see the danger?

"Alexandros?" Asher said, looking from his sister to his mother. He puffed out his cheeks and lowered his brows, very much like the big pagan. "I don't like him."

"I don't either," Mara agreed. She gathered her damp cloak from the floor and shook it hard. If only she could shake some sense into her mother.

Asher squirmed in his mother's arms; she was still crying. Mara loosened Nava's grip on Asher and dragged him from her. "Mama is a little sad, Asher. Go outside and gather sticks. We'll make some breakfast." She sent him on his way with a forced smile and a little swat on his bottom. He crawled quickly through the door, dragging his lame leg behind him.

She crouched beside her weeping mother. "Mama, you can't let him come here again."

"It is for Asher. He needs a father."

I don't believe it. She isn't making any sense. "Asher has a father. Or did you forget about Shaul? You know, your husband?" She took a breath and tried to speak calmly. "Mama, Alexandros doesn't want to be Asher's father. He's not going to marry you."

Nava wiped tears from her cheeks. "At his age, Asher should be learning a trade, not playing with toys. He needs a man to teach him."

"Yes. Shaul is the one who should teach him. If you would just . . ." If she would just get up in the morning and work hard all day. If she would just take care of her children. Then she could send word to Shaul—beg him to come back. They could be happy again.

But Mara couldn't say that. They never spoke of her mother's illness.

Nava lay down and turned her back on the room. She pulled her cloak over her head like a shroud, as though she intended to sleep forever.

Mara blew out her breath in frustration. Nava would not get up again today. Sleeping seemed to be her only refuge from the dark thoughts and sadness that bound her. *Lord, why do we have a mother who is not a mother at all? If she is the one who is sinful, why must Asher and I suffer?*

Mara left the gloom of the house and crouched by the cooking pot. The two looming mountains seemed to press down on her. Would she ever reap the blessings of following God's laws, or would she only see the curses that were sown by her disgraceful mother?

Chapter 2

"Have you been given much food lately?" Leah asked.

Mara lifted one shoulder. "We have enough."

She and Leah sat near the cooking fire. Asher played under the tall cypress trees that stood guard around the house like Roman soldiers. A cool breeze lifted the damp clothes that lay drying on the bushes.

"Don't lie to me, my girl," the old woman croaked. "These people," she motioned toward the village, "they don't abide by the laws they claim so dearly." Leah's withered face dipped close to Mara. "Charity is often their worn-out sandals and rancid oil, I'd guess."

Mara pounded the barley one last time. Taking charity, especially from some, galled her, but without it they would starve. She would beg for food if she must—not for herself—but for Asher and her mother. "The garden is coming along. And Passover is near. People are always generous after Passover."

She didn't want to talk about food. There was something even more important on her mind. "What can I do to help her, Leah?" Mara nodded toward the house where Nava slept through the days and nights.

Leah took a packet of herbs from her belt and poured them into a small pot. She ladled hot water from the cooking fire. "This may help a bit when she wakes up."

The scents of mint and bitter rue drifted over to Mara. But the soothing drink would not help her mother. She needed something stronger.

Mara poured another measure of barley onto the flat stone. The hard kernels cracked and popped under the heavy grindstone. She leaned into her work. How could she ask Leah about the demon? Even thinking of it made her skin prickle. *Please, Lord. Forgive me.*

"What is wrong with her, Leah? Could it be . . ." She felt as if a huge hand were squeezing her chest. "I just want her to be happy again, like before . . ." Before Asher was born.

"What do you mean?" Leah lowered her voice, although not even Asher could hear them.

"I mean . . . I've heard some of the women talking." She sat up straighter. She'd just have to say it. "They say that it's an evil spirit." She swallowed. "That it comes in the night, sapping her strength and leaving her weak. Do you believe that, Leah?"

Leah pursed her lips. She didn't look shocked or outraged. "I don't know." She gazed toward the trees where Asher played. "Many women are like this after the birth of a child. Especially a difficult birth like your brother's. It can last for months. But with Nava, who can explain it? It's been years now. She is not always ill. She eats. She is sometimes well. Then she will lie in bed for days or weeks, leaving her children to care for themselves, pushing her husband away . . ."

Mara scooped the ground barley into the cooking pot. Could an evil spirit live inside her mother—in their house—lurking close to Asher while he slept? If only Nava could be like before. When she sang and smiled. When Shaul was here. She ladled water over the barley and stirred in a palmful of spicy cumin and a pinch of salt.

Leah scooted closer. "You could check for a demon, but the priests disapprove . . ."

She stopped the spoon mid-stir. "I don't know what else to do. Please, Leah." *Anything is better than wondering.*

"There is a way to find out. Then . . . at least you'd know for sure." Leah bit her lip and looked around the empty valley.

"I won't tell anyone, Leah. I promise." She pushed the cooking pot over the hot coals. "Please. Tell me what to do."

• • •

Darkness fell quickly in the little valley. In the bright light of day, talk of an evil spirit had seemed almost foolish. Now, as the night wrapped around the lonely house, the sputtering oil lamp cast shadows that made Mara's blood pound in her ears and her hands tremble.

Mara checked that her mother and Asher were asleep, then carefully scooped the warm ashes from the cooking fire and sprinkled them thickly over the doorstep and into the house.

It would leave claw prints—like a rooster—in the ashes. So Leah had said.

Mara snuffed the lamp and lay down on her thin pallet, wiggling close to Asher. She had laid their sleeping mats close together but as far as they could be from her mother's corner. She lay with her eyes wide open. The moon's light seldom brightened their deep valley, but tonight the blackness weighed on her like a burden of stones.

How big was a demon? She imagined that it would move like a shadow with scaly, claw-like feet and a long sinewy body. She listened for scratching, a hiss, any sign that a sinister creature prowled inside the house. Close by, she heard her brother's gentle breathing and the goats shifting in the lean-to next to the house. The shrieks of the night birds and the clamor of insects usually comforted her, but tonight they seemed to be warning her of danger.

She scooted closer to Asher. She'd heard the priests say it. She repeated it every night. This night, she breathed it over and over. *Watch over your people, oh Lord.*

Mara opened her eyes just to squeeze them closed again. Her mind was full of fearful dreams: giant birds with the heads of snakes flying away with Asher in their sharp talons, village boys chasing them with mattocks and rakes, she and Asher wandering alone in the mountains.

Her heart sped up. Were sharp-clawed footprints scratched in the ashes?

What will I do if the marks are there? What do I do if they are not?

Mara said her morning prayers lying on her back beside Asher, his breath warm on her cheek. Then she rolled off the mat, careful not to wake him. She passed her mother, who was huddled in a ball, as she tiptoed to the door.

The ashes lay smooth and undisturbed, not a mark or scratch to show that something had breached the doorway. She sank to the floor on weak legs. Of course no evil spirit defiled their home. But if not an evil spirit, then what?

She had asked Leah what to do if the prints had marred the ashes. "Some wear an amulet—a locust egg or fox tooth," Leah had answered.

Mara shook her head. "Charms from a soothsayer? We would surely be thrown out of town if anyone found out."

Leah nodded her head. "Yes. Trust in the Lord. Go to the mountain, and ask the Lord to send an angel to fight and vanquish the spirit."

She would go to Mount Gerizim and pray. There was nothing more for her to do. Only a miracle would heal her mother.

Mara took a fistful of ragged straw and swept the ashes from the doorway. Then she stood for a long moment, watching as the sky turned pink over Mount Ebal. The day's work called. She stoked the fire, then milked the wiry-haired goats while the wood burned down to glowing coals. She tipped the grain jar to get every kernel of barley and pounded it fiercely until the faint breeze blew fine puffs of barley flour into the air. Leah was right. They hadn't been given much food for several weeks. But the garden was growing well, the goats were healthy, and she had plenty of wool to card and spin. Aunt Ruth would give her barley and oil in exchange for her fine yarn, and after Passover they would get plenty of charity from their pious neighbors—enough for several months if they were careful.

Mara leaned back on her heels. The morning chores were done, except one. The jug was almost empty again. She would need enough water for today and tomorrow. She stood and stretched her cramped shoulders, looking to the west at the path that wound through the valley. How many times had she wished to see Shaul walking from Sebaste, coming home to them? She shook her head. It was up to her now to keep her family fed.

She stepped through the doorway. Asher was already folding her cloak and rolling their sleeping mats. "Take good care of Mama while I'm gone," she said.

"I will, Mara!" He waved to her.

She started east, up the hill. The two mountains rose on each side of the path, a testament to the Samaritans of Sychar. Mara knew the story as well as she knew her morning prayers, as well as she knew the outline of Mount Gerizim against the sky.

She'd heard the story all her life, how not long after the twelve tribes of Israel had entered the Promised Land, they began to struggle for power. The high priest was frightened that the Ark of the Covenant—the dwelling place of the Word of the Lord—would be stolen. He hid the Ark there, in a cave on Mount Gerizim.

Her people, who had lived for centuries near the Holy Mountain, said that the cave disappeared and the Ark was never seen again. It would remain in the mountain until the coming of the Taheb, the Restorer. But the southern kingdom of Israel said that Jerusalem held the Ark and was the only true place for worship and sacrifice to God. The people were divided and would stay that way until the Taheb came and showed them the true place to worship—Jerusalem or Mount Gerizim.

Generations lived and died in the land that God had given them. In the north, evil queens brought the people the goddess Astarte and built altars to Baal. Some Samaritans embraced the new gods, rejecting the One who had brought them out of slavery in Egypt.

But her people, the people of Sychar, stayed faithful to Yahweh. They built an altar on the slopes of Gerizim, and the village of Sychar grew on Mount Ebal. It remained a town of strict faithfulness to the God of Abraham, practicing a faith as ancient as when Moses first set his eyes on the Promised Land.

Mara hurried along the path. To the south, the crest of the

Holy Mountain of Gerizim caught the morning sun. The white stone synagogue lay in the shadows halfway up its steep side. To the north, clay houses—all larger than hers—were scattered on the slopes of Mount Ebal. The marketplace on the lowest slopes already bustled with merchants and shepherds leading animals to water. Without the life-giving water of Jacob's well, Sychar would be just another empty valley in Samaria.

She reached the wide road called the Patriarch's Highway, watching the ground and thinking of the day ahead. She needed to repair that roof before another rain came. Perhaps Uncle Uziel would help her.

Thoughts of roof repair fled as she raised her eyes from the road. Her heart jumped to her throat. Three tall, burly boys idled at the side of the wide road. They shoved each other as she came closer.

"Nava's daughter."

"Here she comes."

She slowed her steps. These boys were far worse than their mothers, but she would not cower to them. She lifted her head, squared her shoulders, and whispered a small prayer. *Help me, please.*

The boys circled like jackals before a kill. They were almost as old as Mara, old enough to be working with their fathers instead of looking for trouble. They had probably been loitering close to the Patriarch's Highway, lying in wait for traveling Jews to harass. They got her instead.

"Let me pass." Mara hoped they didn't hear the tremble in her voice.

"Where is your mother, Mara? Too ashamed to go to the well?" said the tallest boy with a sneer. "My father says she is nothing but a—a whore."

Amram, the eldest son of Zevulun and Tirzah. He was tall and thick but had the bad manners of a spoiled child. The other two boys gasped, then laughed along with Amram.

Mara's face flushed hot. Her throat closed so tightly that she could barely breathe, let alone speak. She lowered the jar from her head and wrapped her arms around it, shielding herself from her chin to waist. She stared into the eyes of the nearest boy, the smallest. He faltered and took a step back. Amram did not.

Just ignore them. Maybe she'd get by with just a few insults. Quickening her stride, she veered around them, her head high.

Chapter 3

S hem heard the woman's desperate sobs before he saw her.
He and his brother had stayed late at their tutor's house,
debating Aristotle and complaining about the Romans. Now
they made their way through the dark alleys and winding streets
of Caesarea when all the respectable citizens were safe behind
locked doors. Everyone knew that only thieves, cutthroats, and
Roman soldiers prowled the city after sundown.

It was Shem's fault they were late, and he'd pay if his father
found out that he had taken Benjamin through the city in the
dark. But they had only to make their way across the wide, open
forum and down a few side streets before they reached their father's house on the cliffs above the sea. He had his knife if they
ran into any trouble. And he knew how to use it.

The sobs became louder. Drunken laughter rang out. "What's
a fine woman like you doing out in the dark?" Greek words with
a heavy accent, definitely a Roman.

"Please."

The desperate word quickened Shem's pulse. What was going
on here? He pulled Benjamin into the dark shadow of the nearest
building and edged closer to the square.

Under the imposing statue of Augustus Caesar, a woman
knelt on the stone paving, gathering onions and oranges that had
rolled from her basket. Two soldiers stood above her. One held
a lighted torch and swayed on unsteady legs. The other, his hair
the color of fire, bent over the woman, pulling at the rough cloak
that covered her shoulders.

Benjamin tugged on Shem's tunic. "Shem, remember what Father said. One more fight and—"

Shem put his hand to his lips. "Shh. I know."

But Benjamin was right. Their father had warned him. In the past month, he'd come home with two black eyes and a broken nose. If he came home with any more injuries, he'd have to pay his own tutoring fees. But how could he ignore such injustice?

Shem pointed to a dark doorway. "Stay here."

Benjamin was the youngest of Shem's four brothers. At twenty, he was only two years younger than Shem, but his beard was just wispy patches, and his fair hair was as fine as a child's. He stuttered, but only when their father was around. He didn't have any trouble speaking with their Greek tutor. Benjamin needed the escape to their tutor each day as much as he needed the medicine that his physician gave him for his chronic cough. And it was Shem's job to get him safely there and back.

Benjamin plucked at his cloak again. "Shem. Don't do it."

He brushed his brother off. "I'm not going to fight. I'm just going to talk to them."

Shem stepped into the forum.

"Come on. Just one little kiss!" said the redhead.

"Please." The woman shoved the basket toward the soldiers. "Keep the food. Just let me go."

The drunken one lurched forward and grabbed the neck of her cloak. She choked out a scream.

Shem stepped forward. "Let her go."

The soldiers straightened and turned to Shem. Their hands went to the swords that hung from their studded leather belts.

The woman grabbed her basket and ran.

Shem held out his own empty hands. "She's nothing. Forget her." He smiled. "Here," he rummaged in the fold of his tunic for a coin and held it out to them. "Have a drink on me."

See, Benjamin. I'm not starting anything.

The redhead stepped closer to him, his stance relaxing. "You speak Latin well, for a Jew."

Shem let that go. Both Samaritans and Jews lived in Caesarea. The Romans didn't know the difference, and they didn't care. If you weren't Roman, you didn't count. Few Samaritans or Jews spoke Latin, and even fewer spoke it well. Perhaps he'd be able to reason with these men.

The drunk tipped his torch toward the fading patter of sandaled feet. "Longinus, he spoiled our fun. I guess he'll have to make it up to us."

"As I said, have a drink on me." Shem tossed the coin. It clinked on the stone pavers, then rolled and settled at the drunk's feet.

Shem heard the shuffle of his brother's sandals, and the soldiers' attention shifted behind him. He clenched his teeth to stifle a curse. Why hadn't Benjamin done what he was told?

The redhead—Longinus—smirked. "Who's your *mulier*?"

His woman? Shem stiffened and blood roared in his ears. He knew what the Roman was implying. "He's my brother. We're on our way home."

Longinus stepped toward Benjamin.

Benjamin held his ground, but his pale hands twitched at his sides.

"Hey, *cinaedus*," Longinus said. "You're out late with your boyfriend, here." He hacked and launched a wad of saliva at Benjamin.

Benjamin flinched as spittle covered his face.

That was too much. "Leave him alone!" Shem stepped up to the soldier and pushed him in the chest. "Keep your perversions to yourself, you filthy dog."

Longinus stepped behind Shem and wrenched his arms back in one smooth motion. The drunken one threw down the torch and came at Shem from the front.

"Benjamin, get out of here!" Shem yelled before a hard punch to his gut took his breath away.

Benjamin launched himself at the one named Longinus. He wrapped his thin arms around the soldier's neck and held on.

Shem's arms came free. He reached for his knife.

Metal scraped against leather as the drunken soldier pulled his sword from its sheath.

Shem crouched into a fighting stance and circled. It wouldn't be much of a fight. A sword against a blade, but he'd do what he could. A glance behind him showed Longinus throwing Benjamin off his neck.

"Run!" Shem shouted. This time, his brother did as was he was told. He took off, and Longinus went after him.

When Shem turned back, the sword was right in front of him. His distraction had cost him precious seconds. He felt a hot slice, then pain along his cheek. His eyes stung, and blood clouded his vision.

He ducked the second thrust and got in close before the soldier could regain his balance. Up close, he was hardly older than Shem. As he felt the soldier's arm swing back for a strong blow, Shem thrust his blade forward with all his strength. The soldier's eyes met Shem's. His brows came down in confusion, and his sword clattered to the ground.

Shem looked down. His hand was pushed against the soldiers ribs, the knife plunged to the hilt. Dark blood poured out like spilled wine.

What have I done?

He pulled the knife out, and the soldier crumpled to the ground.

"Don't even think about it."

Shem froze in mid-stride at his mother's whispered warning. "I was just—"

"I know what you were doing. And I know why."

Shem turned from the door.

His mother sighed. "You've been stuck in the house for days—you're like a caged lion. But it isn't worth it. You could be seen."

Shem cringed at his mother's anxious voice. "It's not even dawn, and it's raining. Any Roman soldier is probably still sleeping off last night's drunk." Except one. One Roman soldier was nothing but ash on a funeral pyre. Was his mother mourning him?

He shrugged off his cloak and stepped back into the dark house. She was right. It wasn't fair to endanger his family just to get a breath of fresh air. Even if the soldiers weren't up yet, there were plenty of Greeks and even Jews in Caesarea who would gladly turn him in. And then . . . crucifixion outside the city gate, a slow death next to other murderers.

But what did they expect him to do? He couldn't hide for the rest of his life. Shem tried not to be angry at his mother. She had the rest of the family to think about, their safety to consider. He had only himself to blame for this imprisonment. And the Roman legions that infected the city like a pestilence.

He couldn't think clearly in the stifling air of his father's home. His brothers' subdued whispers, worried looks from his mother, and—most grating of all—his father's constant tirades, made it impossible to forget his guilt. He desperately wanted to get out, just to clear his head.

"Come, I want to talk to you," his mother said.

Shem followed her down the wide hallway, past glowing brass lamps and ornately carved doorways. Soft carpets muffled their steps as she led him to the brightly lit kitchen, already bustling with servants and smelling of warm bread.

His mother scooped thick yogurt into a bowl for him. "Don't worry, I won't tell your father that you tried to escape."

Shem helped himself to a round of soft, warm bread. Of course she wouldn't tell. He was her favorite son, after all. Which is why this must hurt her more than anyone else.

"I need you to promise me something, Shem." She sounded serious. She poured a stream of dark honey over the yogurt and put the bowl in his hand.

He nodded as he dipped his bread. He had heard his father ranting late into the night. It wasn't hard to guess that the conversation had been about him.

"Ezra has decided what to do with you."

Shem opened his mouth to speak, but she raised her hand.

"Shem. Don't argue with him. Just do as he says." She laid her hand on his arm. "Please, Shem. He's trying to save your life."

Shem finished his food in silence, then hurried down the long hallway. He couldn't appear before his father with sleep-mussed hair and an old tunic. His father had a plan for him, and Shem doubted that he would like it. But Ezra's word was law.

Shem stepped into his spacious room to find his servant hovering like a wasp in a fig tree. Drusus had already straightened the thick blankets on his bed and tidied the wax tablets and scrolls on his cluttered desk. He buzzed about the room gathering stray clothes and abandoned sandals.

"Good morning, sir. I'm sorry to have left you these past days."

Shem shrugged. A few days without Drusus had been a relief. His servant was a short, wiry Greek who seemed never to run out of words.

"Your father sent me to attend to some . . . family business."

Drusus's hopeful pause meant that he had information to share, but Shem was not in the mood for gossip. Shem rooted through a cedar-lined chest, searching for his best tunic.

"I trust you didn't find my absence a hardship. You are already so terribly burdened." Drusus produced the tunic and a look of concern.

"Of course not, Drusus," Shem snapped. "I'm not a child." He shrugged into the sandalwood-scented linen and dismissed Drusus, wondering at his eager words but determined not to indulge his servant's loose tongue. He would find out soon enough.

Shem adjusted his tunic and glanced in the burnished-silver mirror that hung near his bed. He touched the puckered wound that curved from his temple to the corner of his mouth. The scar would always remind him of his own stupidity.

The familiar weight of guilt settled on Shem as he found Benjamin waiting outside his door. He stopped Shem with a hand around his arm, his grip as weak as a girl's. "Father wants to see you," he said rolling his eyes. "Right away."

Shem frowned. Yes, Ezra didn't like to be kept waiting.

Benjamin coughed and took a deep, wheezing breath. "Mama is there, waiting for you."

Shem steadied him with his other hand. "You should be in bed."

Benjamin waved his concern away. "Remember—"

"I know, I know. Don't lose my temper. Go now. Get some rest and stop worrying about me." He stepped past Benjamin and strode down the long hall toward his father's workroom.

Whatever his father had decided, he would do. Not for his father, but for his mother and for Benjamin. Did that soldier have a brother? *Maybe I deserve to be crucified.* He surely didn't deserve his mother's concern, or his brother's loyalty.

Shem entered his father's workroom to find Ezra behind a vast ebony worktable, frowning at him as though he was a naughty child. He measured at least a head shorter than his son but was more powerfully built. His face was heavy and square, with thick brows and a wide mouth. Scrolls and maps littered his worktable, and an iron-bound money box sat at his feet. From this room, Ezra's commands were carried out by slaves and sons alike as he did business with merchants throughout the Roman Empire.

Shem's mother stood silently at his side, as straight as a tent pole, her hands clutched to her heart. A glance from her reminded Shem of his promise.

"Well, Shem," Ezra said. "You put all of us in danger this time. This trouble is not going away. I've heard that they are still searching for you throughout the city."

His father waited. No doubt for another apology.

Shem said nothing as he perched on the edge of an intricately carved chair.

"The centurion owes me a favor. If they track you here, I can get protection for the rest of the family. But you . . . I can't protect you. You'll hang from a cross outside the city gates."

His mother's quick sob only earned her an irritated look from her husband.

"We need to get you out of Caesarea." Ezra watched Shem with pursed lips, clearly waiting for a response.

Shem twisted the heavy gold signet ring on his first finger. It glinted in the sun, now high enough to pour through the wide windows and heat the already stuffy room. The ring was a sign, his father had said, that Shem was on his way to being an important man in Caesarea. Would that ever happen now?

His father snorted impatiently. "I sent Drusus to Sychar yesterday to speak to your grandfather."

Shem's head jerked up as his heart sank. *Please, not Sychar.* The tiny town where his mother had been born was an intellectual desert, a wasteland of farmers and narrow minds. He was probably better educated than Sychar's high priest.

"Abahu has agreed to take you on as his apprentice in the olive business," his father continued. "With no sons, he is in need of an heir. You will be useful to him."

"But . . . but Father." Shem tried to keep his voice steady. "What can I do there? Pick olives?" Shem heard the note of scorn in his own voice and glanced at his mother.

His father's face darkened and his voice rose. "You are hardly in the position to be selective, boy."

Shem ducked his head, ashamed of himself. His father was right. *But, please, not Sychar.*

"Now," Ezra sent a stern look to his wife. "Your grandparents know nothing of the . . . trouble . . . that you have had here in Caesarea. I ordered Drusus not to go into that disaster. There is no need to alarm them."

His mother's mouth hardened into a thin line. She clearly didn't agree.

Shem knew a little about his grandfather, Abahu of Sychar. He had heard that Abahu had been disappointed when Ezra had taken Dinah, his only child, to Caesarea. Shem could guess that Abahu despaired for his grandchildren. He probably thought they had deserted the Holy Mountain that was central to their faith.

But Abahu was no village idiot. He would wonder why Ezra was suddenly so eager to part with his most scholarly son. Surely Shem would need to give his grandfather an explanation?

"Grandfather will wonder—"

"You will not speak of it."

"But they might be in danger—"

"No." His father slapped his big hands on the table. "Do not tell your grandparents about the Roman." He frowned at his wife. "They will not look for you there. I doubt that anyone here even knows that your mother comes from Sychar. It is not something I brag about."

"How long must I stay?" Shem asked. He would just have to get used to the idea. A few months couldn't be that bad.

His father sighed a bit too loudly. "Perhaps it is a good place for you to live. Your grandfather has a good life there, and he is old. He needs someone to take over the olives for him."

Shem sucked in his breath. "You mean . . ." He looked from one parent to the other. "I will never return here? Never live here again?" This was too harsh. But was it? A knife in the heart was harsh. A funeral pyre was harsh.

"It is the only way," his mother said quickly. "And it is a good place."

Now he understood her earlier request. She wanted him away from the city and with her parents, where he would be safe. And she wanted him to take care of Abahu and his grandmother.

She raised open, pleading hands toward Shem. "My father, he is a good man and will teach you well. Drusus said that he was overjoyed to have you join his family. You will be happy in Sychar. And safe, my son."

How had his mother managed to get his father to agree to this? Ezra had had much grander plans for his well-educated son. He surely wouldn't let the money he had spent on tutors go to waste. Not to mention the bribes he'd paid to get Shem well-placed in the city government.

"Well, we shall see what happens," Ezra said. His face was turned to his wife, but he cast a sidelong glance at his son. Some of the tension drained from Shem's shoulders. No, his father wasn't about to banish him to Sychar forever.

"Leave us now, Dinah. Shem will say good-bye to you before he goes." Ezra dismissed his wife with a curt wave.

She rested her hand briefly on Shem's shoulder. He pressed his own hand over hers for a moment. His father's brows lowered, and his mouth twisted. Ezra didn't approve of grown sons show-ing affection toward their mothers, but Shem had never let that stop him.

With his mother gone, he looked back to his father. "I won't be staying permanently in Sychar, then?"

Ezra shook his head. "I don't think that will be necessary. They won't look for you forever. Once the current legion moves to another area of the province, you should be able to return here. Then we can continue with your education and get you placed in the city."

"But what of Mother and my grandparents?" Shem asked.

"Your mother," Ezra snorted. "She would have you waste your life in the olive grove. I will not let that happen. Any fool can prune trees and harvest olives. I need you here. If you gain your grandfather's trust, you could still inherit the olive groves. We'll hire a steward to manage them. It will be a good income for you."

"So I am to lie to them?" Bitterness filled Shem's throat. *This is wrong.* "About everything?"

"Shem, do not be so childish." Ezra unrolled a scroll and fixed his eyes on it as he spoke. "There is no need for them to know. Go to Sychar, work hard, help your grandfather. I will send word when it is safe to return to Caesarea. And Shem," he glanced up at his son. "Stay out of trouble, for once."

Chapter 4

"I look ridiculous." Shem ran a hand through his newly cut hair. It was indecently short with absurd ringlets arranged over his forehead. His smooth cheeks stung from the scrape of the blade that had taken off his soft black beard.

Drusus adjusted a curl. "Ridiculous? Of course not. You look like a respectable Greek merchant, just as your father ordered."

Ezra stalked into the room. His critical eyes flicked from Shem's shorn head to his sandal-clad feet. "Yes," he said, running a hand over his own full beard. "That will do."

"How will this help me get out of the city?" Shem asked. He touched his scar, a naked red furrow on his smooth white skin. "At least my beard and hair almost covered the scar."

"My informer reported that soldiers are questioning every Jew and Samaritan. From a distance, you look like a Greek merchant."

"What about close up?"

Ezra shrugged. "Don't let them get close, boy."

Shem clenched his teeth. *Easy enough for you to say. You are not the one they are after.* But an argument with Ezra wouldn't help anyone. "How will I get past the guards at the gate?"

"I have a man waiting for you on the east end of the forum. He'll get you out. After that, cross the plain in the dark. You'll be in Sychar by morning."

They walked down the hallway and into the lush courtyard. The high walls protected them from the view of the street. Long shadows stretched over his mother's flower garden, and the evening breeze smelled of the sea.

His older brothers stood under the blooming fig trees. Benjamin and his mother sat close together on the edge of a gurgling fountain. Drusus waited by the gate, a loaded donkey by his side.

His mother rose and stepped toward him, her face already streaked with tears.

"Don't worry." He embraced her, ignoring his father's grunt of disapproval.

He said good-bye to his older brothers as they clapped him roughly on the shoulders. He would miss their fighting and teasing, but he had never had much in common with them. They worked in the shops and ran the businesses that his father owned. They knew of shipping and selling. Shem knew of philosophy and the law. Still, a pang of remorse surprised him.

He turned to Benjamin. He would miss his little brother the most. A lump formed in his throat as he embraced Benjamin's bony frame. "Take care of yourself."

Benjamin nodded, and Shem felt his brother's body shudder.

Shem tipped his head toward their father. "Just stay out of his way. I'll be back as soon as I can."

"Go on now, Shem. Get out of here before the soldiers find you." Ezra checked the buckles on the donkey. "Remember. East end of the forum."

How could he forget? That was where this had all started. "How will I know him?"

A brief, humorless smile flashed across his father's face. "Oh, you'll know him when you see him."

With a last nod to Benjamin, Shem slipped out of the courtyard and into the late-afternoon glow. Drusus walked behind, quiet for once, towing a donkey loaded with gifts for Shem's grandparents.

It took only a short time for them to slip down the narrow alleys to the forum, partially deserted now that the statue of Augustus threw its long shadow over the square. Two soldiers lounged at the northern corner, but their eyes were trained on three scantily dressed women displayed in front of Athena's temple.

Where was the man that his father had paid, probably very handsomely, to get him out of the city gate? All he saw at the east side of the wide square was a filthy tanner standing by an oxcart heaped with sheep and goat skins.

As Shem drew near, the tanner jerked his head up. "Shem ben Ezra?"

The meaning of his father's brief smile hit him squarely in the nose. The tanner reeked of the urine and dung that he used in his trade. His clothes were rags, his feet and bare legs stained yellow from tramping in urine vats all day.

He looked Shem up and down, his grizzled face unimpressed. "Don't look like a killer to me."

The man slapped his ox's bony rear end and turned abruptly down a street so narrow that the rickety cart could barely squeeze through it. He didn't look back to see if Shem followed.

Shem glanced back at the soldiers—they hadn't moved—but Drusus scurried behind him, one hand clamped firmly over his nose.

The clop of the ox's feet rang off the high walls. They walked to the end of the street where they could see the corner of the main gate. Shem squeezed past the ox to peek around the corner. Freedom was just a stone's throw away, but it might as well be across the ocean.

Three soldiers stood at the gate, harassing each passing traveler. A cart heaped with melons rumbled to a stop. As one soldier questioned the driver, the other two plunged razor-tipped spears deep into the pile of fruit. A breeze chilled Shem's neck and sent a shiver down his back. *How will I get past the soldiers?*

The tanner started throwing the heavy skins, covered with dried blood, dung, and bits of flesh, to one side of the cart. The smell of rot and decay intensified. He turned to Shem and punched his hand toward the space he'd made. "Get in, then," he said. So that was the plan. Once again, Ezra had had the last word.

Shem pulled his cloak tightly around his new white tunic and wedged himself into the center of the cart, curling his legs up to his chest. His stomach lurched, and his last meal threatened to come up. He glanced at Drusus. The servant looked as though he was about to faint.

Shem swallowed the bile that rose in his throat as the man covered him with one heavy skin after another, squeezing the air from his lungs. The damp skins pressed close around his face, blocking any fresh air. He took shallow breaths as the cart lurched forward. How long would he be able to last?

The cart bumped to a stop. Shem's heart pounded. Would the soldiers probe the cart with their spears as they'd done with the melons?

"Where are you going?" a deep voice barked in Greek with a heavy Roman accent.

"Taking these skins to my tannery, on the north beach," the tanner replied.

Shem's lungs ached. His stomach heaved and he tasted bile. This must be what it felt like to drown. But in a sea of blood and gore. A sudden jab ripped through the skins, and a flash of pain lanced across his shoulder. He sucked in a breath of hot, fetid air and contracted into a tighter ball. *I'm not going to make it out of the city alive.*

"Roman dogs!" the tanner bellowed. "You're ruining my good skins."

A soldier cursed. The cart jolted, and the tanner grunted like he'd been kicked. The sound of flesh striking flesh followed another jolt to the cart.

"*Merde*! Get this stinking filth out of here, and don't come back if you know what's good for you."

The cart jerked and began to roll. A wave of pain and nausea surged through Shem, and the sounds and smells dissolved in a black void.

Fresh air. Shem took a deep breath. He opened his eyes to the blur of a dirty hand and a sharp crack of pain across his cheek.

"You alive?" The old tanner peered at him with one eye. The other was swelled shut, and his filthy tunic was ripped down the front.

"Should have charged your father more than ten drachma to

get you out." He dragged Shem out of the cart and dumped him on rocky ground. "Ruined five of my good hides."

They were on a road. Alone. And outside the city gates. The tanner was already heading north with his cart.

Drusus knelt beside him, opened his cloak, and checked for blood. "Are you hurt, sir? The soldiers . . . the spear . . ."

Shem pushed Drusus away and clambered to his feet. His shoulder stung, but a quick look showed that the spear had just nicked him. "I'm fine." He shrugged off the stinking cloak and threw it at his hovering servant. "Get rid of that."

A narrow road stretched east, toward Sychar. He stalked down it. Surely, this night couldn't get any more humiliating.

Shem's long, hurried strides slowed after they crossed the Plain of Sharon by the light of the moon and reached the less-exposed hills of Samaria. He threw himself down next to the first flowing stream, plunged his arms in to his elbows, then his head. The icy shock revived him, but no matter how much he scrubbed, he still smelled the stench of death.

He left Drusus behind, preferring to be alone with his thoughts as they trudged the narrow path that wound through the hills.

Mother said that this . . . situation is part of God's plan for me. Hadn't Joseph been exiled into slavery to save his people, she said.

Shem snorted. He was no Joseph. Talk of God's plan was just an excuse men used when their lives didn't work out as they desired. The God of Abraham only acted in the lives of great men like Jacob and Moses.

He hadn't prayed when the soldier drew his sword in the forum. And he didn't pray when he thought he would die in the tanner's cart. Prayers weren't heard by their God. His people had prayed for thousands of years, yet their history was one of defeat and slavery, their land overrun with foreigners. Yes, he believed the God of Abraham was the one, true God, but his God had deserted his people long ago.

They passed Sebaste when dawn showed pink through the eastern clouds. Now, as the sun brightened the rocky peaks and deepened the shadowed valleys, Sychar lay just over the next hill. They passed a little house alone in the valley between Mount Gerizim and Mount Ebal. The tiny hut looked about to fall down, but the neatly tilled garden showed sprouts of green and the fire in front burned brightly.

"What about that hut?" Drusus panted, catching up. "Perhaps we can ask for some breakfast?"

"Whoever lives there can hardly spare us breakfast," Shem said. "Your stomach can wait. We will be at my grandparents' soon." And then he'd have to decide. *Is it right to lie to Abahu to obey my father? And if I tell the truth, what then?*

Shem stopped at the top of the hill. There it was. Sychar, just as he remembered from his few visits as a boy. A cluster of tiny houses, a marketplace, women with water jars on their heads, boys driving goats. *I'm supposed to live here? And for how long?*

"Shouldn't we go through the village?" Drusus whined.

Although early, a few villagers peered out of the doorways. They must have nothing better to do. In a town this small, word of his arrival would be spread before he could even reach Abahu's home on the other side. *I might not care about what these people think, but grandfather surely does.*

"No," Shem said as he started down the hill. "This path skirts the town and meets the Patriarch's Highway. We don't need everyone getting a good look at us before we even see my grandparents." He left Drusus struggling behind him with the donkey.

Chapter 5

Mara measured her steps. *I'm not running away from them.* Just ahead was a sharp curve and then the well. A few more steps and she'd be safe.

She jumped as a sharp stone hit her just above the elbow. Behind her, Amram snickered. Another hit her on her leg, biting into her skin. More rained down on her back and legs. The boys laughed and jeered.

She didn't look back but broke into a run. The tall jar bumped against her hip, slipping from her damp hands. She stumbled and fell to her knees, desperately juggling the water jar to keep it from breaking on the stony path.

A yelp rang out behind her. She glanced over her shoulder. Amram lay splayed on the dusty ground. The other boys stepped back, the rocks dropping from their hands. A man towered over Amram. *Who is that?*

The stranger growled. "Picking on girls? Is that what you do in this town?" He took a quick, menacing step toward the smaller boys. They flinched, then spun around, and ran toward the village.

He turned back to Amram. "What is the matter with you? Do you make your family proud when you throw rocks at girls?"

Amram scrambled to his feet. He stepped forward, his fists clenched. "I know who you are."

"Do you?"

Amram pointed a thick finger. "You've come to live here. My father knows about you. He is the most powerful man in this town. You should know better than to make enemies of me and my family."

The stranger stood still and silent, then glanced over his shoulder at Mara. "Well, now that I'm trembling in fear, you can go report back to your abba. Make sure and tell him you took care of this dangerous girl as well."

Amram sneered once more at Mara, turned, and half-ran back toward the village.

The stranger watched Amram scurry away. When he turned to Mara, she scrambled around the big jar, putting it between them, and peeked over the lip of the jug.

He was young, not a boy but a full-grown man, probably over twenty years. His bright white tunic—made of fine linen—ended at his knees and was belted with intricately tooled leather studded in silver and bronze. An ornate dagger and fat leather purse hung from his waist, and his feet were encased in sturdy Roman sandals.

His face was smooth instead of bearded, and his short black hair curled over his forehead. Serious dark eyes regarded her silently, and straight thin lips remained turned down in anger. Dark brows contrasted sharply with his pale skin—she had never seen such pale skin. An angry red gash marred one side of his face, and one shoulder of his tunic was torn and stained with what looked like blood. She had a fleeting, ridiculous thought of the stories of warrior angels—terrifying and beautiful. Still crouching on the ground, she caught up her mantle and used it to shield her burning face.

"Are you hurt?" His sandals scraped the ground close to her. His words were precise and clipped, unlike the softer inflections of the Samaritans.

She shook her head. *I must look ridiculous, huddled on the ground.*

She held the water jug close to her face with one arm and pushed herself to her feet. *Can he see my legs tremble? Even if I weren't forbidden to speak to a man in public, I couldn't think of one thing to say.*

Another man came panting along the path, trying to keep up with a trotting donkey. "First you wouldn't budge; now you won't slow down!"

This man was small and slight, also short-haired and clean-shaven, but much older, and his clothes were of lesser quality. He yanked the donkey to a halt behind the young man, who stood tense and straight, his fists at his sides. The older man's head swiveled to take in Mara. "What happened?"

The younger man turned toward him. "Nothing, Drusus. Let us get on with our own business." He glanced at Mara, one brow raised, then walked past her.

She ducked her head to hide her flaming face.

Mara didn't move as dust settled around her bare feet and the sound of sandals and hooves faded around the curve in the road. *What just happened? Is he new to Sychar, as Amram said? He's wealthy, certainly, and hardly looks like he belongs here.*

Mara started toward the well. If he was new to Sychar, he would soon find out that he'd chosen the wrong side in this battle. He seemed to regret it already.

Her legs still shook when she reached the well. She searched the women's faces, but no one was drawing water or even spared her a glance. The women and girls were clustered in bunches, chattering in high voices about the handsome stranger who had just passed by.

As Asher played in the afternoon shade, Mara sat by the hot fire, baking enough bread for tonight and tomorrow. Her extra tunic and Asher's white tallith were washed and drying on the bushes, ready for Sabbath prayers. The plump skin of goat's milk hung by the fire, thickening into a sour yogurt.

Mara's hands still shook when she thought of the boys on the path. Her mind swam with sharp words that she could have—should have—used on Amram. She groaned out loud. How ridiculous she must have looked to the stranger.

Nava dragged her thin body out of the dark house as if she were made of stone. Her lips were cracked and dry, her face lined from sleeping, her hair matted to her head. She sank to the ground beside Mara.

Mara kneaded bread dough, beating it fiercely. *Here she comes, looking for food and water after she slept the day away. She doesn't care what I put up with because of her.* She pinched off a knob and slapped it on the hot coals of the cooking fire. Nava had to be made to see reason. The boys on the road were just the beginning if she kept up her acquaintance with Alexandros. Everything she did just made their lives worse. Did she care for her children at all?

Mara turned back to her work without a word to Nava. She could get her own water.

"Asher," Nava said, patting her lap, "come here."

Asher crawled over and climbed into the folds of her dirty tunic, sticking his thumb in his mouth. His eyes flicked between his mother and his sister.

"Mara." Nava laid her hand on Mara's shoulder.

Mara shrugged her away and slapped another round of dough on the fire.

"Mara." She rested her hand on Mara's, stopping her frantic movements. "I'm sorry. I don't know what is wrong with me. Thank you for taking such good care of us."

Mara's angry words drained away. *My mother is sick. Not just her body, her very soul is wasting away.* She blinked back tears and nodded, not trusting her voice. She went into the shadows of the house and brought her mother a dripping ladle of cool water. "Drink, Mama. It will help." *If only I could give her something that would heal her parched soul.*

When evening finally darkened into night, Mara dragged her tired body up the rickety ladder to the rooftop. It was wide and flat, covered with dried reeds. The night was cool and clear, perfect for sleeping outside. She lay down next to Asher.

"Mara," Asher said. His face was pinched and worried. "Are you angry at me?"

She tucked Asher's thin blanket around his shoulders. "No, of course not, little one. Why do you think so?"

"Because you aren't talking. You haven't smiled all day. And you're doing this with your face." He pressed his lips tightly together and lowered his brows.

The laugh that escaped her lightened her heavy heart. "Oh, Asher. I'm sorry. I'm just . . . I'm just angry. Not at you. Not at anyone." Except Amram.

Mara snuggled close to her brother on the hard sleeping pallet. *I will take care of us all, no matter what happens.*

Her thoughts turned to the stranger on the road. His pale skin and fine clothes. Her stomach flopped like a fish on dry sand. He didn't belong in Sychar and probably wouldn't stay long. She'd just have to avoid him.

Shem's grandparents stared at him when he reached their home on the far side of the village. As though he was a stranger.

Shem stood in Abahu's courtyard with Drusus and the donkey behind him. A stone wall surrounded the house and trees, protecting them from curious neighbors. Low rosemary and lavender bushes scented the morning breeze. Flowering fig trees brought to mind his mother's garden in Caesarea, but Abahu's courtyard was much smaller. The walls seemed to close around him.

"Grandfather." Shem bowed his head to Abahu. Abahu did not answer.

"Shem, you are . . . taller than I remembered," his grandmother finally stuttered. She averted her eyes from his face, smooth and beardless, his short dark hair, his foreign clothes and sandals.

Shem took a deep breath and met Abahu's eyes, looking into a face that would be his own when he grew old. But where he was pale, Abahu's skin was deeply tanned and lined like old leather. His thick hair and beard were streaked with more silver than black. His bare brown arms showed ropey muscle that spoke of a life of hard work.

Abahu's eyes narrowed, and his mouth formed a tight line. His sharp gaze took in the blood on Shem's tunic, but he didn't say a word.

"Mother and Father send their greetings." Shem stepped aside and waved a hand at Drusus and the donkey. "Father sent gifts from Caesarea."

Abahu raised one brow as he glanced at the bolts of cloth, jugs of wine, and delicacies sent from the city.

"Grandfather. I—" Shem swallowed. His mind was dulled from travel and lack of sleep, but clearly this was not going well. "I am glad to be here."

Abahu's face softened. He stepped forward and embraced Shem, greeting him with a kiss on his cheek. "You are welcome here." He cleared his throat and walked stiffly to the house.

Shem followed Abahu into the house.

His grandmother rushed for water to wash his dusty feet. Mechola looked older than he remembered. Her soft, whiskery face was deeply lined, but her eyes were still bright and sharp. She had the gentle smile that he remembered from his childhood—so much like his mother's. Her rough brown tunic and plain sandals were simple dress, considering the wealth of their house.

Abahu's house was roomy and comfortable for a town such as Sychar. The thick walls made of sun-dried bricks kept it cool in the summer and blocked the worst of the winter winds. He showed Shem two sleeping rooms, a workroom with a loom and baskets of wool, and a storage room packed from floor to ceiling with food and oil. A small formal dining area with a low table and couches was probably rarely used, Shem guessed. Abahu's home, while one of the largest in Sychar, would easily fit into the courtyard of his father's house in Caesarea.

Abahu sat beside him in silence as Shem ate the warm bread and dried fish that his grandmother served him. He rose quickly as soon as Shem swallowed the last bite. "You'll want to see the olives now."

Shem ran a hand over his tired eyes. Farmers didn't sleep during the day, even when they had been traveling all night. "Yes, of course, Grandfather."

• • •

When night finally came, sleep was impossible. Not because the bed was prickly and hard compared to his soft mattress at home—Shem's body was tired enough to sleep on a bed made of stone. No, his thoughts spun like the wheels of a racing chariot.

The small room was furnished simply with a bed, some hooks, and one lamp set on an overturned bushel basket. His grandfather had no rolls of parchment, no writing desk. Shem longed for his teachers, his fellow students, the libraries and gymnasium that he had left behind in Caesarea, even his brothers. He tried to picture their faces but saw instead the dark eyes of the soldier in the forum. Shem groaned and rolled over.

And then again this morning. How long it would take for the boys from the road to tell the entire town about their encounter? What else could he have done—just walk by and let the boys torture a girl? But he was a grown man knocking down a boy. As if he wasn't enough of an embarrassment to his grandparents already.

Granted, that boy was almost as tall as he and picking on a girl. Shem hadn't gotten a good look at her—just an impression of wild dark hair, brown skin, and dirty bare feet. She hadn't uttered a sound, not even a thank-you.

Not a good beginning in Sychar. *Stay out of trouble, for once, Shem.*

A creak and a groan sounded from the room next to his. The low rumble of his grandfather's voice carried through the thin wall.

"Did you know about this outrage?"

"Of course not!" Mechola whispered. "I'm as surprised as you."

Straw rustled as the old couple settled themselves onto their mattresses. The darkness around him amplified their whispers. "You must admit," Mechola said, "he was polite. This can't be what he's used to. I'm sure he has a very fine room in his father's home."

"He can just go back to his fine room."

Of course Grandfather is angry. Tomorrow all of Sychar will see his grandson, looking like a pagan, at Sabbath prayers.

"Surely you won't send him away because of his hair? His father is more Greek than Samaritan."

"He promised to maintain respect for the law given by Moses. 'Do not cut the hair at the sides of your head or clip off the edges of your beard.'" Abahu sighed. "And what good can a boy like that be to a farmer? I doubt he's done a hard day's work in his life."

Shem's neck warmed. His grandfather was right about that.

At least Drusus wasn't lying at the foot of his bed, listening. He'd sent the nosy servant home to Caesarea as soon as he'd had some food and rest. He'd warned Drusus to go straight home instead of stopping to gossip in the village.

"He can learn. It may take some time. But I have heard you say that there is more work than you and Enosh can do, especially at harvest."

A deep grumble penetrated the wall. "Enosh."

"Enosh is a hard worker, Abahu. It is just his way to be quiet. You know he needs the work. A boy his age is looking to marry in a few years. He'll need a bride price and a home for his wife. He won't earn that as a shepherd."

Shem had liked the tall, quiet boy who had helped them in the olive groves today. Enosh, related in some way to his grandmother, worked hard and didn't chatter. Even better, he hadn't stared at Shem's hair or scar. He was barely a man but worked as hard as Abahu.

"You are right, of course, but what I wouldn't give for a son to inherit my land and trees."

Mechola fell silent.

Pity and shame twisted through Shem's chest. His mother had spoken of a brother who died in childhood. They'd once had a real son to inherit the land and take care of them as they aged— instead of Shem.

"Shem is your son now. I can't help but think . . ."

"What?"

The mattress rustled. "He seems to be searching for something."

"Searching? For what, woman?"

"I don't know. It's silly, but he seems . . . lost."

Abahu grunted. Before long, snores drifted through the thin wall.

He didn't deserve his grandmother's loving words. And what did she mean—searching for something? *All I'm searching for is an answer to this problem.* He turned over, pulling his blanket tight although the night was warm enough.

How long can I live this lie?

Ezra had forbidden him to speak of the Roman. And if he told the truth, Abahu might send him back to Caesarea. He would only endanger his family again if he went back. But could he look into Abahu's face—or Mechola's—every day, pretending that he was their new son? Could he live with being a liar, as well as a killer?

He stared into the darkness. No. He couldn't do it. Ezra was wrong to make him lie. His grandparents were good people and deserved to know the truth. He must tell them, and soon.

But what will Abahu do when I tell him the real reason I'm in Sychar?

Chapter 6

Asher clung to Mara's neck, almost cutting off her breath as she trudged up the last stretch of the path on Mount Gerizim. They reached the clearing in front of the synagogue, and she crouched, letting him slide to the ground.

A few villagers passed by, not looking at her and giving Asher a wide berth as though he were a poisonous snake. She heaved him up in her arms and walked into the building, her head high. They had as much right to be there as any of the villagers.

The building was built of stone—huge slabs that had been dragged up the hill centuries ago. Sandals were strewn on the floor of the anteroom, but since Mara and Asher were barefoot she stopped only to wash their hands in the ritual water vats, then continued into the sanctuary.

Everyone in the village came to Sabbath prayer. Everyone except Nava. The men occupied the middle of the large, square room. At least a hundred men and boys stood facing the stone dais set in the center front. Women and children stood along the walls three deep. Mara breathed a prayer of relief that her mother hadn't come.

Mara hitched Asher up higher on her hip and slipped behind the nearest woman. She made her way toward the front of the room, the women and children moving aside hastily as soon as they saw Asher.

The high priest, Yahokeem, stood on the dais. Behind him hung a heavy curtain, pulled back to reveal a metal case decorated with carved pomegranates. In it were housed the scrolls of the law, the most valuable treasures in Sychar. They were written by Aaron's great-grandson Abisha, not long after the settling of the Promised Land.

She looked over the crowd. Where was Aunt Ruth? There was Uncle Uziel, standing near the front. Beside him was Abahu, the olive grower, and beside him . . .

Mara's back stiffened and she caught her breath. She ducked behind plump Tirzah. The big woman's expensive scent tickled her nose, and she held her breath to ward off a sneeze. She peeked around Tirzah's elaborate hair.

The stranger stood next to Abahu, the olive grower. Their faces—both stern and handsome—were set like stone, ignoring the stares and whispers around them. They stood straight and stiff, taller than most of the other men by a full head. As with all the men, a white tallith lay over the stranger's clothes, and his head was covered. But his smooth, pale face still looked foreign next to the dark skin and full beards around him. She shrank back until all she could see was Tirzah's back.

Adah and Rivkah towered next to Tirzah.

"It's Dinah's son," Tirzah whispered to Adah.

Yahokeem raised his arms. The murmurs of the crowd ceased.

Adah bent her head toward Tirzah. "Which one?" Some of the women looked at her sharply.

"One of the younger ones, I think. He doesn't look like Ezra, does he?"

Rivkah giggled, and Adah poked her with a bony elbow. "What's he doing here? They haven't been here for years. Not even for Passover."

Tirzah shrugged. "I don't know. But every girl in town is talking about him."

Yahokeem lifted an ancient scroll from the elaborately carved chest behind him. He unrolled it and began to read.

Rivkah peered back at Mara with a smirk. As she raised her hands to pat her twisted braids, her silver bangles jingled like bells. Jebus had been generous with his betrothal gift.

And she wants me to know it.

When the last prayer was sung, Mara scooped Asher from his place on the floor and darted out of the building.

A call from the anteroom stopped her. "Mara."

She turned back. Tirzah stood in the doorway, a jar and a packet in her hands.

She shoved the bundles into Mara's free hand. "No matter what your mother does, I won't let children starve in my village." Giving Asher a wary glance, she turned on her heel, and went back into the building.

Tirzah might be the cruelest of the village women, but she never failed to give to Nava's unfortunate children. Mara forced out a thank-you as Tirzah's broad back disappeared. Charity given with a measure of disdain still filled Asher's belly. She juggled the jar and bundle into a more secure position and started back down the path.

"Mara, slow down!" Asher complained, bumping up and down on Mara's back as she rushed down the path. She slowed, glancing back at the synagogue. A crowd of villagers poured out of the doors, spreading down the mountain.

"Sorry, Asher," she panted. "I'm just hungry."

"Me too! I'm hungry too!" Asher clasped her neck, almost choking her. "Go faster, Mara!"

Mara picked up her pace again, sweat trickling down her neck. She didn't want to face anyone right now, especially not the stranger. She should at least thank him for saving her. But in Sychar, gossip traveled as swiftly as the desert lark. If any of the women found out that the newest unmarried man in Sychar had helped her, they would hate her more than ever.

No. She would avoid him and hope that neither he, nor Amram, would tell what happened on the road to the well. Mara breathed a sigh of relief as she reached their little valley and Asher slid from her back.

Sabbath prayers at the synagogue were not as bad as Shem had feared. His grandfather brought Shem to the front of the crowd.

Abahu didn't look ashamed or embarrassed. If anything, his grandfather seemed . . . defiant. He stood near Shem, almost protectively, as the priest read the law and the village men sent him sidelong glances.

Now they walked home in silence. They skirted the village and passed the well. Only a few women filled their jars in the heat of the mid-morning sun.

Abahu nodded at them, and they stared at Shem.

A breeze cooled the air and whispered over the newly greened grass and sprouting crocuses. They reached Abahu's well-tended courtyard, full of flowers in fragrant bloom. Wide, flat rocks made a comfortable place to eat and rest in the shade of spreading fig trees.

"Please, Shem, sit here," Mechola said, hurrying into the house. "I will bring the food and wine."

He sat down with Abahu on the sun-warmed stones. It was time to give his grandfather an explanation. About his hair, his clothes, everything. He deserved it; they both did.

Shem met Abahu's direct gaze with his own. "Grandfather, I am sorry. I know that my appearance has caused gossip. I have brought shame on you and Grandmother."

"Gossip?" Abahu jutted his chin forward. "Do you think I care what the old women say about me while they stand around the well?" He sat up straighter. "And I am not ashamed of my grandson."

Shem's shoulders drooped. *I don't deserve this loyalty.*

"No, and I don't care what the men say in the marketplace." Abahu's voice rose. "Do you know what I care about?"

Shem swallowed hard and nodded.

"What is my son-in-law teaching my grandsons in Caesarea? Does he still teach you of the God of our fathers? Or has Ezra adopted the gods of the Greeks and Romans and turned his children into pagans?"

Mechola came out with the food. She put bread, oil, and dried fish in front of Abahu, then brought sweet melons, a bowl of olives, and honey cakes. She rested her hand gently on her husband's shoulder and frowned as she set the jug of wine before him. A jug of water came next. Mechola withdrew but stood nearby in the shade of the house.

Abahu poured wine and water into both goblets. He sat back, took a long drink, and raised his silver eyebrows. "Well?"

Shem took a deep breath. *Where should I start?* "Grandfather, it is not what you think. This . . ." He gestured to his hair and clothes. "This is my fault. I need to tell you why I am here. Why my parents sent me to you. I am not here to take over the olives. And I am not here to become your heir." Shem fidgeted with his goblet. "I'm here because I killed a Roman soldier."

Mechola drew in a sharp breath.

Abahu faltered, bit into a round of bread, and chewed, his brows pulled down.

Shem's mouth was dry. "I've been hiding for about a week, but they are still looking for me. I cut my hair and shaved my beard to disguise myself. They are looking for a Samaritan, or a Jew. My father thinks they will not look for me out in the country. But you still must know that you are hiding a fugitive. You might even be in danger."

He waited for the outrage.

Abahu leaned forward. "Tell us what happened, Shem."

He's not angry. He's as calm as if we were talking about the price of seed. "I'm sorry. I seem to . . . find trouble wherever I go. I don't want to put you in danger. Or lie to you. But my father . . ."

Abahu raised a hand. "Don't worry about that part yet. Just tell us what happened."

All I can do is tell them the whole thing. Then they can decide what to do with me. "I've been in fights before. Too many of them. I get so angry . . . there is so much injustice in the city. The strong abuse the weak. Greeks and Romans oppress the Jews and Samaritans alike."

Father thinks I look for fights, but he's wrong. Trouble finds me. Sometimes it was Greek traders insulting Benjamin or youths picking on beggars in the marketplace. Sometimes his own brothers teased him once too often. He touched the puckering scar on his temple again.

"There were two soldiers. They were harassing a woman." He clenched his hands into fists. "They—the soldiers—were drunk. They pushed her around. I couldn't just walk by." He raised his eyes. "They were looking for a fight. But it got out of control so fast."

"What did you do, Shem?" Abahu asked.

"I . . . pulled out my dagger, told Benjamin to run . . ." Abahu's face was hard to read. Would he call him a fool, like his father had? "One of them grabbed me, and he had a sword." Shem touched the scar again. "But I got in close. I . . ." He swallowed hard. The look on Abahu's face told Shem that he didn't have to explain.

"We got away. We hid in a warehouse, one of ours. But they have been looking for me ever since. It's all over the city." Shem sat in miserable silence.

Abahu and Mechola exchanged a long look. "So your father sent you here to hide you." His grandfather looked older than he had a moment earlier.

"Yes," Shem said. "But . . . there is more, Grandfather."

Abahu pursed his lips. "More than killing a Roman soldier?"

"My father had Drusus tell you that I'll settle here, take over the olives and the press since you have no sons of your own."

"Yes, that's what your father wants." Abahu nodded.

Shem shook his head. "That is not what he wants. I must tell you that he has other plans for me. Big plans. He's waiting for this to blow over. Maybe a year, he told me. Then he will want me back in Caesarea, I'm sure of it."

"What do you mean? And why didn't he tell us?"

Shem shrugged. Saying anything more would show his father as the liar that he was.

Abahu frowned. "What of your mother?"

"She doesn't know. Really, she expects me to stay here and live with you. She thinks it will keep me out of trouble." Shem rubbed the back of his neck. *And already I've threatened some of the village boys.* He picked up his cup and took a long drink of wine. Strong and sweet, it loosened his tight throat. "But my father . . . well, I am very valuable to him. And yes, I have learned the laws of the Samaritans."

His grandfather grunted.

"But I've also studied with the Jews. Before I left, I was studying with a Greek tutor. I speak both Greek and Latin, as well as Aramaic and Hebrew." Shem fidgeted with the ring on his finger. "I've been promised a place in the city government."

"You are young to know so much, and why you would need to know the laws of the Jews . . ."

"It is helpful in Caesarea." Shem shrugged again. It wouldn't help anyone to tell Abahu that Ezra had dealings with many Jews—Jews that didn't even suspect that his father was Samaritan. "Learning comes easily to me."

"You're saying that you won't be staying here?" Abahu said.

Shem looked at Mechola. Her eyes were downcast, and her mouth drooped.

"I don't know. I must obey my father, but I will not lie to you. If they find me here—the Romans—you both will be in danger." Shem swallowed hard. "I will understand if you want me to leave."

Abahu sat still and silent.

Shem picked up the round of bread. He put it down without taking a bite. He took a deep gulp of his wine.

Abahu sighed, then said gruffly, "You have grown to be a good man. Eat and rest. We will trust in the Almighty. Tomorrow we will get you some sturdy clothes and teach you how to be a farmer."

Mara smiled at her mother. When they had returned from the synagogue, Nava had been awake and dressed. She had already laid out the bread and yogurt in the shade of the trees. Mara knew then that her mother would spend the Sabbath with them, singing songs and telling stories.

They ate together, tearing off chunks of yesterday's hard bread and soaking them in the thick, tangy yogurt. Nava ate little, but smiled and listened to Asher chatter as he stuffed his mouth with almonds. Mara hadn't mentioned the source of the almonds, and Nava didn't ask.

Now they sat in the house as dusk fell. Mara pulled a gap-toothed ivory comb through her mother's tangled hair. Asher snuggled deep in Nava's lap, talking around the thumb that refused to leave his mouth. "Mama, tell us a story, please? Tell us about Mara's abba?"

"You've heard that story so many times, my sweet." Nava tipped her head back so that her long hair fell in Mara's lap and closed her eyes. "Mara's father was very handsome. He was tall and strong, and he made the most beautiful clay jars and pots. He could paint a beautiful garden—greens and golds and pinks—on a water jug. Sometimes he would paint little flowers on shards of clay for me. He would slip them to me in the marketplace. My friends were so jealous of his devotion."

Asher snuggled deeper in his mother's lap. Mara's hand faltered on the comb. Had that been the beginning of trouble for her mother?

"When I came of age, he asked my father for my hand. But my abba said no. You see, Moshe was not a rich man, just a potter's son. My father wanted a better marriage for me. But Moshe, he waited patiently. And finally, Abba said yes." She smiled, and her face became young again. "We were so happy."

Mara stopped brushing. *That's where the story always ends. She never speaks of Moshe's death, nor of the years after it. Is there more that she isn't telling?*

Nava ran her hands over her hair to test its smoothness. She shifted Asher to Mara's lap and took the comb. "Now, let me work on your hair, Mara."

"You now, Mara!" Asher said. "You tell a story now."

Mara smiled at her little brother. He had so few days like this. Thank God the Sabbath required them to rest with no distracting chores. "What would you like me to tell, my sweet?"

"Tell me about my father, Mara, please?"

"No, Asher. You hear this story every day." But never in front of her mother.

"Please, Mara?" Asher squirmed.

Mara remembered Shaul, Asher's father, well. It was the happiest time she had ever known and the most painful of all her memories. And Nava never spoke of him.

Asher took his thumb out of his mouth. "I won't suck my thumb tonight. I promise."

He deserves to hear about his abba. "Alright. Your abba," she began. "Well . . . he was big and strong and very handsome." She looked over her shoulder at Nava.

Her mother's smile was gone.

"And what else, Mara?" Asher asked.

She couldn't stop now. "He loved Mama very much. When they married, I was about as old as you are now. He always laughed and made Mama and me laugh, too."

The tug of the comb in her hair stopped.

"Did he make things out of wood?" Asher hurried her on to his favorite part of the story.

"Yes, beautiful things. Yokes and plow handles and even the stool that we sit on to milk the goats."

Nava put the comb into Mara's hands. Why had Nava pushed Shaul away? *I know she loved him.*

"What else?" Asher said, his cheek dimpling.

"Well, don't you have a little donkey and a little cow that you play with every day?"

Asher nodded his head, too pleased to speak, and pointed to the well-worn toys lying in the corner. Toys that he would have given up years ago if he had a father, instead of a mother who treated him like a baby.

"Those were carved by his hands! I watched when he gave them to you, although you were too little to even hold them. He loved you very much to make those for you."

Nava rose and went to her corner of the room. She spread her mat on the floor.

Asher let out a satisfied sigh. At least he had liked the story. He lowered himself from Mara's lap and crawled to his sleeping mat to lie down beside the beloved cow and donkey. "How did my abba die, Mama?" he asked.

Nava's shoulders slumped under an invisible weight. She dragged her hands over her eyes and forehead. "I think I am tired now. Go to sleep, Asher." She lay down on her mat and turned her back to them.

Mara went to Asher, who was already drowsing. *At least he is unaware of the hurt that his words cause.* She tucked his little blanket around him and traced his peaceful face with one finger. She looked at her mother, curled in a tight ball of misery. Any mention of Shaul sent her back into a private world of darkness. *Lord of all, please help them. Help them both, I beg you.*

Chapter 7

Mara's sack bounced against her leg as she hiked toward the village. The rough-spun bundle held her spindle, a great tuft of carded wool, and three skeins of green yarn for her aunt Ruth. Ruth would send it home filled with barley, oil, and beans. Asher's thin legs slipped from around her waist, and she hitched him higher on her back. *He's so much smaller than other boys his age, but by winter, he'll be too big for me to carry.* What would she do then?

But an even bigger worry weighed on her. *Should I tell Ruth about Alexandros?* It would be a relief to talk about it. Maybe her aunt could get Nava to see sense and send the pagan away for good.

When they arrived at her uncle's courtyard, Mara was panting and covered in sweat. She dropped Asher to the ground and sank onto the bench under a sharp-scented eucalyptus tree. The courtyard was small but full of color. Crocuses bloomed around trees that provided both shade and beauty. Her aunt's loom sat in one corner, a basket of yarn beside it. The smell of baking barley loaves warmed the air, and children's laughter drifted from behind the house.

"Can I go?" Asher asked, looking toward the back garden.

"Yes. Help with the weeding. Be good."

Ruth hurried out of the small house and folded Mara in her soft, plump arms. Mara breathed in her aunt's sweet scent of lavender and barley. It felt good to be held and petted like a child again.

Although younger than Nava, Ruth was no great beauty. Her

body was small and rounded, her brown face creased with laughter, her small, dark eyes full of kindness. Most days found Ruth working in her modest home, surrounded by her children and their friends. Three strong sons and a daughter made Ruth the envy of many women in the village.

Uziel, not rich but well-respected, sold tools from a cramped shop in the middle of the marketplace. He made barely enough profit to support his growing family, but Ruth did her best with what little she had. Their home—only two rooms and a tiny courtyard—always felt cozy instead of crowded.

Mara presented Ruth with the yarn.

"Mara, this is a beautiful color. It will be lovely in the cloth I'm weaving for Matea. But you must let me pay you, my dear." Ruth ran her fingers over the smooth thread.

Mara shook her head. "You give us more than you can spare. Please, I want you to have it."

Ruth sat down at her loom. Clay weights stretched the warp threads tightly downward while Ruth wove the colorful weft threads across the length of fabric. Her daughter, Matea, toddled from the house and settled at her feet. Mara sat under the eucalyptus tree and took her spindle and a great tuft of goat's wool from her bag. The soft breeze and the comforting scents of the courtyard soothed her worried mind. Now would be a good time to talk to Ruth about Alexandros.

Mara jumped as the courtyard door banged open. A shrill voice followed. "Well, well, isn't this nice?"

Adah flounced into the courtyard, her hands empty. She wore a new linen dress, and her wrists jangled with shiny brass bangles. A necklace of amber hung from her skinny neck. Mara suppressed a groan. Adah was here to show off her finery and gossip.

"Mara! How beautiful you are," she said. "You are the image of your mother at your age, isn't she, Ruth?"

Adah ignored her at the well and marketplace, but here, in front of Ruth, she acted like a close family friend. Of course, Ruth knew the truth.

Adah smoothed her dress and sat down next to Ruth. "Except

Nava was already married at your age. In fact, I believe she was twice married, if you count that mess with Zevulun."

Mara faltered and almost dropped the whirling spindle. *What did Adah mean? Twice married?*

Ruth caught her breath and looked from Mara back to Adah.

Adah covered her mouth with her hand, as real remorse etched a furrow over her eyes. "Oh!" She looked to Ruth. "She doesn't know?"

Mara straightened her back. What was Adah talking about? "Of course I know." She met the other woman's eyes with a blank face. Whatever it was, she didn't want to hear it from Adah.

"Adah," Ruth patted Adah's leg. "I heard Jonothon's wife had the baby yesterday?"

"Oh, yes!" Adah turned away from Mara, relief in her voice. "And you wouldn't believe what happened!" She launched into a story about the priest and his wife that she had heard from a very close friend.

Mara gave her spindle a twist and another pinch of carded wool. What had Adah meant about Nava? Ruth would know. *There could only be one reason why she never told me. It must be very bad.*

". . . I would have loved to see Abahu's face when that boy came to his door in his Greek clothes and shorn hair!"

Mara's mouth went dry. Adah was talking about Abahu's grandson. She gave the spindle another twirl. She felt unclean listening to Adah's gossip, but her ears strained to hear about the stranger. Had he said anything about her?

"You know Mechola; she doesn't say much. But I believe she is just as shocked as her husband. Can you believe it? Dinah's own boy, looking like the Greeks of Caesarea! Dinah," Adah snorted. "She was always so smug—and he's old enough to be set in his father's trade! I'd say he's well over twenty. Far too old to be an apprentice, that's what my husband says. And far too learned, from what his bragging servant says, to be picking olives!"

Mara snuck a glance at Ruth. She seemed completely absorbed in her weaving. *Yet I know she listens. A new member of the village affects everyone.*

"And they haven't come to Passover for years! They say he is to learn the olive trade . . . humph! Something isn't right about that, I say. That servant hinted that he might have been rushed out of Caesarea for other reasons . . ."

Mara's heart sank. So he was staying in Sychar. She would no doubt meet him again, and he would remember her humiliation on the road. He might start asking questions about her.

Ruth halted her weaving.

Adah fell silent, and the courtyard seemed to echo with the sudden quiet. She waited for Ruth to speak, her eyes bulging like a hooked fish.

Ruth pointed. "Adah, would you please pass me that skein of green thread?"

Adah handed it to her with a sniff. "Well. You might not care. Your daughter is too young. But he is a catch, rich and handsome. Every girl in town is talking about him. I'd guess they sent him away to put a stop to a bad match. His kind always falls for the wrong girl."

Ruth tied the new thread to her shuttle in silence. Adah sniffed again and stood, brushing her robe free of dust and adjusting her mantle over her thin, frizzy hair. "I must go, dear Ruth. I can't believe I've stayed this long already! I have so much to do today, and Shimon will be furious if he comes home to no bread. That lazy Rivkah can't be trusted to do anything right. I don't know what Jebus sees in her."

She turned to Mara. "Good-bye, Mara, please pass on my greeting to your mother. And, my dear," her gaze dropped to the ground, "I'm sorry that I ever mentioned . . . well, about Zevulun. Please, forgive me." She hurried out of the courtyard without a backward glance.

The courtyard gate slammed shut. Mara stopped her spindle. She opened her clenched hand to find the soft wool crushed and damp.

Ruth put down the skein of yarn and held out her arms. "I am sorry, my dear. She didn't know. Adah's a gossip, but not that cruel. At least not when she's alone."

Mara fell into Ruth's embrace. "What about Zevulun, Ruth? What does he want forgotten?"

Ruth squeezed her tight. "Mara," she finally said, "I will tell you about your mother. But you must try not to judge her. She was very young and foolish. It is best forgotten. But in Sychar . . . nothing is forgotten." Her aunt settled back at the loom.

Mara sat at her feet. Her heart fluttered, and she wrapped her arms around her chest like a shield.

"Nava was a very beautiful girl." Ruth's eyes rested on Mara's face. "Many said too beautiful. You are so much like her. Travelers talked of her beauty to other towns. Strangers would stare, and men of every age were foolish in her presence. But Nava . . . she didn't practice the modesty that women like that must. She knew her own power and used it shamelessly on any man she met, whether old or young."

Ruth wound the green thread around her shuttle. "Our parents could deny her very little—perhaps they spoiled her. Our father doted on her, and mother was so proud of her beautiful daughter." Ruth said this with no bitterness and looked down at Mara with a little smile. "But don't think of her as just beautiful and selfish. She was also so joyful, so full of laughter. You could not be anything but cheerful with my big sister. I adored her."

"I remember what she was like . . . before," Mara said.

Ruth passed the shuttle through the warp, her hands flying faster as she talked. "Nava had given her heart to a handsome and reckless boy, Moshe. His eyes were as blue as the sky, his mouth full of sweet words. They sighed over each other in the marketplace; I could hardly watch them without laughing out loud. All the older girls were even more jealous of Nava. It was so improper, how they acted. But most just looked the other way, because it was Nava."

Matea crawled into Mara's lap and snuggled close, her eyes half closed.

Ruth used the shuttle to beat the green threads tight against the woven cloth above. "When Nava reached marrying age, a man of the village, a very rich one, spoke to our father. They began to make arrangements for his betrothal to Nava. Nava protested. It was disgraceful, really. If my daughter . . ." She glanced at Matea. "Well, anyway. It was Zevulun, of course. He was a widower with no children then. He already had great influence in the village, but, you know, he was not handsome or full of flattering words."

Mara shivered, thinking of Zevulun. Whenever the big man passed her in the marketplace, he scowled.

Ruth reached the end of the green thread and held out her hand.

Mara passed her the next skein, her eyes locked on the thin green stripe that was appearing on the creamy white wool.

"Nava begged Father to change his mind. She rubbed his feet, made him honey cakes, but he did not waver. He wanted her to marry the richest and most powerful man in the village. For once, Father was immune to her charms or her tantrums. She was bound to obey."

No. Please, Lord. It can't be. Mara's stomach twisted, and she pulled Matea closer.

Ruth ran her fingers over the vertical warp threads like she was strumming the strings of a harp. "The betrothal took place after the olive harvest. Before our family and most of the village, Zevulun declared, 'She is my wife and I her husband, from today and forever.' And they were betrothed, bound to each other in the marriage contract."

Her mother had lied to her.

All these years. Nava had been betrothed to Zevulun before she married Moshe. Betrothal meant a sacred contract, broken only by a formal decree of divorce. This was a very different story from the one her mother told. "Why didn't anyone tell me?"

Ruth took a deep breath. "I'm sorry, Mara. We thought that your mother . . . that Nava should tell you, if anyone."

"She didn't."

"She is not well. I'm sorry I let you find out this way, from Adah." She went back to the green thread and her shuttle.

"What happened?" Mara asked. *I don't want to know.*

"They were to be married in the spring. Zevulun refused to wait a full year." Ruth's voice dropped. "The winds of Gadim were bad that winter. It was so cold. Father became very sick. First a cough. Then a burning fever took his life. Nava and I mourned together with Mama. Then we moved to our uncle Lemech's house.

"But she was still so selfish, so caught up in her own misery. To lose her beloved father and also be forced to marry a man like Zevulun was too much for her to accept."

Mara shook her head. She couldn't listen to any more. Matea slumped in her lap, asleep. She gathered her little cousin in her arms and stood, then carried her to a shady corner and laid her on the soft grass. She wanted to scream. To run away. To shake her mother. She slumped on the bench under the eucalyptus and put her face in her hands.

Ruth moved to sit beside her. "I'm sorry, my girl."

"Tell me the rest," Mara said.

Ruth wrapped her arms around Mara's rounded shoulders. "We mourned. And then, when spring came, Nava dressed in her finest clothes. I remember, I asked her where she was going alone. She shushed me and made me promise not to tell Mama.

"She told me later what happened. She went to the market-place and spoke to Moshe. Then she went to Zevulun's house, where she found her betrothed. He was shocked, she said. She demanded, 'Write me a bill of divorce, Zevulun, so that I can marry the potter's son. My father is dead; I will not honor his agreement with you.'"

Mara caught her breath and jerked her head up. No wonder the women hated Nava. Especially Tirzah. Her own husband rejected so shamefully. Nava was a constant reminder that Tirzah hadn't been his first choice of bride. Yet Tirzah still gave them more food than most of the other families. Mara vowed to think more kindly of the woman. At least to try.

And Nava, her own mother, breaking her betrothal vow. Mara had never heard of a woman—anyone—doing something so disgraceful. "What did Zevulun say?" she breathed.

"I can only imagine how furious he was. He is a prideful man. Nava told me that he called her a disgrace to her family, which was true. 'Get out of my house and my sight, shameful woman! May your potter's son be cursed with you.' Then he went to the priest to write out a letter of divorce and sent it to Uncle Lemech."

She remembered her mother's uncle only dimly—a loud, disapproving voice and a deeply furrowed brow. He must have been furious. The family shamed, disgraced, because of Nava. "What happened then?" Mara whispered. "What did Lemech do?"

"The news spread all over the village before the bill of divorce was even delivered. You know how the priests talk. Moshe and Nava . . . they were betrothed at once and married quietly just three months later. She went to live with his family. Of course, Zevulun wanted the bride price returned. Our uncle was humiliated."

Ruth rubbed Mara's cold hands between her own. "Mama was shamed in the village and wouldn't even speak to Nava. I was forbidden to visit. I was about to be betrothed myself—"

"To Uziel? But I thought that was later? After I was born?"

Ruth shook her head. "No. Not to Uziel. To someone else. But that . . . didn't happen."

Didn't happen? Because of her sister's shame. "Oh, Ruth." Mara brought her aunt's hands to her face.

"Don't cry for me, Mara. It was meant to be. Uziel is a good husband." She ran her hands over Mara's hair and sighed. "Nava was young and selfish and very, very happy. Sadly, it did not last long. She was eight months with child—with you—when Moshe went to Galilee for paints. He was attacked by bandits. His body was brought back to Nava. She gave birth during her grieving and named you Mara, for her bitter grief. Moshe had left Nava with little more than the clothes she wore."

Mara clutched her aunt's hands. "And then you married Uziel and took us in."

Ruth nodded. "After Mama died."

Ruth was too kind to say it, but Nava's shame probably killed the grandmother Mara didn't even remember.

Mara buried her face in her aunt's soft shoulder. *I can't tell her about Alexandros.* No one could ever find out, especially not Ruth and Uziel. The shame of the pagan's visits, heaped upon the disgrace of Nava's past, would be too much for the people of Sychar to forgive.

Chapter 8

The afternoon sun beat down on the little house, and no breeze cooled Mara's sweat-soaked back or stirred her damp hair. Asher lay in the shade of the cedar trees. Mara measured lentils and water into the blackened cooking pot, then stirred in spicy cumin and sharp coriander.

They had been eating well. After telling Mara about her mother and Zevulun, Ruth had loaded her basket with barley, oil, and lentils. It had been enough for the last few weeks and, with luck, would stretch until Passover.

She set the pot on the fire. "Let's walk one more time, Asher. Then you can rest."

Asher rolled over. "I'm tired, Mara."

"I know, my sweet. But you are getting too big for me to carry. One more time around the garden. Then, when Mama gets home from the market, she'll be so proud of you."

Today Nava had worked cheerfully alongside Mara, making the mood in the little house light. But how long would her mother's happy mood last? Until the next snub in the marketplace or whispered remark in the synagogue? At least Alexandros hadn't come back. It had been weeks since his last visit. Maybe he'd moved on to another woman. Or been eaten by wild dogs.

Asher still hadn't moved.

Mara walked to the cedars and stood over her brother. "I found some honey on our doorstep this morning, Asher."

"Honey?" He rolled to his knees. "Can I have some?"

"One more time around the garden." She held out her hands. He let her pull him up, then leaned on her as they circled the garden. He ground his teeth together as he limped along, putting as much weight as he could on the tender side of his crippled foot.

"Good. Now rest, and I'll bring you the honey." She found the jar that she'd hidden under a pile of shorn wool and brought it to him. "Don't eat it all."

Mara returned to the garden to pull some green onions. Asher had watered faithfully, and they were already eating some of the early vegetables. She'd sent Nava to the market with thread to trade for some fish. They would have a feast tonight.

She went back to weaving on the rickety loom while the lentils cooked. If Asher could walk, even a little, things would be different. If Asher could work in the village when he grew older, they would have food and clothing without having to depend on the townspeople. Nava would surely get well if she had hope for a better life for them all.

And if Nava got better, she could send word to Shaul. Mara moved the shuttle through the warp. Nava must ask him—no, beg him—to come back to them. He would. She was sure of it. He had loved Nava. The rumors would fade, and they would be a family again. It could happen. Perhaps the worst time had passed.

A shadow passed over the loom. Mara looked up with a smile, expecting her mother, but her heart dropped like a stone. Alexandros stood in the doorway. Had he passed through the village on his way to their home? Had anyone seen him? Surely Nava would not let him stay here again.

"Hello, Mara. You are even more beautiful than the last time I saw you." He stepped inside without an invitation. His eyes took in the empty room. He came closer. "Where is your mother, girl?"

Mara stood quickly, pulling her mantle over her hair and most of her face. He stepped close enough for her to smell the cloying sweetness that always surrounded him. His scent—and the way he eyed her—made her step back.

She took a deep breath and tried to make her voice strong and confident. It came out more of a croak. "She—she went to the market but should be home soon." She slipped along the wall, as far from him as she could get, and darted out the door.

Alexandros's speckled donkey was tied to a bush in front of the house. The animal's back sagged under a load of packets and baskets. She scanned the hill, but the path from Sychar was deserted. Alexandros followed her and leaned his bulky shoulder on the door frame, watching her every move.

"You didn't see her on your way through town?" Mara asked.

"I came from Sebaste today. Your home is first on my agenda," he said, licking his lips.

Mara felt only a moment's relief. At least no one had seen him yet.

Alexandros stepped closer to her. He smiled. "Maybe it is time we got to know each other better, Mara."

A cold wave of fear rose in her. She glanced desperately at Asher, asleep under the tree. Alexandros's eyes followed hers, and his mouth curved in distaste.

"Alexandros!" Her mother's voice rang out from the top of the hill.

Mara sagged with relief.

Nava hurried down the path, breathless and flushed, a smile on her face. "Alexandros, you honor us with a visit again. I heard yesterday that the merchants were expecting you."

Mara stared at her mother. She didn't sound like she was about to ask him to leave.

The big man took Nava's hands and stared at her like a hungry dog stares at meat on his master's plate. "I couldn't pass by without a visit to the most beautiful woman in Samaria."

Nava hurried to the fire. "Come, Mara, why have you not brought bread for our guest and a bowl of water for washing?"

Alexandros raised his brows at Mara, a laugh lurking around his mouth.

"Mama? I thought . . ."

"Mara, do as I say," Nava said sharply.

As Mara brought the washbowl, she tried to catch her mother's eye.

Nava had uncovered her hair. She smiled sweetly and laid her hand on Alexandros's arm. What was she doing?

Nava barely noticed Mara as she served Alexandros the lentils, onions, and bread. She did not speak to Asher or help him with his meal. Alexandros pretended that Asher was not even there, but his eyes rested on Mara when he barked at her to fetch a wineskin from his donkey's pack.

Mara untied the wineskin from the donkey's back. She clenched her teeth and brought it to Alexandros. Did Nava really think that he would marry her and bring them all to live with him in Sebaste? *Living in the same house as Alexandros—seeing him every day—she couldn't do that to us. He would not be good to Asher. And I cannot think of the way he looks at me.*

"Sit with me and eat, Nava," Alexandros ordered, motioning for her to join him.

Mara's mouth dropped open as her mother sat down opposite the man and took bread from his hand.

Nava laughed as he whispered closer to her ear. Mara longed to hear her mother laugh. But not like this. Not with him.

Alexandros poured himself more wine and some for Nava as he told stories of his dealings with cheating Assyrians, evil Egyptians, and the Jews of Jerusalem. Nava listened with rapt attention, sitting closer to him as the evening darkened into night, their faces lit by the flickering light of the cooking fire.

Asher crawled into Mara's lap and rubbed his face. Nava glanced at them. "The weather is fine tonight. Mara, you and Asher sleep on the rooftop."

"But, Mama . . ."

"Do as I say!" Nava's jaw was tight.

What is Mama thinking? With a sick taste filling her mouth, Mara gathered their sleeping mats, leaving only her mother's mat in the dark house. She threw both heavy mats over her shoulder and climbed the rickety ladder to the flat roof, her heart pounding and her cheeks wet with angry tears.

When she'd helped Asher up the ladder, she sang to him and stroked his hair until he fell asleep. *Life was hard enough for us be-*

fore. If anyone finds out about Alexandros, it will be unbearable. Lord, help us, I beg you. Clear her mind. Restore her senses. Let her see what she is doing to us!

Asher slept. The fire below flickered over the faces of Alexandros and her mother. Their low murmurs made her skin feel as though a thousand bugs crawled over it. She couldn't stand being near them, watching her mother destroy any chance they had of happiness. Amram was right. Her mother was a whore. Mara climbed quietly down the ladder and slipped into the dark night. She ran up the hill to the deserted olive grove. At least there she could be alone.

The dark grove surrounded Shem, as peaceful as an empty synagogue. He stepped quietly through the trees, running his hands over an ancient branch. He'd learned a great deal about olives in the weeks since he came to Sychar.

The tree arching over his head had seen more than three hundred years. Ten generations had harvested its oil for their bread and lamps, their medicines and ceremonies. It had been just a seed buried in the ground when Alexander, the great general of Greece, conquered this land and the rest of the world.

Shem sat on a stump that could have been a seedling when Aristotle taught in the temples of Athens. Both trees were already old by the time Pompey captured the Promised Land for the emperor of Rome. The wind lifted his hair and rustled through the dry leaves scattered among the tree roots.

After a few weeks in Sychar, Shem had ceased jumping at every noise, afraid that Roman soldiers had somehow found him. His father was probably right. He would be safe here.

He wondered if he would be in Sychar in the months after the hot summer, when the olives fell from the trees and bright, golden oil flowed through the ancient press. The thought did not make him cringe as it had just weeks ago. His mother had been right; this was a good place.

His body had adjusted surprisingly well to the work of a

farmer. His arms and shoulders had ached at the end of the first days of hard work, but not anymore. His daily labors sent him early to bed with weary muscles and a feeling of contentment unlike any he'd known in Caesarea.

His grandparents lived simply, with none of the wealthy pretensions of his father's house. Unlike Ezra, Abahu never raised his voice or subjected his household to foul moods or tirades. His grandfather was easy to talk to and well-learned for someone who had lived his whole life in Sychar. Mechola was kind and clearly happy to have him in her house.

He still missed his teachers and the comforts of Caesarea—still hoped to return—but Shem could imagine living here, in Sychar. He pictured himself growing old with these trees, raising a family, providing oil for the village. Surely it was more worthy a life than doing his father's bidding, brokering with traders and greedy merchants in Caesarea? Or, as his tutors claimed, a life lived in the pursuit of knowledge for its own sake. But was it enough? Was that God's plan, as his mother had claimed?

He could even imagine marrying a village girl and raising a family in this peaceful village. It wouldn't be hard to find a wife here. Of course he saw the girls that twittered like sparrows wherever he went. He could hardly miss them. He guessed that they were much the same as the canaries that vied for his attention in Caesarea. The girls of Sychar draped themselves in homespun wool and brass bracelets instead of brightly dyed linen and gold, but women were much the same wherever you went.

One would make as good a wife as any other.

Mara's pulse jangled in her ears like a tambourine. She slumped next to a twisted trunk and took deep breaths. Branches wove between the ancient trunks like intertwined fingers. Dead leaves drifted over twisted roots that coiled among the trees.

She watched the moon travel over the sky. Patches of moonlight leaked through the trees and scattered silver shadows on the uneven ground. She tried to pray, but no words came—just anger at her mother and dread of what she would face next.

The moonlight blurred as her eyes filled with tears. Her life would be so different if Shaul had stayed. She would probably be betrothed by now, like Rivkah. Maybe even with children and a house of her own. He would have chosen a good man for her, someone trustworthy and kind.

She would have honored his choice, she told herself fiercely. She didn't need a handsome husband or flattering words. She would have worked hard to make her husband happy. But she would have no husband, no home, no children. She and Asher would be at the mercy of the village, which saw nothing more than her shameful mother and a crippled boy. Or worse, they would be dragged off to Sebaste with Alexandros if Nava had her way.

A twig snapped close by.

Mara held her breath and tried to see through the moon-dappled darkness. She pushed her back hard against the tree trunk, sliding up to a crouch, ready to run. If the wrong kind of man found her—Amram or his friends—she would be in even worse trouble. A cold fear froze her limbs. Had Alexandros seen her leave?

"Who's there?" A man's voice called softly.

She saw a tall form come out of the shadows, very close. Close enough that she could hear his breathing. It must be him. Alexandros. He must have seen her leave and followed her. His words echoed in her ears: *It is time we got to know each other better.*

"Leave me alone," she whispered. She pushed off from the tree and ran. She didn't get far. A grasping root caught her foot, sending her sprawling on the ground. The side of her head smacked against a solid trunk. She lay still for a moment, the pain in her head overpowering her fear. A hand closed around her arm.

Mara jerked around, kicking hard at the figure standing over her.

He released her arm with a yelp.

She got up to her knees. Her mantle was off, and her hair was wild around her face and shoulders. "Stay away from me. I mean it!" She looked around for a stick to defend herself, but he stepped close and reached down to her again.

"What are you doing? Are you hurt?"

He moved into a bright patch of moonlight. It wasn't Alexandros. It was Shem. He took both of her shaking hands in his. She struggled against him.

"Are you insane? To be out here by yourself! Your mother and father . . ." As he pulled her up to her feet, the patch of moonlight fell on her face. He stopped and dropped her hands as though they were hot rocks. His mouth fell open, and the front of his long throat jumped.

She dipped her chin, remembering her humiliation on the road. He had to regret helping her. She had seen by his shocked face that he knew about her . . . about Nava. She tried to raise her head high, to look him in the eye, but she couldn't do it.

He continued after a moment in a lower voice, "They will be worried about you. I will take you home."

"No!" Mara croaked. She kept her eyes on the ground. "I mean—no. I'll go. I'm sorry. I thought you were—I mean, I thought you were someone else." Humiliated twice in front of him. *He must think I'm a fool.* She tried to recover her dignity, but everything—Alexandros, Nava, now this—it was too much.

She covered her face with her dirty hands and burst into tears.

Chapter 9

"Mechola! You never said that your grandson was so handsome!" The tall, bony woman gushed in his grandmother's doorway. Shem had seen her before. She was often in the marketplace with her three skinny daughters, bickering over jewelry and linen.

Shem stood silently with a bucket of still-warm goat's milk. In Caesarea, Drusus had brought breakfast to Shem's room each morning. Here, he milked the short-tempered goat himself. He didn't mind. He gave his grandmother the bucket.

With her back to her visitor, she rolled her eyes at him. "You know I try not to brag about my grandchildren, Adah," she said as she filled a wooden bowl with chunks of fresh melon, then poured on thick yogurt and dark honey before handing it to Shem.

Adah walked farther into the house and resumed her complaints about one of the town merchants. "You know that Canaanite, that one that sells the Nubian beads and bracelets? He said he'd be here yesterday! But he still isn't here, and I promised my daughter . . ." She looked coyly at Shem.

He shoved melon in his mouth and tried not to listen. Abahu already waited for him in the olive grove.

The woman spoke to Mechola, but her words were clearly for Shem. "I hope your grandson knows that I have three beautiful girls. One is betrothed already. And such good wives they will make . . ." Adah let her comment hang in the air a moment before she resumed her complaints.

Shem chewed and thought about the girl in the olive grove.

He had been struck speechless. She was so beautiful, even in the shadowy grove. Her wide eyes were unlike any he'd ever seen. What color were they? Her dark hair had been wild and tangled, framing a perfect face. He had seen beautiful women in Caesarea, but never one like her.

What had she been doing in the grove so late at night? She was afraid of someone, that was certain. She had sobbed for only a moment but hadn't made another sound as he brought her through the grove.

He had stolen quick glances at her as they walked through the trees. If possible, she was even more beautiful with her face streaked with tears. As they had stepped out of the dark trees into the light of a half moon, he saw that her feet were bare and dirty. A tattered brown tunic and a belt of frayed rope hung on her thin frame. He had seen her before; she was the girl with the water jar.

At the edge of the grove, she spoke to him, almost begging. "Please, let me go on alone. Please."

Of course he had followed her, telling himself that he just wanted to make sure that she was safe. He watched her run to the small, shabby house in the valley. A large speckled donkey stood outside the door, loaded with bundles, but there had been no light burning for her.

He swallowed the rest of his breakfast. He wanted to ask his grandmother about the girl, but her friend seemed to be ready to talk all day. She must not know that Mechola hated gossip.

As he turned to go, Adah finished her rant about the merchant. "Well, I just hope he shows up today. I won't hear the end of it. Keep watch for him, will you? He leads a huge speckled donkey loaded with packs."

Shem's head shot up. Could it be the same donkey? Did the merchant know her father? He swung around and blurted, "Oh, I saw that donkey. Outside the house in the valley. It was tied there last night."

Adah turned and stared at him, her mouth pursed in a little circle of surprise. She spoke directly to him, shock prevailing over manners. "What? At Nava's house? The one outside the village? Just when did you see him?"

Mechola put her hand to her forehead and closed her eyes for a brief moment. "Shem really doesn't know his way around the village yet, do you, my boy?" She took his arm and led him to the doorway. "I think your grandfather is waiting for you," she said with a firm push. She shooed him away from the house and turned back to her gleeful visitor.

"At Nava's house? Oh, she is disgraceful," Adah's delighted voice drifted across the courtyard. "I need to go now, Mechola. I have so much to do."

Shem looked back at the house to see Adah hurrying toward the village, a smile on her face. Mechola stood in the doorway shaking her head, her lips pressed tight in a worried frown.

Shem tamped the soil around the olive seedling and straightened, rubbing the small of his back. Planting seedlings was hard work. But at least it kept his mind off the girl. He'd only thought of her a hundred times today. He'd made a big mistake, telling Adah that he'd seen the donkey at the girl's house.

Abahu, Shem, and Enosh worked well together. Enosh, the son of Mechola's brother, Noach, was thin and angular. He had to be close to seventeen, all long limbs and sharp points. A wispy beard showed under his high cheekbones and wide mouth. He rarely spoke, but he smiled often, and his teeth were straight and very white in his dark face. Maybe because he was so quiet, his light brown eyes seemed to see what others missed.

Shem had wondered for weeks if Enosh could actually speak at all, until yesterday when he noticed that Enosh's arms were covered with angry red welts. Shem raised his brows in question as Enosh absently rubbed the swollen marks. "Bees," was his only word of explanation.

Enosh did all he could to help Shem learn the hard work of an olive farmer. Shem was grateful and surprised, for Enosh had good reason to resent him. Surely Abahu had thought of giving his land and livelihood to his nephew. Shem wished he could tell Enosh that he probably wouldn't be in Sychar long enough to threaten his inheritance.

He picked up the last seedling and brought it to where Enosh swung a mattock at the hard ground. "Enosh, do you know the girl that lives in the house in the valley? West of town?"

The mattock hit the ground with a thud. Enosh turned to Shem and tipped his head.

"Is she . . . I mean, is there . . ." Shem's face warmed.

Enosh's forehead wrinkled.

How could Shem ask about her without admitting that he'd been alone with her in the olive grove? That would get her into even more trouble. "I mean, what is her name?"

Enosh's long fingers pried the seedling from Shem's fist. "Mara." He cradled the wilted vine in his hand. "Her name is Mara."

Shem left Enosh and trudged down the hill to Abahu. Mara. Bitter. Her tears had been bitter last night. "The seedlings are planted."

"Good," his grandfather said. He tossed Shem a broken mattock. "Now, take this down to Uziel's shop. See if he can repair it. If not, we'll need a new one. Go ahead home when you're done. We're finished here."

Shem hiked down the hill. When he reached the marketplace, he slowed his pace. An argument was brewing.

A large man with thinning gray hair and fine clothes bellowed before a group of at least a dozen men. His belly jutted over his belt, and his neck draped over his collar in thick folds. Near him stood Jonothon, the youngest priest of Sychar. Small and thin, with a sparse beard, he looked hardly older than Shem. To one side stood Uziel, the friendly tool merchant, his bald head shining in the sun, and the old shepherd Noach, the father of Enosh. Noach was as talkative as his youngest son was silent, despite being stricken with an illness that had frozen one side of his face in a fearsome and permanent frown.

The big man continued to shout. "I tell you, she is guilty of adultery! We all know it!"

Shem stopped just outside the circle of men. Just what was going on here?

"Are we to watch our women make fools of us?" The man's bushy eyebrows were pushed down over his red face. The priest and some of the men shook their heads.

"The Lord has commanded, you shall not commit adultery," Jonothon said to the crowd.

A bent old man stepped forward. "Zevulun, calm yourself. We know nothing but gossip. We cannot convict a woman on gossip alone."

So the red-faced shouter was Zevulun. Shem had heard talk of him. He was the richest man in the village and the father of the bully on the road that first day.

Uziel and Noach nodded their agreement with the old man.

Another man, the old shepherd that lived alone on the other side of Mount Ebal, shouted, "Nava is guilty; we all know it!"

Zevulun held up his arms. "Did she not have the pagan in her home last night? Here." His eyes locked on Shem, and he pointed. "This man witnessed them together! Come here and tell them."

The men turned as one to study Shem.

Shem drew a sharp breath. That woman, Adah, had jumped on his words with glee. This has something to do with the girl, Mara. Who was Nava, and what had he started? And this man, Zevulun, dared to drag him into his battle and order him about like a servant?

Shem threw his head back and considered Zevulun. "You are wrong. I witnessed nothing."

Zevulun's eyes narrowed, then he dismissed Shem with a wave and turned back to the men, "We don't need his testimony. Who among us does not know this is true? She has been this way since she was a girl. She defiles this city with her disgraceful ways!"

Noach stepped up, his permanent scowl even deeper. "Let the woman be, Zevulun. You have held on to your anger for far too long."

Zevulun's face turned a darker shade of red. "What? My—this

has nothing to do with that! You are blinded by her as you have always been! She deserves to be thrown out of this town—no, stoned!"

"Perhaps she is guilty," Noach said, "but what good would stoning do?" He turned to face the milling group of men. "It would leave her daughter and a crippled son with no mother at all." Murmurs of agreement spread through the crowd. "Her husband is gone. He divorced her years ago. How can she be guilty of adultery if she has no husband?"

Zevulun was losing the crowd. He motioned for the young priest to speak.

Jonothon stepped forward quickly, like a dog called by his master.

The men quieted. "For many generations, we have followed the laws of Moses more truly than those who worship in Jerusalem. While the other towns of Samaria fell into the ways of the pagans, we have endured, and God has blessed us. We cannot allow sin to pollute us now."

Some men nodded at this; others looked unsure.

Uziel stepped forward and held up his hands. "Wait. We have no proof of any wrongdoing. Until we do, a trial is impossible. We shall attend to the truth and trust in the Lord. The Passover starts tomorrow, so let us discuss this after the week of Massot."

This time, most of the men nodded their heads, and the crowd began to break up.

Zevulun stepped close to Uziel and glared, his protruding belly almost touching the smaller man. "So be it. We will do nothing for now, Uziel. If it is proof you want, the Lord will provide proof. Then, your sister-in-law will be punished."

Shem backed away. Stoned? They couldn't mean that. But if they did, this woman's death would be his fault. If he had only kept silent. *Why does trouble find me no matter where I go?*

Shem took a warm round of bread from Mechola. He crouched near the cooking fire behind the house as she slapped dough on the hot stones. Shem set the bread aside. He couldn't eat. His mouth felt like a dry streambed.

"So it was because of what I said, about the donkey?"

"Adah is perhaps the biggest gossip in the village. You didn't know, so don't blame yourself." Mechola flipped another hot round of bread onto the growing pile next to her. "That home, the one where the donkey was tied, belongs to the woman Nava. She is alone. Her husband is . . . gone."

Shem's face heated as he understood his grandmother's delicate phrasing. He swallowed hard, then continued. "So Adah told her husband, and now they accuse this woman, Nava, of . . . being with the pagan?"

Mechola reached up to put her arm around his shoulders. "You couldn't have known, Shem. And it probably would have gotten out anyway. This has been coming for a long time."

He couldn't help but ask. "She has a daughter?"

"Yes, my boy. Her name is Mara, and her life, like her name, is a bitter one."

"Why is that?" But he already knew.

His grandmother sighed and shook her head. "Through no fault of her own, my boy. She seems to be a good girl. But her mother is a disgrace to her family."

Mechola busied her hands with the flat rounds of dough. "Mara's father is dead, and Nava's last husband left her. Her little brother is lame and will never be able to provide for them. No man in this town wants anything to do with Nava and a crippled boy. Yes, Mara is beautiful," Mechola glanced at him, "but that only reminds them all of her mother."

"The men—Zevulun and the priest—they spoke of a trial?"

Mechola slapped another round of dough on the cooking stone. "Zevulun hates Nava. He has looked for a way to drive her out for many years. He may just succeed this time."

Shem remembered the cruel boys throwing rocks and Mara's tears in the olive grove. So Mara had good reason to cry. He shook his head to drive her image from it. He had been sent to Sychar to stay out of trouble. And this was definitely trouble.

• • •

"You wanted to see me, Uncle?" Mara stepped into her uncle's cramped shop. It was late in the afternoon, and the slanting rays of the sun lit the shop with golden light.

Hoes and mattocks lined the walls. Hammers and saws hung from nails. Coils of twine and rope were piled in a corner. Uziel sat on a low bench, fitting a mattock blade into a new wooden handle.

"Yes, Mara. Come in and sit."

Mara hesitated. Her uncle was a good man, and kind. He never raised his voice to his children. She had seen him run his hands over Ruth's hair and gaze at her like she was an Egyptian princess. He gave food and oil to her and Asher. But he rarely spoke to Mara. And never alone. Had news of Alexandros already reached him?

She shuffled through the gloom and sat at his feet. Whatever it was, he must be obeyed. He was the head of her family now that Shaul was gone.

"Mara." Uziel picked up a length of twine and wound it into a coil. Then he unwound it. He pulled at it, as if testing its strength. His brows knit together. "Mara. I have received an offer of marriage for you."

Mara felt her mouth drop open. She snapped it shut. Marriage? For her? Who could it be? Her heart raced. Who in the village was of age? She had given up on the thought of marriage. A lightness lifted her heart—a home of her own and children!

But Uziel wasn't smiling. Why wasn't he smiling? This had to be what he wanted. Finally, she would no longer be his burden. And neither would Nava. His hands worried at the twine in his hands. Why wouldn't he look at her?

"Who is it?" she asked. Her joyful hope had shriveled and now sat like a rock in her belly.

He coiled the rope again, then put it down at his feet and finally met her eyes. "Jobab, the shepherd, has asked for you."

The name hit her like a kick in the stomach. Jobab? "But he's—"

Uziel held up one hand. "I know. He's old enough to be your grandfather. His last wife, though, was even younger than you."

His last wife. Dara—dead at the bottom of the gorge. And the wife before that—dead from a blow to the head.

Uziel fidgeted on the bench. "He is old. Yes, I know he is not what a young girl wishes for in a husband. But Mara," Uziel looked behind her at the empty doorway and lowered his voice, "he is very old. When he dies, you will have his flocks, his house. You won't have to depend on others."

Depend on others. He meant depend on him. "Uncle, I can make more thread. I can weave and sell it in the marketplace. I promise not to be a burden on you." *Just don't make me marry that man. The one with two dead wives.*

"It is a good marriage for you, Mara."

"What about Mama? And Asher?"

Uziel dropped his gaze to the floor. "He doesn't want them in his home. He won't take them."

Mara's chest tightened into a hard knot. She couldn't leave them. They would never make it without her. "I can't leave them. They'll never—"

"He did offer a solution." Uziel's mouth turned down like he didn't want to go on.

"What is it?" How much worse could this get?

"He suggested that instead of a bride price, he would agree to provide your mother and Asher with food and oil. As much as they need. For as long as you are married."

No bride price? The dishonor would be known in the village before the betrothal vows were out of their mouths. Her face burned, and her mouth felt like it was filled with ash. "You can't . . . the priests . . . Can he do that?"

Uziel nodded, but his cheeks bore two bright spots of red. "He doesn't have it. His marriage to Dara was only two years ago. And he is anxious to wed soon. He thought that if we knew your mother and brother would be taken care of, we would agree."

The price of their lives was every shred of her dignity. And how would he treat a wife that he had paid for in bread and oil? Better than he had treated Dara, or the wife before her? What if she didn't bear him a son? Would he still feed her mother and brother?

"Mara." Uziel reached out and took Mara's hands. His were small and creased with deep lines. "I want you to think about it. It is my duty to think about your future. And now, with the rumors of your mother . . ."

Rumors of Mama and Alexandros? Is that what he means?

"I must think of your future and my own family as well." He squeezed her fingers. "Ruth is with child again."

Mara's heart jumped at the news. "That is wonderful. I didn't know." It was wonderful news. But also another mouth to feed, and they barely had enough as it was.

"Yes, it is. But we must all do what we have to do. And marriage is what the Almighty calls us to." He pulled his hands away and picked up the mattock blade and handle. "No one knows of this. Not even your aunt. You will consider Jobab's offer. And I will pray about it. He has asked for a decision one month after Passover. If that time comes and there is no good reason to refuse him, then you will be betrothed. I'll insist on a betrothal period of a full year."

A chill crawled down Mara's neck. "Thank you, Uncle." She stepped out of the cool shop and into the late-afternoon heat. One month. It might as well be tomorrow. Nothing would happen in one month that would change Uziel's mind.

Chapter 10

The thirteenth day of Nisan dawned clear and warm, the sky a brilliant blue. It was a good day to celebrate the Passover.

Mara carried Asher to the mikvah for the required cleansing before the feast. Rough stone steps led to a dark cave cut into the hillside just past the olive groves on Mount Ebal. A well of pure, sweet rainwater lapped at the lowest step. Asher grimaced as he dipped into the cold water, then disappeared into the dark to wash.

A few women and children waited impatiently at the top of the steps for their turn; they did not speak to her. She had sensed a change in the village since yesterday. Turned backs and whispers. No one met her eyes. *They must know about Alexandros.* But how could they? He had been gone before the first light of day. Unless he told them himself. A bitter taste filled her mouth as she imagined the man boasting about his conquest in the marketplace.

Mara had not looked at or spoken to her mother at all yesterday, nor today. In fact, she had treated Nava much the way these women were treating her. She didn't know what else to do.

It was Nava's fault that she had to marry Jobab. That she would have to leave Asher. How would he manage without her? Would Nava get up and get water—make food—if she were gone? She tried not to think of the grizzled old man who would be her husband. Or Dara's frightened face in the marketplace just days before she died. What kind of woman gave herself in marriage without a bride price? Only a desperate one. And Jobab knew she was desperate.

Mara dreaded gathering with all of Sychar on the slopes of Mount Gerizim for Passover. She would surely see Jobab. How should she act? And what if she saw Shem? By now he would know all about them and why she had been hiding in the trees that night.

Asher came out of the dark, dripping and clean. Mara entered the dark coolness of the mikvah. If only the water could take away the stain of her mother's sin. Too soon, she was done. Asher climbed on Mara's back. She bent almost double with his weight as she started the long walk to the Holy Mountain.

At the bottom of Mount Ebal, they joined the crowd making its way to the altar of sacrifice on Mount Gerizim. The entire village would celebrate through the night and the next day. Then the men would live on the mountain for the week of Massot, eating unleavened bread and making offerings to the Lord.

Before she started the long climb up Gerizim, she crouched down, letting Asher slide off her back. She needed to catch her breath. *If they do know about Nava, they can't do anything about it until after Massot. Maybe . . . maybe in a week they'll forget.*

Villagers passed by carrying food, tent poles, and water jars.

She bent her back and said to Asher, "Climb up, my sweet."

Instead of feeling his heavy weight on her back, she heard Asher squeal in delight. She twisted to see Enosh, silent as always, swinging her brother into his arms. He was even taller than the last time she'd seen him, when he'd taken her goats for shearing. Would he ever stop growing? It seemed like just last summer they had been children—she teasing him about his long eyelashes, he chasing her around the well as their mothers drew water.

She managed to smile—his dark lashes still reminded her of a she-goat. Enosh said nothing, but a flicker of a smile crossed his angular face as he settled Asher on his shoulder like a lamb.

Mara kept her eyes on Enosh's long back as they passed the synagogue and reached a wide, almost level stretch of ground behind the stone building. Cedar trees stretched high above, and their needles carpeted the open ground and scented the air. The dull thump of hammers sounded against wooden stakes as families erected three-sided tents for the feast.

Enosh marched ahead, looking at no one, to the spot where Uziel and her cousin Yoseph were raising a tent. Ruth unpacked baskets of food. Enosh set Asher near them, making sure he was comfortable. His cheeks were red beneath his thin beard, and his light eyes met hers for a moment before he slipped away through the crowd.

The chatter around them dropped to whispers. In the nearest tent, Amram and his father sat on thick cushions while servants bustled around them. Tirzah stopped what she was doing to stare at Mara. One tent over, Adah pointed to her and whispered in Rivkah's ear.

Mara's throat closed, and her eyes stung with tears. She looked at the ground. If only she didn't have to face this crowd, these people she had known all her life. She knew what they were thinking, and they were right to think it.

Ruth stood and hurried to embrace her. She squeezed Mara more tightly than usual and whispered in her ear. "Is she coming?"

I hope not. If only she would stay home. But she nodded. "By dusk." Ruth gave Uziel a long look.

"Mara?" Asher struggled to stand and slipped his hand into hers. He could probably feel her trembling. "What's the matter, Mara?"

Mara bent to meet his eyes. "Nothing, Asher. Nothing." For Asher's sake, she forced a smile. "You have time to play with Matea for a while."

He wrinkled his brows and squeezed her hand harder.

"Go on," she said. "Don't get dirty."

Asher dropped her hand and crawled to where his little cousin played in the shade of the cedars.

She stood and caught Amram smirking at her. His gaze went past her and changed to a venomous glare. She turned and found herself only ten steps away from Shem, setting up his grandfather's tent.

He looked different. In his new wool tunic and dazzling white tallith, he fit in with the rest of the men of Sychar. His sandals were newly made of carved wood and strips of leather. Short, dark stubble had grown to cover his face, and his skin had darkened enough to almost hide his scar. He looked far more like a village farmer than he had when she had first seen him.

He caught her scrutinizing him, but his eyes narrowed when he saw Amram. He pounded the tent pole into the ground with two heavy swings.

Mara's hands shook as she unrolled her threadbare cloak in the shade of her uncle's tent. She spread Asher's close by. What must he think of her? Had he told anyone? He probably thought she was as bad as her mother, going to the olive grove in the middle of the night. Her face felt as hot as a live coal. She bent her head away, determined not to notice him again.

As the sun dipped low, the mood became festive. Musicians tuned their instruments, a reed flute lilted, a lyre joined in. Men gathered under the cedar trees. Mara joined Ruth, Uziel, and the children in the tent.

As they began the song of praise and thanksgiving, Mara saw her mother hurrying up the steep path. Her heart sank, and the song died on her lips. She had hoped that Nava wouldn't come. Hoped that, just once, Nava wouldn't bring shame on her children. Guilt pressed on her heart. No, it wasn't right to deny her mother the celebration of Passover, the holiest feast.

Singing voices were replaced by whispers. Everyone was watching Nava, talking about her. Nava reached them and embraced Mara. Her smooth skin smelled clean, and her soft hair gleamed. Mara turned her face from her mother's kiss. Nava didn't falter. She bent to kiss Asher, then embraced her sister.

Uziel stood at the entrance to the tent with his arms crossed. His mouth was turned down and his brows drawn together. Was he going to deny Nava the Passover celebration?

Nava approached him, her head bent. "Uziel. Brother. Will you allow me to celebrate the Passover with my children and sister?"

Uziel's hard gaze went from Nava to his wife. The whispers

around them died to silence. Mara wanted to crawl under a rock and hide. It was Uziel's right as head of his family. He could forbid his wife to even speak to her sister. Just as he could demand that Mara marry the shepherd.

Ruth reached out to her husband. "Please, Uziel."

Uziel stepped forward. "I took you and Mara in when your uncle died, Nava. And again I agreed when Shaul left. But there is talk among the men, Nava."

A cold finger of fear brushed down Mara's spine. About Alexandros? Would Uziel reject Nava because of the rumors?

Uziel stepped forward and reached under Nava's chin. He brought her face up to look into his. "Do not bring shame upon my family, Nava."

Nava nodded and crouched down beside her sister. Uziel left to sit with the men. The villagers went back to their songs and instruments.

Mara could breathe again. She scooted away from her mother and busied herself with the children. If she tried hard enough, she could avoid Nava for the rest of the night.

When the first star appeared in the eastern sky, Passover began.

The people left their tents and gathered in the open space behind the synagogue. The priests—Jonothon and Yahokeem— stood on the far side of a deep pit. Mara stood with her mother, Ruth, and the children. She felt a prickle on the back of her neck. She peered around Ruth to see the grizzled face of Jobab. He was staring at her.

The head of each family brought forth a bleating lamb and stood near the trench lined with stones. Jobab held a struggling animal and a gleaming knife. A hush fell over the crowd. The priests gave the signal, and each man cut the throat of their lamb. Blood flowed, and the prayers of atonement were chanted by all.

Mara held Asher high enough to see the priest parting the crowd, carrying a bronze bowl and a branch of hyssop. He walked slowly, solemnly daubing the foreheads of all the first-born sons with the blood of the lambs. Asher received the mark of the covenant solemnly. He touched his forehead, then admired the red smear on his finger.

Mara's stomach grumbled as the men skewered the salted meat on long poles and placed them on the glowing coals of the Tannurim. The pits were sealed over with mud until midnight. As the crowd jostled around the pits, she once again caught Jobab's stare. She didn't like the way he looked at her—like the feast wasn't the only thing he was anticipating. Dread crawled up her back like a poisonous spider.

The people sang the ancient songs of thanksgiving. Flickering torches lit the mountainside. Women stacked unleavened bread in newly woven straw baskets and brought out the bitter herbs. Children fretted in their mother's arms as they waited for the feasting to begin.

Finally, the hour came to break open the brittle mud crust. The smell of roasted meat made Mara weak. Lilting flutes and jingling tambourines mingled with laughter. Mothers called to their children, and men groaned with hunger as women carried the steaming lamb to each family.

All around them, the families laughed and feasted. Mara sat between her mother and Asher in Uziel's tent. She barely tasted the succulent meat or the bitter herbs. She sang the songs of Moses and the Exodus from Egypt, but they failed to fill her with joy. Would the Angel of Death pass over her or strike her down? *Oh, Lord, where is my deliverance?*

When morning came, Mara sat in the shade of the tent with Nava and Ruth. The side panels were lifted to invite the breeze. The nearby tents were full of women and children, while the men sat farther away under the cool breath of the cedar trees. Nava hadn't disgraced them yet. Only a few more hours, and she could take her mother back to their home, away from the watching eyes of the villagers.

Matea settled into Ruth's lap, her eyes drooping. "Tell us about the great flood, Mama."

"No, of Joseph and his brothers!" Asher protested, crawling into the shade. He climbed into Nava's lap, dragging his twisted foot up and rubbing the red sores on his toes. "But why did God let his brothers throw him down the well?"

Ruth settled Matea more snugly in her lap. "Sometimes the Almighty allows bad things to happen in order to accomplish his plan."

Mara rubbed her burning eyes. *Is marriage to Jobab part of the Almighty's plan for me? What good would that accomplish?* She snuck a glance at the old man under the cedar trees. He was watching her again.

A flash of brass and jingle of bracelets warned her that there was more to worry about than the old shepherd. Adah and Tirzah sauntered to the entrance of the tent. "Ruth, my dear." Adah stepped in without an invitation. "What lovely children you have. You are indeed blessed by the Lord."

Tirzah followed, and both women sat down across from Ruth and Nava. Tirzah smiled like a snake, and Adah fidgeted like a guilty child.

Panic stabbed at Mara. *This is trouble.*

"Yes, Adah, they are some of the most beautiful children in the village. And so perfectly formed," Tirzah said, her lip curled as she glanced at Asher.

Asher's thumb went in his mouth, his eyes wide. *Why must they pick on him?* Mara scooted closer to her mother and brother.

Tirzah angled toward Ruth with a bright smile. "Your oldest— Yoseph—is growing tall. In a few years, he will look for a bride." She smoothed her dress over her ample lap. "Isn't it a heavy burden? We all want our sons to make good marriages. But they are so easily swayed by a pretty face."

Nava stiffened beside Mara, her hands clenching Asher's tunic. Mara's legs tightened, and her pulse quickened. She must get her mother away before this got any worse. She glanced outside the tent. They were surrounded. Other women—even some of the men—had stopped talking to watch them.

Tirzah sighed. "Amram has been warned to choose a wife well, for it can bring disgrace upon your entire family to choose poorly."

Adah snickered behind her hand.

Mara slipped her hand into her mother's and squeezed. Nava did not respond. Her eyes were fixed on Tirzah. *Please, Mama, whatever they say, don't lose your temper.*

Ruth took Nava's other hand. Her words were calm and measured. "We trust Yoseph to make a good decision. But he is not yet interested in finding a wife, Tirzah."

Tirzah pulled herself up with a jerk. "Ruth, I would never push my daughters on anyone. That is for him and his father to decide. And a father's decision is law in his family, is it not?" She jutted her chin at Nava. "At least in a respectable family."

Nava's face was as pale as the tent cloth. Her hand trembled in Mara's. How long would these women torment them?

Matea, half asleep in her mother's lap, grumbled. "Mama, I'm thirsty."

Mara moved to get the girl a ladle of water from the jar outside their tent. Perhaps they would leave now that they had humiliated Nava.

"Oh, no," Tirzah said quickly. She sent Matea a honey-sweet smile. "Let me get you all some water, my dear Ruth. It is Passover, is it not? A time to serve the less fortunate among us." She caught the eye of one of her servants, standing in the nearest tent, and motioned to the water jug, her flabby arms flapping like wings. "Hurry up, you worthless girl."

The servant jumped as if she'd been stung by a bee. She brought the jar and a clay drinking cup to Tirzah. Tirzah took the jar without a word of thanks, and the girl backed a few steps away. Mara felt a stab of pity for the poor girl. It couldn't be easy serving Tirzah every day.

Tirzah dipped the cup into the water jar. She passed it to Matea, who gulped loudly. Asher struggled to sit upright in his mother's lap, staring at the dripping cup.

Adah smiled at Tirzah like they were playing a game. "May I have some water?"

Tirzah nodded "We all need some water, do we not, on this hot day?" Tirzah filled the cup and passed it to Adah, then dipped it again and gave it to Ruth. When Ruth had passed it back with her thanks, Tirzah drank deeply herself. She caught her servant's eye and tipped her head toward the jar.

Mara's breath caught in her throat. Nava's hand tightened around hers.

The servant took the cup from Tirzah and bent to lift the jar.

Ruth stopped her with an upraised hand. "Wait. Tirzah, will you not offer water to my sister and her children?"

No, Ruth. They are petty women. Let it go. Mara caught Ruth's eye and shook her head. But Ruth's mouth was set and her cheeks flushed red.

Tirzah clasped her hands together in front of her chest. She leaned toward Nava, but her voice rose like a braying donkey. "Oh, I would. You know that, Nava. I certainly don't hold anything against you." She fluttered her hand to where her husband sat. "But Zevulun . . . I'm sure you understand. He would have us break the cup and the water jar, too. Men are so careful about impurity." Her harsh laugh echoed through the silence.

Nava gasped.

Mara's mouth went dry. She scanned the surrounding tents. Every face was turned toward them. Zevulun's mouth curled into a satisfied smirk. Under the cedars, Abahu, Shem—even Noach and Enosh—were watching.

Ruth struggled to rise with Matea still in her lap. Her mouth moved, but no sound came out. Her cheeks were flaming red, and she pulled a deep breath through her nose. Mara had never seen her placid aunt so angry. She must stop Ruth before she shamed her own family for Nava's sake.

But she couldn't move. Her arms hung like slabs of cold stone. Her tongue stuck to the roof of her mouth.

Nava dropped Mara's hand and scooted Asher into her lap. Nava reached for her sister's shoulders and gently pulled her back down. Nava's face was calm, her chin raised. Every ear waited for her next words.

Please, Mama. Don't make it worse for us.

Nava squared her shoulders and leaned forward. "Tirzah, what you say is true." Her words struck like a hammer on a tent stake.

Tirzah's brows rose, making furrows on her fleshy forehead.

Nava continued. "Men can be unforgiving. Perhaps your husband will never forgive my rejection of him."

Zevulun watched with an open mouth. Abahu and Shem stared. Enosh stood as if to come toward them, but his father's hand on his arm stopped him.

Nava went on. "But I'd rather be hated by Zevulun and everyone in Sychar than share his bed."

Tirzah's chin disappeared into the heavy folds of her neck. Her pink lips dropped open.

Mara pulled Asher close like a shield. Her heart swelled with pride and fear. Nava wasn't afraid of these women. But how much harm would she cause, now that she'd found her voice?

Nava raised her hand toward the queen of the village women. "And you too have good reason to hate me. But I can't help it if your husband still thinks of me before he lies down beside you every night."

Ruth's hand flew to her mouth. Mara choked, and her heart dropped like a stone. Every face in the clearing turned to Zevulun. His neck was purple, and his face burned red.

Tirzah lunged at Nava. Her hand snaked out, cracking across Nava's cheek.

Nava didn't flinch, and she didn't cower.

Mara curled herself around Asher. All was lost. Their beautiful, brave, foolish mother had sealed their fate. She had humiliated the most powerful man in the village on the holiest feast of the year. Pride and despair warred within Mara. *Mama is so brave. She is so foolish.*

Nava pushed herself to her feet. The mark of Tirzah's hand burned bright on her pale cheek. She ran her hand over Mara's hair, then bent to kiss Asher on the cheek. Before Mara could find her voice, Nava stood tall, adjusted her robes, and walked down the mountain, her head held high.

There would be no more charity from the village now, and certainly not from Tirzah. They would be lucky not to be driven out of town. Mara would have to marry Jobab, and soon. They had no other hope.

Chapter 11

S hame needled through Shem as he watched Mara tend her garden. He stood in the shadows of the east grove, looking down on the little house. A pruning hook dangled from his idle hands. A hot wind from the eastern desert rustled through the olive grove and spun fingers of dust in the valley.

What am I doing here? I have enough worries, serious ones like being hunted by Romans. He didn't need to spy on a girl with eyes like jade and amber.

Massot had ended, and the week on the mountain with the men of the village had surprised him. The men of Sychar, at least some of them, were not just dim-witted farmers. They were no scholars, but their faith was real and alive. In fact, some of what they said made more sense than the complex philosophies he had learned at the feet of his teachers in Caesarea. These men, farmers and merchants, had true faith in the God of Abraham. They had prayed, sung, and spoken of many things. But none had spoken of Nava.

Nava's display at Passover had shocked him. Insulting Zevulun's wife—that he could understand. But how could she have so little regard for her children? From what he could tell, they depended on the village for their food. Mara's reaction still made his heart constrict. She had watched her mother go down the mountain, her face drained of all color. She must have been so ashamed.

Nava could not be driven from town only because she had insulted Zevulun's wife, and they didn't seem to have any proof of adultery. But the family could be starved out. Were Mara and her brother hungry right now?

A pang of guilt brought him out of his thoughts. He turned away from the little house and hiked through the trees. He would talk to Mechola about taking food and oil to Mara. He'd buy it himself. *And then I'll try to forget about her.*

As he cut through the grove, he passed the ancient oil press and toolshed. Low voices rumbled from inside the shed. Shem froze. Abahu and Enosh were far away in the east grove today. Was someone stealing his grandfather's hoes and mattocks? He crept around the shed to the small, high window and stretched to peak in. He glimpsed not a band of thieves but a stranger by the door and a rotund figure with his back to Shem. Zevulun's fine robes and thinning hair were easy to recognize. The stranger, heavy and brutish, was bald with a scarred face covered in dark stubble. His dirty clothes and sandals marked him as a Greek.

Shem's heart sped up. He ducked down and pressed his back to the cold stone wall. *What is going on here?*

"What took you so long to report to me?" Zevulun's voice rasped low and furtive.

"I didn't want to interrupt your sacred feast," the stranger said. The big man's voice was like a bleating goat.

"Tell me what you've learned, before someone finds us here," Zevulun growled.

"You told me not to come into the village," the man said. "I checked the grove; there's no one here."

"Just get on with it."

"I've found the man you want," the stranger said. "I'll be happy to tell you the rest. After you pay me."

Zevulun's voice rose. "You! Nothing better than a common criminal, yet you imply that I cannot be trusted?" A muffled jangle and thump followed. Shem risked another glance through the window. The man picked up a bulging coin pouch and weighed it in his hands before tucking it into his belt.

"The carpenter called Shaul does still live in Sebaste," he said. "He works hard, but with little real talent, for the builders of the new temple to Zeus. Most often with wood but also with the stone masons when he is needed."

"Yes, yes." Zevulun's heavy robes rustled. "But is he married?"

"I am coming to that." The coins jingled again. "He lives alone. A few questions led me to a wine shop that he sometimes visits. I waited there and soon fell to talking with this man that you are so interested in."

Zevulun grunted.

Shem almost smiled thinking of how irritated Zevulun must be at the man's disrespect. But where was this information leading? What kind of trouble was Zevulun stirring up?

"Seems that he left his wife and children in another town while he found work at the temple. After a few cups of wine, at your expense, he told me that his wife was very beautiful—the most beautiful woman in all of Samaria."

Shem froze. Could it be Nava? But if she had a husband in Sebaste, why were they so poor?

"Almost broke my heart. Said she didn't love him anymore, he couldn't live with her, he left. Such a sad tale . . . and a daughter and son as well." He laughed. "Soon after that, he staggered home to drown his sorrows in another amphora of wine, also purchased by you."

"But he didn't divorce her? No written papers?" Zevulun asked.

"Couldn't bear to do it, the coward. Said if he couldn't have her, no one else would." The informer chuckled. "It's been an honor doing business with you, sir. Call on me again if you need further assistance."

"Oh, I'll need you again, and very soon," Zevulun muttered.

The shed door creaked. He could make out the informer's heavy steps, crunching through the dry leaves of the olive grove. He was heading toward the path to Sebaste, away from Shem. But Zevulun would walk around the shed and toward the village. Shem crept around the corner and pressed himself against the farthest wall. The big man rustled past, wheezing his way down the hill. Shem slid to the ground, his heart hammering in the silence of the grove. *I have to warn Mara. Zevulun is gathering evidence against her mother.*

• • •

The harsh sun beat down on Mara's bent back as she pulled the last of the stubborn weeds from the baked earth around the cucumber vines. A hot wind whipped her hair into her face and stirred dust that dried her mouth and filled her eyes with grit.

Asher didn't complain as he worked beside her, but she knew he was hungry. They had run out of barley days ago. Every year at Passover, she found grain and oil, almonds, and dried fish on their doorstep after the feast and, again, after Massot. This year there had been almost nothing. Figs and oil from Leah, another jar of honey, and plenty of turned backs at the well.

Mara scraped together what she could from the garden, but the gnawing emptiness kept her awake at night. She couldn't bear to beg Ruth and Uziel. Her uncle was surely disgusted with Nava, and she didn't blame him for it. This would set his mind even more toward her marriage to Jobab. And she couldn't make Ruth choose between her husband and her sister. She was more alone than she'd ever been.

The barley harvest will be done soon. Then we can glean enough for several months. A trickle of sweat ran down her nose. The long, cold days of winter would come, and then—unless the villagers forgot her mother's sins or forgave them—they would starve. Or she would marry, and they would live.

Lord, have mercy on us. Deliver us from this misery, I beg you.

Nava had barely risen from her mat since they had come home from the mountain. She didn't eat; she hardly drank—even as the days turned hot. Her affront to Tirzah had emptied her, like a broken jar drained of water. Why couldn't Nava have used her burst of passion to help her children instead of sentencing them to death?

Asher gathered up the last of the weeds in silence. She helped him hobble to the shade of the cedar trees, where he collapsed and closed his eyes. Would he be able to care for himself and Nava when she married Jobab? He'd have to.

Mara checked the purse at her belt. She knew exactly what it held—their last bronze coin. Barely enough to purchase barley and oil for the next few meals. Should she use it now or save it for winter? Asher was so miserable, but they might need it even more later. Her hollow stomach twisted, hunger battling against panic.

"Asher, I'm going to get us some food and water." They would have a good meal tonight, then trust in the Lord. She picked up the empty water jar and hoped no one would be at the well in the heat of the day.

"Take good care of Mama while I am gone." Not that Nava would notice or even care. She cared about nothing but her own misery.

Asher nodded, too hot and hungry to speak.

Mara started up the path, the jar on her head. The wind had died, but the sun beat relentlessly on her back. Before she reached the top of the hill, a tall shadow broke away from the cover of the olive trees. A man strode down the hill with purpose. Shem. And he seemed to be coming straight toward her.

She looked at the ground and sped up, her bare feet slapping the hot dirt. He veered to intercept her. She must either step off the path to go around him or stop in front of him.

He held out his hand, palm facing her. "Mara, please."

Mara stopped and lowered the jar from her head. She cast a glance behind him. The path was empty for now. *Why is he talking to me? It's not right.* Was he waiting there—hiding in the olive grove? Just like that night. Perhaps he thought she was like her mother. Not respectable.

Her knees wobbled, and she squeezed the jar closer to her. Disappointment vied with fear. After he'd saved her from Amram and helped her in the olive grove she'd thought he was different from the boys in Sychar—better, somehow. But he wasn't. He might even be worse. Maybe he was just like Alexandros.

Shem took one step closer. "Please, I need to talk to you. About Zevulun."

Zevulun? She glanced up at his face but quickly dipped her head again. He was too close. She had seen something in his dark eyes. Worry? And what could he have to say to her about Zevulun?

He leaned toward her, his voice low. "Listen, Mara. I heard him talking to an informer in the olive grove. They spoke of a man named Shaul. Is that Nava's husband?"

Mara could smell the olive grove on his wool tunic. She nodded.

"Did he—Shaul—give your mother a written letter of divorce?"

A letter of divorce? Mara shook her head. "I don't know. He said the priest . . ." She stopped. The way he looked at her . . . his eyes searching her face. Like he was watching for lies. And asking about this, her worst memory. She took a gulp of air and a step back. "It was so long ago."

Shem's shoulders dropped, and he rubbed his hand over his face. "Mara, I think Zevulun is planning something. He seems to be gathering evidence against her. Perhaps to accuse your mother of . . . something."

The unspoken word hovered in the air between them. Adultery.

Why does he care what happens to Nava? To us? Shame burned through her and lit her face on fire. What could she say? Nothing. Nava was guilty of adultery.

Shem's eyes caught hers in a long look that she didn't understand. It wasn't like Alexandros's leer or Amram's scorn. Shem was different from the others. Strength came back to her legs; she didn't need to fear him.

He swallowed hard. "I just wanted you to know." He shifted from one foot to another, pivoted, and took three long strides toward the olives. Mara let her breath out but caught it when he jerked toward her again. He hurried back, swinging a bulging pack off his back. He shoved it toward her. She shifted the water jar enough to gather the pack in her arms, then tipped sideways with its weight. "What—"

As he bent close, his whisper brushed her cheek. "Be careful, Mara. And tell your mother to be careful."

• • •

"Mama. Mama, get up. I need to talk to you."

Mara shook her mother's bony shoulder, rolling her over to face the sun that streamed through the doorway into the little house. The bundle of food that Shem had given her—wheat, oil, even some dried fish—lay discarded beside the door. Food wasn't her greatest worry anymore.

Nava's body felt light and brittle in her hands, like a bird's wing. Her eyes were open; she hadn't been asleep. Her gaze was far away, in another lifetime. She blinked at Mara like she didn't even know her.

"Listen to me. Zevulun is . . . I think they are trying to accuse you of . . ." She swallowed. "Mama, they are going to accuse you of adultery."

Nava's licked her dry, cracked lips, but she didn't speak. She rolled back toward the wall, pulling her legs to her chest.

"Mother!" Mara shook Nava's shoulder, dragging at her mother's thin body again. Nava didn't resist. She was like a dead animal, just muscle and bone with no life within. How could she give up when her children needed her?

Mara rolled Nava on her back. "Mama! What are you doing to us? What would you have us do when they drive us away from here? Beg in the streets of Sebaste? Mama, they will stone you!"

Nava's voice was as lifeless and limp as her body. "I don't care what happens to me."

"You don't care? What about us? Do you care what happens to your children?" Pain twisted through Mara's heart. *Lord, help me. Let her see how much we need her.*

"You'll be better off without me."

A shadow cut through the light from the door. Mara glanced over her shoulder. Asher knelt in the doorway, his mouth trembling. She bent close to Nava and shook her. "You are so selfish!" she hissed. "Can't you see what you are doing to him—to both of us? First you drive away our father, and now we'll have no mother."

Nava wrenched out of Mara's grasp and buried her face in her hands, sobbing.

"Crying isn't going to help, Mama. Not this time." She stalked to the door and scooped Asher into her arms. His scrawny arms wrapped around her neck. Her legs trembled with his weight and her own anger.

"Where are we going, Mara?" he asked in a small voice. "To the well? I'm thirsty."

The well was the last place she'd go today. The women would be right to stare and gossip. No, she needed to hide. Only one person would help them now. What would Aunt Ruth say? Would Uziel refuse them? She would tell him that she would marry Jobab—without the bride price—on one condition. Asher must live with her. But would Jobab agree? "We'll go to Aunt Ruth's; she'll have water."

"But what about Mama? She's thirsty too."

Tears blurred her vision, but she blinked them back. "She can get her own water, for once." Asher stared at her. She didn't care. Nava would have to take care of herself from now on. Just as she had forced Mara and Asher to take care of themselves. Mara had nothing left to give to her mother. Jobab was their only hope. She took one last look at the woman hunched in the corner.

She is right. We would be better off if she were dead.

Mara sat under the pomegranate tree in Ruth's garden, her heart empty and hollow. She had cried all her tears and had nothing left inside her. Ruth hadn't asked any questions, just held Mara in her soft arms, murmuring and patting her like a real mother.

"It's like she's trying to make things worse. Like she wants us to be driven out of Sychar. What is the matter with her?" Mara whispered.

"She is ill, Mara. Her mind is clouded. She wasn't always this way."

Mara nodded. "I know. I remember how she was before. Maybe she's right. Maybe we would be better off . . ." A lump rose in her throat. The thought burned like a fiery brand. *I'm a terrible daughter. It's not her fault.* But it was. It was all her fault.

She hadn't told Ruth about Shem or Zevulun. Ruth knew about Alexandros, and that was bad enough. Ruth scooped steaming lentils into a wooden bowl. Mara took the bowl with shaking hands. The knot in her chest loosened as she ate the spicy food and drank cup after cup of cool water. Asher ate his fill, then played happily with Matea and Tovia, Ruth's youngest son.

Ruth put her hands on Mara's shoulders and said gently, "I know it isn't fair, and she should be taking care of you and Asher. But you are all she has. Leave Asher here now. Go, try to talk to her."

"No." Mara shook her head and slumped against Ruth again. "I just can't. Let her take care of herself for a while." *She'll need to get used to it.*

Mara's head pounded with every new, selfish judgment. Her heart ached. It felt good to let Ruth take care of her, at least until Uziel came home. She closed her eyes and tried not to think of her mother's gaunt body and dry cracked lips. Instead, the image of Jobab's wrinkled face came to her. She would do whatever she must to make him happy, give him an heir, and make sure that she didn't end up like his other wives.

Chapter 12

Nava dragged herself one step closer to Jacob's well. Just around the bend now.

She was as heavy as clay, as empty as the water jar on her head. She couldn't do it anymore. Just a few more steps, and it would be over. She would end the darkness that had plagued her for eight years—end it in the deep pit of Jacob's well.

She rounded the corner. The well shimmered in the heat like an oasis. It was deserted, of course. Who but a crazy woman would go to the well in the middle of the day? The other women—those who were good wives, good mothers, good daughters—they had gone in the cool of the early morning.

But not me. I've failed at it all. I was a disgraceful daughter, a worthless wife, the worst mother. My children will be better off without me.

Just a few more steps and she was there. Why had she even brought the water jug? She wouldn't need it. She set it on the ground next to the dried gourd and rope for drawing water. She perched on the ledge of the rocky opening. The heat pressed down on her, and she pulled off her head covering. It fluttered to the ground like a black shadow. She wouldn't need it anymore either.

She leaned far over the black hole. How far down? How deep the water? A dank breeze stirred from the depths. She licked her cracked lips.

Her body would spoil in the water. Just like Tirzah had said, "Men are so careful about impurity." Now they would have to be.

The women who had made her life a misery these past eight years would have to walk miles to fill their jars. The men would argue. Who would climb down and pull her body out? Not Zevulun, he was too fat. Uziel? *I'm sorry, Uziel.*

She scooted closer to the inner lip of the ledge. A pebble dropped down into the silent blackness. It would be better this way. They all knew it. Mara would take care of Asher. She already did. *Better than I ever have.*

Ruth would take them in. Uziel would have to allow it. And—after a year or so—Mara could marry without her mother's shame hanging around her neck like a stone collar. She would be all right.

A raven landed on the other side of the well, close enough that she could see its bright, black eyes. It opened its coal beak and cawed as though it was laughing at her.

Her sorrow was like a cloak of lead that wrapped around her body, dulling her senses and scattering her thoughts. Why had she let Alexandros into her bed? It had seemed like the only solution. Now, it was just another of her many mistakes, pulling her toward the cool black water.

The hot wind, the sun, her husbands—they'd taken all of her. She was hollow, like a broken jar. Every bit of her leaked out and wasted on the dry ground. Good for nothing but this last thing, this last final gift to her children. Freedom from a disgraceful mother.

Just another moment and she'd feel nothing more. No sadness, no regret. The calls of the birds and the chirrs of insects urged her on. She swayed toward the cool darkness.

"Give me a drink, woman."

Nava jerked her head up and lost her balance. She felt herself falling. A hand closed over her shoulder. It was warm and gentle and pulled her away from the darkness.

She righted herself on the stone ledge. A man stood before her. He wasn't tall or handsome. His dark hair curled around a rough tunic and a dirty traveling cloak. No money pouch hung from his belt—no knife either.

Where had he come from?

Why had he touched her?

She scanned the road behind him. It was empty. She glanced over her shoulder. No one came from the other direction.

"Give me a drink."

She pulled in her breath. He was Jewish. She could hear it in his words. A Jew! Talking to her and touching her. What should she do? What would Ruth do? Or Tirzah? Run for their husbands. But she had no husband. She shouldn't even speak to him. But what did it matter now?

"How can you, a Jew, ask me, a Samaritan woman, for a drink?"

The man looked from her to the gaping mouth of the well.

His deep brown eyes seemed to see into her heart. Did he know what she had been ready to do? How could he?

"If you knew the gift of God and who is saying to you, 'Give me a drink,' you would have asked him and he would have given you living water."

Nava's lips burned, and her throat was as dry as sand. Living water? The gift of God? What was he talking about? There was no running water within an hour's walk. How could he have flowing water?

She leaned away. *He's either mad or possessed by a demon. I don't care. He's just another man to bring misery to me.* "Sir, you don't even have a cup." She waved her hand over the opening. "The well is deep; where can you get living water?" A flicker of anger stirred in her. If only he would go away and let her finish what she'd started. "Are you greater than our father Jacob, who gave us this well and drank from it with his children and flocks?"

Her insult didn't disturb the man's calm. He glanced at the gourd tied to the rope, then back to her.

Perhaps if she gave him a drink he would leave her alone. A hush settled over the birds and the insects, like they were waiting to see what she would do. It was just a drink of water. Then why did she feel like it was the biggest decision of her life?

Nava picked up the gourd. She tossed it into the hole, then pulled it up, dripping and full. She wanted to gulp it down but held it out to the stranger. Would he take it? From a Samaritan woman?

His hand closed over both the neck of the gourd and Nava's fingers. "Everyone who drinks this water will be thirsty again; but whoever drinks the water I shall give will have a spring of water within, welling up to eternal life."

Please, I want that.

A cool shiver began at the top of Nava's head and moved through her like a rippling stream. Her dry throat was quenched, her lips and skin cooled like she had just stepped into the mikvah. The cool wave swelled, lapping at the heaviness of her limbs. And with each surge, it took away her sadness, like the sea eating away at the shore. It washed away her thirst, her weariness, the ache in her head and in her heart. Every pore, every empty, hollow place inside her was filled. It sluiced through her like a spring rain, carrying away the despair like a flood carries away the debris of a lifetime.

She pulled her hand away. The wave of cool water ebbed, but the feeling of lightness, of joy—*I remember this feeling*—remained. Was it sorcery? But sorcery was from the evil one. This did not feel evil. What had he said? *If you knew the gift of God and who was saying to you . . .*

She ran her hand over her hair and tunic. The cracks in her lips were gone; her skin was smooth. Her legs felt strong, like she could run over the mountains. What had this man done to her? What was this living water?

Even her mind felt clear and sharp, as though she had just woken up from a restful sleep. Her eyes fell on the black opening of the well. She stepped back from it. What had she been doing? Had she really thought that was the answer? She covered her face with her hands. And what had she said this morning to Mara?

"You'd be better off without me." Her legs gave way, and she sank to her knees. *Oh, Mara. I'm sorry.*

The man was still there, watching her. Who was he? He raised the gourd to his lips and drank the water down.

Whatever it was that he'd given her in those moments, she wanted more of it. She wanted it every day for her lifetime. She wanted to never again feel the black despair that had almost consumed her. "Sir, give me this water. That I may not be thirsty or have to keep coming here to draw water."

He placed the gourd back beside the well and wiped his mouth with the back of his hand. "Go call your husband, and come back."

My husband? Shame swept through her like a brushfire. Would he take back his gift? The living water? Would she be dried out and empty again if he knew about her? *Please, no.* She lowered her forehead to the ground and spoke into the dust. "I do not have a husband."

The man crouched on the ground in front of her. He picked up her hands and pulled her up until she knelt before him, her face close to his. His brown eyes were as deep as the well beside them, but full of light instead of darkness. "You are right, for you have had five husbands, and the one you have now is not your husband."

He knew about her husbands—all of them. And about Alexandros. But he didn't sound angry. He didn't act shocked. He knew, and still he touched her. Had he been told by someone? But no, he was a Jew. No one in Sychar would talk to him. But how did he know? Could he be a prophet? The Prophet? The one who would tell them everything?

Could he be the One that we've been waiting for? The Promised One?

She swallowed. His hands were warm and callused, just like any man's. His cloak smelled of dust and sweat. Was she, Nava, really speaking to the Taheb? The one that her people had awaited for centuries? "Sir, I can see you are a prophet. I know the Taheb is coming, the one called the Anointed; when he comes, he will tell us everything."

Something in his face told her to ask, but the words surprised her even as she heard them in her own voice. "Are you the Taheb?"

He stood, still holding her hands, and pulled her to her feet before him. "I am He, the one who is speaking with you."

• • •

Mara woke to the slap of running feet and a breathless voice call-ing her name. She was stretched beneath the pomegranate tree, her head resting on a soft pillow. Ruth was at the loom but jumped up as the courtyard door slammed open and Nava rushed through.

"Mama?" *Am I dreaming?* This wasn't the woman she had left wasting away in the dark corner of their home, the woman with gaunt cheeks and dull eyes. The woman who had given up her spirit and was ready to die.

This woman fairly flew across the courtyard. Her dark hair gleamed in the sun, and her cheeks glowed as pink as a child's. Her green eyes sparkled like the waters of a mountain stream.

Nava bent and grabbed both Mara's hands, a smile lighting her face. Even her hands were smooth and soft again. "Mara, come! You must come!"

And her voice . . . she practically sang my name.

Mara let her mother pull her to her feet, surprise flickering through her. *She's strong.*

Nava turned to her sister. "Ruth, you too. I've met a man . . ." She stopped and put her hand to her side, breathing hard.

Ruth's forehead creased with worry.

"No, it's not like that," Nava said, straightening again. She stepped close and clutched Mara's arm. "You must believe me, Mara."

Mara tried to pull away, but Nava held her tight. *Where was the woman who had given up? Who said they'd be better off without her?*

"Mara, after you left, I went to the well. I was alone there when he came. He is a prophet; he told me everything I've done. I think he is, well, I think he is the Taheb. You must come and see him, before he goes."

Another man? They didn't need another one of her mother's men in their lives. Mara pulled her arm away. What new trouble was her mother making? Whatever it was, she wasn't having anything to do with it.

"The Taheb?" Ruth reached out to her sister. "Nava, what are you saying? How did you meet him? And why do you think he's the Taheb?"

Nava ran her hands down her sister's arms, then embraced her like she hadn't seen her for years. "He talked to me at the well. He knew me. I mean, really knew me. Everything I've ever done, each of my husbands . . ." She turned to Mara again and grabbed her above the elbows. Without dropping her eyes, she said, "Even about Alexandros."

Mara stiffened. How could she mention Alexandros in front of Ruth? Had she no shame? If the stranger knew, would he tell anyone? But her mother didn't even pause.

"He is a Jew, a Galilean." She pulled Mara toward the gate. "You must come; then you'll see that I'm speaking the truth."

Mara wrenched her arms away. She wasn't going anywhere. Certainly not to the well to meet a Jew who'd spoken to her mother. Jews don't even speak to Samaritan men—never to women.

Ruth patted her sister's arm, her frown deepening. "A Jew?"

Mara caught Ruth's gaze and held it. Her aunt was worried too.

"I will get Uziel; he'll know what to do. Then we'll go to-gether." Ruth hurried out of the courtyard.

Mara studied her mother's flushed cheeks and bright eyes. She reminded Mara of the woman from her childhood, the one that she wished for every day. No. Her mother hadn't changed in an afternoon. This was just more of the same trouble. One man couldn't change her mother, at least not for the better. Mara turned and walked away.

Nava's sandals slapped behind her, and strong arms wrapped around her waist. Mara pried at her mother's hands, but Nava held tight.

"Mara," her mother pleaded, "will you forgive me? I feel like I've woken from a dream, a nightmare. I am so sorry. Please, Mara, believe me. I am changed."

Just like that, Mama? You've changed? Nava would have to show her more than a strange Jew to make her believe that.

Chapter 13

Mara rounded the corner to the well. The Taheb? The One whom they had awaited for thousands of years? It couldn't be. Nava pulled at one arm, dragging her into a run every few steps. Ruth and Uziel hurried behind with worried frowns.

Five men—were they all Jews?—stood at the well. One stood apart. He was not young but had no gray in his dark, curling hair or his full beard. He looked strong, like a laborer. Taller than Uziel, but not as tall as Shem. He dressed no better than the other men, but they all watched him as Nava approached.

Nava pulled Mara to the one who stood apart, then fell to her knees, her head bowed, her body still.

"Is this the man that you say is the Taheb?" Uziel asked Nava.

She seemed content to kneel at his feet forever. "He told me everything I've done. And he told me that I was speaking to the Taheb, the one we've been waiting for."

Mara took one step closer. Was this just another man who would bring shame upon her mother? His dark, deep-set eyes regarded Nava. He smiled and held out his hands to her.

What was he doing? Surely he wouldn't touch a Samaritan woman.

Nava put her own hands into those of the Jew. He helped her to her feet, his smile never faltering. Mara glanced over her shoulder. Her aunt's face was pinched. Uziel's brows pulled together. The other men stepped back, and their mouths dropped open. *So they are* all *Jews.*

Abahu, Mechola, and Shem came around the bend behind

her aunt and uncle. Shem walked in front, hesitating a step when he saw Mara. His forehead creased, and his mouth turned down. Word of the strangers must have spread quickly.

The priests and Zevulun came next with a clamoring herd of villagers. Their shouted questions stopped abruptly when they saw the stranger holding Nava's hands. The villagers crowded on one side of Jacob's well, the group of Jews on the other. Mara and Nava stood between the two, Nava's hands still clasped by the stranger.

Jonothon pushed forward. "What is this?"

The stranger raised his brows at the young priest. His lips twitched as though he might be holding back a smile, but he did not release Nava's hands and did not reply. The men around him shifted and looked at each other.

"You are Jews. Where do you come from?" Jonothon asked, a little more politely.

A rough, burly man stepped toward the Samaritans, towering over the little priest. "We travel from Jerusalem. We journey home, to Galilee."

Yahokeem shuffled to the front of the villagers. He squinted at the strangers and lifted a trembling hand to the mountain behind them. "But where did you come from? Did you come from the mountain, from Gerizim? How can you claim to be the Taheb if you come from Galilee?"

The man holding Nava's hands said, "We are weary. Will you let us rest in your town?"

Jonothon and Yahokeem didn't answer.

Abahu stepped forward. "Please, master, come to my home."

The man nodded as if he had been expecting Abahu to say exactly that. "Thank you, my friend. I am Jesus, of Nazareth."

Abahu turned and started toward his home. The stranger— Jesus—fell into step next to Abahu. His friends trailed behind, shrugging and muttering to each other. The priests and some of the villagers followed, passing Mara with murmurs and questions.

"Jews entering a Samaritan town?"

"Who do they think they are?"

Nava pulled Mara behind the crowd. She caught up with Mechola as they neared the village. "May I help you serve your guests, Mechola?" she asked breathlessly.

Mechola stopped abruptly and turned to Nava. Nava stood her ground, but Mara shrank back. Mechola wouldn't want Nava in her home. Most of the village women wouldn't even speak to her. What had gotten into her mother?

The old woman reached out and touched Nava's chin with her wrinkled hand. "Yes, thank you, Nava. I will need help with all these hungry men to feed." She turned to Mara. "I could use your help, too, my dear."

Mara swallowed and nodded. She followed Mechola past the men settling into Abahu's enclosed courtyard. At least ten fig and pomegranate trees blossomed overhead and still left room for a dozen men to sit. And the house was bigger than the synagogue! With so many windows, there must be four or five rooms inside. Only three people lived here?

"If you could pour the water for washing?" Mechola asked Nava, pointing toward a tall water jar and a stack of clay bowls.

Nava nodded and hurried to pour water as the travelers untied their sandals.

"Mara," Mechola said, as if Mara were a familiar visitor, "get some olives from the storage room. Just back there." She motioned with her head toward the rear of the house.

Mara walked hesitantly toward the back of the big house. The arrival of the strangers had pushed Shem from her mind, but now she worried about seeing him. Why he had warned her about Zevulun? And had he told his grandparents?

She peeked into a room, and her mouth fell open. The tiny room harbored more food than her family saw in a year. Stacks of dried fruit, baskets of grain, and crocks of honey covered the shelves. Baskets of beans, pistachios, and almonds filled an entire wall. Cakes of dried grapes, dates, and figs were stacked in towers, while urns of oil and wine lined the floor.

Mara shut her mouth and lifted the lid off a large cask. She found a cup, dipped it into the briny liquid, and heaped olives into a large wooden bowl. She hurried back to the courtyard in time to see the man named Jesus accept a cup of water from Mechola.

Jews and Samaritans alike fell silent as he drank deeply and wiped his mouth with the back of his hand. "Good water comes out of Jacob's well," he said to Abahu.

An astonished murmur raced through the courtyard. A Jew, drinking from a Samaritan vessel!

The big rough man burst out, "Master! How can we take food and drink from Samaritans without defilement?"

Jesus laughed and threw his arm around the big man. "Nothing that goes in a man can defile him, Peter. Only what comes out can defile."

Whispers of outrage swirled around the courtyard as Jesus passed the cup to Peter. The big man's face pinched, and his brows pulled down, but he drank. The other Jews hesitated just a moment before following his lead.

When the shadows grew long, Jesus and his followers walked up the Holy Mountain to the synagogue. Nava and Mara followed along the path worn smooth by centuries of pious feet. The stone slabs of the synagogue still radiated the warmth of the sun, but the interior was cool and shadowed.

After washing their hands in the anteroom, Nava dragged Mara into the dim interior, already crowded with villagers. Women stepped back, giving them a wide berth. Mara pulled on her mother's hand, bewildered by Nava's bright eyes and flushed cheeks. What had gotten into her? First approaching Mechola, now pushing to the front of the synagogue. Would this Jew be another reason for the villagers to despise her mother?

The air hummed with excited talk about the stranger.

"Is he really the Taheb?"

"The Promised One?"

"What does Nava know? Why should we believe her?"

In the front of the room, Zevulun, Amram, and Shimon stood with Jonothon, their arms crossed and their faces fixed in stern masks. Noach and Enosh stood on one side of the Galileans, Uziel and Abahu on the other. Shem slouched behind, his brow wrinkled in a skeptical frown.

Where had he been while Jesus and his friends had eaten and rested at Abahu's house? Wasn't he curious about the Jews?

Yahokeem hobbled up on the raised dais. He pulled back the curtain and opened the case that housed the scrolls. He chose a crumbling scroll, then raised watery eyes to the crowd. "Let us hear from the one who claims to be the Taheb."

Jesus stepped up next to him and took the scroll from his wrinkled hand. A grumble of anger churned through the crowd. A Jew reading from—even touching—the ancient Samaritan scrolls?

Nava's hand was tight around Mara's, her body straining toward this strange man who commanded every eye in the room. The silence stretched, but Jesus seemed completely at ease in silence.

"I am the light of the world." He didn't shout, but his voice filled every corner of the room. "Whoever follows me will not walk in darkness but will have the light of life. I came into this world as light, so that everyone who believes in me might not remain in darkness."

Murmurs filled the room as Jesus stood tall and straight, his dark eyes resting on each person in turn.

Jonothon stumbled up on the dais, his face flushed and his mouth pulled into a hard line. "What do you mean? Who are you?" He waved his arms at the crowd, and the murmurs dwindled. "If you really are the Taheb, as you told this woman—" He jerked his head toward Nava. "If you are the one who will bring about the age of favor for Abraham's children, then where is the true Ark? Are we right to worship on this mountain, as Joshua commanded, or are the Jews right to worship at the temple in Jerusalem?"

Jesus responded, "Do the prophets not say, 'The heavens are my throne, the earth my footstool'?" He glanced around the room. "The hour is coming when you will worship the Father neither on this mountain nor in Jerusalem. You people worship what you do not understand; we worship what we understand, because salvation is from the Jews."

Angry cries broke out, louder than before.

"Who does he think he is?"

"Look at him; he looks like a beggar."

"Are we going to listen to a Jew?"

Mara glanced at Shem. His gaze was turned toward Jesus' friends as they shuffled closer to their leader. Were they preparing to protect their teacher or hoping that he would protect them? Shem backed away from the Jews.

The crowd quieted as Yahokeem held up a wrinkled hand. "Tell us clearly." He stepped closer to the Jew. "Are you truly the Taheb, the one called the Anointed, who will tell us everything?"

Whispers and murmurs ceased, and the shuffling crowd stilled. Could it be? Had her mother met the Restorer at Jacob's well?

Jesus lifted his chin, and he seemed to grow taller. Mara caught her breath. He looked—just for a moment—like a king.

He said into the silence, "I am."

And at that moment, Mara could almost believe that it was true.

Chapter 14

S hem opened his eyes and rolled over, his straw mattress rus-
tling. It was still dark. Maybe he could escape to the olive
grove before Jesus and his friends stirred.

The Jews had talked long into the night with Abahu, Uziel, and
Noach. Shem had listened, silent and uncomfortable, through the
evening meal but afterward had fled to the olive grove. When he
snuck back to his room very late, they were still gathered around
the fire in the courtyard. He had slept restlessly, trying to shut his
ears to their talk and laughter.

In Caesarea, he had enjoyed debates with his teachers, be they
Samaritan, Jew, or Greek. So why did he feel this overwhelming
need to avoid the Jewish teacher and his friends? Of all the men
in this backward village, he was by far the most learned. But he
didn't like the way the Galilean looked at him—like he already
knew all about Shem. When those dark eyes rested on him, Shem
heard the young soldier's dying breath and saw the life go out of
his eyes.

Shem jerked his tunic over his head. There was nothing new in
the Jew's teaching. Just more of the same tired claims that priests
and prophets had spouted for hundreds of years. *The man calls
himself the Taheb, the Restorer. But he'll have to do better than that.*

Shem left his room and found his grandmother again at the
fire in the courtyard, surrounded by the warm smell of baking
bread. The travelers had already descended from their sleeping place on the wide, flat roof. They were crouched under the
trees, eating and laughing, but Jesus was not among them. Shem
greeted them with a nod and sat down a few steps away.

These men—two sets of brothers—were obviously not scholars. He could tell by their accents that they were from Galilee. But they were gracious guests, despite their country ways. They seemed to have overcome their aversion to Samaritan food and vessels, for they ate a great deal and with gusto. Every Jew knew the saying: "The water of Samaria is more unclean than the blood of swine." They were either very sure of their prophet or couldn't resist Mechola's cooking.

"Where is your teacher?" Shem asked, accepting bread and watered wine from his grandmother.

"Went to the mountain," the one named Peter answered around a bite of bread. "He prays alone." He finished chewing and turned to the one named James. "I agree with John," Peter said. "If he says he is the Taheb, then he is also the Messiah."

Peter grabbed a handful of almonds from the one sitting next to him, Andrew. They were so alike with their long noses and wide eyes. Brothers more at home hauling nets and cleaning fish than sitting at the feet of a teacher, Shem guessed.

"But they are different," James said. He accepted another round of bread from Mechola. "The Messiah will overthrow the Romans. He will be a king, like David. The Taheb," he nodded to Shem, "the Taheb is a prophet."

Shem didn't respond. *I'm not getting into this argument.* But James was right. The Taheb that the Samaritans waited for was to be a prophet, the second Moses, the Restorer of peace and an age of favor for those who kept the Lord's commandments. The Messiah that the Jews awaited was a warrior king. One man couldn't be both.

James's brother, John, frowned. John was younger than the rest, much younger, probably close to Shem's age. "And what about the water? Again, yesterday, there was water. He is telling us something."

James shrugged. "How do you come up with that?"

"The first time was at the Jordan," John said. "I heard the voice of God when he came out of the water. 'This is my son,' He said."

Shem tensed and leaned forward. John had heard the voice of God?

"Many say it was only thunder," James said around a bite of bread.

"On a clear day? I was there!" John slapped his hand on his knee. "I tell you, God spoke. And it was when Jesus emerged from the water."

God spoke? And what was Jesus doing in the Jordan?

James held up his half-eaten bread like a shield. "We're not doubting you, it's just—"

"And then there was Cana." John raised his brows at Peter and Andrew.

They both looked away.

Shem had to know. "What happened in Cana?"

"Again with water. At a wedding we went to in Cana. The wine ran short, but Jesus told the servers to fill the washing jars with water. And when they drew it out, it was wine. And good wine—the best I've ever tasted."

James pushed him in the shoulder. "I think you had already drunk your share."

John pounded his brother's shoulder with his fist. "You were there. You saw it."

Turned water into wine? No. That sounded like a story made up by some drunk friends of the groom.

Peter shook his head and frowned like a father at bickering children. "John's right, though. There is something about water that he is trying to tell us. Yesterday he met the woman at Jacob's well. She said he asked her for water and promised her living water."

James wiped his hands on his robe. "You are making too much of it. Coincidence. Nothing more."

Andrew spoke for the first time. "Peter is right. And so is John. If the Rabbi says that he has living water, we should listen."

Three of them agree. That probably didn't happen often. "Tell me," Shem said, "do you understand all that he says? Do you truly believe that he is the Messiah, the one who will deliver the Jews? Or the Taheb, as the Samaritans say? Or both?"

The men seemed to be waiting for Peter to answer, but the big fisherman stuffed his mouth full of bread and shrugged while he chewed.

John spoke instead. "We don't know. Each day he reveals just a little more to us. But we know this—he has the words of everlasting life."

"Everlasting life?" Shem asked. *Surely not that. Not here, in Sychar.* "Does he believe in the resurrection of the dead?"

"Yes. He says that he is the resurrection and the life. But . . ." John contemplated his hands. "We don't know what he means."

These men were more foolish than Shem had ever imagined. Talk of eternal life could only bring trouble. Rome had no patience for Jewish prophets. More than one had been put to death for stirring up trouble in the province. But they were Galileans, and everyone knew that Galileans had more muscle than sense.

Peter finally spoke up. "A prophet or a king—I don't know. But he is the one promised by the Lord. That I believe. We have left everything—our homes and families, our boats, all we have. We will follow him wherever he leads."

"Even if he leads you into trouble? To death?" Shem asked.

They nodded in unison, their eyes shining with fierce purpose. Shem took a bite of his bread, but it tasted like straw in his dry mouth. He felt like he had as a child when his older brothers trooped off to their tutors, leaving him behind. But why be angry with these rough fishermen? He certainly didn't want to be one of them.

Besides, he was far more educated than any of them. Educated enough to know that this Galilean, however wise, was not the Taheb. These men had given up everything to follow a false prophet. And perhaps to their death. Then why did he feel like he was the fool being left behind?

Shem lengthened his stride to keep up with Abahu. "There is much to be done in the olives, Grandfather." And he would rather be doing it than attending evening prayer in the synagogue.

"It will be there tomorrow. Let us see what Jesus says today."

He says that he is the resurrection and the life. Jesus had best not speak of that here in Sychar. On this point the Samaritans agreed completely with the strict Sadducees of the temple. Eternal sleep was their hope; anything else, blasphemy.

Shem just wanted Jesus and his friends to leave. If this man stayed much longer in Sychar, he would draw the notice of the authorities. Romans didn't like Jewish prophets. Roman soldiers in Sychar could only mean trouble for him—and his grandparents. And he'd had enough trouble to last a lifetime. Just when he'd finally found some peace, this man—this false prophet—had stirred in him a storm of unrest.

Abahu stopped abruptly at the top of the path. Outside the synagogue, an argument brewed.

Zevulun bellowed at a crowd of men, his rolls of jowl and neck as red as a pomegranate. "Was it not just a few years ago that our families lost their husbands and sons? Cut down by the Romans on the Holy Mountain? And a man who claimed to be the Taheb was the cause!"

Many nodded their agreement. Shimon pushed his way to the front and faced the crowd. "All of Samaria believed that false prophet. He said that he knew where the Ark had been buried by Moses. But instead of proving that Mount Gerizim is the Holy Mountain, they were surrounded by Pilate's soldiers and killed. Many of our sons—my own brother—died! Are you willing to bring the wrath of Rome onto our heads again?"

Zevulun's voice lifted to a roar. "We should run this man and his disciples out of our land. Let him go back to the Jews and bring the Roman swords down on them!"

Abahu tensed beside Shem and stepped forward. Shem put a restraining arm on his grandfather. This wasn't Abahu's battle, even if the Jew was staying at his home. It would be better for everyone if Jesus and his friends just left.

But Uziel squirmed through the crowd to stand next to Zevulun and Shimon. He raised his arms, and the crowd quieted. "Zevulun, you are wise," he said calmly. "We must be careful of false prophets. But I have listened carefully to this Jesus. He doesn't ask us to fight the Romans; he doesn't speak of revolt at all. He seems to speak more to us of prayer and healing our covenant with the Lord."

Others murmured their agreement with Uziel, among them Abahu. Shame warmed Shem's cheeks. Uziel was right. This prophet didn't seem to have any motive of self-interest. He did not ask for money, power, or recognition. He didn't ask for them to rise up against the Romans. But he did proclaim himself the Taheb, the Promised One. He was a contradiction. Why was he staying in Sychar? What could this Galilean possibly hope to gain?

Shem pulled Abahu toward the door of the synagogue. He would listen to the Jew, but he would not believe his outrageous claims. The sooner the Galileans left Sychar, the better.

Mara squirmed through the crowd with Nava, as impatient as her mother was to see the Jewish teacher. She had thought of nothing else since the night before. And today! Nava was like a different person. She had awakened early, rushing through the chores so fast that there had been little left for Mara to do. Song and laughter had filled the house. Mara wondered if she were living in a wonderful dream.

Had this man really changed her mother? She needed to find out more. Perhaps he really was the one they had been waiting for, the Taheb.

Mara's pulse quickened as Jesus' words rang out in the crowded synagogue. "He is not the God of the dead, but of the living. No one can come to me unless the Father who sent me draws him, and I will raise him on the last day."

A hiss of astonishment rippled through the people. The women pressed close around Mara and her mother. They ducked their heads together and whispered. The men in the center of the room shifted closer to the front, where Jesus stood alone on the raised platform. Angry words flew like arrows.

"What do you mean?"

"Blasphemy!"

Nava clutched Mara's arm, squeezing hard. Was Jesus saying that he would raise the dead? Give them life again after death? Surely he must mean something else? And what would this mean for them? Nava had brought this man into their town. She would be blamed.

Jonothon spoke, his face mottled with red. "Are you saying that there is a resurrection of the body after death?"

Yahokeem stepped forward. "And what of the day of vengeance? If you are the Taheb, when will God deliver his people and punish their enemies?"

Jesus raised his hands to the people, reaching out to them, and waited for them to quiet. "The reward of the righteous is now at hand. The hour is coming when all who are in the tombs will hear his voice and will come out, those who have done good deeds to the resurrection of life." His gaze drifted over the crowd, stunned into silence. His eyes stopped at the small knot of men that included Zevulun and Shimon. "But those who have done wicked deeds to the resurrection of condemnation."

Jonothon and Yahokeem stared at him with open mouths.

Mara's heart pounded in her chest. He seemed to already know who was wicked and who was righteous. Or he was foolishly making enemies of the most powerful men in the village.

Zevulun's outraged bellow broke the silence. "Throw this man from our holy place!" He stomped up on the dais and advanced on Jesus until his face was only a hand's breadth from the Jew's. "We will not listen to his blasphemy." Spittle flew from his mouth with every word. "This is not the Taheb! A Jew, a—a carpenter from Nazareth—he will end up like all false prophets, hanging on a Roman cross!"

Mara and the women around her were pushed back to the wall as the men surged forward. Mara's heart lurched as Nava stepped toward the angry mob, but she grabbed her mother's hand just in time to pull her back.

Thank God Asher is safe at Ruth's house tonight. Would they beat Jesus and throw him out of the town? Or something worse? The penalty for blasphemy was death. Even a Jew knew that. And then what? Would they take out their rage on Nava? On her children?

Disappointment crushed the hope that she'd brought into the synagogue. She'd been wrong and so had Nava; this man couldn't be the Taheb, the Restorer that they'd waited for. But he'd seemed so wise, so sure. He'd done something—something very good—to Nava, but the Taheb wouldn't let himself be stoned by an angry mob in Sychar.

We should leave now, before this gets any worse. She pulled at Nava. "Mama, we must go. Now." But Nava pulled her hand from Mara's and shook her head, her eyes locked on the Jew in the front of the room.

Jesus stood tall and calm as his friends fought through the angry mob. Abahu and Enosh reached him first, holding back the men and allowing Jesus to step down from the dais. Shem reached him next, but the Jews were too far away to help. *There are too many. They are going to attack him, pull him out of the synagogue.*

Mara closed her eyes. *Lord, if he is your Anointed One, save him.*

She waited for the crowd to close in on Jesus. But no, as he stepped forward, the pressing crowd parted around him. He walked calmly through the mob, his hands at his sides while a clear path opened up before him. The angry faces turned confused, and the outraged cries dwindled into silence as he walked past them unharmed, through the open doorway and into the twilight.

Mara sucked in a breath, her heart filling with wonder. How had he done that? Was it an answer to her prayer? Could he really be the Taheb?

Mara grabbed Nava's hand and pulled her toward the door. It was impossible to believe, but it must be true. *The Taheb had come, and Nava was the first to be restored.*

Shem dropped his hands to his sides. One minute, the crowd was on top of him, and Jesus was in danger of being stoned. The next, they were watching him walk, unharmed, out the door. What kind of magic did this Jew possess?

The crowd poured out of the synagogue. Shem followed slowly with Abahu. Jesus was walking down the pathway as though he hadn't just been in danger of stoning. Men and women gathered in knots below the cedar trees. Their voices carried through the shadows.

"Who is he?"

"What did he mean?"

"Blasphemy!"

Others—Uziel and Enosh, Noach and his other sons—followed closely behind Jesus and his friends. Were they there to protect them, or did they want to hear more of his unfathomable words? Other groups of two or three—men, women, and children—brushed by Shem and hurried after Jesus. More stood around the synagogue, their arms crossed over their chests, their heads bobbing.

Abahu jerked his head toward the path and started down it. "Let us go home."

Where the Jew is waiting with more of his ridiculous claims?

"This Jesus is unlike any Jew I've ever heard of," Shem said, catching up to his grandfather. A cool breeze ran through the cedars as the sun dipped behind the mountain. "The Samaritans expect a Taheb. They—we," he amended at Abahu's sharp frown, "we wait for a Restorer. Jews pray for a Messiah—someone to overthrow the Romans. This man, though," Shem shook his head, "he does not seem to be what anyone is expecting. If he is a fraud, he is not a clever one, because he is not giving anyone what they want."

"What he says, though," Abahu said slowly, "it strikes me as the truth."

The night birds called and the insects chirped as they wended through the empty village streets toward Abahu's house. Yes, Jesus seemed more than just clever. He didn't speak in tired phrases they had all heard before. His words were surprising, even shocking, but they rang true.

Shem just didn't know what they meant.

They pushed through the gate to find Abahu's courtyard teeming with people. Jesus sat under a spreading fig tree in the center of the courtyard. At least a dozen men were at his feet, including Uziel, Noach, and their sons. More leaned against the walls and crouched in groups, watching him. He might be barred from the synagogue, but there were still many who wanted to hear his words.

A knot of women stood off to one side. His grandmother, Uziel's wife, an old woman with silver hair, and—his heart dropped at the familiar tattered robe and striped head covering—Mara. Beside her stood Nava, who had brought this man into their town. Now Zevulun had even more reason to hate her.

Jesus raised his head, his expression untroubled. "Abahu. Will you too send me away?"

"You are welcome here for as long as you wish to stay," Abahu said with a nod. Shem couldn't help the quick scowl that crossed his face. He looked at the ground, feeling like a rude child.

The crowd quieted as Jesus turned to them. "Moses wrote the law of your fathers on stone tablets. I will write my law not on stone, but in your hearts. I say to you, blessed are the poor in spirit, for theirs is the kingdom of heaven."

Abahu lowered himself to the ground next to Uziel. Noach shifted to make room for Shem. There was no choice; he'd have to stay and listen. As Shem settled next to his grandfather, Jesus went on speaking of the meek, the hungry, the merciful. These were not the words of someone wanting to inspire a rebellion.

Jesus' eyes shifted to Nava. "Blessed are those who mourn, for they will be comforted."

Then Jesus turned to Shem. "Blessed are those who are persecuted because of righteousness, for theirs is the kingdom of heaven. Blessed are you," he continued, "when people insult you, persecute you, and falsely say all kinds of evil against you—because of me."

Shem shifted uncomfortably. *Why is he saying these things to me?*

Jesus spread his hands to the crowd, as if he were appealing to them all. "Rejoice and be glad, because your reward will be great in heaven."

Rejoice in insults? Rewarded in heaven? Shem could stand it no longer. "Teacher, what do you mean by this? That we are to rejoice in persecution? That we are to welcome abuse? What good does that do?"

Jesus leaned toward Shem, his voice softening. "Unless a grain of wheat falls to the ground and dies, it remains just a grain of wheat. But if it dies, it produces much fruit."

Shem crossed his arms and lifted his chin. "Forgive me. This makes no sense to me. For a man to die at the hands of his enemy is the greatest good he can do in his life? How can we help our people by dying?" Could he have helped his brother by dying? Wouldn't that just be two dead Samaritans instead of one dead Roman? Should they not fight those who seek to kill them? "For hundreds of years, we have died at the hands of our enemies. That has not brought our people a better life."

Murmurs of agreement rose around him, but not from Abahu.

Jesus ignored the crowd, keeping his dark eyes on Shem. "You have heard it said, 'you shall love your neighbor and hate your enemy.' But I say to you, love your enemies, and pray for those who persecute you, that you may be children of your heavenly Father."

Shem shook his head. This was no prophet. He seemed so certain, so authentic. But his words were contrary to everything Shem had learned from hard experience. Shem stood up. "I have heard enough. I have no patience for your riddles."

He banged through the courtyard door and stomped toward the olive grove. This Jesus was no prophet. He was a fool. *And he's trying to make a fool of me.*

Chapter 15

Mara sat next her mother, stripping dried beans from their husks and throwing them in the cooking pot. Nava had been up before the sun, cooking barley and milking the goats before Mara had even stirred from her pallet.

"Jesus left Sychar this morning to go to Nazareth," Nava said.

Joy and regret filled Mara's heart. Joy that Nava had come back to her and Asher. Regret that Jesus would not stay with them forever. In just two days, her life had changed. She had listened to Jesus and watched her mother. He had restored her. Whatever the illness was that had taken her strength and sense, it was gone.

The memory of her anger at Nava ached like a scar on her heart. *How could I have wished her dead?*

This was the mother that Mara remembered from her childhood. The mother she had missed every day since Asher had been born and the mother that Asher had never known.

I wish that I could catch his words from the air, hold them in my hand, and examine them as often as I want. I have my mother back. He is the Restorer. Perhaps the future might not be one of despair and poverty, but one of hope.

Soon Nava would send word to Shaul in Sebaste, and he would surely return to them. Asher would have a father and learn a trade. Mara would speak to Uziel. If Shaul returned, their lives would be better. Now that Nava was restored, everything was different. Surely he would see that she didn't have to accept Jobab's offer.

They weren't hungry anymore. Shem's gift of wheat, oil, and dried fish would last for several more days. Other villagers—the ones who listened to Jesus' words of forgiveness—had given them gifts of barley, almonds, and figs. Best of all, Mechola and Abahu treated them as friends, and some of the others looked on them more kindly.

"Will you go to the well with me?" Nava asked.

Mara poked her head around the corner of the house. Asher worked in the garden, planting a new crop of beans. She put the tall clay jar on her head, and together they climbed the steep path and followed it around the village.

As they rounded the corner of the Patriarch's Highway, raised voices came from the women clustered at the well. Mechola and Leah faced Tirzah and Adah. Other women and girls stood nearby, silent and watchful.

"I only know," said Mechola, "that my heart filled with joy at his words."

Leah nodded. "He did not ask for us to forsake our beliefs, but to live them more faithfully."

Tirzah grimaced. "My husband and sons say he's a disgrace. You are fools to let yourself be swayed by a Jew." She spit out the last word. She jerked around and saw Nava and Mara. "And at the word of a woman like that." She raised a hand at them. "She may have known many men, but we can hardly trust her to know the Taheb when he comes!"

Mara held her breath. *No, Mama, don't let them get to you.*

Mechola's mouth turned down, and the creases in her brow deepened. Several women stepped up behind Tirzah; some drew closer around Mechola. Adah looked uncertainly at Mechola, then took half a step toward Tirzah and her allies.

Nava set down her jug. "You are right, Tirzah," Nava bowed her head. "I have offended many of you and disgraced my family."

Tirzah's mouth dropped open.

Nava raised her head. Her eyes shone with unshed tears. "But when I spoke to Jesus at the well, he knew of all my sins. He did not condemn me but called me to repent and start again. He forgave me."

Tirzah drew her large body upward with a sharp breath. Her

florid cheeks turned a darker shade of red. She seemed even more enraged at Nava's humility than she had been at her pride. "Forgave you!" she sputtered. "Who is he to forgive? In this town, we punish those who break our laws!"

She turned her back on Nava with a stamp of her foot. She jerked her head toward Adah—"Zevulun and Shimon will hear about this"—and marched away without a backward glance.

Mara threw her arms around her mother, pride and love filling her heart. *I should be afraid, but I'm not.* They were still in danger. Even more danger than before Jesus came. But because of him, her mother was a different woman—a forgiven woman. And that was all that mattered.

Mara hurried into the dim house. She had gone to Ruth's to take her some more green thread and tell her about what had happened at the well that morning. She'd rushed back, not even staying to eat the midday meal.

But something was wrong. The fire was out, and the water jar lay on its side in the middle of the room, a wet puddle all that was left of the day's water. "Mama?" *Where is Asher?*

Mara's eyes adjusted to the gloom to see Nava huddled in the corner, Asher clutched in her arms. Her face was buried in his neck, and she quaked with sobs. Mara rushed to them. "Mama . . . what is it? Is Asher hurt?"

She untangled Asher from her mother's arms and ran her hands over his bare legs and arms. "Mama?" Her throat closed and she worked to swallow, her mouth as dry as ashes. Were the days of having her mother restored to her over? Had the illness come back as soon as Jesus was gone? She took Nava's chin in her hand. One eye was swollen shut and turning an ugly dark red.

"What happened, Asher?"

"It was the bad man. Mara, he hurt Mama! I tried to take care of her, Mara . . . I couldn't . . . I'm sorry." He burst into tears and threw himself into Mara's arms.

Nava wiped away her tears with shaking hands. "I'm all right,

Mara. Please, Asher. You were a good boy. You did just as I said."
She sat up straighter, taking a deep breath. "It was Alexandros.
He—Mara, I don't know why I did the things that I did. I can
hardly remember. But I did, and it was wrong. And now Alexandros . . ." She put her hands over her face.

Mara squeezed Asher tight in her arms. "What did he do?
Mama, tell me."

"He was here. He wanted to . . . stay here tonight. I told him
no. I said he couldn't." Nava took her hands from her face and
straightened. "I told him that I'd changed, that he couldn't visit
here anymore."

Mara freed an arm from Asher and put it around Nava. *Thank
you, Lord. We'll never have to see him again.* A surge of warmth
filled her.

Nava took a shaky breath. "I told him to never come here
again. He said I'd be sorry. That the priests would punish me, and
he would be there to . . . to laugh as they stoned me." Tears slid
down her face again as she looked from Mara to Asher.

Mara's joy melted like water into the dry ground. *We are still
in danger.* Jesus had changed their little family forever, but some
in the town of Sychar were very much the same. The ones who
mattered—the ones with power—still hated Nava. And Alexandros would know just who those men were.

She rocked with Nava and Asher in silence, thinking hard.
Zevulun hated Nava even more than before. She had brought
a man into the town, a Jew. He had disagreed with the priests,
humiliated Zevulun, and divided the town. He'd find a way to
punish her.

Mara rested her forehead against her mother's hair. But because of Jesus, they seemed to have more friends now. She could
count on Abahu and Mechola—and Ruth and Uziel, as always.
Perhaps even others.

She sat up straight and smoothed her mother's hair. "Maybe
he was just angry. I didn't pass him, so he didn't go toward the
village. Maybe we will hear nothing more from him," Mara said
hopefully.

Nava nodded, but she didn't meet Mara's eyes.

She doesn't believe that any more than I do.

Nava drew a shaking breath and covered Mara's hand with her own. "We must trust in the Lord and face whatever comes. If you and Asher can forgive me, I will be content . . . no matter what happens."

"Mama . . ." Mara gazed at her mother's beautiful face, her green eyes still bright with tears. "I have forgiven you. And I won't let anything happen to you."

Chapter 16

Shem labored in the hot morning sun, sweat pouring off his face. He, Abahu, and Enosh had carried at least twenty heavy jars full of water to the wilting seedlings in the north grove, and they had at least another ten to carry. The Jew and his friends had left two days ago, thank the Almighty. *I'd rather carry a hundred jars than listen to any more of his wild claims.*

He straightened from his task to see Mechola hurrying up the side of the hill, her face red. What was she doing here? And why did she look so worried?

Abahu followed his gaze, and his silver brows drew together. Mechola did not smile when she saw them but set her mouth in a grim line and quickened her steps. Enosh flashed Shem a frown and set his jar on the ground.

Abahu started toward Mechola. Shem followed, and Enosh's footsteps rustled behind him. Abahu took her by the shoulders, guiding her to sit on a stump. Her breath came hard and fast.

Shem bent over her. "What is it?" His arms and legs tensed. Could Roman soldiers be in the village, searching for him? He checked down the hill. The olive groves and barley fields lay silent and empty. Apart from Mechola's wheezing, he heard only birdsong and chirping insects.

"It's Nava."

"What happened?" Abahu and Shem asked in unison.

"I heard from Adah—and I think it's true—I heard that the priests are calling a trial. For adultery."

A trial? Shem had told Abahu about the informer and Zevulun. Abahu had agreed that they would need proof. "But they must have some proof to convict her. Did you hear anything about evidence?"

"I don't know. But Adah said . . ." Mechola grimaced. "She said that the priests were going to—well, I can hardly believe it." She shook her head.

"What?" Shem closed his hand over his grandmother's soft shoulder.

"Adah seems to think they are going to give her the bitter water test."

"What?" Shem jerked upright. "That is absurd! That test hasn't been used for a hundred years!"

Abahu shook his head. "Perhaps not in Caesarea, but here it is used still. I've seen it twice in my lifetime, but I've never seen it prove the innocence of a woman, only guilt."

"I haven't seen Nava since the day before yesterday, at the well." Mechola wiped her damp forehead with her sleeve. "Adah said that the priests sent a messenger to her, commanding that she come to answer for her sins. Midday at the synagogue."

"But I haven't heard of a trial." Abahu ran his hand over his gray beard. "They would have called us—all the men of the village—to hear the evidence."

"Perhaps," said Shem. "Unless they weren't interested in justice—only punishment. Or they have called only those who will agree with Zevulun."

For a moment, only the saplings rustled in the breeze, and the dry leaves whispered on the hillside. Abahu turned to Shem. "We must help her. If the Taheb doesn't hold her sins against her, neither can we."

Shem looked at the sun, which was already well above the eastern horizon. *I don't care what the so-called Taheb said. I just know Mara needs help.* "We don't have much time."

"I'll get Uziel," Abahu said, helping Mechola to her feet. "We'll find as many men as we can. If we have enough, we can stop the test. Zevulun doesn't have as much support as he thinks, but we'll need every friend we can get."

"You can count on me. And my father and brothers."

Shem started at the sound of Enosh's deep voice. He thumped the quiet youth on the back. He was old enough to lend his voice. They would need their friends' support, but they would need more than that. Zevulun was cunning; they needed the law on their side.

Abahu turned to go down the hill and motioned for Enosh and Shem to follow.

"Grandfather," Shem said.

Abahu turned back.

"I know the law. If I could talk to Mara's—to Nava—I could speak to her, prepare her. It might go better for her if she knows what to say."

"Yes." Abahu nodded decisively. He looked to Mechola. "Go with him to Nava. Quickly now. Talk to her. We'll meet you at the synagogue."

"Mara, I'm afraid I'm not feeling very well today." Nava sat at the loom, but her hands lay limp in her lap. "Would you mind gleaning the barley while I stay here with Asher?"

"Of course, Mama." Mara wondered at her mother's strange tone. Mara had done the gleaning by herself for many seasons while her mother was ill. In the days since Alexandros's attack, Nava had been very quiet. Mara pounded the measure of grain one last time. That should be enough for their bread today.

Mara took up a large basket. They would need as much barley as they could gather for the long months ahead. She kissed the top of Asher's head. "Take care of Mama today." As soon as the familiar words left her mouth, she regretted them. Since Alexandros's visit, Asher had watched over Nava like a Roman guard. He had stopped sucking his thumb and abandoned his toys. He crawled across the floor, his face set in a determined frown, and stationed himself at Nava's feet.

To her mother, she said, "Try to rest. The weaving will wait." She turned to leave, but Nava caught her arm and pulled Mara close. She held her in a long embrace, squeezing her tightly. Mara leaned back and looked hard at her mother.

"Don't worry about me; I'm just being foolish." Nava laughed, but it sounded more like a sob. "I do love you so much, Mara."

Mara frowned. *Why is her smile so forced?* "Are you sure? Maybe I should stay?" She brushed her fingers over the purple and green bruise high on Nava's cheek.

"No, we need the barley. Don't mind me. Now go, and fill your water skin at the well as you pass. It will be hot today."

Mara trudged up the path. Nava didn't seem ill, not like before. She would almost say that Nava was hiding something from her. She shook her head. Her mother was fine; she was well again. There was nothing to worry about.

The barley field lay on the eastern end of Sychar, a long walk. She quickened her steps. If she was fast and the gleaning was good, she could get home by early afternoon. *Please, Lord, send your angels to keep watch over them.*

As she neared the village, she raised her eyes from the path to see Shem and his grandmother walking toward her. As always, a rush of heat flooded her face when she saw Mechola's grandson.

Mechola stopped in front of her. "Why, Mara, where are you going?"

"I'm going to the barley field to glean." Mara tipped the basket toward the older woman. *What a strange question.*

Mechola cast a sideways glance at Shem, who raised his eyebrows and shook his head. Mechola fluttered her hands in Mara's direction and leaned toward her. "Forgive me, my girl. It's just so very hot to be working in the fields. Is your mother gleaning with you today?"

"No . . ." Mara said. *Why is Shem looking at me like that?* She focused on her dirty bare feet, flustered by his dark eyes. "No, it's a long walk—the field is a long walk, and she isn't . . . isn't feeling well." *I sound like an idiot.*

Shem took his grandmother's arm and pulled her gently. "We should let Mara get to the fields, Grandmother, before it gets even hotter." He prodded Mechola again, and they hurried away. As Mara watched them go, she saw Mechola peer back over her shoulder, her brow furrowed like a newly planted field.

Where are they going? Surely not to her house. Maybe to one of the olive groves. The odd meeting only increased the tightness in her chest.

Shem and Mechola walked past the olive groves and up the hill. A lizard skittered away from his foot and rustled into the dry grass. Mara was going to glean barley instead of to her mother's trial.

"She doesn't know," his grandmother said.

"It's better this way," Shem answered. Mara would be spared the humiliation of the trial. If it went well, she would be glad; if it went badly . . . well, at least she wouldn't be there to see it. But she would be angry.

It was his fault that Nava was in this mess. If he hadn't been so stupid . . . At least he could keep Mara out of it. At least he could do that for her.

Cresting the hill, he saw Nava sitting on a bench outside the little house below, holding Asher in her lap. His squeal of delight floated up the hill along with Nava's low laugh. Shem and Mechola trudged down the path and into the valley.

Nava fell silent when she saw them heading toward the house. Her smile faded as they passed the cooking fire, and she stood, settling Asher on her hip. Asher stared at Shem with wary eyes.

How beautiful she was, this older version of Mara. Then Shem saw the dark bruise under her eye. His hands clenched into fists. Who had done that?

"Good morning, Nava," Mechola said. "You know my grandson, Shem."

Nava nodded politely. He bowed his head in return.

"We are here to help, Nava," Mechola said simply. "Abahu is gathering men who will be fair and just at the trial. We will go with you and stand by you, no matter what happens."

Nava swayed, her face crumpled. Shem stepped forward and took Asher from her arms. She covered her face with her hands. "I didn't think—I wasn't sure I could do it alone."

The birds twittered in the tall cedars. Asher pushed away from

Shem. Shem hitched him higher. The boy was heavy. How did Mara carry him all over the village?

Nava dried her eyes with her rough sleeve. "I sent Mara away. She has been through enough."

Mechola nodded. "Yes, we met her on the path. We didn't tell her." She motioned for Nava to sit. The sun had climbed high; they didn't have much time.

Mechola sat down next to Nava, and Shem settled Asher in his grandmother's arms. He crouched in front of Nava, meeting her worried green eyes, so much like Mara's that his heart beat faster.

"What did the priest's messenger say?"

Nava jumped at his voice. She was frightened, and with good reason. He tried more gently. "Please, Nava. I need to know his exact words."

Nava took a deep breath. "He came yesterday. Mara wasn't here. It was the servant of Jonothon." She thought for a moment. "He said, 'Jonothon orders you to the synagogue tomorrow at midday. You are charged with the sin of adultery.'"

"Nothing else?"

She shook her head.

"He didn't name your accuser?"

"No," she said. "But . . . wouldn't it have to be Shaul? We are still married, even if he has been gone since Asher was a baby. He never actually divorced me."

Shem frowned. "They would need the testimony of two witnesses. Would they be able to find two witnesses?" he asked as gently as he could.

"I . . . I don't think so," she stammered, dropping her gaze to the ground. Her face turned red.

Mechola scooted over and put her arm around Nava's thin shoulders. "He is trying to help. Don't be afraid, my dear."

"But you know . . ." Nava swallowed. "You know that I am guilty?"

Shem regarded the beautiful, sorrowful woman in front of him. Here was why Zevulun had hired the informer to find Shaul.

This was serious. "That will be hard for them to prove," he said with more certainty than he felt.

The sun had reached its zenith. A hot wind from the east swept dust into Shem's eyes and dried his mouth as he walked up the Holy Mountain. "Be respectful, but do not admit to any sin," he told Nava. He carried Asher easily on his shoulder, adjusting his long strides to keep pace with Nava and his wheezing grandmother. "Be respectful, no matter what they do. Or what they say." He slanted her a glance, thinking of her outburst at Passover.

Nava lowered her head. "I understand."

Shem stopped walking and turned to Nava. "This is important. We must hope that they do the bitter water test. If they do, you will go free."

Nava's face froze. She looked terrified. She shook her head. "No. I won't."

"Yes. Believe me." Shem reached out and put his hand on her shoulder. "Just drink the water. It will taste bad, but that is all. They say that if you are guilty, the water will hurt you. But it is just used to frighten a guilty woman. Drink it. Nothing will happen, even if you are guilty." She needed to trust him on this. He gripped her shoulder hard. "The worst thing you can do is refuse to drink it. That is an admission of guilt."

Nava bit her lip and stepped back from him. "Wouldn't Shaul—wouldn't my husband have to agree to my punishment?"

"Yes," Shem answered. "That's why Zevulun went to such trouble to find him."

Nava shook her head. "I can't believe that Shaul would agree to . . ." She glanced at Asher. "He wouldn't do that to me or to Asher."

"I hope we don't have to find out."

A crowd had already gathered outside the synagogue. Shem directed his grandmother to a shady spot under a cedar tree. He settled Asher on the soft carpet of needles.

Nava crouched down and stroked her son's soft face. "Asher, stay here," she said softly. "Mama will be gone for a little while."

Mechola patted his shoulder. "He'll be fine. We will sit in the shade and wait for you to come back to us." The old woman put her arms around Nava's shoulders and pulled her close. "May the Lord be with you."

Shem gave Mechola what he hoped was a reassuring smile. It felt forced and unnatural.

They couldn't convict Nava without two witnesses—it was the law. If they did find two people who would swear that Nava had committed adultery, then they could drive her from Sychar. But only if enough men agreed to the punishment. Abahu would make sure that didn't happen. There weren't enough men in this village who would follow Zevulun's lead.

And stoning? It couldn't happen. Roman law forbade the death penalty without permission from the local governor. Everyone knew that. Even Zevulun wouldn't go that far.

He whispered to Nava, "Don't worry. Just drink the water."

Chapter 17

Zevulun swaggered toward them, dressed in a finely embroidered robe, his jowls swaying. He pointed a fat finger at Nava. "There she is! Now you will answer for yourself, disgraceful woman."

"Let us take this to the priests," Shem said. His voice came out strong and firm. The big man narrowed his eyes and looked from Shem's face to his rough tunic and farmer sandals, then turned and stalked toward the crowd.

Nava stood rooted to the earth, her face pale. She pointed weakly at a big Canaanite in the center of the crowd. Her hand went to her bruised eye. "Alexandros," she whispered.

Shem tightened his fist at his side. Had the pagan done this to her?

"And there is my husband, Shaul." Her eyes rested on a man standing apart from the others. Short and barrel-chested with a large, square head and heavy brow, he had the air of one who worked hard and drank harder. His attention was on Nava, his thick arms crossed over his chest.

Energy charged through Shem's veins. He would protect her. Zevulun may have been waiting for his chance, but it had been Shem—his own thoughtless words—who had brought Nava to this. He lifted his chin and motioned for Nava to follow him into the synagogue.

The sanctuary swarmed with men, but who were they? A few he recognized from Sychar, but the rest were strangers dressed in rough workmen's clothes. These were not the merchants and farmers of Sychar but what looked like stonemasons and builders from Sebaste.

One scarred face was familiar to Shem. It was the informer, the one who had spoken to Zevulun in the toolshed. He darted from one man to another, whispering to them and encouraging the taunts and leers as Nava passed by.

Nava moved closer to Shem. "So many . . ."

Shem caught sight of his grandfather standing with Noach, Enosh, and his brothers. Uziel stood at the front of the room, stretching to see over the crowd. At least they had some friends here. But not enough. He sent his grandfather a questioning glance. Were these the only men who would stand for Nava?

Abahu returned a worried look. There were at least thirty strangers gathering around Zevulun and Shimon. Where had they all come from?

Had Zevulun brought in men from outside Sychar, promising them . . . what? A spectacle? One thing was certain; they weren't there to help Nava. Some spit at her as she walked past. Others muttered insults. Nava shrank away from them, her hands shaking as she pulled her mantle around her face.

Shem and Nava reached the dais where the priests stood. Yahokeem demanded quiet, and the angry buzz of voices died away. Nava swayed slightly beside Shem. She was the only woman in the room.

Yahokeem raised trembling arms. "Let us put on fear of him before we speak of him. Let us search for the truth and learn wisdom, that no apostasy will be found in us. Let us attend to the truth and trust in him, our Lord and Maker."

The men answered in unison. "He is God, and there is none beside him."

Yahokeem leaned heavily on Jonothon's arm. "The charge is adultery. Who brings forth this woman for trial?"

"I do." Shaul stepped forward. In his hand he held the cereal offering.

"How do you know this woman?"

"I am her husband." Shaul's voice broke. He looked not at

Nava's stricken face but at Zevulun. Zevulun scowled and nodded, jabbing his finger toward Nava. Shimon stood by him, urging on the angry men.

"Are there any witnesses to her sin?" asked the priest.

"Yes, I am a witness," Alexandros said, too loudly, as if he'd been coached. "This is the whore who enticed me to her bed only a few weeks ago. And I doubt I'm the only one." His thin lips dipped down at the corners, as if he were trying to hide a smile. Shem's pulse hammered in his ears, and his fists ached to wipe the sneer off the pagan dog's face.

Zevulun stepped forward, his face triumphant. "There is your proof. What more do you need? She is guilty of adultery. Let us now decide her punishment."

Shem couldn't believe his ears. Decide her punishment? They hadn't even proven her guilt. This was no trial. These rough, agitated men clearly had no interest in justice. He raised his hand to the crowd. "Wait! Is this how you conduct a trial in Sychar?"

Zevulun turned on him. "And who are you to speak in defense of this woman?"

Abahu pushed toward the dais, tall and erect. He ignored Zevulun and directed his words to the priests. "He is my grandson and lives in Sychar. He knows our laws. Zevulun," he added with a look of disdain, "why are you leading this trial? You are not the wronged husband." He towered over the now-speechless Zevulun. "Let Shaul speak against Nava, if he will. Shem will speak for her. You have done enough for today."

Zevulun's face turned scarlet. He turned to the crowd of men and bellowed. "I only seek the Lord's will. If this woman has sinned, the Lord will see her punished. If she is forgiven, he will save her." He lowered his voice and inclined his head to the priests. "Let the Lord's will be done."

As Zevulun stepped back from the dais, the crowd settled, and Yahokeem motioned for Shem to continue.

He took a deep breath. He'd questioned his teachers and scholars of Caesarea hundreds of times. He could do this. "Do you punish one of your own on the testimony of a pagan?" He stood tall and pulled his shoulders back. "And what of the second witness that the law requires?"

Yahokeem's brows twitched lower. Shem felt a whisper of hope. But then Jonothon stepped forward and flicked a hand at Yahokeem. The old priest shuffled behind Jonothon with a tired sigh.

The younger priest cocked his head at Zevulun, then turned to Shem with a patronizing smile. "You are correct," he said. He looked over the waiting crowd. "We cannot convict a woman solely on the word of one man. Are there any other witnesses?"

The crowd murmured, but no one came forward. Nava stood with her head down, her shoulders sagged. Shem breathed a sigh of relief.

Jonothon raised his hands. "No? Then let us give her the bitter water test."

A deep rumble went through the crowd of men. Nava's face drained of all color. She shook her head.

Shem nodded to her. "Drink it," he whispered. "Trust me."

Jonothon took up a large earthen cup. He and Yahokeem proceeded through the men, to the center of the sanctuary. "Come forward, Nava, daughter of Naftali, and stand before the Lord."

Nava's eyes met Shem's before she turned and walked through the hushed crowd.

"On this scroll is written the accusation of adultery." Yahokeem unrolled the scroll and held it open. Jonothon poured water over the parchment and caught the stream of ink and water in the earthen cup.

Shem shook his head. *I don't believe it. This test is ancient history.*

Jonothon scooped a handful of dust from the floor of the sanctuary. Sprinkling it into the cup, he said, "If you have not gone astray by impurity while under the authority of your husband, be immune to the curse of this bitter water." He swirled the mixture. "But if you have acted impurely, Nava, daughter of Naftali, may the Lord make you an example among your people by causing your thighs to waste away and your belly to swell! May this water, then, that brings a curse, enter your body."

He pulled off Nava's mantle, threw it to the floor, and held out the cup. Nava jerked back like it was poison.

Shem clenched his jaw. *Just drink it. Please.*

Every eye fixed on Nava. She stood alone amid the crowd of men. She took the cup in her shaking hands and raised it to her lips. She closed her eyes for a moment before she let the cup fall from her hands. The inky water pooled in the dust.

"No. I will not drink it." Tears leaked from her eyes, but her voice rang out strong in the silent room.

Shem's heart pounded. *What is she doing?*

"Then you must be guilty!" Zevulun shouted. He waved to the surrounding men, and they stepped closer to Nava.

Nava ignored Zevulun. She took a deep breath and looked sadly at Shem. She seemed to be begging for his understanding. "I will not drink it. I am guilty."

Shem's heart seemed to stop beating. *I don't believe this. How can she do this to her children?*

Nava knelt before Jonothon. She bowed low, her forehead touching the dirt. "I only beg that you take my children into consideration as you decide my punishment. I have changed. Please." Nava could not see the smirk of satisfaction that crossed Jonothon's face, but Shem did. And the glance that passed between Jonothon and Zevulun.

"She admitted it!" Zevulun shouted, his large body jerking in a triumphant dance.

But Nava wasn't done. She crawled through the dust on her knees and stretched out on the ground before her husband. She reached out a hand to touch his foot. "Shaul, I do not deserve your forgiveness, but for the sake of your son, will you defend me?"

Shaul's face pinched, and he blinked. His throat worked but no words came from his mouth. He leaned down, his hand stretched out toward her dark hair.

Zevulun pushed Alexandros forward.

"Far be it from me to tell you, priests, how to punish your own people. But even the pagans do not allow their wives to flaunt themselves to other men. I had no idea that she was married." Alexandros shrugged, and a smile twisted his lips. "She was willing enough."

Shaul's face hardened at Alexandros's words. He jerked away from Nava's prostrate body. The cereal offering fell from his hand. "How could you? When you knew how much I . . ." He swallowed and looked from his wife to Alexandros. "How do I even know Asher is mine? You were not a proper wife to me, and yet I did not divorce you. I always hoped . . ." His voice dropped to a whisper. "You could not bear for me to touch you, yet you allowed this pagan in your bed?" He worked his mouth and spit on her.

"She has admitted it. She is an adulteress!" Zevulun crowed. "There is only one punishment in Sychar for adultery. May the priests do their duty now and condemn her to death."

They can't do this. Shem's mouth went dry. These men were using the laws of Moses for their own gain, their own revenge.

The room erupted in confusion. The crowd of rough men began to shuffle toward the center, closing in around Nava. Shaul covered his face with his hands as though he couldn't bear to watch.

"Wait!" Shem pushed the nearest men away from Nava, trying to keep the panic from his voice. "You cannot order the death penalty. What of the Roman law?" Zevulun stepped up and dug his fat finger into Shem's chest. "What do the Romans care for one disgraced woman in Sychar?" He looked around at the crowd. "Will you tell the Romans about this?" he asked a rough man near the front, who shook his head. "Will you?" he asked another.

He leaned in close enough that Shem could smell the sweat that beaded on his forehead and soaked his linen collar. "And you won't, will you, Shem, son of Ezra? Surely you—of all the men here—would not want to bring Roman attention to Sychar?" Zevulun's mouth curled into a sneer.

Shem stepped back in surprise. A chill whispered up his spine. So Zevulun's informer had been busy. And he was right. Shem couldn't go to the governor. Neither could Abahu if he wanted to keep his grandson safe. They were helpless, and it was all his fault. If he hadn't come to Sychar, Nava would be safe in her home with Mara. He couldn't bear it. *Not another death on my head.*

Jonothon raised his hands. "You, Nava, daughter of Naftali," he intoned, "are condemned to death by stoning."

The men stormed around Nava, pulling her up and dragging her to the door. The tide of men pushed Shem to the back of the crowd. "Get to her!" he shouted, catching sight of Abahu. Enosh and his brothers struggled through the crowd. Uziel was flattened against the farthest wall.

"Shaul, help me!" Nava called to her husband. One man dragged her by the arm, another held her by her hair. Shaul turned toward his wife, his face twisted in indecision. Too late, he held out his arms toward her, but the space between them was already too wide.

Shem rammed through the rest of the crowd and out of the synagogue. He glimpsed Zevulun and Shimon throwing Nava to the ground before the crowd surrounded her.

I have to stop them. Shem rushed toward the mob. Pain shot through his jaw, and he was on his back on the dusty ground, tasting blood.

Amram stood over him, his fists raised. "Your turn to lie in the dirt."

Shem scrambled up with a rush of anger. If Amram wanted a fight, he'd get one. He sidestepped the sluggish fist that Amram threw at him and lashed out with his own. He felt a satisfying crunch, and blood spurted from Amram's nose. Shem turned and plunged into the crowd. He craned his neck to see over the crowd.

Nava struggled to her feet. "No!" she cried. "My children, think of them . . . have mercy! Please, I know that I've sinned. Jesus, the Taheb, he knew my sins. But he did not condemn me. Please." She turned to Shimon. "You know. He forgave my sins."

Zevulun's face turned from red to purple. "Forgave your sins!" He covered his ears with his hands. "A Jew from Nazareth forgave your sins? That is blasphemy!"

Zevulun ripped off his cloak and threw it to the ground. Shimon, Jonothon, and Alexandros piled their own coats at his feet. Men and boys fetched armfuls of stones. Zevulun hefted one in each hand, and the others did the same.

Shaul darted to the edge of the crowd. He pulled at the nearest bystander. The man knocked him aside. Shaul waved his arms at Zevulun. "Stop! Don't hurt her!"

No one took any notice of him.

Shem shouted, "Stop! Listen to this man."

Zevulun's head jerked up. "Get that one out of here!" He pointed to Shem. A huge man with arms like tree trunks waded through the crowd toward him. Who was this? No one from Sychar. This moment had been carefully planned by Zevulun and his cronies.

But where was Abahu? He spotted two rough shepherds dragging Abahu and Enosh toward the cedar trees.

The goliath grabbed Shem by the neck of his tunic, choking him as he dragged him farther away from Nava. Panic gave Shem strength. He twisted suddenly and slammed his elbow into the man's face. He heard a low grunt, and his tunic came free.

Shem couldn't see Nava, but he heard her screams. Abahu was huddled on the ground behind the crowd, protecting himself from a round of vicious kicks. Enosh was holding his own against a man twice his size. Shem hesitated. Which should he help first? He stumbled out of the crowd and brought Abahu's attacker down with one blow. A hard kick kept him down.

"Are you hurt?" Shem helped Abahu up.

Enosh limped toward them, holding his ribs, but his attacker lay motionless on the ground. "I'll stay with him."

"Go," Abahu coughed out, pushing Shem toward Nava.

Shem heaved himself through the shouting mob. *Please, don't let me be too late.*

He glimpsed Zevulun hurling a massive, jagged stone. It hit the side of Nava's head, and she fell to her knees. Alexandros smiled grimly as he threw two huge rocks at Nava's bent body and reached for more.

The angry crowd closed in. Harder and faster they threw. Their cries grew less human, like the shrieks of buzzards fighting over a carcass.

Finally, Shem reached the inner ring of the crowd. He froze. Blood matted Nava's dark hair and flowed down her arms. A deep gash covered half her face and poured blood. She scrabbled through the dirt on her hands and knees, trying desperately to crawl away under the rain of stones.

Sudden pain shot up his arm. Amram had found him again, and this time, he had the help of the angry giant, his nose still spewing blood. The giant wrenched both Shem's arms behind his back. Amram grabbed his tunic and pulled it tight against his throat. Shem struggled but couldn't move. He could hardly breathe. "Let me go!" he croaked.

"It's too late," Amram sneered. "She'll get what she deserves."

"Finish it!" Zevulun roared. Huge stones hit her like battering rams. Small ones flew like arrows.

Shem pulled hard, cursing, trying to wrench his arms free, but Amram and the giant held tight. Despair squeezed his chest like a vice. He couldn't save her now. He had failed her. Then Shem heard another voice, small and high. It came from near the ground.

"Stop hurting my mama!"

No, not Asher. His blood surged, panic rose in his chest, and he strained against the hands that held him. A flash of dirty tunic caught his eye—Asher, crawling through the legs of the tightly packed crowd. As Shem tried to get enough air to cry out, to stop him, Asher reached the open area where his mother cowered. He took no notice of the flying stones but scuttled toward Nava.

Nava caught sight of her son. "No, Asher!" she screamed. She reached weakly through the rain of stones. Asher threw himself at her. Nava, with what seemed the last of her strength, pulled him close, pushing her bleeding body over his small one.

"Stop—the boy!" Shem yelled. Could anyone hear him? Didn't they see?

Finally, some men backed away, stones dropping from their

hands. But not Alexandros. The big man hurled one last stone with all his strength. Nava saw it coming. She curled around Asher. The stone met her skull with a crack. Her body stiffened, then went limp and still.

Shem slumped to the ground. He had failed. Nava was dead. He hadn't put a knife in her heart like the soldier, but it was his fault just the same.

Mara couldn't move. Her feet had turned to stone, her bones to water. What—who was that? Who was lying in a heap in front of the synagogue? She forced a foot one step forward, her legs suddenly weak and trembling.

Worry had plagued her in the barley field. Finally, at midday, she took her half-filled basket and walked back to the village to find men and women hurrying toward the synagogue. A small boy streaked past her, running in the opposite direction. "Tovia!" she snagged his arm as he passed her. "What's going on?"

"Mara, hurry!" said the boy, breathing hard. "Your mother . . . go. I need to get Mama." He gave her a push toward the mountain and ran toward Uziel's house.

My mother? At the synagogue? The basket dropped from her head, and barley sheaves scattered on the ground as she raced out of the village toward the Holy Mountain.

Now the sea of bodies parted to form a wall of silent spectators on each side. The figure lay in the dirt, unmoving. It was Nava's tunic, pushed high above her knees, her legs streaked with red. Stones of all sizes surrounded her still body, and a dark pool seeped into the dust around her wild black hair.

Mara took another step on legs that felt as weak as a newborn baby's.

The crowd around her stood silently, watching. She heard only one voice, her own, whispering her mother's name. Her feet shuffled toward the crumpled body. What was that? A small, twisted foot lay under the blood-soaked arm, a scrap of tunic that she knew so well.

Her heart stopped. "No." She dropped to her knees beside her mother. "No, please, not Asher." She peered up at the strange, ugly men looming over her. Who were they? *Am I dreaming?* "Help me! Please, someone!"

Then Uziel knelt beside her. Blood trickled from his nose, and his tunic was ripped. He gently rolled Nava to the side, exposing Asher.

"Asher, Asher, please talk to me." Mara cupped Asher's cheek, covered in dirt and streaked with tears. His eyes were squeezed shut, his hands clutched Nava's bloody fingers.

"Don't hurt my mama," he said, without opening his eyes.

She breathed again. *He's alive. Thank you, Lord.*

Mara turned to her mother's body. Uziel held his hand over her mouth. "She breathes. She's still alive," he whispered.

How did this happen? Alexandros hurried down the mountain. Zevulun stood slightly apart, brushing dust off his linen robe. Shem staggered toward her, his mouth was bleeding, his face streaked with dirt and—were those tears? Enosh and Abahu knelt on the other side of her mother. Uziel put his arm around her shoulder and pulled her close. But another man came forward. She reached out to him. "Shaul? Abba? Why are you . . . ?"

Shaul didn't even look at her. He threw himself on the ground and buried his face in Nava's blood-streaked hair. A low keening rose from his body.

What had happened? She turned to Uziel. "How did this—"

He shook his head. "I'm sorry, Mara. I don't know . . ." He ran his hands over Asher's hair and face. "He's cut and scraped, but I think that's all."

Asher's lashes fluttered. His small mouth worked to swallow, and his hand jerked. Mara caught it in her own. He squeezed her fingers and opened his eyes. "I took care of her, Mara. I did."

Uziel slipped his arms under Nava's slack legs and shoulders. He tried to lift her, but she was too heavy for him. He looked to Enosh for help.

Shaul pushed himself up from the ground. "Let me carry her."

Uziel frowned but he nodded. "To my house."

Shaul lifted Nava easily. Her head tipped back, and her blood-soaked hair hung down, almost brushing the ground. One arm swung limp and lifeless. Shaul choked back a sob, then started down the mountain with his burden.

Mara's body was numb. What happened? Why was Shaul here? Who were all these strangers? Still kneeling in the dirt, she put her arms around Asher. She buried her face in his neck, fighting to breathe.

"Here, Mara, let me." A gentle hand closed over her shoulder. Shem. She didn't need his help. He had known about the trial this morning, but he'd let her leave. He'd seen her go to the field. She jerked her shoulder free and tried to get to her feet, holding Asher close. Her legs buckled, and she sank to the ground.

Shem untangled Asher's clutching hands from her hair, scooped him to his shoulder, and offered her his other hand. She took it, pulling herself to her feet. He winced, and she glanced at his hand. It was swollen and bloody.

"I'm sorry, Mara," he said, his voice breaking a little. "We tried to stop them. They must have . . . they had it planned. There were too many . . ."

"You knew," Mara said. They all knew. Everyone but her. "She knew, and she sent me away. Why didn't you tell me?"

Shem stared at the ground. "Don't blame her, Mara. She wanted to protect you. I wanted to protect you. I should have told you, but we—none of us thought it would come to this."

Come to this. Stoning. But she had known. She had always known it would come to this. Even after Nava had been healed by Jesus, she had known that they were still in danger. Why hadn't she been there to protect her mother?

Mara sat on the floor next to her mother's still body. A bloody mask hid her mother's beautiful face. A long deep gash formed an ugly scab from her temple to her mouth. One eye was swollen shut. Cuts and scrapes covered her soft brown skin. Leah had bathed the wounds and applied salves. She had tried but failed to get Nava to drink water steeped with herbs. There was nothing left to do but wait and pray.

The evening breeze cooled Uziel's crowded little house. In the corner, Asher sat silently in Mechola's lap, staring at his mother. Leah tended to Noach and his sons, cleansing and wrapping their wounds. Outside, in the courtyard, Mara could hear Uziel, Shem, and Abahu.

"Zevulun planned it all," Uziel declared. "He tried to convict her with witnesses. When that didn't work, he was ready to do the bitter water test."

Shem's voice rang through the soft evening. "Yes, he was ready. He found Shaul. Alexandros was happy to help. He must have brought in twenty men from Sebaste. He probably paid them. He is the one who should be stoned!"

Mara wondered dimly at his anger.

"He had Jonothon and Shimon on his side," said Abahu. "And he was ready for anyone who would try to stop them."

"She could have just drunk the water," Shem said. "I told her to do it. It wouldn't have hurt her. That test is just to scare the guilty."

"And it worked," Uziel sighed. "No, there's nothing we can do about Zevulun. She admitted her guilt. And we can't prove that he paid men. It's over unless we want the village full of Roman soldiers asking questions. That won't help Nava now."

"But we can't just let Zevulun get away with it. He used the law of Moses for his own revenge. He deserves to be punished!" Shem's voice rose and fell as he paced around the courtyard.

The silence stretched out for several long moments. Her mother would not have feared the curse of the bitter water. The new Nava would not deny her guilt, not even to save her life. Not now. Not to men like Zevulun and Shimon.

"These are people we live with, whom we eat and drink with!" Abahu said suddenly, fiercely. "They worship on the mountain with us, with her . . ." Disbelief echoed in his voice. "How could they do it? I'm ashamed to be living in the same village as those murderers."

Mara winced at his last word. She put her hand on her mother's chest. Nava still breathed. *Thank you, Lord.*

Mara rubbed her hands down Nava's cold arms. She pulled the blanket up around Nava's shoulders and lay down close beside her, praying that her own warmth and strength would seep into her mother's weak body.

She must have slept, for suddenly the house was quiet. Nava's shallow breath still moved against her body. Sleep had brought a dream, one that she tried to hold, one that teased her with an elusive sense of hope, a deep familiar voice. She tried to call it back, but it drifted away like smoke.

She opened her eyes but didn't move. A single lamp burned in the room, sending its golden glow over Mechola—still huddled in the corner, but without Asher. Her eyes were closed, and her chest rose and fell in a peaceful rhythm. The songs of night birds and insects drifted through the dark window like a mother's lullaby.

Gratitude swelled in Mara's heart, so strong that tears stung her eyes. *Thank you for Mechola. For Abahu and Noach. For Shem.* They had fought for her and Nava and Asher like a family. Uziel had stood against the village, jeopardizing his livelihood. Enosh and his brothers had risked their lives for Nava. Mara wasn't alone anymore.

She heard quick footsteps and closed her eyes. Someone stood in the doorway, breathing softly. She didn't want to talk to anyone; she didn't want to cry.

"Try to sleep," Mechola whispered.

"I can't." It was Shem's voice. He sounded tired. "Every time I think of Zevulun . . . I could have helped her more. I should have seen this coming."

"You did all you could."

"But what can I do now? I need to do something." Footsteps paced the length of the small room and back again.

Why did he need to do something? She was grateful for

his help. But what more could he do? And why did he think he should?

"There is nothing to do now," Mechola answered. "We can only wait. And pray."

Mara heard a frustrated snort close by from Shem.

"Has she—do you think she'll wake up?" he asked. "Have you ever seen this kind of injury?"

Mechola sighed, and her slow footsteps scraped across the floor toward Nava and Mara.

Mara kept her eyes closed.

"I have seen it once before," Mechola answered her grandson softly. "A little boy, many years ago." Her voice dropped even lower. "He had been with Noach, helping watch the sheep. He loved the lambs. He tried to rescue a lamb from a rocky cliff and fell.

"We tried everything. He never woke up. He lived for almost a week, but we couldn't get him to drink or eat. He died in your grandfather's arms. Our only son."

Mara opened her eyes a crack. Shem put his arm around his grandmother and pulled her toward him. The old woman wiped her eyes with the back of her hand and gave her grandson a shaky smile. "Don't tell Mara. She has enough to worry about. We must get Nava to drink, somehow. She has lost a lot of blood. If she doesn't drink, she will die quickly."

Mara squeezed her eyes shut as panic rose in her chest. She wished for sleep to come again. But sleep wouldn't rescue her from this nightmare. She opened her eyes as Mechola unwound the strips of linen from her mother's head. Shem was gone.

"Is there any change?" she asked.

Mechola felt the swollen wound on Nava's temple, then shook her head.

The familiar voice spoke like a whisper in Mara's mind, the same voice that had come to her in her dream. She remembered it now. She'd heard it before. Her heart sped up, and urgency filled her like a rushing river. He was calling her, she was sure. And she knew what she had to do.

She pushed herself up and scooted close to Nava's head. "How long does she have?" she asked. "Please. Tell me the truth."

Mechola's busy hands stilled. "She's lost a lot of blood. She's already weak. Three—perhaps four—days."

Mara stroked her mother's hair and kissed her battered face. "I am going to get help." She stood up.

"Where? Who can help?" Mechola put her hand gently on Mara's arm.

"I will go to Jesus. If he can't help her, no one can."

Mechola's face creased in thought but she showed no surprise. "To Jesus," she said. "Yes. But Mara, you cannot go. If they find out, you'll be—"

"I know. But I have to take that chance."

Mechola shook her head. "No, my dear. It's too much of a risk. Let's send Uziel or even Shem."

"No, it must be me. Don't you see? They don't believe in him. They don't believe he is the Taheb." Mara took a deep breath. "I heard his voice—just now—in my dream. He called me, not them."

Mechola didn't scoff but moved her warm hands to Mara's shoulders. "My dear, do you even know where to go? Jesus could be anywhere by now. He's been gone for three days."

"His disciples said that they were going to Nazareth, to his mother. I will go north, to Galilee, then follow the road to Nazareth. Someone will know where he is."

"Maybe you should wait . . . ask Uziel?" Mechola said hesitantly.

"He'll forbid it." Mara threw on her cloak. "No one needs to know."

"Mara, wait. Just a minute." Mechola hurried out the door and came back a few moments later with a water skin, a round of bread, and a pair of sturdy sandals. The sandals were too big, but Mara buckled them on. Even her toughened feet wouldn't do well on roads full of sharp rocks.

Mechola filled the water skin from the jar near the door. She tucked it into Mara's belt and smoothed her cloak more tightly around her shoulders.

Was this what it was like to have a grandmother? Mara slipped her arms around Mechola's waist and hugged her close. "Don't worry. I'll be back soon."

Mechola squeezed her back. "What way will you leave the village?"

"I'll go through the olive grove, then on to Sebaste by the road." After that, she didn't know how to get to Galilee. But she would find a way. She stepped toward the dark doorway. "Pray that I find the Taheb." She looked once more at her mother. "And please take good care of her," she whispered.

Chapter 19

Mara hesitated in the olive grove as her eyes adjusted to the dark. The stars were a milky ribbon in the sky. Their brilliance seemed to light the way north over the rise of Mount Ebal, the mountain of curses. The moon shone full and bright enough to turn the trees to silver and cast their bent shadows on the hillside.

Would she ever see Sychar again? And if she did, what would she come home to? She crossed her arms over her heart. It thumped like an animal caught in a trap. If the people of Sychar found out that she'd left—and traveled alone to find a man—they would accuse her of impurity. And they would find out. *Every man in town will despise me, even Jobab.* She had no choice—her mother's life in exchange for the only thing she ever wanted, a husband and family of her own.

Again she heard the voice, calling her name. Was it real or the memory of her dream? No matter, she would follow it. She set her eyes on Mount Ebal and took a deep breath. *Lord, help me find your Anointed One, the Taheb.*

She walked quickly, her feet remembering the path through the familiar olive grove. She would find him. He would save her mother.

Heavy footsteps pounded behind her. Her legs trembled, and she swallowed hard as she stopped and turned toward the sound. How would she explain herself to Uziel? How could she make him understand?

The shape that came out of the darkness was taller, thinner.

The voice was one she had heard before in the darkness of this same grove.

"Wait, Mara!" Shem stopped a few strides from her, breathing hard. "You cannot do this."

"What? It is the only thing I can do." *Why is he here?* She turned away. She'd run if he tried to stop her. But how far would she get?

Shem grabbed her arm. "Mara, stop and listen to reason!"

She tried to pull away, but his fingers clamped tighter. Her heart hammered in her chest. He was too strong. "Why are you here? Did Mechola tell you to . . . ?"

"Yes, she did. Someone needed to stop you. You could be killed!"

"This isn't your problem. You aren't even from Sychar. Please." She glanced down at his hand, still holding her arm, and swallowed. "I'm begging you, Shem. Please. Let me go."

Mara's plea tore at Shem's heart. She was wrong. This was his problem. Her tears reflecting in the silver moonlight were his fault. If anyone deserved to die for their sins, it was him, not her mother.

But this idea of hers was madness. How could she go all the way to Nazareth alone? Shem tried to make his voice calm. "Mara. Do you even know where you are going? It is too dangerous for a girl. You are a target for jackals—animal and human."

She didn't look afraid.

There must be some way to change her mind. "If something happened to you . . . what would become of Asher?"

Mara's eyes filled with tears. Her lips trembled. "I have to try. She is dying."

Shem swallowed hard. *If only he could take back those thoughtless words he spoke to Adah.* This was his fault, and he would put it right. If Mara ended up dead like her mother, his guilt would be too much to bear. "I'll go. I know the way to Nazareth."

She jerked away from him. "No. You can't."

"Why not? Better I go than you." What was he saying? He was

safe here in Sychar, but outside, on the road? Would any Roman soldiers still be searching for him? No, not after all these weeks.

"Shem." She stepped closer to him. "Do you even believe that Jesus is the Taheb?"

He tried to think of an honest answer that would satisfy her but couldn't.

"I didn't think so. He cured her once; I know he did. He will again, but you must have faith in him. You don't. So it has to be me."

This crazy, stubborn girl refused to listen to reason. There was only one option left. The one his grandmother had already decided on when she woke him. "We aren't going through Sebaste, then."

"We? What do you mean?"

"It is a city full of vice and pagans. We'd never make it through alive." He checked for the knife at his belt. At least he'd have that. But could he use it again if he had to? Even to defend Mara's life?

She raised a hand as he turned toward the top of the hill. "Wait, Shem. You can't. Your grandparents. If someone finds out we're together . . ."

"My grandmother already knows. She'll tell Uziel and Abahu. If we hurry, no one else will even know we're gone. There's a trail, just a path, that cuts straight north from Ebal to Engannin, then meets up with the road through Galilee. It will save some time." Then they would have to travel on the open roads, such as they were. Most were just beaten tracks, but they had plenty of traffic, especially Jews going back and forth to Jerusalem—maybe even Roman troops. It couldn't be helped, though. Cutting through the wilderness would surely get them lost or attacked by something with sharp teeth and claws.

She shook her head. "No. I can't let you. You don't need to help me. If someone sees us it's too much of a risk for you."

What was she talking about? "A risk for me?" Did she know about the Romans that searched for him? But no, her head dipped, and she wouldn't meet his eyes. Something else worried her. "You mean if the villagers find out we were together?"

She nodded.

Yes, the laws of Sychar were far stricter than those of Caesarea. If anyone discovered them traveling together, the consequences for him would be lifelong. But that was the least of their worries. "Just let me worry about that," he said abruptly. He stepped closer to her. If he was going to risk his life, she needed to understand the real danger. "Listen, Mara. I'll get you to Jesus. But you must obey me. These roads are dangerous, especially for a girl like you—"

"Like me?" Her eyes widened, and she shrank back. "What do you mean?"

Shem drew in a sharp breath. She really didn't understand. "Mara, don't be an idiot." He caught her chin in his hand and held it. "A girl like you . . ." He pulled her chin up until he could stare into her amber and jade eyes. "One look at you, and I'll be left bleeding to death in a ditch while you are taken in chains to the Damascus slave auction." Understanding flared in her face. And fear. At least the girl had some sense. "Now, do what I say, and I'll find your Taheb."

He brushed past her and started the climb up Mount Ebal.

Foolish girl. He might deserve to die—it was his fault after all—but she didn't. He'd get her to her Taheb, then safely back to Sychar, or die trying. Maybe she'd forgive him when she found out what he'd done to her mother. And when they returned, whether Nava lived or died, Zevulun and Alexandros would be punished.

He catalogued their sins. Zevulun, using his money and power to concoct that mockery of a trial and, worse, using the law of Moses for his own revenge. The rich and powerful preying on the weak—just as in Caesarea. And Alexandros, a pagan, using Nava, then joining in as the men of her village turned against her. She might be—she surely was—guilty of adultery, but they were guilty of even more despicable sins. He didn't know how, but he would make sure they paid for their sins just as they had made Nava pay for hers.

• • •

Mara stayed close to Shem as they walked, almost bumping into him in the dark. Why was he helping her? Didn't he know what he risked? His family was wealthy and important, both in Sychar and Caesarea. If they discovered that he had traveled with her, alone and unmarried . . . he would spend the rest of his life regretting this night.

The full moon shed just enough light to see the path ahead. Her breath made little puffs of mist in the cold air. She pushed her chilled hands deep in the folds of her cloak, pulling the thin fabric around her body. He'd said he knew a faster way. *Please, Lord, help us find the Taheb in time.*

Barley fields stretched out below them, the cut stubble glowing gold in the moonlight. Had it just been yesterday that she had started home, hot and tired with her basket of grain? It seemed like a childhood memory.

The sharp scent of terebinth brought her out of her thoughts. Shem stopped suddenly at the edge of a grove.

"This is the path," he said. "I would be far happier to travel it when morning comes."

She shook her head. "No, please, we must hurry," she said.

He sighed. "Stay close, then." He stepped into the darkness, moving quietly and studying the dark shadows between the trees.

They traveled the dark path in silence. It wound up and down the valleys and hills like a meandering stream. The bright moon lit their way in the open spaces but made the shadows of the oaks and cypress darker and more menacing when they picked their way through wooded hollows.

At each narrow valley, Shem stopped and held his finger to his lips. He stood still, his head cocked toward the darkness, before stepping through the thorny bushes and overhanging trees. Mara shivered. He was listening for the rustle and growl of wild beasts. Or even the whispers of bandits. What would they do if they were attacked? She closed the short distance between them.

Wild dogs howled in the distance, but no animals crossed their path. Her body warmed at the brisk pace, but her eyes felt gritty and her legs already ached with weariness. The borrowed sandals rubbed her ankles until every step brought a sharp pain. She pushed one foot in front of the other and stayed close to Shem. What was he thinking? Did he already regret helping her?

As the eastern sky faded to a lighter shade of black, the morning birds began to sing in the bushes and trees, growing silent as they passed and then taking up their song again. The path climbed sharply up a rocky hill, and Mara scrambled up, clutching at sapling vines to keep from sliding backward.

Shem reached the top, then turned around and offered her his hand. It was warm and rough. More like a farmer than a scholar. He winced but easily pulled her up. They stood together, catching their breath. The faintest hint of ocher showed that dawn would soon flare in the eastern sky. And they weren't even to Engannin yet.

"Mara, sit and rest," Shem said. His voice was gentle, as were the hands that pushed her to sit on a stone ledge. He settled himself beside her and pulled out his water skin.

Mara looked to the east. The sun was rising on her mother's still body. "There isn't time to rest," she whispered. But she perched on the cold stone with a tired sigh, put her elbows on her knees, and rested her forehead in her hands. Her legs ached, her head pounded, her blistered feet hurt most of all.

Shem put a firm hand on her shoulder, as if she had tried to rise. "You won't make it at all if you don't rest. It is a long walk to Nazareth, and we've barely started." He handed her his water skin. "I'm surprised you could keep up with me."

Mara nodded at the water skin and the purse tied to his belt. "You planned to go all along?"

"I planned to make you see sense. But Mechola warned me that you were stubborn." He frowned at her as though she was a willful child.

She turned her head away before he could see her blinking back tears. He was angry with her. He regretted helping her already. She took a long drink of water and gave the skin back to him. He probably didn't want to speak to her at all, but she had to know. "Shem . . ." She hesitated, looking at his swollen hand and grazed knuckles. "What happened at the trial?"

Shem rubbed his battered hand. "I don't know exactly. Zevulun . . . He had too many men. They had it planned. She confessed—then everything happened at once. They grabbed me, Abahu, anyone who wasn't throwing rocks. By the time I got away . . . I'm sorry, Mara." He looked down at the ground.

Mara puzzled over his words but didn't ask the question hovering on her tongue. Why was he helping them? It didn't really matter. He was the answer to her prayer even if he didn't believe in the Taheb. "Thank you, Shem," she said, almost whispering. "I've been nothing but trouble to you."

Shem's mouth twisted into a half smile. "Don't thank me, Mara. Trouble would find me with or without you."

Chapter 20

S hem checked on Mara, trudging behind him. She was still close, her shoulders hunched and her head down. The rocky path wound around hills and dipped through ravines and brushy screes. As the sun streaked the sky with pink clouds, a dry desert wind came out of the east, blowing dust into his burning eyes and parched throat.

Zevulun won't get away with it. I will get justice for Nava. But how?

If only they could report Zevulun to the Romans. He would be punished—severely—for carrying out a stoning. But Zevulun's threat echoed in his ears, *"Surely you, of all the men here, would not want to bring Roman attention to Sychar?"* No, he couldn't report Zevulun, but neither could Zevulun report him. Any Roman intervention would doom them both.

Zevulun was a merchant. And so was Alexandros. Why didn't he think of it before? He knew of history and languages, not business. But he did know someone well-connected in the world of buying and selling. He'd send word to his father. Ezra was good at revenge; he'd heard him rant of it often enough. With Ezra's connections, they would find a way to make Zevulun and Alexandros pay.

They wouldn't have to involve Rome. Shem and Ezra would exact their own justice, and quietly. Shem had seen his father stoop to threats, bribery, even blackmail to get his way in business. They would kick Zevulun and Alexandros where it hurt the most—in their money pouches.

He could send a messenger from Engannin to Caesarea. A fast

horse would get there by early evening. Then, when he returned to Sychar, he and Ezra would find a way.

They were moving fast and would reach Engannin soon. Then the open road—with new dangers—that led to Nazareth. And then . . . then they could go home. Hopefully with the prophet, this Jesus who Mara so desperately believed would heal her mother.

What made her think that Jesus could do such a thing? Jesus had not even spoken of healing while staying in Sychar. He had performed no miracles. There had been the talk of the miracle at the wedding in Cana. Turning water into wine. But nothing about curing the sick. No. This was a fool's journey, and he was the fool. At least they would get justice when they returned to Sychar.

Shem didn't want to see the prophet again. He didn't like how he felt when Jesus looked at him. He felt afraid. Not afraid of the man, Jesus, but afraid of something. He rubbed his stinging eyes. There were plenty of real dangers to fear on this journey.

"This is bandit country, or worse." He jerked his chin to the hills, pockmarked with dark caves. Mara shuffled closer. What would she think if he told her that the real danger to them would be Roman soldiers, searching for a Samaritan with a scar?

As they labored up the last hill before Engannin, Shem saw a group of men advancing toward them. "Mara!" His arm shot out to stop her.

"Unclean, unclean!" the men cried.

"Step back!" Shem called out to them. He took Mara's arm and slowly advanced toward them. "Lepers," he whispered. "Don't worry; they won't hurt us."

The men backed away, their threadbare clothes and stained bandages whipping in the hot wind. They continued to cry out and lament, asking for mercy from God and man. One tall man stood apart from the rest, watching in silence. His embroidered cloak was finely made, but his face was wrapped in soiled linen.

As Mara and Shem reached the top of the hill, they could see down into a narrow valley. More lepers lay on the ground near poor huts and dark caves. Their arms, feet, and faces were wrapped in cloths. The stench of putrid flesh reached them even from a distance.

"Is that where they live?" Mara asked, her face pale.

"It is where they die," Shem replied. "They are Jews and Samaritans together, here in Dotham." *And the God of Abraham doesn't hear the prayers of either.*

He fumbled with his money pouch. "There are probably more in the caves. I've heard that there can be as many as a hundred lepers living here together." His heart pinched in pity for the miserable people. "These are the lucky ones." He nodded to the group still crying out to them on the ridge. "Those—lying on the ground—they will not live much longer."

"May the Lord have mercy upon you," he raised his voice to the lepers. *The Lord has had little mercy on them so far.* But if God wouldn't help them, at least he could. He shook two silver shekels from his purse, chose one, and returned one to his belt. He laid the coin on a flat stone near the path. Mara gasped, her eyes wide. It was a great deal of money, but these poor wretches needed it more than he did. One shekel would be more than enough to accomplish what he needed in Engannin, with plenty left to get them to Nazareth and back.

Shem urged Mara on. He looked over his shoulder to see the tall man retrieve the coin that would be enough to feed them all for weeks, then bow deeply to Shem. His words carried over the wind, "Perhaps one day we can return your kindness."

Returning the bow, Shem suppressed a grimace. How could a band of dying lepers ever help him on this ridiculous journey? Unless they could go to Sychar and infect Zevulun and Alexandros with their disease. They, at least, deserved a long, tortured death.

"We're leaving Samaria now, almost in Galilee," Shem said as they came within sight of the gates of Engannin. It would be more dangerous here. Not for her, but for him. It was true that Roman soldiers usually ignored the Jews—unless they were hunting one.

He pulled his head covering closer, glad that his hair and beard had grown during his weeks in Sychar. His dark curls were almost long enough to hide the scar from any passing Roman soldier.

They reached Engannin just as the sun rose fully above the horizon. As they stepped onto the broad highway, Shem motioned for Mara to adjust her mantle and cloak. That would have to do. He'd like to hide her face from every man they passed.

Shem adjusted his belt and strode toward the village, ignoring Mara as any good Jewish or Samaritan man would do. Roman soldiers, wild dogs, bandits, slave traders. It was just a matter of time before their luck ran out. If God had no mercy on the lepers, who had done nothing wrong, he would have none on Shem. No, it was up to him to finish this foolish journey and get Mara back to Sychar safely. And then, whether Nava lived or died, he'd see justice done.

Mara stood in Shem's shadow as he pointed to almonds and dried figs at the first shop they found in the Engannin marketplace. She kept her eyes down. Could they tell that she was Samaritan? What would they do if they found out? Run her out of town?

Shem could pass for a Jew from any of the big cities—Caesarea, Jerusalem, even Damascus. She shifted impatiently as Shem fumbled for his money pouch. The sooner they got out of Engannin, the safer she would feel.

Shem handed the shopkeeper the bright silver coin. The greasy man's jaw dropped, and his eyes bulged. He hurried to gather enough bronze to exchange for the shekel.

"Is there a messenger that will go to Caesarea?" Shem asked as the man poured a handful of bronze into his open hand.

The shopkeeper eyed the gleaming coins in Shem's hand. "Yes. Yes, sir. I can get a message to Caesarea."

A message to Caesarea? What was he doing? Perhaps sending word to his family that he had left Sychar. He wouldn't tell them why, would he?

"How fast?"

"I have a fast horse. I could get it there by tonight, sir. At the latest."

Shem raised his brows. "A horse? In this town?"

The shopkeeper bobbed his head so hard that his head covering flapped around his ears.

Shem chose two bronze sestertii from his hand and poured the rest into his money pouch. "Get me something to write with."

The shopkeeper scurried away. He came back with a scrap of well-worn papyrus, a lump of what looked like burnt wood, and a split reed.

Shem took the materials and crouched down on the ground. Mara leaned over to watch him spit on the cake of black coal and stir the reed in the liquid. He smoothed the papyrus over his knee and began to write with sure, quick strokes.

It was like watching a dancer or a skilled musician. She'd seen writing before, but the priests in Sychar labored over each mark on the paper. Shem's message flowed from the reed to the papyrus in just moments. When had she started thinking of him as a farmer? He was a scholar, better educated and more skilled than any of the priests in Sychar. And destined for more than olive farming.

The shopkeeper hovered nearby with the stub of a beeswax candle. Shem rolled the papyrus into a tube. He tipped a dribble of hot wax on the seam, slipped the gold ring off his finger, and pressed his seal into the wax.

The shopkeeper held out his hand.

"Let's see that horse first," Shem said, tucking the rolled message in his belt.

The man bowed and called down a dank alleyway. A small boy—hardly older than Asher—scurried up leading a battered donkey that wouldn't make it to the next town, let alone Caesarea.

"This is your horse?" Shem looked doubtful. "And this boy is your messenger?

The man nodded. "He'll ride hard. He'll be there by nightfall or get a beating when he comes back." He eyed the coins in Shem's hand like a starving man watches meat roasting on a spit.

Shem crouched down beside the boy. "Get this to Ezra ben Aaron, the merchant." A flash of bronze passed between him and the boy.

The boys eyes widened. He slipped the coin into his mouth and ducked his head.

Shem slapped the other coins into the man's hand. "If the message doesn't reach my father tonight, I'll be back to talk to you about it."

He prodded Mara into the street.

What was he doing? What was all that about? He'd just given most of his coins away. But Shem didn't explain his actions to her as they marched through Engannin under the watchful eyes of every merchant and villager.

And he didn't explain when they reached the outskirts of the town and filled their water skins at the well. It was none of her business. She was just a Samaritan girl. Why should she expect him to tell her what he was doing?

When they had walked well past Engannin, Mara let Shem guide her to a stand of laurel trees. The sun, now their enemy, blazed well above the horizon. She sank down into the soft, shaded grass with a sigh. She might just never get up again.

She surveyed the land around her as she ate. So this was Galilee, ruled by the half-Jew Herod Antipas. She had heard stories of his wickedness and had pictured Galilee as a smoking Sodom or Gomorrah, but it was beautiful. A stream sparkled in the lush green meadow. Crocuses and lilies glowed in the marshy ground. She breathed in the perfume of the sweet fennel and cool, clean mint that sprouted around them.

Shem blessed and broke the round of bread sent by Mechola and gave her half, along with the almonds and figs he had bought on the way through Engannin. "Here. This will help."

Mara snuck a glance at Shem. He watched the road, rubbing his short, smooth beard. Should she ask him what the message was about?

Abruptly he turned to her. "You should not speak, I think."

"What?" She fumbled with her bread. "I wouldn't—I mean, I don't." What did he mean? She hadn't spoken to any of the people they had passed. She couldn't. A woman didn't even speak to her own husband in public. Only in the privacy of their home or among other women could she speak freely. Did he think she didn't know that?

"No." He raised his hand. "No, I mean when we meet others on the road or in the towns. They might be Romans or Greeks. They might speak to you." His eyes rested on her face.

"Your accent will give you away as a Samaritan. We'll be safer if you let me talk, now that we are in Galilee. I don't have the country accent that you do. We could pass for Jews, here, and be safer."

"Oh." Heat crept up her cheeks. "I thought . . ." What did she sound like to him? A dim-witted country girl? She inspected her hands, clutched around the bread. They were dirty and callused, and her nails were ragged. He was so learned, so polished, and she was so—well, a poor Samaritan girl. One that wasn't even offered a bride price. She nodded silently.

He propped himself up against the trunk of a tree. "Get some sleep," he told her.

"Sleep? Can't we—"

"Mara." He interrupted her with a flash of impatience. "Don't argue. You can't walk all night and all day. Just rest a little."

His tone stung, but she knew he was right. She lay down on the soft, cool grass. Her eyes were so heavy. Just a little while, she promised herself. Then they would get to Nazareth, and the Taheb.

Doubt wrapped around her like a dark mantle. What if Jesus wouldn't even speak to her? He was the Taheb and she was just a worthless girl, despised even by her own people. And traveling alone with a man who wasn't her husband. She wasn't even worthy to speak to him, let alone ask for a miracle. What made her think that she deserved it?

• • •

Shem leaned back on his elbows and watched Mara sleep. *Someone has to stand guard.* She slept so peacefully, the lines of worry finally smoothed from her face. What had her life been like? Harder than his, he was sure. She probably thought him the spoiled son of a rich man, and she was right; the last few weeks had seen the only hard work he'd ever done.

He pictured the pampered girl that his father had chosen for him in Caesarea. Her family owned ships that went to ports throughout the Roman Empire. She would be a pretty, obedient wife and spend her days trying to please him. The thought of her stirred nothing in him. Even dirty and tired, Mara was beautiful, and she didn't even seem to know it.

He sat up straighter and ripped a handful of leaves from the bushy plant beside him. The cool scent of mint drifted over him. He should tell Mara the truth. She deserved to know about him. But she looked at him with such gratitude, almost with awe. She wouldn't be so grateful if she knew that his stupid words had brought her mother to trial.

He crushed the leaves in his hand. And what would Mara think if she knew that soldiers still searched for him in Caesarea and maybe even Galilee? If she knew he had murdered a man? And if Nava died, he'd have another death on his head.

Trouble found him, he'd told Mara. But what if it was the other way around? Did he really find trouble, as his father claimed? Here he was again, putting himself in danger. If they were attacked, he'd have no choice but to fight back. He might end up killing again.

Shem jumped as Mara sat up with a startled breath. "Did I sleep long?" She looked at the sun, still near the top of its downward slide to the west. "We should go; we must hurry." She struggled to sit up and adjust her mantle and tunic.

Shem's gaze dropped to her feet as she uncurled her legs. Her ankles were covered in bright red blisters crusted with blood. "You're bleeding, Mara." Why hadn't she told him? He rolled to his knees and cupped her ankle, all sharp bones and sinew.

"Please, don't. I'm fine." She pulled her foot back and tried to tuck the tattered garment over it.

He tightened his grip. "Wait. I mean it. Let me see." He shook his head. "These sandals . . . they don't even fit. Of course they gave you blisters. What were you thinking?"

"I . . ." She bit her lip. "I didn't have any. Mechola gave them to me."

He swallowed, silently cursing his stupid mouth. "Well, you can't go barefoot on this road. Look, let me do something." He reached to his belt and pulled out his dagger.

Mara sucked in a breath. "What are you going to do?"

She stared with wide, frightened eyes at the blade in his hands. What did she think he was going to do to her? "I'm just getting you a bandage. You can't walk like this." He nicked the hem of his tunic with the knife, then ripped off a long strip of linen.

"Oh," she cried out. "Your tunic." She reached out toward the now ragged hem.

Shem couldn't believe his ears. Every stride up and down those hills must have felt like walking through hot coals. She protested as he wrapped the linen strip around her blisters, but he ignored her. He carefully treated both ankles, wrapping extra cloth around them to keep the sandals from rubbing. There. That would have to do.

"Better?" he asked, glancing to her feet as they stepped back out on the road.

She nodded. "How much longer?"

"We'll be in Nazareth before mid-afternoon. But we'll need water and food before then." Shem checked behind them. No dust clouds on the road. Little could be seen around the bend ahead of them. Meadows stretched to either side, empty of all but green grass and singing birds. So far, they were safe. But it was still a long way to Nazareth and back.

By now, the boy would be on his way to Caesarea with the message. He would get there by tonight, and Ezra would be waiting in Sychar when they returned from Nazareth. He would hear the story from Abahu and see his father-in-law's bruised face.

Ezra wouldn't like that. When they returned from Nazareth, Mara would have her prophet, and they would know if Nava would live or die. But either way, Shem would make a plan with Ezra to ensure that Alexandros and Zevulun were brought to justice.

Now, all he had to do was get to Nazareth and back without running into bandits, soldiers, or any other kind of dangerous animal. He'd have to be careful with the money he had left, but it would be enough.

Finding the Taheb was what Mara had to do, and he'd help her, even if it were a useless journey. But getting justice for Nava was what he had to do. It would help if he knew why Zevulun hated Nava so much. There was more to that story than Mechola had revealed. He would need to find out. And Mara was the one to tell him.

Chapter 24

The sun beat hot on Mara's face, and sweat trickled down her neck as she dragged herself up yet another steep hill. On one side of the road, a flock of sheep grazed on green grass; a shaded cedar grove stretched out on the other. The rest and the bread had helped. Her ankles throbbed dully with every step, but they bothered her less than the thought of Shem wrapping her dirty feet in his own clean linen.

They would be in Nazareth by mid-afternoon, and then she would see Jesus again. Her heart sped up at the thought of approaching him, of speaking to him. She knew he could help her, but would he? He had spoken to a Samaritan woman. But dare she speak to a Jewish man? Would he know her thoughts? That she had wished her own mother dead at the very moment he healed her?

They passed a group of travelers going the opposite direction. Shem called out a greeting while she watched her feet kick up ribbons of dust. When they had passed by, Shem slowed his pace until they walked shoulder to shoulder.

"Mara," he said. "Why does Zevulun hate your mother so much?"

Mara lengthened her stride. Shem easily matched it. Of course he would want to know. She just didn't know how much to tell. Finally, she said, "Please don't judge Nava too harshly."

He didn't say a word as she told him of her mother's betrothal to Zevulun, her betrayal of her vows, and her marriage to Moshe. "Zevulun had every right to be angry at her," she said. "But Zevulun," she scuffed a few steps along the road, "it's been so long. He held on to his anger for all these years."

Shem still didn't speak.

She glanced at him. He didn't seem shocked. "But Moshe died before I was even born. On his way to Tiberius. Probably on this road." She tried not to sound bitter. Her life would have been so different if he had lived. But she wouldn't trade a better life for one without Asher.

"What happened then?" Shem finally asked. "Was Shaul her next husband and Asher's father?"

Mara's steps faltered. How could he not know? It was the best-loved story in the village. "You have lived in Sychar for weeks and don't know of my mother's other husbands?"

Shem's eyebrows shot up. "How many did she have?"

Mara watched her feet and chewed on her lip. He really didn't know.

He said more gently, "I live with my grandmother, remember, who does not gossip. My grandfather would rather speak of olives than people, and the only other person that I see is Enosh. I don't think many of the others like me."

Mara didn't have to answer, for at that moment she raised her head and her mouth dropped open. A caravan bore down on them. Shem's arm shot out to quickly guide Mara off the dusty track and into the prickly brush. Thorns bit into her ankles as she stared.

"Babylonian traders," Shem whispered at her side. He bowed in greeting to the leader of the caravan, who was riding a huge donkey. He was the tallest man Mara had ever seen. Long brown legs stretched almost to the ground. His ebony skin glowed against bright silk robes, embroidered all over with gold and silver thread. A heavy gold ring pierced his hooked nose, and his fingers and arms were spangled with jeweled rings and gold armbands. He glittered in the sun.

Laden camels, more donkeys, and servants followed his majestic lead. The animals were loaded with intricately woven baskets and carved chests strapped in bronze. They passed close enough for her to reach out and touch their rough, hairy hides. Beside the procession rode four armed men. Swords were strapped to their sides and gauntlets of silver protected their arms and legs.

"Keep your head down." Shem stepped close to her. His eyes were on the guards, and his hand rested on his knife.

The air echoed with the shouts of servants and the slap of leather on hairy flanks. Thudding hooves kicked up clouds of dust. Mara's curiosity tormented her until she raised her eyes to stare at the passing strangers. A guard rode so near she could feel the heat of his horse. He glanced warily at Shem, then turned his head just in time to meet her eyes. She looked down, but not before she saw a leer on his scarred, brutal face.

The procession passed quickly, and Shem hurried her out of the brush and back onto the road as soon as they were gone. He walked quickly through the dust, watching the retreating caravan with a tight mouth and worried eyes.

Why did the travelers worry him? Surely they were not interested in two poor Samaritans. Mara hurried to catch up to Shem and kept her questions to herself. Maybe he would do the same.

Shem looked over his shoulder at the receding caravan. He increased the pace so that Mara had to break into a short run to catch up to his long strides. "Then what happened?"

He was helping her; he deserved to know the rest.

"After Moshe died, my mother didn't want to remarry," Mara continued. "My grandfather and grandmother were dead, and Moshe's parents moved away from Sychar. They never liked her, Mama said.

"My aunt Ruth had married Uziel. She begged him to take pity on us. He is a good man, from a respectable family. He allowed us to live with them until my mother finished mourning and remarried." *And he's taken care of us many times since.* What would Uziel do when she returned home so disgraced that even Jobab wouldn't take her?

"But Nava would not accept any of the men who came to Uziel for her hand. She was very proud. They said she angered the Lord by her refusal to marry, and she disgraced her family even more." Mara snuck a glance at Shem. He was scowling at a rocky hillock on their right. Was he worried about bandits or disgusted with her mother?

"When I was about three years old, Uziel ordered her to marry. She could not continue to live with them." Mara shook her head. "Ruth told me that she chose the richest of her suitors, a merchant of fine cloth and carpets. I don't think she cared for him at all."

They passed a lone terebinth tree, stretching its gnarled red branches into the sky. She remembered Gershon only faintly as a tall, silent man. He was even quiet around her mother. His eyes often rested on Nava, and in her childish way, Mara had thought he looked sad.

They had lived in a large, fine house with many servants. The tile floors were covered with wool rugs. Verses of the law were engraved in stone in each room of the house and embroidered onto cloths that hung among the rich furnishings.

"Was he good to you?" asked Shem.

He had so many questions. Why was he so interested in Nava's past? "Well, yes." Gershon was probably her favorite of her mother's husbands, next to Shaul. "I don't remember much. I had pretty clothes and even toys. I remember being happy." It wasn't as hard as she thought it would be to tell Shem her story. Especially when he watched the road ahead instead of her.

Gershon's house had been stern but never unkind. They observed the Sabbath strictly and had gone on pilgrimages to Mount Gerizim often. In his household, even the youngest fasted on the Day of Atonement. Gershon lived his faith, giving much to the poor and following the law. He never shouted or raised his hand to her or her mother.

"We lived with Gershon for two years. I didn't know; I was so young. But Ruth told me that . . . My mother, she was not a good wife to him."

"They had no children?"

"No," Mara replied. "My aunt says that it was my mother's

fault, that she refused to have children." Mara pressed her lips together. She shouldn't have said that. Her cheeks reddened, and she glanced sideways. But Shem just nodded, his eyes on the road ahead.

She told him the rest. "Ruth said that Gershon was divorcing her. But before he did, he was killed by the Romans in the revolt of Mount Gerizim."

"Gershon died in the revolt?" Shem asked, twisting to look at her.

"Yes. With many others: Uziel's younger brother, Noach's oldest son."

"That's why there are just old men and boys in Sychar."

"Yes." *Very few men of marriageable age.* "And when the Romans learned that Gershon had been a rich man, they confiscated all his gold, his carpets, everything. Fortunately," Mara went on, "Mama kept the house and livestock. Many people—the villagers—said it was more than she deserved."

And maybe Shem would agree. Especially when he found out the rest of her mother's story. And if Shem regretted helping Nava, perhaps Jesus would too. How much mercy would the Taheb have on a woman who had sinned so many times?

Chapter 22

S hem heard pounding hooves coming toward them before he saw the cloud of dust kicked up not far ahead. The flash of a metal helmet made his heart leap into his throat.

He grabbed Mara and pulled her off the road. They stumbled through the brush as he searched for a place to hide. Stinging nettles burned his feet and calves. "Here!" he scuttled behind a flowering mustard bush, pulling Mara down just as four galloping horses swooped past them with creaking leather and clanking armor. His legs were weak, and blood pounded in his ears. That had been close.

"Roman soldiers," he said, choking on the dust. "It is best if they don't see us."

They waited until the sound of the horses had died away before creeping out from behind the branches of yellow flowers.

"What would happen if they did?" Mara asked, rubbing her leg. "They wouldn't have a reason to stop us, would they?"

A rash needled over Shem's sandaled feet and up his ankles. "They are Romans. They don't need a reason." They would need no more reason than to look at her. Then one look at him, and they would both be captured, tied to a horse, and dragged to Caesarea. He pictured his punishment, probably crucifixion. Mara wouldn't be so lucky.

She pursed her lips, clearly ready to ask more questions that Shem didn't want to answer. He guided her back to the road. "Gershon died on Mount Gerizim. Then what happened? Did you go back to Uziel?" He had seen the house where they lived and knew that it was not that of a wealthy merchant.

"No, Gershon had a brother."

Ah. That made sense. A widow always had the option of marrying her dead husband's brother. "So, a Levitical marriage. Who was he?"

"He is Shimon, Adah's husband now."

Shem groaned as the pieces of the story fell together. Nava had offended two very powerful families in a few short years. The scene at Passover made sense, now. The village had good reasons to reject her. But still, Zevulun had no interest in justice; that much had been clear at the sham of a trial. He was only concerned with his injured pride.

Mara stared straight ahead, her mouth drooping. This must be hard for her. She had done nothing wrong, but she faced the consequences of her mother's sins.

Mara went on so quietly that he had to walk closer to hear her. "By that time, the villagers thought she was cursed. Some thought that she might have an evil spirit. She knew that her only hope was to marry Shimon, to claim her rights to a Levitical marriage."

"But Shimon was not like his brother. He was . . . unkind. He announced that he would take on the disgraceful widow and her child. Like he was helping us." Mara's voice turned bitter. "He only wanted his brother's house and livestock. But he told everyone he would make her into a proper wife."

They reached the top of a hill and started downward. Shem's sandals slapped against the packed dirt. "And that didn't happen."

"No." Mara fell behind again. He slowed until she caught up. "She was not a proper wife to Shimon. It was less than a year when he divorced her."

Shimon was not a gentle man. He'd been as eager as Zevulun at the trial and had been throwing stones at the front of the mob. How badly had Mara been treated at Shimon's hands? Was he as culpable as Zevulun for Nava's injuries?

Mara's face was pinched, and she stared blindly at her trudging feet. "It is our law that the husband gives half the bride price to the bride's family but keeps the rest in reserve in case of divorce. He gave that to Mama, as he should. The priests agreed that it was fair. We also kept the household goods and a couple of goats. That's when we started living in the valley."

"Just you and your mother?"

Mara nodded. "Shimon was fair to us, but not generous." Mara glanced warily at him. "I'm not sure that she deserved any better."

Shem couldn't believe it. A woman and small child left alone, practically in the wilderness? How had Mara felt, shuffled from one father to another, from house to house? He felt a rush of anger toward Nava. Perhaps she did deserve some punishment. "It must have been hard for you."

Mara shook her head and her brows came together. "I don't know. Most of the time I think I was happy. Mama was always good to me. Even when we were on our own, living in the little house, she was a wonderful mother. We sang and worked together. She never raised her voice or her hand to me. I loved her—love her—so much." Her voice broke and she swallowed hard.

"How long was it before she married Shaul?" Shem asked. "That would be her—," he counted on his fingers. "Zevulun, Moshe, Gershon, Shimon—fifth marriage?"

"It wasn't long. Shaul came here—I mean to Sychar—to work with the carpenter Yaakov. He is a cousin to Uziel. He knew of my mother's story—everyone knew—but he didn't care. I think he really . . . Well, I think he really loved her."

Shem struggled to adjust to this new picture of Nava. She had sinned and deserved at least some of the punishment that she received. But so had he. And even more seriously. How could he cast the first stone at this woman when he had killed a man? No, he couldn't condemn Nava so quickly.

Shem needed the rest of the story. What had happened with Shaul, the man who condemned his wife to death? "If he loved her . . ." He tried to say it as gently as he could. "Why did he leave?"

• • •

Mara couldn't answer Shem's question right away. It brought back her saddest memory. How much more should she tell him about Nava's final marriage? He'd be right to despise Nava as the rest of the village did. She would understand if he was disgusted with her mother. Would he be shocked to hear what her life became after Asher's birth? Would she, too, disgust him? But she couldn't lie. Not after all he'd done for her.

She looked at the high grassy slopes dotted with large, fat-tailed sheep. Between the hills lay wide valleys planted with golden wheat and blossoming blue flax. She would just tell him the rest as quickly as she could. He didn't need all the details. "We were so happy with Shaul. He was like a real father to me. He would come home and throw his arms around Mama. She laughed and sang all day." Mara turned to him, smiling at the memory.

Shem stumbled a little on the smooth road.

"Mama got pregnant right away." She remembered the birth clearly. Her mother smiling even through the pain. Leah's face when she saw the baby. She rubbed him with olive oil and salt to harden his muscles, wrapped him, and laid him in Nava's arms. *"It must be God's will,"* Leah had said in a shaking voice. Nava began to wail, her cries waking the newborn.

"Mama knew what they said in the village. That her sins had poisoned her firstborn son. She had disgraced her family and broken her vow to Zevulun, and this—Asher—was her punishment."

Mara trudged on with leaden feet, the weight of her sad memories pressing hard on her shoulders.

"Then what happened?" Shem asked softly.

She had never told another person the rest of the story. Her mother—her laughing, beautiful, joyful mother—had wrapped herself in misery. She had turned from her children and her husband on that day and hadn't emerged from her cocoon of despair until she had met the Taheb, the Restorer.

Mara swallowed hard. "She couldn't get over it. The guilt or the shame, I don't know which. She loves Asher; I know she loves him. She just couldn't look at him, or hold him. She just . . . left us." Nava had left them. She had turned her back on her daughter, her newborn son, her husband. She slept all day and wept all night. She let the fire die, refused to make meals, and watched the garden fill with weeds.

Mara had tried to hide her mother's failings. She was old enough to keep it a secret. She ground the grain and had bread baked by the time Shaul returned from his work at the carpenter's shop. Mara set Asher at his mother's breast when he cried in hunger. She worked the garden, cleaned the small house, and brought wood for the fire, every day hoping that Nava would get better.

"I did everything that I could." The fields of blue flax blurred. "But it wasn't enough." Would this journey be enough? Or just another failed attempt to save her mother?

When the lump in her throat had loosened, she continued. "Shaul was understanding at first. He said, 'Give her time.' But when time didn't heal her, Shaul lost patience. He was angry, and she cried more. I didn't know what to do.

"One day, he came home in the middle of the day. Asher screamed in my arms as Mama sat by the fire, just staring. Shaul sat down by her." Mara's voice fell to a whisper. Shem came closer and ducked his head close to her.

"He said, 'I can't go on this way. I can't help you, and I can't bear to see you so unhappy. Maybe it is better if I go away.' She didn't even look at him. He said that he'd spoken to the priest and was going to divorce her. He had found work in Sebaste. He was leaving us."

"What did she do?" Shem asked.

"She didn't do anything!" Mara still couldn't believe it. *How could Mama have let him go?* He was so good to them. "I begged him not to go. I begged her to stop him. But she just sat there." *If only he had stayed.*

She had thrown herself at Shaul, pleading with him. He had squeezed her in his strong arms, telling her that it was best, that the priest had told him to begin again in Sebaste. They didn't see him again . . . until yesterday.

"How old were you?" Shem asked as they reached the top of

another rise. The land and the sky stretched out around them, gold and green and blue.

As the days had gone by and Shaul had not returned, she had taken care of her little family as well as she could. She washed their clothes and carried them up the shaky ladder to dry on the flat roof. Other days she chopped at a fallen log or gathered dead branches to provide enough fuel to make the bread.

She pulled the weeds in the garden and turned the hard red soil. Beans, onions, and cucumbers sprouted, and she watered them with rainwater from the cistern. She harvested chickpeas and fava beans that kept well through the long winter months. She took the first fruits of every plant and set aside the required tithe to bring to the priests.

Every day she went to the well, often covered in dung and dirt, dreading the pitying stares of the women and the whispering girls who had once been her friends. Every day she brought home water to keep her family alive. Every day, she hoped—she prayed—that Shaul would come back to them. But he didn't.

"Mara? How old were you?" Shem asked again.

"I was seven when Asher was born, so about eight when Shaul left."

Shem let out a harsh breath. "Why didn't they help you?"

"Who?"

"The villagers. My grandparents. Your aunt and uncle should have taken you in, at least. You were just a child!"

"Oh, they did. They helped," Mara said quickly. "Some of them, sometimes. We would have starved without them. Ruth gave us food often, whenever I asked. But her family was growing. Sometimes they didn't have enough for themselves.

"And some of the villagers were generous, especially at first." She thought of Tirzah, who had good reason to despise them, yet gave them wheat and almonds every week. Until Passover, that is. And it was hard to blame her for stopping after what Nava had done. "Your grandfather still is very generous. He gives me enough oil to light the Sabbath lamp for the whole year and more for cooking."

She didn't speak of the many hungry days when she had wondered where the next meal would come from. She didn't have to; it seemed that Shem already knew.

"But you went hungry."

Mara didn't want to seem ungrateful. "It was easy for them to forget about us, I think, because of where we live. Most of the time we had enough: a round of bread or a jug of beans on our doorstep. Sometimes it was good food. Honey or almonds. But some days . . ." She stopped, thinking of the rancid oil and moldy bread that some people called charity.

Shem snorted.

"Some days were good, though," she said, trying to sound less pathetic. "Mama would wake and help with the garden or weaving." Most days, though, her mother didn't wake until midday and then sat like a statue, staring into the fire. "My mother is not actually a widow, as you know. She is still married. And Asher isn't an orphan. But for the most part, the villagers helped us anyway."

"Noach and Enosh help me with the goats. I don't know what I'd do without them. They take them in the spring, and I get a kid or two by fall. They help me sell it for a good price. Enosh always shears them for me. He brings me their wool and more—enough to spin all year long. I sell the cloth or trade it. We were managing. Until Alexandros."

She snuck a look at Shem's unreadable face. She shouldn't have said so much.

"Mara," he put his hand on her arm. "I didn't realize . . ."

She jerked away and walked faster. "I don't want pity," she choked out. That's not why she told him her story.

He caught up to her easily. "Mara . . . slow down. You are right. You don't deserve my pity."

"What?" That stopped her. What did he mean by that? Would he turn around now? Make them both go back to Sychar? He would have every right, and she wouldn't blame him if he did.

"Look what you've done. You could have given up, but you didn't. You took good care of your mother and Asher. You were hardly more than a child. I don't pity you, Mara, I admire you."

Mara blinked. Heat rushed up her neck and face. His words echoed in her ears. Never had another person admired her, ever. She hadn't even known that she wanted to be admired. It was like being handed a cool cup of water when you were too hot and tired to even know you were thirsty. And the water was even sweeter coming from a man as learned and worldly as Shem. The man that every girl in Sychar had tried to impress admired her.

Chapter 23

Is this the town of Jesus, the teacher?" Shem asked at the first merchant's tent in Nazareth. *This is where Mara is putting her hope for her mother?* The Taheb couldn't have come from here. It was even worse than Sychar.

Nazareth was little more than a collection of caves and poor houses carved into a hillside. A jumble of covered booths and tents littered the square. Men lounged in the shade, slapping at flies, while women drifted from booth to booth. Shem had hoped to find Jesus without attracting attention, but every eye in the tiny marketplace watched them already.

"Jesus ben Joseph? The carpenter?" the man asked, lowering his pipe and spitting out the words like they had a sour taste.

Shem nodded. He had heard the disciples say that carpentry was Jesus' trade. "My sister and I seek him."

Mara leaned forward. The merchant's eyes went to her, and his face changed.

Shem gave her a stern glance and stepped in front of her.

"Pah." The man raised his pipe again. "He is no teacher. Just the son of a poor carpenter." He looked more carefully at Shem's fine clothing and cloak. "What do you want with him?"

Shem drew himself up to his full height. He expected a more respectful tone, and he didn't like the leer that the old man had given Mara. "Our business is our own," he snapped. "Can you tell us where he is, or shall we buy elsewhere?"

The man eyed the money bag on Shem's belt. He shuffled forward, bowing his head. "Forgive me, sir. I can tell you only this: he came through town a few days ago. Heard he was going to Capernaum with that band of his."

Shem closed his eyes for a moment as a wave of despair washed over him. Mara let out a muffled gasp. "So you are sure he is not here, in Nazareth?"

The man shook his head. "No. His mother, Mary, still lives here. But she's gone today, visiting family."

Shem pointed to some dried figs and pistachios and reached into his money bag. Ten bronze sestertii left. Plenty to get them back to Sychar. But what would he do with Mara? Shem tapped his fingers on the tent pole, waiting for the slow merchant to gather the food.

A choked sob sounded behind him.

Shem turned to Mara. Tears trembled on her lashes, and her lips moved soundlessly. He had to get her out of the square. Finally, the merchant tumbled the fruit and nuts into his hands. Shem tucked the food in his belt and hurried Mara away.

He turned down a line of poor houses. As soon as they were out of sight of the marketplace, he took Mara's arm and helped her to a shady spot under a fig tree. He lifted her water skin from around her neck.

"Sit. Stay here. I'll be right back."

He went to the well, surrounded by women. They fell silent as he approached, their eyes traveling over his fine traveling cloak and money pouch. A mother pushed her pretty daughter forward. The girl smiled at Shem and took the water skins from his hand. He avoided looking at her as she dipped water and shot him sideways glances.

On his way back to Mara, he saw an old woman sitting in a doorway. "I am seeking Jesus ben Joseph," he said, crouching down in front of her.

"He is not here," she answered. Her wizened old face turned to the east. "He went to do his father's work, he said. In Capernaum."

"His father's work? Is his father there?"

She shook her head, and her lips stretched into a toothless smile. "Find Jesus, and you find his father, my boy."

He shook his head. More riddles. He thanked the old woman and plodded down the narrow street. What would he tell Mara? She would want to go on to Capernaum—that was certain. He couldn't go there. It was too far, too dangerous, and they were both too tired. He hadn't slept for days. *At least I won't have to face Jesus again.* His last words to the teacher had been like those of a spoiled child.

He must insist they turn back and take her home to Sychar. They hadn't seen any soldiers yet, but his luck would surely run out if they went all the way to Capernaum. He had done his best; he had kept his promise to her. They would return to Sychar and hope for a miracle for Nava. He'd work on justice for her killers.

Shem found Mara crumpled next to the tree, exactly as he had left her. "Mara, drink."

"Thank you." She took a long drink. Her dusty cheeks were streaked with tears. "Shem," she said, "thank you . . . for every-thing. But now . . ." Her voice broke and she pressed her lips together for a moment. "You've done so much for me, but I can't ask you to go on." She hid her face in her knees, but her body shook with sobs.

Shem bit hard on his lip, wondering what to do with this heartbroken girl. There were only two choices. Go back to her mother, dead or dying, or go on to certain danger for both of them. If she didn't find the Taheb, Mara would always blame herself. *When she should be blaming me.*

"No, Mara." He set his hand on her shoulder. He could feel her bones, sharp and birdlike. "We're going to Capernaum." If she thought her only chance was in this prophet, he would find him for her.

Mara jerked her head up and stared at him.

They could make it work. "We can get near Tiberius tonight, find a place to stay, then be in Capernaum by tomorrow midday." His father would wait for him in Sychar. They would only be a day or two late. He'd have to be careful with his coins. An inn for two nights would take all he had.

"I can't ask you to—"

"You aren't asking me." He grasped her hands and pulled her sharply up. "I'm telling you. We are going on." He turned and stalked down the road, leaving her to follow in silence.

After a steep climb that took all their breath, they passed the tiny town of Cana. The road turned sharply east, and the rutted road began to descend through the rocky hills. Lush grass blanketed the narrow valleys, and vineyards clung to the steep hills.

Shem glanced back at Mara, lagging behind again. What was he thinking? How would he get this exhausted girl to Capernaum by tomorrow? He slowed his pace and waited for her to catch up to him.

"Mara," he said, getting an idea. "Do you see this land around us?"

Her gaze didn't waver from her feet.

"The Greeks have a story that explains this land. They say that one of their gods, a Titan, was walking the earth, carrying a load of rocks that he was to spread over the world. But while he walked here, his sack of rocks broke. The whole mass of rocks tumbled out between the Jordan and the sea, making this land of plains and rocky hills."

Her head came up, and she looked around. Her steps quickened just a little.

Shem thought a moment. "Do you know the Greek story about the creation of man?"

She shook her head, but interest sparked in her face.

He increased their pace. "There were two brothers, Prometheus and Epimetheus. They were given the task of creating man by the ruler of all the gods, Zeus. So Epimetheus made a man out of mud, and another god, named Athena, breathed life into the man. Then Zeus gave Epimetheus gifts to give to all the creatures of the earth. He gave swiftness to the deer, strength to the bear, cunning, fur, wings to other animals. But when Epimetheus got to man, he had given away all the gifts and had none left."

Mara walked close beside him and seemed a little less miserable.

"Now Prometheus, the brother, he loved man more than the gods. He wanted to help the mortals. So he made man able to stand upright as the gods did, and he gave man the greatest gift of all—fire. Fire had only been allowed to the gods, so Zeus was enraged. He wanted to punish Prometheus."

Shem saw a small group of travelers approaching them—a man walking with a woman and child on a donkey. He greeted them politely.

After they passed, Mara asked, "What did Zeus do to Prometheus?" She said the strange Greek words carefully. They were walking quickly again.

Shem told her that Zeus made the first woman, Pandora. "She was very beautiful," Shem said. His eyes rested on Mara for a long moment. "But Zeus had a plan. He also made her very curious. Then he gave her a jar, but she was forbidden to open it. He sent her down to Epimetheus, who fell in love with her beauty."

They started up another steep hill, but Mara seemed not to notice the climb.

"Now the brother, Prometheus, was much smarter. He didn't let Pandora's beauty blind him. He warned his brother not to accept gifts from Zeus, but Epimetheus didn't listen. Prometheus warned Pandora over and over not to open the jar, but her curiosity could not be denied. Finally, she opened it."

"What was in it?" Mara asked, her eyes stretched wide. "Something bad?"

Shem nodded. "Yes. All the evils of the world—sorrow, disease, hatred. They flew out of the jar, never to be recaptured. They went all over the world, spreading and multiplying. That— according to the Greeks—was how evil came to the world."

He stopped there, suppressing a smile at her crestfallen face. It was a good story, one of his favorites. "But," he finally continued, "at the very bottom of the jar, there was one good thing." He increased the pace again. "One good thing that made the world a better place."

"What was it?" she asked, running a few steps to get closer to him.

Shem smiled. "It was hope."

Mara thought about the pagan story. Hope was all that she had now. Hope that her mother survived long enough for Mara to get to Jesus. Hope that they would find him in Capernaum. Shem didn't have hope for Nava. She could tell by the way his mouth twisted every time she spoke of Jesus. But he would see. When they found Jesus, he would believe.

Her heart sped up as she remembered Shem's words before Nazareth. He admired her. Someone like him admired her. She picked up her shuffling feet and forced her sluggish body to move more quickly. But why was he helping her if he didn't even believe in Jesus? She thought back to Sychar, before the stoning. He had been kind to her, even then. Maybe he . . . could he feel something for her? Was that why he was here? She pushed the thought away, but it stayed buried in her mind, like a seed waiting for water and the warmth of the sun.

They descended through a brushy ravine into a deep valley. A cedar grove cast long shadows over the road. Shem turned to her and motioned toward a shady spot. She dropped down into the long, cool grass. Her mind told her to hurry, but her body ached and her eyes longed to close and sleep.

Shem spilled figs and pistachios into her lap, then settled down with his back against a tree. She crunched the nuts and chewed the figs in a sleepy haze while bees droned and the sweet smell of cedar and myrtle filled the air.

Shem would be a good husband.

Don't be ridiculous. Even if he stayed in Sychar, he would marry a girl from a good family. She could name several who would be perfect for him. If she were very lucky—if they got back to Sychar without being missed—she would marry Jobab and try to outlive him. The Greek story came back to her. Hope. She could hope that Shem was different than the men of Sychar. That he knew she wasn't like her mother, that he knew she would be a good wife. Mara's eyes drooped closed, and her head lolled forward.

She shook herself awake.

Shem sighed and got to his feet. He squinted at the sun, dipping down toward the west. "It would be good to find a place to stay before dark." He checked up and down the road once, then again.

"Can we stay in Tiberius?"

Shem rubbed the back of his neck. "I would not choose to stay in Tiberius. It is an evil city, full of every sort of malice. Besides, no Jews stay in the city because it is unclean—it was built over a burial site. We will find a place outside the city."

He stretched his arms to the sky, his back cracking, then turned and offered her his hand. She hesitated before putting her sticky one in his and letting him pull her to her feet. She found herself close enough to see the red scar through his dark beard. How did he get that? She dropped his hand as her heart sped up and her face heated. It was none of her business.

She stepped back. "Then to Capernaum?"

"Yes, we'll start out early. We could be there by midday, if all goes well."

"Midday. She can make it until then," Mara said to herself. She ran through her mother's injuries again—the swollen knot on her temple, the wound at the base of her neck, the long, deep gash down her face. How many broken bones were hidden under the bruised and scraped skin? Had Mechola been able to wake her, to make her drink?

"Mara," Shem interrupted her thoughts, "I pray that your mother is still alive. But you must know that—if we find him— we still have almost two days to bring Jesus back to Sychar."

"Back?" Mara looked up at him. Maybe he didn't understand. "But Shem, don't you see? We don't have to bring him back. Jesus is the Taheb, the Chosen One of God."

Shem brushed grass from his tunic. "So he says."

Mara ignored his tone. "He doesn't need to be in Sychar to heal her. We need only to ask him, and he can heal her tomorrow."

Shem turned to her, his face as confused as if she'd spoken another language. "What?"

Mara squared her shoulders. "He can heal her tomorrow, Shem."

Shem's jaw tightened and shifted, as though he was grinding his teeth. "Mara, tell me this is not what you are hoping for? You don't believe that man, Jesus, can heal your mother from Capernaum?"

"Yes. I do believe that." Mara stood tall and stared him in the eyes. What had he thought? That Jesus would come and give her mother an herbal potion, like Leah? He was the Taheb, not a midwife.

He gave a short bark of laughter and stepped closer to her, "Mara, that is not just foolish. That idea is completely absurd." He took her by the shoulders and gave her a little shake. "Mara, be sensible!"

If sensible meant giving up all hope then, no, she wouldn't be. Her voice rose to match his. "It is the only way, Shem, don't you see? If he is the Taheb—the Promised One—he can do this. Why don't you believe in him?"

For all his talk of hope, he had none himself.

She pushed past him, out of the shadows of the cedars and into the hard, bright sun. She started up the next hill, anger pushing her legs to longer strides. If he didn't believe in the Taheb, she would get to Capernaum by herself. Of course he didn't believe. She'd known that all along. She was a fool to have let herself trust him—even dream of a future with him. He was just like every other man she knew. But the question that had followed her all the way from Sychar still nagged. *If he doesn't believe in the Taheb, then why is he helping me?*

Shem couldn't believe his ears. She must be crazy. "Mara, wait." He ran a few steps to catch up with her.

She sped up. "You don't need to come, I've told you that." Her sandals slapped on the ground.

He regretted his harsh words, but she had surprised him. He'd had no idea that she thought Jesus could do such a miracle. Heal someone from a distance! "Mara, I'm sorry. Please, stop."

She stopped.

He put both hands on her elbows and turned her toward him, holding her there.

She kept her face turned away. *Stubborn little thing.*

He pressed his lips together and took a deep breath through his nose. "I just don't understand, Mara." He tried hard to keep his voice calm. "I saw Jesus. I heard him speak, and he was . . . wise. And yes, good. But a miracle worker? What makes you think he can do that? He never even claimed to be a healer."

"I just know, Shem." Her green and amber eyes were bright, but not with tears.

Shem could see in them the determination that had kept her family fed and clothed for so many years.

"It's the only chance she has, the only thing that I can do for her. I just know that he can help her."

"You just know?" How like a woman to set out on a hunch. To risk both their lives on a hope.

She nodded once, then pulled away from his hands and continued up the hill.

He sighed. Fine. They would go to Capernaum and see just what this Jesus could do.

Worry coiled in Shem's chest like a viper. Every step brought them closer to Tiberius, closer to a whole garrison of Roman soldiers. His father had many friends in the city, but also enemies.

Mara's outrageous hope ate at him, and the thought of the city turned his stomach. Every step seemed like a bad idea. Tiberius was a beautiful city, newly built by Herod, but a brutal and dangerous place. He had been there several times. Would word of one soldier's death in Caesarea have reached Tiberius? Would they be looking for a tall, dark-haired Samaritan with a scar? He hoped not.

The traffic on the road became heavier. They met with Greek traders on laden donkeys, tax collectors escorted by well-armed guards, and groups of pilgrims on their way to Jerusalem. A fast-moving caravan came from behind them, forcing them off the road and covering them in dust as it passed by.

Shem's eyes burned from the constant dust, gritty wind, and lack of sleep. He tried to stay alert, but his mind felt dull. The cliffs they passed were pockmarked with caves. Any one of them could be hiding a pack of bandits, ready to kill them both for the coins in his purse. *I doubt I could put up much of a fight.*

The road wound downward now into the valley of Jezreel, but they were still so far from Tiberius. He would need to find a place to stay, and soon. He glanced at Mara. She looked like she was about to break. He could pay for a good inn tonight. He'd worry about the return trip when the time came.

"There is a spring up ahead, I think. We can rest there," he said.

She dropped behind him again. She hadn't said a word to him since their argument. He shouldn't have been so harsh with her, but he couldn't help what he believed. This was indeed a fool's journey.

He kicked at a loose stone on the road. He was doing his best, trying to make up for what he'd done to her mother. But she was making it harder with her ridiculous faith in the Jew.

Where did her stubborn belief spring from? Had Jesus performed more of a miracle in Sychar than he realized? Yes, Nava had seemed better. But enough that Mara believed him a miracle worker? She was letting her own desperate wishes rule her mind. But turning around was no longer an option, unless he wanted her to believe for the rest of her life that she had failed her mother.

They'd come this far. Whether or not Jesus could help Nava didn't matter, as long as Mara believed she'd done all she could for her mother. And then he would do all he could for Mara.

Chapter 24

Shem . . ." Mara swallowed hard. "I can't go on." She couldn't go another step. Her head pounded, her legs felt like they were made of stone, her feet were on fire. She would gladly make the dusty road her bed.

He nodded. "I know. Just a little farther, and you can rest."

She could tell that he regretted helping her now. He had walked silently, hardly speaking since their argument. He must wish that he were back in Sychar, that he had never met her. She heard the echo of his words and harsh laughter.

He didn't admire her now.

He thought she was a fool. He had said so, and maybe she was. Now they would never reach Capernaum in time. The sun already touched the western horizon, and they weren't even near Tiberius.

"I can't." She heard the sob in her voice but couldn't help it.

"You can see it from here," he said, his voice gentle. "Look." He put his hand under her elbow. It helped, somehow.

At first she saw only a cloud of dust in the valley below. But then—Eden. A broad stream of water gushed out from a mound of boulders. It flowed into a quiet pool fringed with lush grasses and oleanders. She forced her leaden feet down the road, fixing her eyes on the sparkling water and soft grass. Shem kept his arm under hers, helping her forward.

The caravan that had passed them earlier clustered around the standing water. Donkeys brayed and lowered their heads to the pool, their sharp hooves sinking into the spongy soil. Servants chattered and filled water skins.

Shem guided Mara to the scented shade of a tamarisk tree, away from the crowd. She collapsed on the grass. She had never felt anything so soft and cool.

Shem took her water skin from her. "I'll be right back. Don't move."

Mara felt a bubble of foolish laughter rise in her throat. Don't move? She would never move again. She closed her eyes, listening to the sounds of the animals and the voices of the travelers. Sleep wrapped around her like soft wool until a strident shout wrenched her awake.

"Shem ben Ezra!"

Mara's eyes snapped open and found Shem only a few steps from her but turning back toward the crowded spring. She raised herself up on an elbow and peered around him. A huge man strode toward them.

His fine clothing and short, smooth hair marked him as a Greek, and a rich one. He stood almost as tall as Shem, but his shoulders were broader and his belly protruded like a pregnant woman's. Dark red lips curved into a broad smile that didn't reach his hard, gray eyes.

Shem pulled his shoulders back, and his hands squeezed the water skins. The big man embraced Shem, then stepped back to look him up and down. He spoke rapidly in Greek, a note of surprise in his loud voice.

Shem responded fluently in the same language and stepped to the side, cutting off the man's view of Mara. It didn't work.

The big man seemed to sense Shem's protective stance and peered around him. His brows arched in surprise, and he turned back to Shem with a suggestive smile and a low comment.

Shem's short, angry reply brought only a laugh as the other man raised his hands in a motion of innocence. His small, sharp eyes slid back to Mara as he clasped Shem on the shoulder, speaking rapidly, his voice insistent. Shem seemed to disagree with him and shook his head. The big man just spoke louder, and finally Shem nodded.

Shem turned and waved her up from the ground.

She glanced at the big Greek as she got up; his eyes swept down her body.

Shem came close and spoke softly, his voice urgent, "Mara, listen carefully and do exactly as I say. This man knows my father and recognized me. He insists that we stay with him tonight."

She didn't like the way the stranger looked at her; he reminded her of Alexandros. Shem's mouth was a thin line, and his eyes were tight with worry.

They walked toward the caravan, and Shem whispered quick and hot in her ear. "Don't speak. Don't even look at him."

A cold shiver passed through her as she fixed her gaze on the ground.

Huge, meaty hands lifted Mara onto a scrawny donkey. The big man snickered at her gasp of surprise, and his hands lingered on her waist.

A cowering servant ran up, towing a larger, long-legged donkey. Shem jumped up easily on the animal, then spoke firmly to the big Greek. The man wrenched his eyes away from Mara and passed Shem the lead rope for her donkey. He sauntered to his own mount, bellowing orders to his servants.

The caravan moved slowly away from the spring, but the animals gained speed as they spread out on the wide road. Mara watched Shem, waiting for an explanation.

"Hold on," was all he said. He kicked his mount firmly on its rounded belly.

She clutched her donkey's coarse mane. They lurched into a trot, and she had to press her legs around the donkey's sides to stay upright.

Mara watched the ground race under her; they were traveling at least twice as fast as they could walk. She stayed silent, although a thousand questions flew through her mind. How did the man know Shem? And why was Shem's jaw tight and his hand clenched in a white fist around the lead?

The sun dipped low behind them, and the cool evening wind freshened the air as the procession descended rapidly through the hills. The Greek rode at the head of the column, surrounded by armed guards on horses. Shem and Mara trotted not far back, followed by more donkeys under swaying loads. At least six camels lumbered behind, laden with oak chests strapped in iron. Wiry boys ran behind the camels, shouting and beating them with sticks to keep their pace up to a quick trot.

Shem's mount drifted close, and he whispered in terse, quick sentences, keeping his eyes on the guards and servants. "His name is Silas. He is a cloth merchant who sells to my father. Or he did. My father does not trust him, nor do I."

They rode in silence for a few minutes before he went on. "I told him you were my cousin, but I don't think he believed me. He has a good memory for women. I explained that you are a mute and unwell. That we are going to a healer in Damascus."

Mara heard the worry in his voice. But at least they were riding instead of stumbling along the hard road. Her eyes drifted closed as the rocking motion of the donkey lulled her tired body and mind. She swayed sideways. Shem's warm grip bit into her shoulder, and her eyes snapped open.

He leaned close to her, his mount brushing against hers. He looked into her eyes for just moment, then dropped his hand and moved away. "Just try to stay on; we'll be there soon."

Stay awake. Don't fall off.

Her head bobbed along to the rhythm of the donkey. Rocky hills gave way to neat fields of wheat and flax and, soon after, whitewashed towns smelling of fish. As they rounded a curve, her drooping eyes popped open at the sight of the sparkling waters of the Galilee. The deep blue water glinted gold in the setting sun. Mount Hermon rose on the distant shore, its snowy peak painted pink with the last blush of the sunset.

Like a swift shadow, darkness slid over the land, and a chill breeze blew off the water, making her arms prickle with cold. In the distance, she saw the dark bulk of a city, sprinkled with lights. Tiberius.

Before they reached its gates, the caravan veered sharply away from the water. A long, curved pathway led through a vineyard.

They passed under an arched entrance between high walls and into a small village. But was it a village? It was like no town Mara had ever seen.

Instead of houses built of wood or clay bricks, the structures clustered around the courtyard were built of glittering black stone. Fires blazed in a courtyard of gushing fountains and lush vegetation. An army of torches flashed as servants rushed out of doors, hurrying to meet the travelers. Was this vast compound a home for just one man?

Mara stayed on her donkey as the rest of the travelers jumped down and jabbered in Greek. What was she supposed to do?

Silas appeared at her side like a leering giant, his great hands reaching for her. He clamped them around her waist and pulled her from the donkey, setting her down close to his big belly. A chill shuddered down her body as Mara stepped back, pressing herself against the steaming donkey. *This man is* worse *than Alexandros.*

Shem slid from his mount and spoke lightly to their host in Greek. He sounded almost happy. He was ignoring her completely. Couldn't he see what Silas was doing? Silas laughed and stepped away, his thick arm sweeping over the courtyard, and they walked side by side toward the house.

Mara followed slowly. If only Shem would look back at her, tell her what to do. Was she to go into the house with them? Her legs felt like mush and her body hurt all over. She would be happy to find a bed in the servants' rooms. Anywhere. Even with the animals.

A roar from Silas made her jump, but it wasn't directed at her. Immediately, three women rushed from the house. They were thin and haggard, dressed in rough wool tunics. He snapped what seemed to be many orders at them, pointing a finger at Mara. They hurried to her, took her by an arm, and led her toward a door on the other side of the courtyard.

Mara craned her neck back toward Shem. It was quick, but she thought she saw him nod. Silas stared at her as she was pulled past him, his eyes gleaming in the firelight.

• • •

"My luck is finally changing," Shem said to Silas with a long-suffering sigh. "I was dreading another night in a vermin-infested inn. This," he gestured widely to the sumptuous home they had just entered, "is just what I need."

"I've been looking forward to hearing your story, my boy. How did you come to be traveling like a farmer—and with a beautiful girl as well?" Silas threw his arm over Shem's shoulder like an old friend.

Shem ground his teeth and tried not to flinch from the man's heavy touch. He was ready for Silas's questions. He just hoped he could buy them some time. As long as Silas thought him a spoiled, ignorant boy, Shem would have a chance to get Mara away from the big Greek's lair.

"Believe me, it is a long and tedious story. And the girl . . . Well, I'm just glad to get away from her for the night."

Silas arched a brow. "Now I am intrigued. But let us bathe and change as you tell it. You need a haircut and a shave, my friend, if you are to stay with me."

Silas glided through a labyrinth of passages like a serpent, servants scattering like terrified mice before him. Shem walked beside him, memorizing each hallway and door. His host was more dangerous than any roadside bandit. Silas was a shrewd businessman, but not one to be trusted if the rumors of his connections with Eastern slave traders were true.

And the way the man looked at Mara! Shem's blood pounded in his head, and his hands tightened into fists. But he couldn't afford to lose his temper. He would have to be very careful. Silas was the sort of man one took care not to offend. Rejecting his offer of hospitality would have been offensive. As would demanding he keep his eyes—and hands—off Mara.

"It is good to live outside of Tiberius," Silas continued. "The hot springs here provide warm water for my baths." Silas walked Shem into the most extravagant bath he'd ever seen.

Billowing steam greeted them in the first chamber. The black tiles on the floor and wall wept with moisture. Glistening stone benches lined the walls. Through the arched doorway, Shem could see the gleam of water in a bathing chamber as big as his grandfather's courtyard.

Silas clapped his hands, and several male servants appeared with towels. "Let us wash off the traveling dust and get ready for a feast." One of his servants began to undress him. Another waited to assist Shem.

Shem let him take his cloak and tunic. For now, he would have to play along.

"So, I heard that there has been some trouble in Caesarea." Silas lowered himself to a bench, steam billowing around him. "With one of Ezra's boys." He smirked and raised his brows.

So Silas did know. Word traveled fast among merchants. Shem kept his face calm, but sweat beaded on his skin, and it was not from the heat of the room. "I'm sure they've stopped searching for me by now. But my father—it disrupted his plans and so ..." He shrugged and settled on the steam-warmed bench.

"He sent you away from Caesarea until it is safe to return?"

"So he says," Shem stretched like he was enjoying the steam. "He always overreacts. I'm not worried."

Silas rubbed his chin. "There are many soldiers in this area. What if they are looking for you?"

Shem's jaw clenched, but he shrugged. "I doubt that one Samaritan is of much interest to the Romans. He said that traveling as poor peasants would keep us safer. But I know that he just wants to see me miserable." Shem tried to sound petulant and added a scowl for good measure. "This is his idea of punishment. Sending me on a fool's errand with my dim-witted cousin."

Silas laughed loudly at that. Shem smiled. Maybe he was a better liar than he thought. "I have to take her to some friends in Damascus. They are expecting us tomorrow or the next day."

"Expecting you?" Silas rested his chin on one hand, his finger tapping his full lips. "You should stay with me for a few days. You deserve some luxury after such a journey."

Shem frowned. A few days here, and no one would ever see

him or Mara again. "We can't; my father would be very angry."
He cocked his head and pursed his lips. "Then again . . . it might
make this miserable journey worthwhile. I certainly deserve it,
after what I've put up with." He twisted his mouth into what he
hoped was a conspiring smirk. "Yes . . . we will stay a few days
with you, my friend."

Chapter 25

The women stripped Mara of her cloak and unwrapped her belt from her waist. Mara pressed her lips together before she could utter the protest that almost slipped from her mouth.

She stood in a sumptuous room, larger than the entire house she shared with her mother and Asher. Smooth tile floors were strewn with soft carpets. Flickering bronze lamps sat on ornamental tables, and a massive brazier glowed in one corner, making the room as warm as a summer day. On one end, she saw marble steps leading to sparkling water.

The oldest of the women, a crone with deeply lined skin and frizzy gray hair, pointed to herself. "Berenice," she croaked, then pointed to Mara. They all looked at her. She covered her mouth with her hand and shook her head. Berenice seemed to understand. She explained something over her shoulder to the other servants, and they made sympathetic noises. Berenice spoke sharply to the youngest servant, sending her out of the room with a flutter of her bony hands.

The two women turned back to Mara, clucking in disapproval. Their hands pulled at her clothes and tangled hair.

Mara crossed her hands over her ragged tunic, clutching it in her fists and shaking her head, but they took no notice, unlocking her arms and lifting her tunic off her with one swift motion. They chuckled, but not unkindly, as she tried to cover her nakedness.

Berenice took pity on her, wrapping her in a cool linen sheet. The other opened an ebony chest inlaid with lustrous stones to divulge a treasure of sponges, alabaster jars, and jewel-like bottles.

They chattered to each other as they led Mara to the bath. Mara resisted. A pagan bath must be unclean, but the water looked so clear and tempting. Finally, as the women's voices rose and their prodding became more vigorous, she dropped the sheet and stepped into the water. It was warm and wonderful and swirled around her like silk. She sank down on the smooth marble and stretched until the water covered her from toes to chin.

The servants nodded and set to work, pouring water over her hair and rubbing it with sweet-smelling soap. They sluiced water through it again and again. Mara's eyes closed, and she became lost in the blissful sensation. She could stay in this spot forever. But when a soapy sponge slid over her arms and shoulders, she came out of her trance. She grabbed the sponge from the old woman and scrubbed the rest of her body. She wasn't a child, and it couldn't be right to have the other women wash her.

They pulled her out and wrapped her in dry linen. Now, finally she would be able to sleep. But the clucking women weren't done with her. Berenice guided her to a low bench, and they huddled around her.

Berenice pumiced the calluses from her hands and feet and shaped her ragged nails. The other woman gave her sharp-flavored anise seeds to freshen her breath, smoothed her long black hair with an ivory comb, and anointed her with sweet almond oil. Berenice slipped a narrow band of black silk over her forehead to hold her hair in place.

Mara sat dull-witted on the bench as they attended to her. She could hardly keep her heavy eyelids open. The warm bath had soothed her aching body; now she just wanted to find a bed and sleep. Why were they continuing to pamper her as if it were her wedding day?

The two servants eagerly brought out a casket of small pots and bottles. They offered inky black antimony to darken her lashes and red *sikra* for her lips and cheeks, but Mara shook her heavy head. When she put up her hands to protest their offering of sweet, musky scents in alabaster pots, the women exclaimed to each other with raised eyebrows but finally shrugged and gave up.

A wave of dizziness passed over her. Perhaps she would join the woman of the household for their evening meal. That must be it. What would the wife and daughters of a man like Silas be like?

They were slipping ebony bracelets on her reluctant wrists when the young girl returned with her arms full of silk and linen. Mara was not too sleepy to notice the fine weave and expert dye of the cloth. These clothes were finer than any she had seen.

The women slid a sleeveless linen shift of deep blue over her head and fastened it at the shoulders with golden clasps. The shift barely covered her knees and left her shoulders bare. Mara shook her head and crossed her arms in front of her. *I can't wear this; I can see right through it.*

Berenice ignored her. The old woman rummaged through the pile of shimmering cloth again, choosing a flowing silk, sea green and embroidered in gold. She draped it over the tunic, then wrapped a deep green sash high around her waist. That was better, but not by much. Mara pulled at the fabric, trying to cover more of her exposed skin.

Finally, tutting at the red sores on her ankles, the old servant kneeled and slipped delicate sandals encrusted with pearls on her feet. She smiled, lurched to her feet, and motioned for Mara to follow. She lifted a salver of brightly polished silver from a table and brought it close to Mara's face, wagging her head in approval.

Mara studied the image reflected in the burnished surface. She saw wide eyes of green flecked with golden light and smooth, high cheekbones. Her silky hair shone blue-black in the lamplight, and her honey skin glowed. It was Nava's face reflected back at her. Nava, whose beauty had done nothing but make her family miserable.

And now here I am, dressed as the harlot that everyone in Sychar believes Mama to be.

She pushed the mirror away and closed her eyes. Panic and despair clutched at her heart, overwhelming her. She didn't want to be here. She needed to get to Capernaum. She thought of her broken mother lying in a dark room in Sychar. What were they doing right now? Did Asher think she had deserted him?

Berenice stroked her gnarled hand down Mara's hair, murmuring soft words. Mara didn't want to seem ungrateful to this strange woman. She had been kind, in her way. Mara brushed the tears away and offered a tremulous smile. Berenice gripped her arm with her clawlike fingers and pulled Mara out of the room.

Mara stumbled after Berenice. Her mouth fell open as they hurried through one lavish room after another. Silken cushions littered the floors and benches. Wild beasts seemed to watch them with glittering, jeweled eyes from the mosaic walls. The corners held chests covered in iron and gold. Their steps were hushed by thick carpets, but she could hear voices and music ahead. Her heart thumped, and her hands turned clammy as she recognized the booming voice of their host.

She could not be eating with the men.

But Berenice stopped at a bright doorway where men's voices and the sounds of the harp and lute drifted out of the room. She pulled Mara toward the opening. Mara planted her feet and shook her head. She wouldn't go in there; she couldn't. Not dressed like this—like a pagan whore.

Berenice's hand tightened on her arm. The woman looked almost afraid.

If only Mara had her robe. It was dirty and ragged, but at least it covered her. Her heart sped up, and her legs trembled. She couldn't turn back and run away; where would she go?

Berenice pushed her firmly at the small of her back, forcing her fully into the room. Conversation stopped, and three sets of eyes turned to her. Silas at the head of the table, Shem on one side, and a blond woman with a pinched face on the other.

After the first heart-stopping glance, Mara saw nothing but Shem. He reclined on a couch, his farmer's tunic replaced by fine linen. His face was again smooth-shaven, and his hair was shining clean and clipped short. He was a stranger again.

He held a goblet of wine as if frozen. She didn't understand the look that flared on his face as his eyes traveled from her face to her toes, just a flash, quickly replaced by a deep frown. His throat worked convulsively, and his eyes veered to Silas.

Mara's stomach churned, and her knees trembled as she turned her gaze to the big Greek. He licked his red lips as if he were surveying a feast. She'd seen that look before. On Alexandros. On Jobab.

Silas had changed from his traveling clothes into an even finer ensemble of gold and purple. Each meaty hand boasted several rings with huge glittering stones. Gold embroidery stretched across his protruding belly as he rolled to one side of his couch to appraise Mara.

Mara's face burned as Silas's greedy eyes traveled from her face down her body. She pulled her garment around herself and turned a pleading face to Shem. He scowled and spoke to Silas in clipped, short words she didn't understand.

She blinked her burning eyes. Shem was angry with her. If only she could explain. These clothes were not her doing. She didn't want to be here. She wasn't like her mother—what her mother used to be. She just wanted a bite to eat and somewhere to lay her head.

"Oh, but we are Greek, my dear Shem," Silas answered in thickly accented Aramaic. "We allow our women to eat with us, especially such a beauty as this one. I'm sorry that you wish to be rid of her for a night."

He said that? He wished he could be rid of her?

"And, my boy," Silas continued, his voice smooth, "you must know that I am a greedy man. I desire all my senses to be gratified at once. Your cousin will delight my eyes as sweet music pleases my ears and food satisfies my mouth." He patted his belly and laughed, but his eyes stayed on Mara. "And we will speak the language of your land, in honor of your . . . cousin." His lips twitched into a smirk at the last word. "Doris," he grunted to the other member of the group, "give this beauty your couch. You sit farther down."

Mara turned to the third diner. A small, thin woman glared at her from the other side of Silas. Doris lounged on the couch dressed in golden silk that left her neck and shoulders bare. Ringlets of golden hair were piled high on her head, but her pretty face showed marks of age under her heavy makeup. She set her red mouth in a stubborn line and shook her head.

Mara did the same, fluttering her hands in wordless protest.

Silas took no notice of either woman's pleas. He snapped at Doris in Greek. She stood sullenly and walked past Silas to recline on the other side of Shem, leaving the more honored spot for Mara.

Mara sat carefully on the couch. She'd never reclined to eat before. She stretched out on her side and scooted toward the table, pulling at the neck of her dress to keep decently covered.

"You are wise, Shem, to not have taken a wife." Silas didn't take his eyes off Mara. "Cousins are so much more . . . agreeable."

Mara saw Shem's throat jerk, but he just shrugged.

Silas moved his bulky body to the foot of the couches and reached for Mara's feet.

She pulled away. What was he doing now?

"Don't be frightened, my sweet," purred Silas as he unfastened the pearl sandals and gave them to the waiting Berenice. "It is the privilege of the host to remove your sandals and make you more comfortable." He ran his fleshy fingers over her ankles, chuckling as she flinched. He lay back down on his couch, raised just a handbreadth above the others, and barked a command at a servant. The man jumped and hurried from the room.

The servant reappeared in moments at Mara's side with a goblet of ruby wine. She surveyed the sumptuous banquet before her, and her stomach squeezed tight, but not in hunger. Her body seemed unable to move; she could hardly breathe. Shem wouldn't look at her. Silas wouldn't leave her alone. She felt like she was drowning.

Chapter 26

Mara tried to eat as the servants offered platters of exotic foods, each more sumptuous and delicate than the last. Silas served his guests first, dipping into the dishes with carved ivory spoons or his own hand, then bestowing morsels on Shem's and Mara's gilded salvers. *I can't eat all this. Would it be rude to refuse?*

Shem did not admire her now; he was too busy admiring Doris. For all his talk of danger before, he seemed to be enjoying himself. With his easy manners and relaxed pose, he looked like he belonged here. They whispered in Greek, and Doris laughed, stroking his bare arm with her pale fingers and smirking over his shoulder at Mara.

Mara's face burned. Were they talking about her? About how stupid and clumsy she was? Would Doris ask him how he got stuck with such an ignorant girl?

The meat on her plate swam in a sauce that smelled of cumin and cinnamon. She glanced up to see Silas watching her closely, his face flushed and glistening with sweat.

"Eat it! It will not bite you back. I promise there is no pork on this table, but as to your other restrictions, tonight you must forget them." He reached over and ran his huge hand from her shoulder to her elbow, laughing again as she shrank away from him.

Mara hurriedly scooped up the meat and shoved it in her mouth, barely tasting the unfamiliar flavor. She nodded to her host, trying not to meet his eyes. The meal continued with more food and wine than Mara had ever seen. Spiced peahen eggs, roasted hare in fig sauce, lamb covered in olives and capers, antelope cooked in milk and flavored with anise. The pungent aromas choked her, and her mouth burned with heat.

Silas insisted that she try each dish, followed by a sip of the dark, strong wine. Mara's head swam as the servants brought out roasted vegetables and strong cheeses sprinkled with pomegranate seeds. Doris seemed as determined to keep Shem's attention as Silas was to have Mara all to himself. The big man drank far more than he ate, his voice becoming lower and his comments more suggestive as the meal continued. Seeing her blush with discomfort seemed to delight him.

As the servants removed the trays of cheeses, Shem caught the attention of one and spoke quietly to him, flicking his hand toward Mara. The servant returned with a pitcher of water, with which he diluted her wine. She sent Shem a grateful look, but he turned away from her.

"Watching out for your charge, eh, Shem?" Silas laughed, waving the servant away. "Isn't she old enough to drink undiluted wine?"

"I just don't want her to get sick on me," Shem said with a shrug. Why was he being so cruel? Was he the grandson of Abahu or the cold-hearted son of a rich man?

Silas put down his wine and contemplated Mara. He touched her hair, running his fingers over it and weighing it in his thick hand. "She is well past the age to marry. Why is it that she is still a maiden?"

"As I said," Shem answered, sounding bored, "she is unwell and as dumb as a walking stick. Believe me, few men want a wife like her."

Mara felt tears prick at the back of her eyes. Dumb as a walking stick? Shem's face was turned away. *Why won't he look at me?*

She blinked back the tears and took another drink of wine. She had to get away from this table. If it was sickness he was avoiding, perhaps sick was what she should be. It would be easy enough, given the way her stomach lurched. Then maybe she could escape this nightmare and get some sleep.

• • •

Shem ground his teeth together. Silas was worse than he remembered. He hadn't taken his eyes, or his hands, off Mara during the meal. It took all Shem's control not to crawl across the table and choke the fat pig.

He had to get them out of here. But how? And Mara . . . It was hard not to stare at her himself. She looked like a goddess, but he had to force himself to pretend that he didn't even notice her.

"I would think," Silas laughed, "that a woman who couldn't talk would be in the utmost demand! She is beautiful, that is true, and those eyes . . ." Silas put his hand under her chin and pulled it up. Mara's skin paled where his thick fingers dug into her chin.

Blood pounded in Shem's head, and his fist tightened around his goblet. *Let go of her, or I'll show you what it feels like to be helpless.*

Mara wrenched away from him, and he laughed again. "Yes, a woman who is beautiful and can neither complain nor nag—that is truly a rare and valuable pearl!" He pursed his lips, shiny with wine. "Yes, indeed," he said softly, "this one is a real treasure."

A shiver ran up Shem's back and prickled his neck. Silas wanted Mara, and he'd get rid of Shem to have her. Would he have the guards kill him here or turn him in to the Roman garrison in Tiberius?

Whatever Silas planned, perhaps Shem's act as the spoiled, oblivious lout had bought them some time to get away. Silas seemed to have dismissed him as any threat. He might wait until tomorrow to have Shem killed, then do what he wished with Mara.

Shem took a deep breath, forcing a hard voice and a scowl toward Mara. "She is unwell, and believe me, no joy to travel with. Her illness is very unpleasant."

He raised his glass and eyed Doris with what he hoped passed for a drunken leer. "Here's to a few days of good company before putting an end to this foolish journey." He slurped his wine and pretended to sway in his chair as Silas laughed and raised his own glass. Mara turned pale, and her bottom lip quivered. *Mara, it's just an act. I'm doing it for you.* Surely she knew that.

Silas had drunk enough wine for three men. Hopefully, he would sleep hard tonight. Then they could escape. He turned again to Doris. She would be no help; she was terrified of Silas and not too smart. He forced himself to smile at her again and tried not to cringe when her cool hand touched him.

He only half listened to Doris as she purred a suggestion into his ear. Mara didn't look good. Her eyes closed, and she swayed sideways. He rolled from his couch and bolted around Doris, but not fast enough. Silas was already holding Mara's limp body in his arms. Her head lolled to one side.

He put his hand on her cheek. "Mara!"

Silas pulled her body closer. "It seems your charge can't hold her wine." He stepped back. "I'll take the poor girl to a room to sleep it off."

"No!" Shem's heart pounded. He slid his arms under Mara and pulled. Silas did not release her. "No, give her to me."

Silas arched a brow at Shem and pulled back. "I thought you wanted to be rid of her for a night?"

What could he say? Silas had him trapped like a mouse. "I do, of course, but she is ill. Believe me, it is not a pretty sight. It starts with this." He shook her a little. "Then the fit comes on her."

Silas's grip loosened.

Shem grimaced. "And vomiting, sometimes worse."

Silas let her go, disgust twisting his face.

Shem shifted her closer to his chest. "I know how to take care of her." Was it really the wine? Or had the torturous journey been too much for her? How could he get her out of here like this—limp and unconscious?

"Berenice!" Silas roared. The old woman who had brought Mara to them scurried from the doorway. Her old face wrinkled in concern, and she ran her gnarled hand over Mara's slack face.

"Take them to a room in the east hall."

Shem bowed as well as he could. "Thank you, my host. I will see to her."

"We will talk in the morning." Silas turned back to his wine.

Shem nodded and hurried after the servant. *We'll be far away by then.* As they rushed down the hallway, Shem held his breath and dipped his head close to hers. Her breathing was fast. Did her lashes flutter?

"Is he gone?" Mara whispered through barely moving lips.

She had been pretending? He let out his breath in a whoosh. *Good girl!* She had gotten them away from Silas and given him an excuse to leave as well. Now they just had to get out of the house without being seen.

"Shh," Shem whispered. "Stay still."

Berenice bustled in front of Shem, leading them through dimly lit rooms and glancing back with concern. She pointed through a doorway into a small bedchamber. Mara's breath brushed against his neck, and her eyes stayed closed. He lowered her onto a thick, soft mattress. One bright lamp glowed on an ornate table.

Berenice hovered. Maybe the old woman could help them.

Shem fished a bronze coin from his belt. "I need her clothes and shoes."

"The dress, we threw it in the fire." She stepped back as if expecting a blow.

"Just bring what you can find." He pressed the coin into her bony hand. "And Berenice? Please don't tell anyone." She patted Mara's still shoulder and left the room.

"Mara," he said, kneeling next to her. Was she really sick or was it all an act? "Talk to me. Are you really ill?"

Her eyes opened slowly, as if they were weighted with stones. "I don't know . . . the wine and food. I'm so tired." She closed her eyes again.

"Listen." Shem shook her. This was no time to sleep.

She opened her eyes halfway.

"I have a bad feeling . . . We're not safe here. We should leave now, Mara."

"You leave." She rolled away from him. "Then you can be rid of me." She curled up in a ball, her back to him.

How could she believe that? Shem gripped her shoulder. "Mara, I said those things to protect you. I didn't—Mara, we have to go. Now." He rolled her back toward him.

"Leave me alone."

"Mara, we don't have time for this. We must leave. Remember Nava? Your mother needs you."

"Yes, she needs me." Mara's head nodded as her eyes closed. "We must hurry." Her body went limp, and her face relaxed.

What could he do? She was in no shape to travel. Would they have enough time if he let her sleep just a little while? He was weary as well. He stepped out into the hallway and checked up and down. The house was quiet. Perhaps they could afford to rest a bit. Surely Silas was passed out by now.

He slid down the wall outside the room and curled in a ball in front of the doorway. At least he could make sure that no one visited Mara while she slept. He'd just rest. Not sleep. Someone had to stay awake and keep them both from getting killed.

Mara's eyes snapped open. Where was she? The room was dark. Heavy blankets pressed on her arms and legs, weighing her down as memories of the night filled her mind. Where was Shem? He had wanted to be rid of her. But he had also been worried; he had wanted them to leave. She bolted up and threw the blankets aside.

A creak and a jingle sounded through an open window high on the wall. Then, unmistakably, a horse blowing and stamping. She climbed up on the bed and straightened slowly to peer through the small square.

The moon gleamed low in the sky, but the courtyard was lit by more than its thin white glow. Torchlight fell on three men just dismounting from horses—Roman soldiers in full armor and plumed helmets, swords glinting at their sides. Silas stood at the door, beckoning them in, his words low and rushed. Where was Shem? The soldiers were not here by chance.

She stepped off the bed and felt her way to the door. How

would she ever find him in this sprawling house? She stumbled over something big and firm that blocked the doorway.

It grunted.

The dark shape uncoiled at her feet and came at her. She didn't think, just ran, veering around it. It grabbed at her, snagged her arm, and swung her around. A hand closed over her mouth. She went for its head, clawing desperately.

"What? Mara, stop it!" Shem hissed and pushed her back into the room. He lifted his hand from her mouth as she stopped struggling.

Relief made her legs weak. "Why . . . what were you doing there?"

"Making sure no one visited you."

She didn't want to think about that. She pointed to the window. "Shem, there are soldiers out there."

They both climbed on the bed and peeked out the window. The soldiers were gone, but the steaming horses stood waiting.

Shem went back to the door and peered into the hallway. "This is bad," he whispered. "We need to go. Now." He picked up the bundle from the foot of the bed. "Take this."

It was her cloak and new sandals, smaller than the pair Mechola had given her. How had those gotten here?

"Go through the window. I'll be right behind you."

She pushed the bundle through the window, watched it drop into the bushes below, and glanced back at Shem.

"Hurry," he mouthed.

Mara hoisted herself up to the thick sill and pushed herself head first through the small window. She slid slowly down the outside wall until her upper body was free, then fell with a thud. Dull pain shot through her shoulders, and thorny branches scratched her bare arms. She patted the dark ground, found her bundle, and crawled behind the nearest bush.

She waited. A jackal howled in the distance, and the horses snorted and stamped. Her heart pounded in her chest. Any moment she would hear a shout of discovery.

Shem hit the ground beside her with a muffled grunt. He

was up in an instant. He pointed at the arched entrance to the courtyard and ran toward it, hunched close to the ground. She followed, blood roaring in her ears. They passed under the arch and veered into the dark shadows of the high walls.

Shem crouched close to the wall, breathing hard. "Mara, listen. We'll run through the vineyard. Keep low, and stay close to me. Head for the trees there." He pointed to a dark mass of forest. "But Mara, if they come after us—if they catch me—keep running. It's me they want, not you. Run to the water, and ask for a man named Ezekiel. He's a friend. He'll help you."

Go on alone? "But I—"

He held up a hand. "Mara, I mean it. I won't let them catch us both . . . they'll give you to Silas, and I won't be able to protect you." He swallowed hard. "Promise me you'll run."

Why were they after him? And what was he planning to do, give himself up? For her? Whatever it was, he didn't look ready to answer her questions. Doors slammed, and feet hammered on the tiled surface of the courtyard. Deep voices shouted orders. She nodded. "I'll run. I promise." *And if we make it to safety, you'll tell me what this is about.*

Chapter 27

Shem moved fast, listening to Mara breathe hard behind him. No pounding hooves sounded in the black night. If the soldiers had found them, would he have been able to give himself up and let Mara get away? *Thank the Lord it hadn't come to that.*

He stopped in the darkness of a cedar grove. The carpet of needles was soft underfoot, and the scent brought back memories of Sychar. *I never thought I'd wish to be in Sychar.* Through the trees lay the road to Tiberius. "We will skirt the city and go to the water. From there we can look for Ezekiel. Pray that he is fishing today."

That had been close. Too close. If Mara hadn't woken him . . . Did Silas tell them his name? Would they send men to his home in Caesarea? His father would be able to protect the rest of the family—Ezra's connections in Caesarea assured it—but Shem would never be able to go back to the city.

He felt only relief at that thought. This journey was the worst idea. If they could get away—if he could get Mara back to Sychar—Shem knew exactly what he wanted to do with the rest of his life. Not just to Zevulun and Alexandros. But for Mara. If he was honest with himself, he'd known for a long time.

They scrambled along the trees and bushes that flanked the road. The briny smell of the water grew stronger. As they came within sight of the gates of Tiberius, ramshackle warehouses replaced the trees. Shem crouched behind one, hoping they couldn't be seen. He snuck a look around the corner at the empty road.

This would be dangerous. The soldiers must have finished

searching the house by now. Would they try Tiberius or look for them to the north, on the road to Magdala? There was no way to know.

"We need to get down to the water," he said when they'd both caught their breath. He needed another of Ezra's connections to get them to Capernaum. That is, if their luck held and he could find Ezekiel before the Romans caught up with them.

Mara threw her cloak over the thin dress and buckled her sandals. Across the wide road, a narrow rocky beach harbored a scattering of fishing boats. The sun peeked over the distant mountains, and the pink sky reflected on the smooth water.

"Shem," Mara whispered.

He didn't look at her, didn't want to see the questions that he knew would come. "Shem," she said again, more insistently, reaching out to touch his arm. "What is going on?" she asked. "Why are they after you?"

He didn't answer. What could he say?

The sound of pounding hooves startled them both. With no better place to hide, they pressed themselves close to the building. If the soldiers decided to go around the building, they would be found.

The clatter of hooves stopped near enough that they could hear the creak of the leather saddles.

"Longinus," one soldier commanded, "check with the city gatekeepers. We'll ride toward Magdala."

Longinus? From Caesarea? It couldn't be.

One set of hooves thundered toward the city walls, while the other two soldiers whirled their horses and bolted in the opposite direction.

Shem held his breath, then peeked around the building. The soldier disappeared inside the gate; the other two were already out of sight. "Now." Shem grabbed Mara's hand and hauled her toward the road. "He won't be in there long. Now is our only chance."

They sprinted to the water's edge. Shem searched desperately for a boat—any boat that would take them away from shore. A fisherman mending a net on the narrow beach eyed them. Shem veered toward him. "Do you know of a man called Ezekiel, a fisherman, and his sons?" he asked.

The man worked at a knot. "Ay, I know him."

"Is he here? This morning?" Shem looked over his shoulder at Mara and, beyond her, at the looming gate. They would be in full view if the soldier came out of the gate at this moment.

The man finished tying off a knot before breaking the line with his teeth. "He usually comes in about now." He tipped his head down the beach.

Shem followed his gaze, and his heart jumped. A boat was rowing into the shallow water. He grabbed Mara and ran down the rocky shore.

"Stay here." He planted Mara at the edge of the water and waded out to meet the boat. A huge, burly man crouched at the prow while three other men gathered nets into the flat-bottomed vessel. Shem hadn't seen Ezekiel since last winter when he had made his annual trip to Caesarea to do business with Ezra, but there was no mistaking the big fisherman. He silently thanked his father for keeping his Samaritan heritage quiet. Ezekiel was a Jew, and a Jew wouldn't lift a finger to save a Samaritan—even from the Romans.

The bearlike man looked twice at Shem. "Shem? Ezra's boy?" At Shem's nod, he jumped into the water and splashed toward him.

"Ezekiel." Shem gripped the man's massive shoulders. "Please. I need some help. Can you take us out in the boat? My companion and I?" He glanced back at the city gate, then at Mara standing on the beach, her arms wrapped around her body. It wasn't fair to put them in danger, but he had no other choice. "I'm in trouble."

Ezekiel looked at Mara, raising his bushy brows. "Get in, boy. Then tell us your story."

Mara splashed through the shallows behind Shem, the cold water well above her knees when she reached the boat. Before

Shem could help her up, huge hands lifted her. They stayed on her waist while she gained her balance in the rocking boat. But Ezekiel's smile spread wide and fatherly on his bearded face. He wasn't a bit like Silas. She felt like throwing her arms around him in thanksgiving.

But they weren't out of danger yet. She glanced back at the city gate. No sign of the soldier, just a tanner's cart going through the narrow opening to the city.

Two young men with bare, hairy legs and wild, curly hair stared at her with open mouths. They looked enough alike to be brothers, and an older version stood nearby, clearly their father. And these men were Jews. Did they know that they were helping Samaritans? Mara wrapped her cloak around her clinging dress as the father barked an order at the gawking young men. They jumped and went back to work on the nets.

Shem edged her past the fishermen to the back of the boat. "Sit here. I need to talk to them."

She settled on a pile of wet netting that sparkled with fish scales and smelled of the water. Would these rough men really help them?

As the others made the boat ready to set out again, Shem put his head close to Ezekiel's, talking quickly. The fisherman glanced at Mara while he answered, then to the gate. He clapped Shem on the back with a massive paw and went to work on the sail.

Shem climbed over the nets toward her. His mouth smiled, but his eyes were still worried. "Ezekiel will take us to Capernaum. And the other one, Zebedee"—he raised his chin toward the father—"he knows Jesus, and he knows where he is. You will see him this morning."

Mara gasped. They had done it. They would see him. But what would she say? What would Jesus say? Her stomach twisted like the tangled nets at her feet.

As the fisherman readied the sail, a shout came from the shore. A Roman soldier barreled down the beach on horseback, coming straight toward them. His sword glinted in the sun as he turned his sorrel mount into the lapping waves, urging it toward the boat. Mara clutched at Shem's arm and pointed.

Shem jerked to his feet.

The soldier was close, and the sail wasn't even up. He'd be on them in a moment.

Shem called out to Ezekiel. "It's me they're after." His hand went to the knife at his belt. "I'll buy you some time to get away. Please, take care of her." He grabbed the side of the boat, ready to jump into the water.

Mara grabbed his tunic and pulled. "Shem, no!" What was he thinking?

He leaned down and spoke in a harsh whisper. "I have to. I can't let them arrest everyone! I can't let them take you." He took her hand and pressed it to his cheek—so fast that she had only a quick impression of smooth, warm skin.

"Hold on there, lad," shouted Ezekiel, working furiously to raise the sail. "Here in Galilee, we don't give the Romans what they want if we can help it!"

The brothers whooped and took over the sail.

Zebedee picked up an oar and motioned for Shem to grab the other. "Go deeper. Now!" He stuck his oar in the water and pulled hard.

Shem fumbled with the other oar.

The soldier had almost reached the boat. He was close enough for Mara to see his angry blue eyes and the bright red hair curling below his helmet.

She couldn't just sit there. He was almost on them.

Her hands found a cast net. She lurched to her feet, lifted it high, and threw it with all her strength.

It landed on the horse's outstretched head. The horse reared and splashed, trying to toss off the clinging web. The sword flashed and dropped as the soldier tried to control his horse and not fall into the water.

The wind caught the sail, and the boat jerked into motion, sending Mara tumbling back onto the nets. The Roman gave what sounded like a curse and turned his struggling horse back to shore.

The wind rippled through the sail, and the water slapped at the prow as they skimmed over the waves. The five men stared at Mara, their mouths hanging open. Mara squirmed and twisted her hands in her lap. Why were they looking at her like that?

Then Zebedee began to laugh. "Hoho! What a woman you have brought with you, young man! If you aren't already married to her, my boys could use a wife with her quick wits!" The other men joined in, the brothers eyeing her with extra appreciation.

Shem gave her a shaky smile. He heaved a sigh and turned to the other men. "I'm sorry that I brought this trouble on you."

The big man shook his head, his grin flashed white against his beard. "This isn't the first time we've had trouble with them soldiers. And it won't be the last, either!" He clapped Shem on the back, almost knocking him from his seat. "We'll get you to Capernaum, my boy. And your . . . ?" He raised his brows at Mara.

"Cousin."

"Your cousin . . . she can ride in our boat any time. She'd probably make a fine fisherman."

Shem shipped his oar and moved closer to her. He covered her shaking hands with his. "Mara, you . . ." He blew out a little breath, shaking his head like he didn't know what to say.

He looked at her as he had on the road. As though he admired her.

But those Romans were after him for a reason. It was time for him to tell her what was going on. "Shem? Why are they chasing you?"

His grip on her hands tightened, and his face turned serious. "They've been searching for me since I left Caesarea. Silas knew." He shifted on the pile of nets. "He probably hoped for a fat reward for me . . . and a good price for you from the slave traders."

Since he left Caesarea? "But why?"

Shem dropped her hands and twisted his own into the nets. "Mara." He didn't look at her. "I was sent to Sychar to hide. I killed a soldier. I didn't mean to—that is why I had to cut my hair, shave my beard. My parents sent me to Sychar to protect me."

Killed a soldier? A Roman? "You killed a Roman? How? I mean, why?"

Shem pulled at the twisted nets, tangling the fine cords with every word. "It was stupid. I tried to help a woman. My brother was there—he was drunk. The soldier, not my brother. I didn't mean to kill him."

He wasn't making any sense. "So you were supposed to be hiding in Sychar? But you insisted on coming with me? If they had captured you . . . If they find you . . ." Mara struggled to catch up, tensing as she realized the meaning of his words. "Shem. You'd be crucified."

"I know." He stood like he wanted to walk away. But there was nowhere for him to go. He sat down again. "And I've put you in even more danger now that they've seen you. They'll be heading to Capernaum. I'm sorry, Mara. I've done a terrible job of keeping you safe."

But he was wrong. He'd carried her to her room, slept outside her door, protected her. He'd risked his life to help her and her family. The tiny seed of hope, planted along the road in Galilee, sprouted. Without her permission. Without warning. *He really does care for me.* She'd asked herself all along why he was helping her, and now—as hard as it was to believe—she thought she knew. She had to ask, had to know for sure. "Shem, why did you come with me?"

He took a deep breath and stared at the floor of the boat. "I didn't want to tell you. Not now. Not like this." He leaned forward. "It is my fault that your mother was stoned."

Shem's fault? No. It was Nava's sins, Zevulun's pride. Not Shem's fault.

His words came out in a rush, as though he'd been holding them in. "I didn't know . . . I followed you from the olive garden that night. I saw Alexandros's donkey at your house. The next morning, Adah was visiting my grandmother. She was looking for him, and I told her . . ."

Mara's breath clogged her throat. He saw Alexandros. He was the one who let the secret out. *He thinks the stoning was his fault.*

She shook her head. No. This wasn't what she had hoped to hear.

"Yes. It was me. I told her that he was there, at your house. I didn't know just you and your mother lived there." He let the rest of his breath out in a whoosh.

The sprout of hope shriveled and died.

She dragged in enough breath to speak. "You came with me, because you felt guilty? Because you thought it was your fault?" Not for her. Not because he cared for her. Out of guilt.

"Please forgive me, Mara."

Of course she forgave him. There was nothing to forgive. He was a good man. It hadn't been his fault, but he thought it was and he had tried to make it right. It was her own foolishness that she couldn't forgive.

She crossed her arms over her heart. "Shem, it wasn't your fault. It would have happened someday, probably soon. My mother is—was—unwise. You know that she had enemies who wanted this to happen. I just wish . . ."

"What?" he urged.

I wish you'd told me before. In the dark, in Sychar. Not in the bright light, with the water all around them. Not where she had to look at his face. Not where she had nowhere to run. She scooted away from him on the damp netting. He didn't believe in the Taheb, or Nava, or her.

"I wish you had told me this before we left."

"I'm sorry. I didn't know how." Shem spread his hands wide. "I don't know any other way to help you, Mara, so I will get you to Jesus. It is the least that I can do for you and your mother."

The least he could do. To alleviate his guilt. Of course he had his reasons for helping her. What did she expect? That he would put himself in danger just to be near her? Men like Shem—respectable, rich men from good families—didn't help people like her without a reason.

It was ridiculous to feel disappointed, as though he had let her down. Finding Jesus was all that mattered—healing her mother. A thought nagged at her, circling and pecking like a desert vulture. Maybe Jesus wouldn't help her. Why should he?

Zebedee walked gracefully down the length of the rocking boat. "I hear you go to see the Rabbi, Jesus?" he asked Shem.

She sat up straighter. Maybe he knew something of Jesus. Shem gave her a warning glance, and she bit back her questions.

"Do you know him?" Shem asked for her.

"My oldest boys follow him," he said, with a hint of pride. His bushy beard and unruly hair gave him the look of a wild animal, but his smile was kind. "Many come to him. He can hardly stay in one place without crowds following him."

"Why do they come?" Shem asked abruptly, then, "I mean, he is wise. Do they all come to hear his teaching? That is a surprise among the working men of Galilee."

Zebedee grunted. "Yes, it takes more than wisdom to bring Galileans out of the water. We are not known for our scholars, but for our strength and toughness." He flexed a burly arm, and at the last word, his laugh sounded more like a growl. He looked from Shem to Mara. "No. Have you not heard? He cured an official's son. The boy was near death just days ago."

Mara sucked in her breath and leaned toward the older man.

But Zebedee directed his story at Shem. "One of the officials of Capernaum—Chuza is his name—he knew Jesus, had welcomed him into his home many times. His son was very sick, near to death, we heard. We told him that Jesus had been expected back from Jerusalem for days but wasn't here yet.

"The man was beside himself with worry. Chuza said he'd ride out to meet Jesus and his followers. I heard from my boys after—he'd found them in Cana. Chuza begged Jesus to come back with him, to cure his son. Jesus just said, 'Go back. Your son will live.'"

Mara reached out to Shem, clutching at his arm. Jesus had cured a dying boy. She may have been wrong about Shem, but she was right about Jesus. He was the Taheb.

Shem's brow creased, and his eyes narrowed. "What happened?"

Zebedee sat back on his heels with a satisfied grin. "Chuza came rushing home, and his servants met him halfway. They said that the boy had sat up, and the fever left him just at the hour that Jesus had spoken the words. He's fine now. I've seen him myself when I delivered fish to Chuza's house. It's that big estate on the hill above Capernaum. Chuza is a good and upright man."

A good and upright man. Mara's confidence ebbed. Would the Taheb have mercy on Nava? He knew of her sins, she said, and had forgiven her. But that was then, in Samaria. Would he cure a Samaritan—an adulterous Samaritan woman—here in Galilee?

Mara's own guilt seeped through her like venom, poisoning her thoughts. At the very moment that Jesus had cured her mother, she'd been wishing her dead. *We would be better off without her, that's what I thought. And I'd meant it.* Why should the Taheb help someone like her? Wishing her mother dead, traveling with a man, dressed like a harlot?

Shem was not smiling. He rubbed the back of his neck. He was doubting, but not for the same reasons. Shem doubted the Taheb. Mara doubted herself.

Chapter 28

Mara watched the rocky beach grow closer as the sun burned away the last wisps of mist curling over the waves. Bobbing boats and a scattering of huts along the beach gave way to narrow streets and squat-roofed houses. Shem and Zebedee's sons rowed the boat into the shallow waters and threw an anchor overboard. This was Capernaum, where they would find the Taheb.

Anxiety squeezed her throat like an icy hand. She couldn't even swallow. What if she came all this way and failed?

Zebedee jumped into the water and stretched out his arms to Mara. She put her hands on his broad shoulders and let him lift her off the boat. Zebedee held her arm as she waded to the rocky shore.

"Are you all going with us to see Jesus?" Shem asked.

"The fish will wait," said one of the sons. "We will say good-bye to the Rabbi and our brothers before they leave for Jerusalem. I hope we haven't missed them."

Mara trailed behind the hurrying men. Her legs trembled, and her feet felt like they were made of stone. They passed drying shacks where great piles of scales and fish guts reeked in the morning sun. In moments, they were turning down a narrow street. Walls rose on both sides, and the smell of fish faded.

Zebedee opened a high gate without a pause and entered a courtyard overflowing with flowering shrubs and trees. He ushered Shem in, and Mara slipped after him like a shadow. There were so many people! Men who looked like fishermen, others dressed in fine robes and gold rings. There were James and John, saying good-bye to women and children. They called out a welcome when they saw Zebedee, then all the men seemed to be talking at once.

Mara shrank back into the shadow of a fig tree. Where was Jesus? Perhaps he wasn't here. Relief whispered through her. If he was gone, she wouldn't have to talk to him.

Finally, Zebedee remembered his guests and waved Shem forward. Shem took Mara's elbow and pulled her with him. Her feet dragged, but her pulse pounded.

Zebedee put his hand on Peter's shoulder. Peter listened as Zebedee spoke in his ear, his surprised gaze going to Shem. He didn't even glance at Mara. "From Sychar? Abahu's grandson?" He wasn't unkind, but he was loud. The good-byes and chatter faded. Every face turned to her and Shem.

"You're Samaritans?" Zebedee asked, his bushy brows raised in surprise.

One of the finely dressed men stepped back from them. "Samaritans!"

A woman pulled her child closer. "Don't touch them."

Shem curved his arm behind him as if to protect Mara from the crowd. But then the crowd parted, and one man stepped forward.

There he was. Jesus. The Taheb. Mara's heart lodged in her throat.

"Jesus, travelers from Samaria, asking to see you." Peter turned to Shem. "Be quick, we leave for Jerusalem now."

Shem stepped forward.

"Here you are, Shem." Jesus' face creased into a smile. "It is good to see you again."

Mara stepped back. She inched behind a big man in a fine linen robe. She couldn't talk to the Taheb. Not now. Not with all these people around. All these Jews who hated them.

Shem didn't make a move toward Jesus, but Jesus went to him, pulling him into an embrace and whispering into his ear. Shem's face contorted, and he tried to pull away. He asked Jesus a question in Greek.

What was going on? Shem's face was hard and blank. His body went rigid like he was ready to run.

Jesus seemed to be giving instructions. Were they talking of Nava? Mara heard the word "Jerusalem," and Shem tried to step back from Jesus. Jesus finished speaking but kept his hands on Shem's shoulders. Shem nodded but looked bewildered.

Jesus turned to his followers, his right hand still on Shem's shoulder. "He will be named Stephen, and he will be the first of many. Stephen," he said to Shem, "I will see you in Jerusalem."

What was that about? Jesus—the Taheb—wanted Shem to go to Jerusalem? Jesus acted like he had been waiting for Shem. Like he'd called Shem to Capernaum. But Shem looked confused and something else. She'd seen that look before. He was angry.

He twisted around and spied Mara. He reached her in one stride and pulled her from her hiding place. "Jesus, this is why we are here. This girl needs to speak to you."

The people stared at her. She could feel their eyes on her hair, the black ribbon on her forehead, her flimsy dress. She glanced down. Her robe gaped open, showing too much skin. Doubt filled her throat, choking her. She was sinful, too. She'd traveled alone with a man. She was dressed like a pagan whore. She had wished her mother dead. He had known of Nava's sins; he would surely know of hers.

She dropped her head, staring at the ground, and tried to swallow. The words she had prayed a hundred times screamed in her mind. *Jesus. Taheb. Please. Heal my mother.* But nothing came out.

Mara squeezed her eyes shut. She heard the breathing of the men around her, their hushed expectation. She smelled the dust and the faint odor of fish, and felt the warm sun on her face. No. She was not worthy to speak to the Taheb. Not Mara, the daughter of Nava. Her heart had brimmed with hope when she heard him call, but now it was full of nothing but doubt and guilt.

She twisted and ran through the crowd, pushed through the gate, and rushed blindly down the narrow alley.

She reached the beach, the sun hot on her shoulders. Salty

tears ran into her mouth, and the smell of dead fish flavored every gasping breath. Why had she thought she could speak to the Taheb? She wasn't worthy. She must have been wrong when she thought he'd called to her in her dream. But it had been so real. She had been so sure.

She was a fool. Her mother would die. Any hope of a respectable life in Sychar was over if they found out she was gone. If she were lucky—if he would still have her—she would marry Jobab. But who would care for Asher? All because she thought that the Taheb—the Chosen One of God!—would help her, a stupid, ignorant girl. She wasn't worthy to touch him. She crouched down on the beach and wrapped her arms around her legs, curling into a ball.

It was over.

A rough shake roused her from her misery. Shem towered over her.

"There you are. What are you doing? Come! We can catch him on the road if we hurry!"

She wrenched her arm away. "No."

"What do you mean?" He pulled at her hands, but she hooked them around her drawn-up knees. "This is what we came for, Mara. What you wanted. Come on!"

The clatter of iron-shod hooves on stone made them both freeze. Shem moved first, pulling her up and pointing to a drying shack down the beach. They sprinted to it and ducked through the low door.

Slatted walls were hung with drying racks from floor to low ceiling. Mara put her hand over her nose and crouched in the farthest corner. The smell of fish wrapped around them like a damp blanket. Through the gaps in the walls, they saw the two soldiers that had gone north from Tiberius. Shouts in Latin were followed by familiar voices, Zebedee and his sons.

"A man and girl?

"Hmm. Did he have a scar? Yes?"

Mara clutched at Shem's arm. Would Zebedee betray them now that he knew they were Samaritans?

The fisherman pointed away from the beach. "Might have seen them north of the city. Heading to Damascus."

The clatter of hooves receded until only the buzz of flies, and their own frightened breath filled the silence. They were safe for now.

"Mara," Shem whispered. "What happened back there?"

She could ask him the same thing. What had the Taheb said to him? Why had he looked like he had been waiting for Shem to arrive? "I couldn't ask him. He . . . wouldn't heal her."

"What?" Shem started upward, then lowered his voice and glanced out at the road. "So you don't believe that he's the Taheb?"

"Don't believe—" She stared up at him. "Of course I believe. He is the Taheb. That was why I couldn't ask him."

What, exactly, had happened back there in the courtyard?

"There you are, Shem." He'd said it like he'd been waiting for Shem. Like he'd known that Shem would come. And he had.

Shem grabbed her hand and pulled her out of the shack. Zebedee and his sons were already in the boat, waving to them to hurry. They splashed through the shallows, and Shem heaved Mara into the boat.

Zebedee pulled Shem up. "The teacher told us to get you out of Capernaum. Not to Tiberius," he added. "We'll take you to a cove near Magdala." One of the sons watched the beach while the other one and his father hurried to raise the sail.

Shem pulled Mara down onto the nest of fishing nets. She dropped her head close to his and whispered, "What did he say to you?"

Shem jerked back like she'd bitten him. "Who? Jesus?"

"The Taheb. What did he say to you back there?"

Shem scooted a handsbreadth away. "Nothing. Nonsense." His face turned angry again, just like in the courtyard. "Something about going to Jerusalem, to a man named Joseph of Arimathea. Of meeting him there."

"He changed your name. Why?"

Shem raised his hands. "I don't know. He speaks in riddles, as always." He pushed his hands through his hair. "Said that I would be the first of many. Blood and water and his church. Sacrifice." He closed his eyes and pinched his fingers on the bridge of his nose. "He's crazy."

The pieces started to fit together, like mending a broken cup. She had thought all along that she'd been called to Jesus. Called to help Nava. But that wasn't it. She had been called for a reason—of that she was sure now—but the reason was Shem.

The boat pitched and rocked. Mara grabbed the side with both hands.

Of course Jesus wanted Shem to follow him. He was a good man. Well-learned, just, full of compassion. But Shem needed a reason to go to Jesus. And that reason was her. Now Shem must follow his call. Shem must go to Jerusalem and do what Jesus had asked. He was to be part of the Taheb's plan for his people.

So, was all the rest—the stoning, her own hopeless situation—also part of the Taheb's plan?

A gust of wind filled the sail, and the boat glided into deep water.

Sometimes the Almighty let bad things happen to accomplish his plan. Joseph had to be in Egypt to save Jacob's family, the Chosen People, from the famine. But he didn't go there on his own. No. His brothers threw him down a well. They sold him to the Ishmaelites, and he was made a slave. Only then could he rise to lead the Egyptians and show God's power.

Mara leaned back, adjusting to the rhythm of the waves hitting the prow. "What, exactly, did he say?"

Shem let out a breath as though he'd rather talk of anything else. "He said, 'Your time will come soon. Your suffering will be united to mine.'" He rested his forehead on his hands, "What is that supposed to mean? I don't believe any of it."

Mara's heart constricted. What could it mean? Would Shem help the Taheb usher in the age of peace? Would he reveal the truth to his people? "Shem, you must go. Like Joseph. Go to Jerusalem."

"What?" He grabbed her hand. "I'm not going to Jerusalem. Stop talking nonsense. I'm taking you back to Sychar. I won't leave you."

Won't leave me? Joy flared in her. Had her hopes been right about him? Could he really care for her? His hand was warm and felt good and right wrapped around hers. Yes, something more than guilt had brought him on this journey. She could see it in the way he looked at her; she could feel it in his touch. But her joy just as quickly dimmed. *It doesn't matter now.* She must make him see—he had been called by the Taheb, to Jerusalem. To do what, she didn't know any more than he did. But it was important. More important than her dreams of a life with him. Those were foolish dreams, anyway.

If he wouldn't follow Jesus' call, everything she'd given up— her mother, her chances of happiness in Sychar—would all be in vain. She pulled her hand out of his grip. "You will take me home, Shem. Then you'll go to Jerusalem."

Chapter 29

Women. Who could understand them?

She had to get to Jesus, because he was the Taheb. Then she couldn't speak to him, because he was the Taheb. Now she was going on about Joseph and a well and Jerusalem. What was she thinking? That he would leave her and follow this madman? *I'm not going to follow him. Not now. Not ever.*

Zebedee guided the boat into knee-deep water. "The path goes up the hill. From there, you will find the road to Cana." He pulled Shem into a rough embrace. "Safe journey, my son."

Shem nodded. *We aren't safe anywhere.* Where would the soldiers be by now? "Thank you for your help." Jews helping Samaritans—another surprise in a day full of mystery.

The big man grasped his shoulders and leaned close. "Look after the Messiah in Jerusalem. And be careful. He has many enemies."

Shem hopped out of the boat, then helped Mara into the water. The men pushed the boat out into the lake and were gone. He waded ashore, holding Mara's arm until she got her footing on the beach. *I don't need more enemies. And I'm not going to Jerusalem.*

Now, when they were almost to Cana, the sun blazed over their heads. His eyes burned from the glare, and dust coated his mouth. He'd spent the last of his money on food. Now it too was gone, and they dare not stop again. Those soldiers could be right behind them.

Taking this road was a mistake. If Shem were a soldier, he would be searching the towns around the Lake of Galilee, asking questions, looking for two strangers. It would be just a matter of time before they found answers. Their luck couldn't hold for much longer.

His thoughts chased each other in circles like a pack of wild dogs. *"You will be the first of many,"* the Jew had said. What did that mean? Shem had gone over the words of Jesus a hundred times, but they still didn't make any sense.

And the things he had told him to do. Told him—not asked. Why? Why should he turn his back on everything—everyone— and follow this madman to Jerusalem? They would be lucky if they even made it back to Sychar alive. And if they did, he would stay there . . . with Mara.

He turned his scrutiny outward. They were still in danger. The cliffs on each side of the road were dotted with dark mouths of caves. Anyone could be hiding in them. He studied the road ahead of them, then the hill they had just climbed. Not a single soul. Not even the dust stirred.

They had passed only a few travelers since Magdala. None had given them more than a second glance. Perhaps they *would* be able to get to Sychar before the soldiers found them.

The sun dipped toward the west while the road rose upward again. At the top of the hill, the slap of Mara's sandals ceased. He turned to see her standing, hunched and panting, in the middle of the road. He strode back to her, pulling at the cork on his water skin.

He gave it to her, and she took a long drink. Sweat trickled down her face. Her eyes were glassy and unfocused. "How much farther?"

"Not much farther to Cana. Then it will be easier—downhill. We'll stop in Nazareth."

"Why Nazareth?"

"Jesus gave me a message for his mother. And she'll give us food and a place to rest." He'd give Mary the message from her son. That he could do. But that was all. Jesus' other demands were out of the question. Behind Mara, the lush valley of the Jordan wound its way to Jerusalem. No. He wouldn't go there.

"Can you go on?" he asked.

She nodded, and they fell back into line—he plodding ahead, she following a few steps behind. No stories or talk broke the silence as it had when they had followed this road just yesterday. When Mara had spoken of hope and had been so sure of the Taheb. What had changed her mind?

They reached the cedar grove where they had eaten figs and pistachios. The last time they had passed this spot, he had told Mara that it was ridiculous to hope for a miracle. Had she actually believed him? Was he the reason she had run from Jesus?

Before them, Galilee stretched green and gold, and far in the distant west glowed the blue haze of the sea. The rolling hills of Samaria flowed to the south, where they would find her mother. And what if they found Nava still unconscious or, worse, dead? It would break Mara's heart. But he would make it up to her. He would make her and Asher safe and happy in Sychar.

He plodded down into the next valley. Ezra would be in Sychar when they returned. He'd help Shem get justice. Then Shem would settle in Sychar with his grandparents. He would be happy, raising olives and children with Mara. He didn't need to follow a charlatan to Jerusalem and get into more trouble.

They reached the gate of Nazareth as the shadows began to grow long.

"Where is the house of Mary, the mother of Jesus?" Had it been just yesterday that they had spoken to the same surly shopkeeper?

They walked through the narrow streets to a tiny clay house. No courtyard separated the house from the dusty street, but flowers bloomed around the doorway.

"Are you Mary, the mother of Jesus?" Shem asked the woman who came at his first call. Dainty, bare feet peeked out from under her plain, coarse tunic. Although small and delicate as a girl, she had to be at least as old as his own mother. Soft brown eyes that were very much like her son's appraised him.

"You must be Shem," she said.

He stepped back. What was this? Some kind of magic? "How do you know me?"

"A man came, around midday. He asked for you and said you'd be traveling with a girl." She tipped her head around Shem to smile at Mara.

A man? "A soldier?"

"No, not a soldier. Tobias, the tentmaker, offered him food and rest. You might still find him there." She pointed back toward the market. "The big house, with the fountain in front."

Ezra? Here in Nazareth? He could have decided to track Shem down after not finding him in Sychar. That would be very much like his impatient father. Shem turned to Mara. She was pale and swayed on her feet.

Mary held out her hands. "Come, child. Stay with me and rest."

Shem put his arms on Mara's shoulders and guided her to Mary. "I thank you. And when I return, I have a message from your son." He squeezed Mara's shoulders. "Stay here. I'll be back soon."

Shem found the house with the fountain in front. It was the largest he'd seen in Nazareth, but hardly big. A rotund man with a hooked nose and very crooked teeth welcomed him inside the courtyard.

"Ah! You are Shem. I told your friend that you would come through Nazareth again, and here you are."

"Is my father still here?"

"Your father? I—"

"Shem!" A shout rang out from inside the house.

Was his father that happy to see him? But it wasn't his father's bulky form that rushed out the door.

"Drusus." What was he doing here?

"I'm so glad you are here. I didn't know what I would tell your father." Drusus said in slurred Aramaic. He carried a cup in one hand, an empty wineskin in the other.

"Where is Ezra? Is he in Sychar? Did he get my message?"

Drusus looked about to fall down. The tentmaker watched them, his curved nose pointing first at Shem, then at Drusus.

Speaking Greek, Shem said, "Come with me." He dragged the servant to the farthest corner, waving away the tentmaker's offer of food and drink. Drusus had clearly had enough of that.

When they were seated on a bench, he leaned over the little man. "Where is my father?"

"In Caesarea."

Shem clenched his jaw. What had gone wrong? "Did he get my message? I asked him to meet me in Sychar."

Drusus cowered and snuck another sip of his wine. "Yes. He got the message. I'm surprised you didn't hear his roar. He said he was through getting you out of trouble."

"Getting me out of—" Shem slammed his hand on the bench. "This isn't my trouble." But it was, wasn't it? "This was an unjust trial. These men deserved to be punished. He has to help me."

"He said the only help you'd get is coming back to Caesarea with me. And that I'd better return with you, or you wouldn't see another sestertius from him."

"What?" Shem grabbed Drusus by the shoulders. Drusus lost his grip on the cup. It dropped on the bench, and red wine splashed over Shem's cloak. "What do you mean? I'm not going back to Caesarea. I'm going to Sychar. To make sure these men are punished."

"Not according to your father, you aren't." Drusus upended the wineskin in his mouth, then dropped it to the floor. "He said to let the men in Sychar handle the women. He wants you back. Said you need to be where he can keep an eye on you. So you don't get into any more trouble. Says you have a soft spot for loose women."

"Loose women!" Shem's voice rose in the stillness. "Where did he hear that?"

"Word travels fast."

He felt like he'd been kicked in the gut. His father didn't know the whole story, and he wasn't even willing to listen. Why did he ever think Ezra would help him? "What about the Romans? They are still after me."

"The centurion said there's trouble in Jerusalem. They are sending troops there—only a few left in Caesarea. Plus there was a string of murders in the Greek quarter. They aren't searching for you anymore."

At least three are. And the red-haired one—Longinus—has good reason to keep searching.

Drusus's eyelids drooped. "He said to get you back by tomorrow. We could stay here tonight. Start out in the morning." He slumped against the wall and closed his eyes.

Shem stood and paced in front of the bench.

He'd never blatantly disobeyed his father. He tapped his hand against his thigh. He could take Mara to Caesarea with him. They would marry and live with his family. But what about Asher? Ezra wouldn't welcome a crippled boy; he could hardly tolerate Benjamin. Mara would be miserable, and so would he.

I won't leave her. Not after what happened in Capernaum. She'd need him more than ever now. Ezra had let him down. He wasn't interested in justice, just his own agenda. Shem owed him nothing now, and he'd make sure that his father knew it.

He bent over Drusus and shook him. "Drusus."

The man's head wobbled back and forth, and his eyes opened a crack.

"Go back to Caesarea. Tell my father I'm betrothed to the daughter of that loose woman."

"Whaa?" Drusus sat up straight. "But he'll—he'll . . . Please, Shem." He clutched at the front of Shem's tunic. "Don't make me do this."

"Tell him exactly this." Shem waited for Drusus's full attention. "Tell him I'll be the best-educated olive grower in Sychar, thanks to him."

Drusus paled.

"And tell him—by the time he gets the message, I'll already be betrothed, and there is nothing he can do about it. I'll send mother word of the wedding. She'll want to be there."

Shem left Drusus groaning on the bench, his head in his hands.

He'd never again have to take orders from Ezra. And he'd

have to support himself and a family. Abahu would take him in, even without Ezra's blessing. Abahu would help him get the bride price. Mechola would welcome Mara and Asher into their home. *I'll have my whole life to find a way to get justice for Nava. My whole life with Mara.*

Mara shuffled through the tiny house behind the dainty woman. Was she really the mother of the Taheb? *As long as she has a little food and a place for me to sleep tonight.*

The patch of garden behind the house smelled of rosemary and barley. Mary slipped off Mara's cloak. She washed the dust from Mara's feet and hands with lavender-scented water, then guided her to a woven rug under the shade of a fig tree.

Muscle and bone protested as Mara lowered herself to the ground. Her body hurt from the soles of her feet to the crown of her head.

From the cooking pot over the fire, Mary spooned hot fava beans onto a round of warm barley bread. She sat beside Mara in silence as she ate. What did this good woman think of her revealing Greek dress? Or her traveling with a man?

She finished her food and drank three cups of cool water. "Thank you. I'm sorry . . ." She fluttered a hand over the front of her dress.

Mary shook her head. She pulled Mara toward her, resting her head on her shoulder and stroking her hair. "Rest, child. You traveled far to see my son."

Somehow, she knew this woman already. Like a friend she hadn't seen in a long time. "But my mother will still die. She may be dead already."

"My son says that not even a sparrow falls without his father's knowledge."

Mara's eyes closed, lulled by the sound of the droning bees in the garden and Mary's soft hands on her hair.

"He is really the Taheb? The Messiah?" She cracked open her eyes.

Mary nodded.

"He told Shem to meet him in Jerusalem. But Shem says he isn't going."

Mary smiled. "I have seen many come to believe in my son. And many who reject him. I think that, for some, faith is a gift. For others, it can only enter a heart with great effort. Some run to him; others turn away. But he keeps calling."

A shuffle and a low voice called from the front of the house. Heavy footsteps followed. Shem appeared in the courtyard.

Mary rose, brought water and food, and set it before Shem.

He ate quickly and in silence. His movements were jerky, and his mouth turned down. Mara knew that look. He was angry. More angry than she'd ever seen him. Whoever had been waiting for him did not have good news. Was it about Nava?

Shem finished, wiped his mouth, and spoke to Mary. "Jesus asked you to meet him in Jerusalem. He left this morning, by the Jordan road." He held out his bowl to Mary. "Thank you for the food and rest. We must go."

"Do you not want to stay here tonight? Mara is—"

"No." Shem shoved the bowl into her hands. "We must go now."

Mara stifled a groan. There was no sense arguing with him when he was like this. She let Shem pull her up. Her legs were stronger. The hollow feeling in her middle was gone, and her throat no longer felt coated with dust.

Mara embraced Mary. "Thank you. For everything."

Shem was already shifting from foot to foot and inching toward the road.

Mary pulled her close and whispered in her ear. "Pray. Help him to hear the call. And do not be afraid when the time comes."

To Shem, she said, "Good-bye, my son. We will meet again soon."

Shem jerked his head down in what might have passed for assent. He turned and almost ran toward the marketplace.

Mara hurried to catch up. *Do not be afraid when the time comes.* She would not be afraid anymore. *He keeps calling.* She would make sure Shem listened. She would persuade Shem to follow Jesus to Jerusalem—somehow—no matter what the cost.

Shem's pace slowed as they approached the city gate. A crowd had gathered, and angry shouts rang through the air. Her heart sped up as she peered around him. Was someone looking for them?

Voices rang out from the crowd. "Stay away! Get away from here!"

About ten paces away, a group of men were pushed up against a wall of rock. They held their hands over their heads and faces, protecting themselves from a rain of stones, but even from a distance Mara could tell they were lepers.

"What is going on here?" Shem muttered. "Stay here." He pushed his way to the front of the mob.

Mara craned her neck to watch him.

He knocked the stones from the hands of those in front. "Stop! What have these poor wretches done to deserve this?"

"They were entering the town! They will spread their disease among us!" A few more stones flew through the air.

Shem turned to the lepers. Some were injured already. Blood soaked their bandaged hands and faces. "What is the meaning of this? Why are you here?"

One man stepped forward to speak. Mara caught her breath as she recognized the dignified leper from Dotham. He bowed to Shem, "Thank you for your help, again," he said. "I am Melech. We seek the healer, the Nazarene. We were told he was here."

"You seek Jesus?" Shem asked.

The lepers nodded; there were at least ten of them in the group.

A man behind Shem shouted, "Go away! He's not here!"

Shem turned on the man with a look that made him step back. "I'll take care of this. Leave now. Go about your business."

The men in the crowd grumbled but scattered. Some spit in the direction of the lepers; some shook their fists at Shem.

Mara crept closer as the crowd broke up. She stared at their leader. His mouth and eyes were the only parts of his face not misshapen by the disease. His nose, cheeks, and chin were covered in crusted red sores and black decaying flesh. On one hand three of his fingers were gone; the rest were wrapped in dirty linen.

Shem stood only a few paces from the lepers. "Jesus is not here."

Melech's shoulders sagged. "We were told that he could heal us."

Shem glanced back at Mara. "Go back to your home."

Should she tell them? She hadn't even had the courage to ask Jesus to heal her mother. How could she offer hope when she had none herself? She pushed in front of Shem. "We spoke with him this morning. He is traveling to Jerusalem. You could find him there."

The men murmured hopefully to one another.

Shem gripped her arm and pulled her back. "What are you doing? These men can barely walk. Don't send them on a foolish journey to Jerusalem."

She ignored him and gazed into the ravaged face of the man in front of her. "Do not be afraid; he is the Taheb, the Messiah."

"Thank you." Melech bowed. "Bless you. We are again in your debt."

Chapter 30

S hem led Mara south toward the hills of Samaria. He walked fast, his feet trying to keep up with his racing thoughts. He cringed at the thought of Ezra's rage at his message. *I only hope Benjamin will stay out of his way.* But Ezra deserved it. *He abandoned me, just when I needed him the most.*

Mara walked beside him, her steps sure and even, as though she'd received more than food and rest in Nazareth. What had gotten into her? Sending the lepers to Jerusalem on the flimsy hope of a cure from a man who claimed to be the Taheb. A man she hadn't even been able to ask to cure her mother. Her foolish faith made no sense.

And what of Jesus' mother, Mary? He knew one thing. He wouldn't meet her again soon. Not in Jerusalem, at least.

As the road curved sharply, they rounded the bend. Just ten steps away, a soldier bent over a spring. His horse stood close by, slurping water from the shallow pool.

Shem jerked to a stop. *How could I be so careless?*

The horse snorted, and the Roman looked up, straight at them. Red hair framed his pale face.

Shem froze. Longinus.

For a moment, the soldier's blue eyes were blank, then recognition flashed—first at Mara, then at Shem. "You!" he shouted in Latin, drawing his sword at the same time that he lunged toward them. He grabbed Mara before Shem could even pull his knife. His thick arm wrapped around her waist, and he pulled her close to him, holding the sword at her exposed neck.

Shem gripped his knife in shaking hands. The soldier circled around him, dragging Mara.

"The gods smiled on me for staying behind. Now I have two prisoners to take back to Caesarea. The man who killed my friend and"—he squeezed Mara closer—"this pretty girl."

"Go," Mara mouthed silently at Shem. "Run."

As if he would leave her. Shem stepped forward. "Let her go. Now," he said in Latin. So this was it. He would have to pay for his sin. But he would not make Mara pay as well. At least he could do that for her.

The soldier laughed. "Put that little dagger down, and I won't have to kill you with it. I'm not drunk. You won't win this time."

Shem raised the knife higher. *I don't plan on winning. And I won't kill again.*

Mara struggled, and Longinus pulled her tighter against him.

A burn of anger crept up Shem's spine. "It might be difficult to get us both. There is only one of you. Let her go; it's me you want."

The soldier glanced over his shoulder at the empty road. No help marched down the road from Nazareth. Mara struggled again, and he growled a curse.

"I'll make you a deal," Shem said. "You can have me without a fight. But you can't have her. Let her go, and I won't fight." He hoped Mara didn't understand what he had just said.

"You are not in a position to be making deals," the soldier growled, but his hand tightened on his sword. The polished metal flashed as the sword dug into Mara's skin. A thin line of blood trickled down her neck. She didn't cry out, but her frightened eyes locked on Shem's face.

"You can have me. Without a fight. Or take your chances against us both. You know she's not afraid to help."

Longinus glanced behind again at the empty road. He loosened his grip. "It's your lucky day, girl. Get out of here." He pushed her away. "Now, drop the knife."

Shem's shoulders sagged, and he dropped his knife on the ground.

"No!" Mara stood between them, looking from one to the other.

"Go, Mara," Shem said, his eyes still on the soldier. "Run."

Mara's mouth tightened into a stubborn line. "No."

His glanced flicked toward her. "Go. Now." *Please, Mara. Please, go.*

She crossed her arms like a stubborn child. "No, Shem. I won't."

Frustration rose up in his throat. Couldn't she see this was the only way?

But Mara's eyes widened, and her mouth dropped open as she looked past the triumphant soldier, where the road curved behind his back.

Shem followed her gaze. Around the bend in the road, an unlikely army marched to their rescue.

Dark rags flapped in the wind, revealing dirty white wrappings on faces and hands. The lepers approached.

What were they doing? They were on their way to Jerusalem, of course. They must have been close behind all along. The leader, Melech, held up his hand to slow his raggedy band. He looked from Shem to the soldier to Mara. "Do you need some help, here, my friend?" he called out.

Shem lunged for his knife and stepped in front of Mara as the soldier spun toward the lepers. "Get away, filthy dogs!" the soldier shouted in stilted Aramaic. "This is not your concern."

"Oh, but it is," Melech replied. At a quick command from him, the other lepers moved in fast, surrounding the soldier, cutting him off from Shem and Mara.

"Get . . . get away, I said!" the soldier swung his sword at the approaching men. His movements were uncertain, and his voice held a note of panic.

"Let our friends here go, and we'll be on our way as well," Melech advised.

"Get away from me, I tell you. I'll cut you apart!" the soldier yelled. The lepers surrounded him in a tight circle.

"Go ahead," one of the lepers taunted. His face was covered in sores, and where his nose had once been there was a gaping black hole. "You'd be doing me a favor. I'd rather die a quick death by a Roman sword than a lingering one like this. But know this: I'll make sure my blood gets on you. You'll look just like me within the month!"

Shem backed away. He must protect Mara from the soldier and keep her away from the lepers. The road was right behind him. But how could he get Mara out of this mess without leaving the lepers to fight and probably die?

The soldier's horse stamped and whinnied.

Melech darted up to the big animal. As he pulled its head down and whispered in its ear, the horse calmed and stood still. "Get on, both of you," Melech ordered.

Steal the horse and run away? Let them fight for him?

"But your men—"

"Go! We'll worry about the soldier."

Shem looked from the soldier—screaming at the lepers—to the horse. He'd ridden before, but never one this big. The square, four-horned saddle seemed very far away. But what other choice did he have?

Shem grabbed the dangling bridle. Melech held the horse's head, keeping well away from Shem. Shem jumped, throwing himself on the saddle. He pulled himself up and threw a leg over, bunching up his tunic and cloak.

"Mara! Come on!" he yelled, holding out his hand to her. She stepped away from the big animal. Shem urged the horse closer to her. "Jump!" he said.

She took a deep breath and jumped, grabbing the back pommel with her other hand. He pulled hard, and she landed half on his lap, half on her side in front of him. He gave the horse a kick while she pulled her body over the saddle.

He raised a hand to Melech. "Thank you, my friend."

"Ride!" the big man yelled. He might have been grinning.

Shem pulled the horse around to face the road ahead and kicked it, hard. The horse didn't need urging. Shem held on to

Mara with one arm, the other fist clutching the saddle horn and reins as the frightened horse took off at a gallop. Shem prayed that they wouldn't fall off.

Mara could barely breathe. She lay twisted on her side, halfway in Shem's lap. Her head hung over one side of the horse, and her legs bounced against the other as the horse jerked and swayed. The front pommel of the saddle bit into her rib cage. She felt herself slipping and clutched at the horse's flying mane.

"Hold on," Shem yelled.

They thundered down the road for what seemed like forever. Finally, Shem slowed the horse by pulling back on the leather straps of its headgear. It snorted and pranced. He glanced behind them.

"Hurry, Mara," Shem said. Mara gasped as he put his hands under her arms, pulling her up to sit in front of him. "Here, throw your other leg over."

Mara pulled up the blue silk tunic, now covered in dust. She tucked it around herself and adjusted her cloak to cover her bare knees. Finally, she was sitting in front of Shem, her back pushed up against his chest. She could feel his heart pounding against her shoulder blades. Her own heart seemed to have stopped.

She looked over her shoulder at his face, so close she could see the dark stubble on his chin and feel his warm breath on her neck. This didn't seem right, it felt . . . indecent. But what could she do? They had stolen a Roman horse. If they were caught now, they would both be executed.

"What did you say to him?" she asked, although she already knew.

"What?" Shem asked, gathering the straps again and kicking the horse back into a trot.

"You gave yourself up, didn't you?"

She felt him take a deep breath. He didn't deny it—he didn't say anything.

"How could you do that?" She twisted to see him, but he

wouldn't meet her eyes. "How could I have faced Mechola if you had been taken?" How could she have gone on at all? She turned away, gripping the saddle pommels in front of her. "I never . . . I wouldn't have left you."

"Mara," he said in a sigh that drifted over her hair. "I couldn't let him take you. I couldn't even stand to see him touch you."

Instead of joy, his admission filled her with sadness. Once she'd hoped against foolish hope for tender words from him, but now she knew she could never accept them. They galloped up a hill, then down.

Silas, the soldiers, Ezekiel's boat, and the soldier again. This wasn't the first time on this journey that they had escaped capture. And it wasn't coincidence. It was the hand of the Almighty. He was giving Shem another chance.

"Can't you see it, Shem?"

"See what?"

"It's the Taheb. He saved you."

"It looked to me like a band of lepers saved us."

The horse snorted and shied from a shadow. "Shem. They were looking for Jesus. They helped you. And before, with Silas, we barely escaped. And on the boat. Can't you see? They were all miracles."

"Mara. That is absurd. A band of lepers and a mad Greek doesn't mean anything. I'm not being called anywhere. I'm being chased. Stop trying to convince me. Jesus called the wrong man. I'm not who he thinks I am, and I'm not going to Jerusalem. I'm going to Sychar. And I'm staying there." Shem nudged his heels into the horse's sides, and they broke into a gallop.

The thought of home filled her with dread. What waited for her there? Her mother, dead. Outraged villagers who would condemn her to a life of shame. How could she tell him to go to Jerusalem when Sychar without him would be like exile into the desert?

His arms tightened around her as they passed through Nain. A few women at the well craned their necks to watch them pass. He relaxed when the village was behind them.

She would have to let him go. Somehow. He had been called by the Taheb. *Pray. And do not be afraid when the time comes.* "Shem?"

He grunted in her ear.

"What would it take to get you to go to Jerusalem?"

"Mara," he sighed like she were a very ridiculous child, "it would take a miracle."

A miracle. They'd been given many miracles already, but he refused to see them. *Please Lord, give him the miracle that he needs to follow the Restorer. And give me the strength to let him go.*

She breathed in his warm smell of cedar and sandalwood and settled more comfortably into the saddle. The horse swayed in a steady gate, and her eyes drooped. Shem held her tight against his warm chest, and his breath touched her cheek. She would let him go. She would make him go. But for now, she let herself relax in his arms.

Shem checked over his shoulder for the hundredth time. The road behind was shadowed and empty. They had stolen a Roman soldier's horse. If they were caught, they would be killed on the spot. He didn't think that he could be in any deeper trouble, yet here he was. And this time, he'd brought it on Mara as well. But what else could they have done? The lepers could only hold off the soldier for a while, not long enough for them to gain any distance on foot. They hadn't had any choice.

The Sabbath horns blew, and the dark wrapped around them. *Add yet one more to my list of sins: traveling on the Sabbath.*

Mara curled up against him, her body limp, her head bobbing against his arm. His other arm wrapped around her, holding her upright in the saddle. How could she sleep at a time like this?

Now he had to find a place to get rid of the horse before they got too close to Sychar. He didn't want to lead more soldiers to Mechola and Abahu. Or to Mara.

At least they could travel fast for now. The horse's stride was strong and steady. He seemed not to even notice his two passengers. Mara was lighter and thinner than he had even guessed, all hollows and bones. She must have gone without food more often than she admitted.

He'd never been this close to any woman. His arm wrapped around her, easily circling her ribs. He could feel her hip against his leg, and her bare calf rubbed against his. The rise and fall of her breath merged with his own. He dropped his chin enough to feel her soft hair against his cheek; it smelled faintly of almonds and myrrh.

"They were all miracles," she'd said. What was she talking about? Why was she so sure that he should follow the Taheb? How could she ask him to give up everything he'd just found? And for what? To follow a false prophet? *No. She's wrong. She's distraught over her mother.*

He thought about marriage to Mara; he'd thought of almost nothing else since Capernaum. He could make her so happy. She would never have to worry again if there would be enough food or a man to teach Asher a trade. They would be content raising olives and children.

But—maybe she didn't even want him. He'd been arrogant, rude—had even ridiculed her. He wouldn't blame her if she was glad to be rid of him. He hadn't been so rough on her that she would refuse him, would she? A worm of doubt made him flinch. Surely she knew how he felt about her? He'd talk to her before they got to Sychar, before they saw her mother. If Nava was dead—and he feared she was—Mara would need him more than ever.

He'd talk to Uziel tonight, and they could be betrothed tomorrow. He might get Uziel to agree to a short betrothal. They could be married within months. Then she'd understand why he didn't want to follow Jesus. He looked at her peaceful face nestled into his arm. For now, she could sleep. He pulled lightly on the reins, and the horse slowed its pace. No need to gallop all the way to Sychar.

Chapter 31

Mara climbed the hill outside Sychar, close behind Shem. They had left the horse outside Sebaste, tired and grateful for grass and a drink from the stream. Then they had crept away and followed the path east.

When they passed the little house in the valley, it was dark and deserted. Nava and Asher must be at Uziel's house. What would she find there? Her stomach twisted like the tangle of roots at her feet. Whatever it was, she would accept it. This journey had been for Shem. She knew that now. But because of her, Shem had closed his ears to the Taheb. Now she would have to help him hear the call. And then she would say good-bye.

A rustle in the dry branches on the lower slope halted her.

Shem froze and raised his hand to his lips.

She scanned the trees. A wild animal? Or someone from the village up to no good in the middle of the night? All it would take would be for just one person to see them together. Her heart hammered. She could not let that happen. They were so close.

But the olive grove slept, silent and empty.

Shem moved away from her. "Just the wind. Come on."

When they were almost in sight of Uziel's home, Shem took her arm and guided her to one of the old trees. "Mara, sit. We need to talk."

What did he want to talk about? She was certain she knew. This was her chance to change his mind—about her and about the Taheb. She slid down, her back against the trunk and her knees pulled up.

He knelt in front of her with a flicker of a smile. "We met the first—no, the second time—right here."

She remembered. She had been crying then. "Shem, you don't need to worry. I won't say anything, to anyone." She wouldn't say a word about their journey. Shem had to be free to leave for Jerusalem.

"Worry? I'm not worried, Mara." He took a great breath and reached for her hands.

She should pull away. With him so close, her thoughts were jumbling inside her head. His hands were so warm. She hadn't even realized how cold she was.

"Mara, I need . . . I want you to understand something." He kept his eyes on their hands. "I told you that I've learned the laws of the Samaritans and the Jews. I know the philosophies of the Greeks and Romans. But they were just meaningless words. I have never . . . truly believed in anything. I have never—had never—found anything that makes me complete, that I can truly love with all my heart. Until now."

She closed her eyes. *Please, let it be the Taheb that you love with all your heart.* But she knew it was not the Taheb. Not yet.

He gulped another big breath and squeezed her hands. "You, Mara. I love you. And I want you to marry me."

Mara pulled away. But he held her hands, and the sturdy tree trunk pressed against her back. Even as her suspicions were confirmed, disbelief whispered through her—men like Shem didn't love girls like her. Even as sadness told her she could not accept him, joy sang out too. He loved her, maybe even as much as she loved him.

The ripple of sadness grew to a roar. He was not for her. He might have given her his heart, but his soul was meant for the Taheb.

She didn't speak, couldn't even form a word.

"I have been watching you since we met that night, here." His dark eyes flicked away and then back to her. "I had planned—hoped—to ask Uziel's permission to marry you. That is, if you were willing. I know I'm not always the easiest man to be around . . ."

A choked protest came from her throat. That wasn't it. That wasn't why she had to say no. *But how can I make him understand?*

"I just . . . want to stay in Sychar with you, become an olive grower . . . have children."

Her face warmed at the thought of Shem's children. Her children. Little boys that looked like him and little girls that looked like her. A house of their own. A man to teach Asher. A lifetime with Shem. But a lifetime knowing that she had taken him from the Taheb? That he had turned his back on his people?

They could not marry. Not now. Probably not ever.

"Your time will come soon. Your suffering will be united to mine."

Shem must go to Jerusalem with a free heart, not one tied to her. A heart for the Taheb. She must give him up completely. And he must give himself completely to Jesus. It was the only way.

He pulled her hands to his heart. "Mara, we can be betrothed tomorrow. I'll speak to Uziel. I promise to be a good husband. Will you be my wife?"

Her heart fluttered like a captured bird. She slipped a now-warm hand from under his and brushed a soft black curl from his temple. Her fingers trailed over the furrow of the scar, down his beardless cheek.

"He will be named Stephen, and he will be the first of many." She could not say yes. But how could she say no? "Shem, I do love you."

He pressed his cheek into her hand and closed his eyes.

"But, Shem, I can't—"

A shout ripped her gaze from Shem.

"There they are!"

A scattering of torches flickered on the lower slopes.

Shem lunged to his feet, then pulled Mara up. "Stay behind me."

The torches converged and headed toward them. Mara looked behind them at the dark summit of Mount Ebal. They couldn't find them. Not now. She pulled on Shem's hand. "We have to run." She stumbled two steps toward the upper slopes.

"Stay there!" an angry voice shouted.

Shem grabbed her arms. "Mara, don't run. They'll only be worse. Don't worry. I'll take care of you." He pushed her partly behind him and faced the approaching men.

No. You can't. But the torches were almost there. She could see faces now, flickering in red and yellow light, like demons. Amram, Jonothon, Zevulun, and Shimon. *Please, Lord.*

Amram reached them first. "There they are! I told you they were together."

Jonothon came next. His hair stood out from his head in wild clumps.

"I saw them," Amram huffed as though he'd been running. "They were lying together."

"You lie." Shem stepped toward Amram with a closed fist.

Amram lowered his flaming torch at Shem.

Jonothon pulled Amram back. "Shem, grandson of Abahu, do not shame your grandfather. Have you," he jerked his head toward Mara, "and Nava's daughter been alone together?"

No, Shem. Don't answer him. Mara closed the neck of her cloak with a tight fist under her chin.

Shem raised his chin and stepped forward. "Yes."

"For how long?"

"Three days."

Amram crowed. "I told you."

Shimon spat on the ground in front of her feet. "She is just like her mother."

"Let us see the woman," said Jonothon.

Zevulun's hand snaked around Shem and closed over Mara's arm. He pulled her into the circle of men and tore her cloak from her shoulders. The blue silk dress glowed in the torchlight, and the gold clasps flickered against her bare skin.

"What is this?" His eyes narrowed. "Have your turned yourself into a Greek whore?"

Mara locked her shaking knees and crossed her arms over her pounding heart. Her tongue stuck in her dry mouth. She knew what she looked like. But what could she say that wouldn't make things worse?

"Take these two to the synagogue and wake the men. Let's put an end to this." Zevulun closed a fleshy hand around Mara's wrist and twisted. She cried out and stumbled as he pulled her down the slope.

"Let her go!" Shem shouted.

Amram jabbed Shem in the back.

He turned on the boy. "Don't touch me. I'm going."

They marched down the hill and into Sychar's empty marketplace. The sky was lightening behind Mount Gerizim, but the village on Mount Ebal was still dark and cold.

Shem scowled over his shoulder to Jonothon. "I demand that you get my grandfather and Uziel. And Yahokeem." Maybe the old priest would calm these men down.

Jonothon didn't answer.

Shem's longer stride brought him up behind Mara as they climbed the worn path to the synagogue. Her head was down as she stumbled behind Zevulun. New anger flared at the men's accusations. Marriage to her was no punishment. This way, they would just be married sooner. But it was more than that to Mara. She would always have the stain of shame upon her. Just like her mother. *Don't worry, Mara. I'll make it up to you. And, somehow, I'll make these men pay.*

The synagogue was cold and dark. The men slipped off their shoes but didn't wash their hands in the cisterns. Amram circled the main room, setting the wall torches ablaze with his own. Soon the room was full of light, smoke, and the smell of burning animal fat.

Zevulun pulled Mara to the front and shoved her up on the dais.

Shem stepped up beside her. Her lips trembled, and a sheen of perspiration shimmered on her face. "Don't worry," he said. In a few minutes, they'd be betrothed.

Mara's chest rose and fell like a trapped animal. She didn't speak as townspeople trickled through the doors in rumpled tunics. Zevulun's wife and son. A dozen more men and women that he didn't know.

Where was everyone else? Abahu and Uziel?

Yahokeem and Jonothon came forward dressed in their priestly robes. Yahokeem settled on a bench. Jonothon approached Shem. "Who will speak for you?"

"I will speak for myself. But we will wait for my grandparents and Mara's uncle."

"We will do this now, before the Sabbath prayers." Jonothon moved to the center of the dais. He prodded Mara to stand at his left, Shem at his right. "Shem, son of Ezra. Answer me. Were you alone with this woman, daughter of Nava, during the last three days?"

Ah, there was his grandfather. Abahu and Mechola pushed through the doors and made their way to the front of the synagogue. Abahu's brow was furrowed, and his mouth was turned down. Mechola rushed toward Mara, but Amram stepped in front of the dais with crossed arms.

Shem faced Jonothon. "I take responsibility for this girl. She is not to blame."

"But were you alone with her. Overnight?"

"Yes. We traveled together. But she is—"

"Fornicators!" Zevulun pointed to Mara. "She is a disgrace. Just like her mother."

"No, I—"

"You." Jonothon turned to Mara. She seemed to shrink into herself. "Come here." Mara stepped back, her head down and her arms curled over her chest. Jonothon nodded to Amram. Amram grabbed a handful of Mara's hair and yanked her toward the priest.

Mara made a sound like a wounded animal.

Shem started forward. *They can't treat her like this.* Zevulun caught his tunic and wrenched him back into place.

"You, Mara, the daughter of Nava. You are a shame to us, as your mother was. You're nothing more than a whore. Just like her. You deserve to die as she did."

Mara's face drained of color, and she slumped down, her legs buckling beneath her.

That was enough. Shem jerked himself away from Zevulun. He rushed at Jonothon and was on him before anyone could react. He landed a fist in his face. Hands pulled him off the priest and threw him to the ground.

He crawled to Mara and pulled her into his arms.

"She's dead," she sobbed into his neck.

I'm sorry. Mara, please forgive me.

"Get away from her!" Amram dragged Mara away.

Two shepherds hauled Shem a few paces away and pulled his arms behind him. A rope tightened around his wrists.

Jonothon scrambled up, wiping his bleeding lip. "Keep him under control." The shepherds wrapped strong hands around each of his arms.

Shem struggled to control his breathing. "You cannot stone her. That is not the law."

Jonothon raised a hand. "I said she deserved to be stoned. But the Almighty is merciful. The law says that a man found guilty of fornication with a maiden shall marry her. He can never divorce her." Jonothon pointed to him. "You will be saddled with this disgraceful woman for all your life, Shem ben Ezra."

His heart leaped. "I am glad to marry her. And honored to have her as my wife. Bring out the marriage contract, and let us be married tonight. Right now."

Shouts went up from the crowd.

Mara closed her eyes and slumped to the ground.

Shem strained against the shepherds, but they held tight. *She mourns her mother. Mara, I promise to make it up to you. I will be a good husband. We will have a good life together.*

Amram pulled at Mara's arm, but she didn't rise. Zevulun took the other arm, and together they pulled her up. She sagged between them, her hair covering her face.

Jonothon raised his arms over Mara. His eyes traveled over her Greek dress, her bare shoulders, and his mouth twisted. "Mara, daughter of Nava, you are ordered to marry Shem, son of Ezra, for your shame. The Lord is merciful, woman. It is a better marriage than you deserve."

He turned to Shem. "Shem ben Ezra, you—"

"No."

Shem jumped like he'd been hit. The word was small, but as deadly as a stone thrown from a sling.

Jonothon turned to Mara, his mouth still open. "What?"

Mara raised her head. She freed her arms from Zevulun's and Amram's slack hands and pushed her hair away from her face. Her green and gold eyes reflected the torchlight as she turned them on the priest. "No. I will not marry him."

Mara kept her eyes on Jonothon. She could not look at Shem.

Shadows stretched high on the walls. At least twenty men and as many women stood in shocked silence. Her knees threatened to buckle. Her breath came in short gasps. *I couldn't save Mama. But I won't let this happen. He cannot marry me. Lord, give me the courage to stop this.*

"No, I will not marry him."

"Mara, what are you doing?" Shem sounded betrayed.

I'm sorry, Shem. He had told her he loved her. He must think she didn't love him. But she did. So much that she had to do this for him.

"But you must. It is the law!" Shem said.

She steadied her breathing. She couldn't stop now. "No. It is the law that you must marry me." Was she right? Could she refuse him?

Jonothon frowned at Yahokeem. "Is that true?"

Yahokeem rose from his bench and shambled to Mara. He leaned close and spoke so low that she had to watch his lips to understand him. "Child, you must marry him. If you refuse, it will go badly for you. Marry him and you will live."

"What is it? Can she refuse?" Jonothon shifted toward them.

Mara clenched her teeth. She must do it. Whatever the consequences.

Yahokeem turned to the other priest. "If she refuses, we go to the unmarried men of the village. If none will take her, then she is the same as an adulteress. She will be stoned."

"No, Mara! Don't do this." Shem struggled against the men who held him. "You know I want to marry you. You said you love me. Mara, look at me!"

She did. That was a mistake. His face was pale, his mouth a grim slash. His dark eyes were bright with unspilled tears. Her own tears welled up and ran down her cheeks.

Do not be afraid when the time comes. "I do, Shem. But I will not marry you."

"Enough!" Jonothon turned to the crowd. "Is there a man in this room who will take on Mara, daughter of Nava. She will receive no bride price, for she is no virgin. She is a fornicator and a disgrace."

"Wait!" Shem dropped to his knees. "Please, Mara."

Mara pulled herself up. She stood in the center of the dais like a lamb offered for sacrifice. She was not afraid of these men. She had chosen her fate, and now she would trust in the Almighty.

Shimon yelled out. "She is a whore like her mother. And stubborn. We all saw that."

Shem pulled toward her, his neck taut with strain, his mouth working but silent.

Amram paced in front of her. He leered at her and flicked a finger at the gold clasp on her shoulder.

No, please not Amram. She swallowed and tipped her head up.

"I wouldn't take her if you paid me the bride price." He laughed and hopped off the dais to snickers from his friends and some of the other men.

Mara scanned the crowd. Would no one help her? Her gaze stopped on Jobab. He was ancient—wrinkled and stooped. But if he would still take her, she would marry him. He stepped up on the dais.

When Shem saw him, his back stiffened, and he lurched back to his feet. He sucked in a breath. "No. No, Mara."

"I need a son." Jobab's eyes rested on her exposed neck and shoulders.

She raised her face to him. *If he is to be my husband, so be it.*

"But not badly enough to marry a whore." Jobab spit in her face.

She flinched as his saliva hit her and slid down her cheek. Relief weakened her limbs. Or was that fear?

Shem struggled against the ropes on his wrists and stepped toward Jobab. Amram pulled him back.

"None will take her. Let us end this. Now," Zevulun called out.

Jonothon raised his hands, and the people quieted. Was that Mechola weeping?

"Mara, daughter of Nava, you are condemned to death by stoning."

Jonothon's words hit her like a kick in the belly. Her legs would not support her for a moment longer. She crumpled onto the hard wood dais. *Lord, give me the strength to do this.*

"Bring her."

Amram dug a hand into her hair and yanked. Pain bolted through her. She saw only a sea of faces, heard a swell of voices. Shem, throwing off the shepherds, lunging for her. Shem on the floor, bleeding. Shouting men, crying women.

She stumbled and lost her footing. Amram caught her wrist, twisted it, and pulled. The sea of faces blurred; the voices roared. *Let it be over quickly.*

Chapter 32

Shem's head smacked against the hard wood, and he tasted blood. He pulled his knees to his chin and slipped his tied hands under his feet. If he could get free, he could help her. He brought his hands to his mouth and worked at the knot with his teeth. He wouldn't let this happen again. Not to Mara.

A shout rang out from the back of the room. "Stop!"

Shem raised his head. He jumped to his feet and off the dais, pushing people out of the way with his bound hands.

Mara was free. She stood wrapped in Uziel's arms, her face buried in his shoulder.

Amram lay on the floor, blood spurting from his nose.

Noach stood over him, rubbing his bony hand.

"What is this, Noach?" Jonothon stalked to the old shepherd, blood still trickling from his mouth. "We have pronounced her punishment. Do you have anything to add to this trial?"

"He doesn't." A deep voice came from near the door. "But I do."

Enosh strode through the scattering crowd. His chest heaved. His hair stood out in wild tufts. He had no belt over his tunic.

"He can talk?" Adah's whisper carried through the silent room.

The men stepped back, their mouths hanging open.

The crowd parted as Enosh passed Noach. Uziel brought Mara to the front, and Shem followed. He stepped close to her, but she kept her face hidden in Uziel's cloak. Abahu and Mechola moved to his other side. Noach and his sons pressed behind him. *Finally, some help to stop this travesty.*

Enosh jumped up on the dais. He looked different, older than when Shem had seen him just three days ago—taller and broader as he turned to the crowd. What had loosed the quiet young man's tongue and put fire in his eyes?

"You stiff-necked people," Enosh said. His deep voice carried to the far corners of the synagogue. Men stopped talking and turned shocked faces toward him. "I have lived here with you all my life. I have listened to you in this synagogue, in the market-place. You talk, but your words mean nothing. You say that you live by the law. You punish according to the law. I say, it is not the laws of God that you obey, but your own."

Murmurs rippled through the center of the room. Women along the sides turned to each other and whispered.

Zevulun raised his hand in a fist. "Who are you to—"

"Silence!" Yahokeem pointed at Zevulun. "Let him speak."

Enosh bent his head to the old priest and waited for the whispers to cease. "You wait for the coming of the Restorer. Yet you did not heed him when he came. You have eyes, but you did not see. You have ears, but you did not hear. His message was not of punishment, but of mercy. You ate bread with the man, you drank wine together, yet still you threw him from your synagogue."

Shem could see the people around him tense. No. Bringing the Jew into this was a bad idea. *That won't save Mara.* What was Enosh thinking?

Jonothon barged forward. He grabbed Mara by the arm and yanked her away from Uziel. "The Jew is gone, and good riddance. What does this have to do with the girl?"

Enosh didn't move, but Shem saw his hands close in fists. "I'll tell you." His light brown eyes swept the now-silent crowd. "People of Sychar, three days ago you stoned a woman—an adulterous woman—right outside this synagogue."

Zevulun yelled out. "She deserved what she got!" Next to him, Shimon and some of the other men nodded their heads.

There had to be thirty men against them. Too many to fight if they turned against Mara. Shem worked on the knots. What was Enosh getting at? That there had been enough death in Sychar?

If Enosh's argument fell on deaf ears—and it would with these stubborn people—they would have to fight their way out of here. Mara would not endure Nava's fate. Not if he was alive to stop it.

Enosh pointed to Zevulun. "Perhaps she did. Perhaps she received exactly as the Lord thought she deserved."

Zevulun puffed himself up. "Yes, that is what Moses told us. And she admitted to her sin. Her punishment was just as the law required. The law of the Almighty."

Enosh shook his head. "No. What happened here was not the law of the Almighty."

Men near the front murmured and stepped toward Enosh. Over his shoulder, Shem saw raised fists and angry faces. The crowd pressed forward.

He finally speaks, and his words will get him killed. He is going to be dragged out of here and beaten. That won't help Mara.

Enosh stood his ground. He swept his hand over the room, stopping on Jonothon. "What I saw that day was the law of Zevulun, the law of Shimon, the law of this priest."

He took a deep breath and spit his words at the crowd.

"No. It was not the law of God that I saw. It was the law of revenge."

Enosh's words hit Shem like a lightning bolt. *He's talking about me.* He froze as the last knot came loose and his bonds fell to the ground. *I'm just like Zevulun. Just like my father. I tell myself that I want justice, but I want revenge. I do not follow the law of God, but the law of Shem.* Another thought nagged at him. Had his desire for revenge deafened him to another call? The call of Jesus? That call that Mara had heard but he had not?

Outraged cries split the air.

"Blasphemy!"

"How dare you?"

Enosh stood tall.

How did this man—barely a man—see so clearly, when Shem was all but blind? *I am no better than the men that killed Nava.*

Enosh stepped off the dais.

What was he doing? The men surged toward him. Shem

spread his arms to hold back the crowd. Abahu and Uziel pushed back with him.

Enosh bent close to Zevulun, but his words rang out clear and strong. "Let us remember your very words in this room, Zevulun. 'If she has sinned, the Lord will see her punished. If she is forgiven, he will save her.'"

The angry cries dwindled; faces pinched in confusion. Men stepped back as Enosh walked toward the anteroom.

Where is he going? Shem followed the tall young man with his eyes but stayed close to Mara. They could still turn on her at any minute, just as they did with her mother. As Enosh passed the anteroom and pulled open the outside door, the weak light of dawn made an arc of gold in the shadowed room. He stepped back.

Exclamations pulsed through the crowd.

Through the wide door, with the morning light glowing behind her, came Nava. Beautiful and whole. Not a scratch on her face or arms.

"Look," Enosh said, taking Nava's hand and pulling her into the room. "Look at his power and forgiveness."

No. It couldn't be. She had been almost dead. He had seen her, not three days ago. *But she is healed. He healed her.*

"Mama!" Mara stepped out, but Zevulun clamped his hand around her arm and jerked her back.

"Zevulun," Nava said, "take your hands off my daughter."

Zevulun's chin disappeared into his neck.

Mara broke free, then froze as Nava turned back to the door and held out her hand.

Asher stepped into the room, his hand clutching his mother's, his eyes searching the crowd. "Mara!" He dropped his mother's hand and ran—*ran*—across the rough stone floor. His legs moved in a blur. He leaped into Mara's arms.

The crowd, silent as Asher had sprinted past them, burst into a flurry of sound and movement.

What just happened? Shem rubbed a hand over his eyes. Asher had run to Mara—in the blink of an eye. Asher, who had never walked faster than a tortured limp, had jumped into Mara's arms.

Mara struggled to untangle herself from Asher's embrace. She crouched down and stood him on the ground.

Shem pushed up Asher's tunic.

Mara gasped and dropped to her knees.

The boy had two plump, strong legs. He had perfect, straight feet. He had ten matching toes. Shem wrapped his hands around the leg that had been so thin and twisted. It was firm and warm. A miracle. But from Jesus? She hadn't asked Jesus for this.

Asher bounced out of his grip.

"Mara, Mara, I run fast now!" he said, his voice high and breathless.

Mara's breath was ragged, as though she was about to cry. Or laugh. Nava reached her, and Mara threw her arms around her mother. Enosh stood behind them like a guard.

Zevulun blustered. "This is the work of the devil!" His face turned red, and his eyes darted wildly from Nava to Asher.

"Speak not of the devil!" Yahokeem rose from his bench, pointing his gnarled fingers at Zevulun. He hobbled to Asher. "The devil does not heal; he only destroys. Let me see them." He bent and ran his wrinkled hand over Asher's leg. He turned to Nava and touched her smooth face.

She stood tall, her chin raised.

"Tell us, Nava. How did this happen?"

Nava slipped her arm around Asher. "It was Jesus. He is the Taheb. Mara went to him," she held out her hand to Mara. "You found him, didn't you?"

Mara nodded.

Shem caught her eye. She'd found him. But she didn't speak to him. Didn't ask him to heal Nava, let alone Asher.

Nava took Mara's hands and helped her up. "Yesterday morning—just after sunrise—I woke up. I felt a joy, a heat rushing through me . . . I can't describe it. My wounds were gone."

Just after sunrise. Just as they had found Jesus in Capernaum. Jesus the Taheb. A shiver passed through Shem. His hands started to shake, and his knees weakened.

Nava was smiling now. "Then I saw Asher—running and

jumping! I knew that it was a miracle. And when they told me where you had gone," she looked to Ruth and Uziel, "I knew you must have found him."

Mara gripped her mother's shoulders. "Both of you. He knew. Without me saying a word. Mama, he answered the prayer of my heart."

Shem's body shook as if a thunderstorm rumbled through him. He fell to his knees. *No, this couldn't be happening.* But Nava and Asher were healed. Yesterday morning, Jesus had healed them from Capernaum. And she hadn't even asked.

Asher skipped in circles around his mother and sister. "My leg was hot, Mara!" his words tumbled out. "I thought I was burning! I woke up and my leg was hot, and I looked down at my leg, and it was different, and I got up and, and . . . I *ran!*" His eyes went big and round.

Women craned their necks. "How can this be?"

"Let me see!"

Men pushed forward, their faces full of wonder. "The boy is healed."

"It is a miracle."

Shem couldn't breathe. The room spun around him. Nava and Asher were both restored. If Jesus was the Taheb . . . Shem thought of his disbelief and cringed. But if he was, then the things Jesus had said—all of them—were true. He had told Shem to go to Jerusalem. But why him? What did Jesus want from him? And what was wrong with him? He should feel joy—the Taheb, the Messiah, has come! But all he felt was very afraid.

"I have prepared a place for you." What did that mean?

"You will be called Stephen, and all generations will remember you." Why?

God changed Abram's name to Abraham; Jacob had become Israel. They were important men, part of the history of God's people. But Shem? Why him? And why now, when he'd found everything he wanted here in Sychar?

And what about the rest of what Jesus had said? The words that made Shem's heart hammer and his mouth go dry? The words he hadn't told Mara. *"The blood of those who believe in me will be the water that nourishes my Church."* What did that mean?

A hand on his shoulder steadied him. Mara. Tears glistened in her eyes.

Jesus was the Taheb and had called him—commanded him—to go to Jerusalem. He had changed his name. But Shem was afraid. Jesus had chosen the wrong man. He was a sinner. A killer. He would fail the Taheb just as he had failed Nava. Just as he had failed Mara.

Yahokeem turned slowly to the crowd. "The Lord has indeed made his judgment on this woman. She accepted the punishment for her crime, and he has shown her his mercy and forgiveness."

Zevulun pushed forward. "What? Forgiveness! She's nothing but a—"

Yahokeem cut him off with a raised hand. "Let no man question the Almighty."

Zevulun closed his mouth, but his face turned a darker shade of red. "This is all well and good, but this girl is still a fornicator." Zevulun jerked Mara out of her mother's arms.

Shem jumped to his feet and knocked Zevulun's hands from Mara. Jesus never said that he had to go to Jerusalem alone. They could go together. He could even face the Taheb if he had Mara by his side. He gathered her hands in his. "Mara. Marry me. Please."

Mara tried to step back, but she was surrounded. Zevulun beside her, Amram behind. Uziel and Nava—all of the townspeople—were watching him beg Mara to marry him. The men murmured; the women whispered. *I don't care. I won't lose her.*

He rubbed Mara's cold hands. "You were right; he is the Taheb. We'll go to Jerusalem together. Look," he pointed to Nava and Asher, "look, your mother is well. And your brother. They will be safe, won't they, Enosh?"

Enosh stepped back and swallowed, then nodded. He had lost his voice as quickly as he'd gained it.

"Please, Mara. Please marry me and go to Jerusalem."

Mara's chest rose and fell as though she'd been running.

"Shem. No. You have been called," she said. "By the Taheb, Shem. The Taheb." She slipped her hands out of his and put them on his shoulders. "That is your mission, your purpose. He needs you free to do whatever he has planned for you."

"But we can—"

"Shem." Her hands tightened on his shoulders. "I know you. I know that if I were with you in Jerusalem, you would not be free. We both have been called by the Taheb. You to go." She dropped her hands. "And me to let you go."

Zevulun yanked her away by one arm. "Enough of this nonsense. We have declared your punishment."

Nava clutched at Mara, but her grip was broken. "Shem, help her!"

"Stop him!" Amram yelled. The two burly shepherds stepped behind Shem and wrenched his arms back.

Zevulun dragged Mara two steps toward the door.

No. He would not let this happen. Not again. Not to Mara. Pain like a dagger stabbed his heart. Pain so real—why wasn't blood flowing from his side? She was right. He could not have both a life with Mara and the life that the Taheb was offering. He had to choose.

But he couldn't. He wouldn't. And so Mara had chosen for him.

How could she do it? How could she give up everything—her own life—to see that he followed Jesus? She would die at the hands of these people to make sure that he did. Where did she find that kind of courage? That kind of faith?

"No!" Shem struggled against the strong hands that held him. "Stop them!"

Nava cried out. Abahu charged after them. Uziel stumbled behind. But Enosh had already stepped in front of Zevulun.

He put his hand on the big man's chest and leaned into him. "Let her go. There is a man who will marry Mara."

"Who?" Zevulun reared back and eyed Enosh.

Enosh straightened his shoulders, but he did not look at Mara.

"Not you?" Zevulun poked a fat finger into Enosh's chest.

"You are too young to marry. You're just a shepherd boy. Where would you live?"

"I will work. We will manage. That is"—Enosh's lean face reddened as he ducked his head and looked at Mara from the corner of his eye—"if she will have me."

Shem's captors dropped his arms. He tried to breathe, but the dagger of pain twisted in his chest. *Enosh marry Mara? To save her life, I must give her to someone else?*

Mara's breath caught in her chest. Her lips parted, but no words formed.

If I will have you? The boy who chased me when I teased him about his eyelashes? Who sheared my goats and brought me wool? The boy who never spoke but saved my life with these words?

Zevulun's hands squeezed tight around her arms. Shem stood not two paces away, free but unmoving. Enosh stared at a spot just in front of her feet, his eyes veiled by those long, dark lashes. The clamor in the room faded into the background.

Jonothon reached Zevulun's side. "You will take this woman? This defiled woman?"

Enosh scowled at the priest. "I will take this woman who knows more about mercy and love than you do. I will take her, and I will give her mother and brother a home as well."

Thank you, Enosh.

Enosh finally raised his face to her. The sun glinted through the synagogue windows, turning his eyes the color of honey. "And I will pay the full bride price. Somehow, I will, if I have to sell every one of my goats to do it. She is worth that and infinitely more."

Enosh. I don't deserve you.

Enosh freed Mara's arms from Zevulun's grip. He picked up her hand and placed it on his chest. His heart beat like a hammer against her palm. His eyes met hers, and his throat jerked as he swallowed.

"Mara, I don't have much. But I give it all to you if you will have me."

High-pitched whispers coursed through the women like a fast-moving current.

Mara couldn't help it. Her gaze flew to Shem like an arrow to the heart.

Shem's jaw clenched tight, and he leaned toward her. "Please, Mara. Don't do this. Go to Jerusalem with me. You are mine, Mara."

Mara's vision blurred. She blinked, but one tear slipped out. "But you are not mine."

Shem turned to Enosh. "Enosh. Don't take her from me."

Enosh faltered and took a half step back. His grip on her hand loosened.

Mara could see doubt in his eyes. Doubt and pain. *Enosh, I will never give you another reason to doubt me.* She folded both her hands around his. "Yes, Enosh. I will be your wife."

Shem slumped to the ground.

Enosh let out a breath and dropped his chin to his chest. Uziel slapped him on the back while Nava and Mechola swooped in on Mara. Jonothon turned to Enosh. "Boy, are you sure? You can never divorce her."

Enosh straightened to his full height. He stared down at the priest. "I've never been more sure."

Jonothon shook his head and pointed to the dais. "Then let us finish this."

Uziel took Mara's arm and took her to the center of the dais. Nava put her arm around her. Ruth and Asher stood beside her. Enosh stepped up in front of her, followed by Noach.

Shem hadn't moved from his place in front of the dais, his body bent as though a heavy beam of cedar weighed on his shoulders.

Yahokeem parted the curtain behind them and opened the great carved chest. He came back with an ancient brown scroll. "In the name of the Lord God of Israel we begin and end."

The men responded in unison. "He is God, and there is none beside him."

Yahokeem spoke to Enosh. "What is the betrothal period?"

Enosh dipped his head toward Mara. "Mara will decide."

Mara jolted a step back. *Me decide?* That was the right of the groom and the bride's father. Uziel nodded to her. She could feel every ear in the room straining for her answer.

How long?

No one would begrudge her a year. A year to live with her mother and Asher. A year to mourn Shem. A year to look at Enosh and see a husband instead of a friend.

Enosh shifted beside her. His eyes went to Shem, then met hers. Was that doubt? Were they all remembering Nava's betrayal of her vow to Zevulun? Did even Enosh worry that she was like her mother?

Shem raised his head, his shoulders lifted. One year for Shem to wait and hope.

One year for Enosh to wait and despair.

The song of a single lark floated through the window.

She swallowed. Her voice must not falter. "One day."

Shem caught his breath and stiffened, as if she had just stabbed him in the heart. Astonished whispers swept through the room. Some of the men snickered.

Enosh stared at Mara for a long moment.

Will he trust me? When he knows I love Shem, will he marry me tomorrow? Never to divorce?

Enosh reached out to her. His warm palms folded around her hands, and his honey eyes searched her face. "Are you sure, Mara?"

She squeezed his hands and beheld the face of the man who would be her husband—the man she would respect and honor for the rest of her life. "I've never been more sure."

Chapter 33

The watery light of dawn seeped through the chinks in the roof of the clay house. Mara pulled Asher's warm body closer to hers. Nava slept close by, her hands thrown over her head, her hair spread out like a dark river.

Her mother and brother were safe and healthy. Tomorrow she would be waking up next to Enosh. Married. Why wasn't she happy?

Shem is leaving today.

She would never see him again.

Was it just yesterday, the Sabbath, that they had stood in the synagogue? That she had vowed to marry Enosh?

After the betrothal ceremony, she had stumbled home with Nava and Asher. Deep, dreamless sleep had claimed her weary body and mind. She woke once at midday, calling for Nava. She touched her mother's cheek, ran her hands down Asher's strong legs, and drifted back to sleep.

Again, late in the afternoon, she dragged open her heavy eyes. Golden sunlight slanted through the doorway. Was that Mechola's voice that she heard, murmuring with her mother?

"Uziel will hold the feast, of course. But Abahu has offered to provide the food and wine."

"Thank you, Mechola. But . . ." Nava paused. Mara snapped her eyes closed just before a shadow blocked the light.

Nava's steps receded. "What of Shem?" she continued. "Won't he—?"

"He'll be gone. He can't bear . . . Well, he's leaving tomorrow morning."

Now, well before dawn on her wedding day, Mara slipped her arm out from under Asher and rolled to her knees, then tiptoed past her sleeping mother. Would Shem leave her without saying good-bye? Was he going to Jerusalem? Surely he couldn't deny the Taheb still, not after yesterday. She had to know.

Even on her wedding day, they needed water. She would go to the well. Surely one of the women there would know if Shem had left and where he was going.

She scooped up the water jug and started up the path. Birds warbled in the cedar trees. Pink clouds edged Gerizim, the mountain of blessings, but darkness still weighed on Ebal, the mountain of curses. She reached the top of the hill and looked down on the village where she would spend the rest of her days with Enosh. Gratitude vied with sadness, in the way of a sunrise invading the dark sky.

She passed the village. Women stopped grinding grain to stare at her. Men leading animals turned to watch her. She forced her head up. They had no power over her now. Her lips moved over her morning prayers. The Taheb—the Promised One—had come! *Thank you, Lord. For Asher. For Mama. For Enosh.* Her throat tightened. *For Shem.*

She rounded the bend and faced the well. A few women already stood around the low wall. Rivkah and her friends, Tirzah and Adah. Of course, yesterday's events in the synagogue had yielded a rich harvest of gossip. But would they know of Shem?

The younger women huddled together, their eyes darting to her. Could she ask about Shem? No, anything she said would get back to Enosh. She would have to listen and hope they mentioned him.

As Mara sent the gourd down to the bottom of the well, Rivkah sidled up to her. "Mara," she said with a smile, as if it hadn't been ten years since they'd been friends, "you are blessed, indeed. Enosh will be a good husband, although he is so young."

Mara tried to smile back. "Thank you, Rivkah."

"All the girls are talking about it. Two men, fighting over you in the synagogue."

Was that what they thought? That Enosh and Shem were fighting over her? She pulled the gourd up from the darkness. Sychar would never change.

She sent the gourd back down as the chatter resumed around her. She heard Abahu's name, and Mechola's. But no mention of Shem. As she poured more water into the jar, a shadow fell on the well, and the talk around her halted. She looked up.

Shem stood in front of her, his familiar water skin in his hand.

Her heart jumped to her throat. His dark eyes watched her. The mouth that she knew so well curved, but it wasn't a smile. Would this be the last time she saw him?

She was staring. She glanced at the women. Every face was turned to them, every ear listening.

He held out his empty water skin.

Mara took it and sent the gourd back down the well. She couldn't talk to him. Not now, with all these women watching, ready to run back to their husbands and neighbors and report every word. Even if she could, what would she say? It had all been said yesterday in the synagogue. She poured the water in the skin and glanced at his face. His forehead was creased, his mouth pursed. What was he thinking? Where was he going?

Mara gave Shem the full skin of water, then finished filling her jar. Shem didn't move. The women around the well whispered. The girls giggled. Mara's face began to heat.

Mara lifted the jar to her head and started back along the road toward Sychar.

Shem fell into step beside her.

"Shem? I can't . . ." she whispered. It wasn't right. She shouldn't talk to him. They were still watching. She could not dishonor Enosh.

He didn't turn his head. "Shh . . . just walk with me a little."

They had traveled far together. Would one more short stretch of road be enough to say good-bye? Would Enosh understand that she had to talk to him, this one last time? Or would he doubt her again? Mara felt the stares of the silent women on her back, heard the whispers as they walked slowly down the road.

Was Shem going to Jerusalem? To do the Taheb's will? And what would that be? *"Your suffering will be united to mine."*

They rounded the curve in the road, and Shem stopped. No one could see them now.

She had to know.

She couldn't bear to know.

"Shem, tell me. Are you going to Jerusalem?"

Shem reached for Mara's water jar and set it on the dusty ground. "Yes, Mara. I am going to Jerusalem. To the Taheb. Because of you."

Her breath caught in her throat. *This is what I wanted. Why do I feel like I'll never breathe again? Shem, always willing to fight for justice, now will fight for the Taheb.* What greater battle was there? But what would happen to him in Jerusalem? She wanted to tell him to be careful, but being careful wasn't his way. She wanted to tell him again that she loved him, but that would only hurt them both.

She swallowed the knot in her throat and forced a breath past the tight pain that filled her chest. Shem had come to Sychar thirsty—for justice, for truth, for something to believe in. He had found Jesus, the living water, and now Shem would never thirst again.

But what of me? Can I drink of the living water?

The answer came like a whisper. She already had. The Taheb had restored her as surely as he had healed her mother and Asher. And now she could joyfully live the life he had given her.

Peace trickled through her, washing away the anguish of good-bye. She and Enosh would be happy. She knew it as she knew the path to Jacob's well. Her life was here, in Sychar. With Enosh and Nava and Asher. She could say good-bye to Shem now.

"I am happy for you, Shem." And she was. "Go to Jerusalem. The Taheb has chosen the right man."

Shem battled the doubt that cut through him like a sword. Could she be right? Had Jesus chosen the right man?

Mara had believed when he had refused to. It had taken a

miracle—several miracles—for him to understand. He was no better than Zevulun, than Alexandros. He thought he wanted justice, but all he'd wanted was revenge. Because all he believed in was himself.

Now, his faith was still not great. It was like a tiny mustard seed. Mara's was like a mountain—faith enough to offer her own life to make sure he went to the Taheb. And so, he would go. Because of Mara, he'd give that mustard seed a chance to grow. Jesus had claimed Shem's soul in Capernaum. Now he would willingly give the Taheb his heart as well.

He didn't deserve Mara. But Enosh did.

Shem had said his good-byes to Abahu and Mechola as dawn brightened the eastern sky.

His grandfather had embraced him. "Send us word from Jerusalem." He held Shem a moment longer, crushed him a measure closer. "I'm proud of you, son."

I promise you, Grandfather, I'll make sure you stay proud of me.

Mechola had gathered him in her arms and hidden her wet eyes on his shoulder. Shem kissed her downy cheek. "Watch over Mara for me," he whispered.

Shem had left the peaceful courtyard with a mind full of turmoil. He had come with so much. A donkey loaded with riches. A bright future in Caesarea—or at least as heir to the olive groves of Sychar.

Now he had nothing.

His father had, by now, received his message and would never speak to him again. Mara was betrothed to another. He was leaving with nothing but his cloak, his dagger, and the few coins that Abahu had given him. And to follow a man he didn't even know.

He pushed open the gate. Enosh stood just outside it, as though he had been waiting for Shem.

The boy—no, the man—who had taken Mara from him. His heart wrenched inside his chest. *Mara will marry him today instead of me.*

Shem tried to brush past him, but Enosh put a hand on his shoulder.

"Shem. She just went to the well. Go. Say good-bye to her."

Say good-bye to Mara? Could he bear it?

Enosh's grip tightened. A muscle twitched in his jaw.

He knows I love her. The whole town knows that she loves me. How can he bear that? And yet he grants me permission to say good-bye to her. Enosh would always put Mara before himself. Even before his own fears. Enosh had everything that Shem wanted. Why did his face seem to mirror Shem's agony?

Enosh stepped closer. "Shem, know this: I have loved Mara since we were children. I have hoped for this day. She is all I've worked for. I've saved every shekel for her bride price. But I thought, surely, she would marry before I could speak for her."

Shem looked away and stepped back. *I don't want to hear this.*

But Enosh didn't let go. His hand tightened, sending a jolt through Shem's shoulder. "I will be a good husband to her, Shem. I promise."

And he would be. But that didn't ease the anguish in Shem's heart.

Now Mara stood before Shem on the road where they first met. No longer a frightened, cowering girl but a woman—sure and strong and full of faith in the Taheb.

He loved her.

She would marry another man today.

He was leaving and would never see her again.

"Mara. You were right. You were right all along. You were right about Joseph." His brothers threw him down the well, sold him into slavery. He thought his life was over. But just when he'd lost everything, God gave him a way to save his people. The Taheb had finally come. Shem would follow him to the end—to death if he'd meant what he had said to Shem in Capernaum.

Shem stepped closer. "When Jesus came to Sychar, I fought against believing in him. It was ridiculous. A Jew—a carpenter—from Nazareth? A man of no learning? I ran from him. But you did not run from him. You ran toward him. You could see what I—with all my learning—could not."

Mara met his eyes. "And now? Now what do you believe?"

Shem blew out a long breath. "He is the Taheb. Just as you said." He raised his face to the synagogue on Mount Gerizim, still shadowed in darkness. "The priests said that when the Taheb came, he would show them the location of the Ark that housed the word of God. But it is not on the mountain or in Jerusalem. It is him. Jesus is the Ark." He stepped closer. "Mara, I can't deny him now any more than the Jordan can leave its banks and run through the mountains."

She nodded as though she knew exactly what he meant. "Then do what he asks of you, Shem, whatever it is."

A hawk screamed from high in the pink and gold sky.

Shem swallowed hard. "He said something else, Mara. He said, 'The blood of those who believe in me will be the water that nourishes my Church.'" *The words that terrified me.*

She brought her clasped hands to her heart. Tears spilled from her eyes and slid down her cheeks. "Unless a grain of wheat falls to the ground and dies, it remains just a grain of wheat."

She understands his words better than I do. He cupped her chin in his hand and brushed his thumb over her cheek, smoothing away the tears, as his voice dropped to a whisper. "Mara, you are not the only one who can give your life for love. You were willing to die for me—a selfish, spoiled man who didn't believe in anything. I can give my life for the Taheb if that is what he asks."

He stepped back and took a deep breath. He could do this. He could leave her now and follow Jesus. "Say good-bye to me, Mara."

She pulled in a shaky breath, straightened, and raised her eyes to his. "Good-bye, Shem. And thank you. For taking me to Jesus, for everything."

He tried to smile. "I might have taken you to Jesus, but you brought me to the Taheb."

A blaze of daylight broke over Mount Gerizim, melting the shadows and bathing Mara in its glow. Once he had seen the beauty of just her face. Now he knew that her beauty was in her courage, in her unwavering faith.

That is what he would take with him from Sychar. The courage and faith that Mara had given him.

Shem etched the memory of her into his heart, then turned and walked away. Away from Mara. To Jerusalem. To Jesus. To a new life with a new name.

Whatever Jesus has planned for his people, I will be a part of it. I will be called Stephen, and I will be the first of many.

Epilogue

JERUSALEM, 35 A.D.

Cursing and screaming, the crowd of men push me through the stone gate. Outside the walls of the city, the blue sky arches cloudless and infinite. The Promised Land stretches out in golden fields and silver-green hills.

The men in front pick up stones and throw them. The first one strikes me, heavy and sharp, tearing into my flesh. It hurts even more than I expected.

They really are going to do this—these men who hate me, who hate the Christ most of all. But I don't regret what I said; it was all true. My trial before the Sanhedrin had been unjust—a travesty. But this time, I didn't care. Jesus prepared me for this, and I am ready. Ready to be the first of many to die for him.

"Your blood will be the water that nourishes my Church." Now, finally, I understand what he meant.

Then come more blows. One jagged rock after another batters me, scraping skin, drawing blood. They rain down, their weight bruising muscle and bone. A big man in front shouts a curse and hurls a rock the size of a melon. It strikes my knee and brings me to the ground.

A shout goes up, and the enraged mob surges around me. Stones come from all sides as men surround my bent body. The rocks tear open my skin and crack my bones as I am beaten into the ground. I taste blood and dirt.

A heavy stone smashes into my temple, then another. Pain

surrounds me, engulfs me like a whirlwind of fire. I give up, lying still. A hot stream of blood runs down my face and pools next to me on the dusty ground. The sound of the crowd is drowned out by the ringing in my ears.

I bring her face to my mind one last time. *You see, Mara? I too can give my life for love.* Love for my king.

There he is, the king victorious. Sitting at the right hand of God, just as he promised. He waits, far clearer than the faces of the men around me. More real than the thud of rock on flesh and bone.

"Lord Jesus!" I can barely lift my heavy hand to him. "Receive my spirit." A rush of peace flows over me like a river of living water.

I cannot raise my head from the dirt, but I have one thing left to say to these executioners who surround me. One thing before I leave this life. I struggle to get enough air to make myself heard. "Lord, forgive them," I say as loud as I can. My mouth moves stiffly, as if in a dream. My voice is barely more than a whisper.

The angry cries quiet; the faces around me become clear. The men pause, hands raised in mid-throw, faces twisted in anger.

"Forgive them, Lord Jesus," I say again—stronger, louder. "Do not hold this sin against them."

Jesus holds out his hand, and I push myself up from the dust. It is finished.

I have fulfilled his purpose. Behind me, my body sleeps, broken and empty. Before me—stretching out as endless as the sky—is the Kingdom, the Power, and the Glory, forever.

SAINT STEPHEN, FIRST MARTYR
Ora pro nobis

Acknowledgments

Without a doubt, this book came about through the work of the Holy Spirit. Thank you, Holy Spirit, for bringing people into my life who sparked ideas, lifted me up, gave me courage, made me reach further, and helped me to persevere.

I'm thankful for my husband, who lays down his life every day for me. Thank you, Bruce, for twenty-three years—every single one of them good. Thank you to Rachel, Andy, Joey, and Anna. For some reason, these kids believe that their mom can do anything. Because of them, I believe it too.

To friends who give me courage and lift me up when I most need it: Laura Sobiech, Anne Greenwood Brown, Wendy Tarbox, and Regina Jennings. And to Wacek Kucy, who may have made this book a reality by the sheer power of prayer.

To Rachel Youngquist, sister and friend. Your wisdom and counsel sustained me many a day. Thanks, also, to my parents, Bill and Jeanette Wetzel, who measure success in faith and family. You are the richest people I know.

Thank you to my critique groups. The day I gathered my courage to read the first chapter of *The Well* to The Scribblers at Stillwater Library, I felt like this crazy dream might come true. To Robert Harley, critiquer extraordinaire, and to my SCBWI group: Wynee Igel, Pat Gilkerson, LeAnne Hardy, Celia Waldock, Sarah Nelson, Mark Zukor, and Lorenz Schrenk—thank you for your honesty, skill, and friendship. And to Loretta Ellsworth, my mentor, for spot-on advice and the kick in the pants that I needed to move forward.

Cathi-Lyn Dyck of Scienda Editorial, you are a godsend. The

story of how you came into my life and ripped my manuscript to shreds is too long for this page. Thank you, Cat, for pushing me further than I dared go.

And to you, Chris Park. How we found each other might remain a mystery, but I'm so glad we did. Every writer needs an agent like you to turn her into an author.

Finally, my heartfelt thanks go to Becky Nesbitt, Jessica Wong, and the team at Howard Books. Thank you for your wisdom, expertise, and enthusiasm. I look forward to every page we work on together.

The WELL

Stephanie Landsem

Reading Group Guide

INTRODUCTION

In the small Samaritan village of Sychar, the well is the place where women gather to draw their water and share their lives with one another—but not for Mara's family. Shunned for the many sins of her mother, Nava, Mara struggles to keep her family alive in the face of starvation and the threat of exile. Then their lives are forever changed with the arrival of two men: Shem, a wealthy young man from Caesarea with an air of mystery; and Jesus, a Jewish teacher who transforms Nava's broken spirit with his talk of forgiveness. When Nava is stoned for her mistakes, Mara embarks with Shem on a journey to seek Jesus' help—a journey that brings unexpected love and unimaginable heartbreak.

TOPICS & QUESTIONS FOR DISCUSSION

1. Nava's family is both shunned and sustained by their community. Discuss how charity is often a double-edged sword in the novel.

2. In the novel, marriage and friendships play an important part, especially for women. How has this changed from Mara and Nava's time to today? How is it the same?

3. Did hearing it from both Shem's and Mara's points of view change the story for you? Did hearing it from Nava's point of view for one chapter make you more sympathetic to her? Is there another character you would have enjoyed hearing from?

4. How would the novel be different if it were told from Nava's perspective, given that she is the most affected by Jesus' arrival? Do you think readers could sympathize with her as much as they do with Mara?

5. Jacob's well is important both as a source of water and gossip and as the site of Nava and Jesus' meeting. Is there a modern equivalent in your community?

6. What surprised you most about life in Sychar?

7. How does Shem's attitude toward the simpler life of his grandfather change throughout the book?

8. Would Mara have married Jobab if she hadn't met Jesus or Shem? Is finding a place in the community and supporting her family worth the loveless marriage?

9. When Jesus first arrives in Sychar, no one believes Nava when she says the Taheb has arrived. "Jews don't even speak to Samaritan men—never to women" (p. 108). What parallels do you see to the tensions between religious groups in modern society? Do you think the author has done this deliberately?

10. "She must make him see—he had been called by the Taheb, to Jerusalem. To do what, she didn't know any more than he did. But it was important. More important than her dreams of a life with him" (p. 235). Do you agree with her? How does she hope to accomplish this?

11. When attacked by Tirzah, Nava acknowledges her faults, even though she risks death or exile for her family. She says Jesus "did not condemn me but called me to repent and start again. He forgave me" (p. 127). Would you have the strength to admit your sins to someone out for revenge? If it meant your family might suffer?

12. Do you think Mara is right to marry Enosh, given that she loves Shem? Why, or why not?

13. Does Shem have a more difficult time accepting Jesus and his faith because he is a scholar? Discuss the differences among Mara's, Nava's, and Shem's acceptance of Jesus as the Taheb.

14. Did the epilogue surprise you? Discuss your reactions as a group.

ENHANCE YOUR BOOK CLUB

1. Discuss the story of Stephen, the first martyr of Christianity, and compare his life and death as related in the Bible to his youth in *The Well*.

2. Mara and her family survive because of the grudging charity of their neighbors. In keeping with the tradition of being a "good Samaritan," volunteer with a group that helps those in need.

3. Create a virtual trip that follows the path Shem and Mara followed to find Jesus. Imagine what their journey must have been like by researching their trail.

A CONVERSATION
WITH STEPHANIE LANDSEM

The Well is your first novel. Did your original plans for the novel differ from what you ended up with?

I was very much surprised with how the novel changed and developed as I wrote it. Research is a great source of inspiration for me. As I dug into the history and culture of Samaria, I found fascinating story elements just waiting to be used. I love it when that happens! As to the characters, they changed as well. Mara became stronger while Shem showed more of his weaknesses. Asher's role expanded, probably because I just loved him so much.

What inspired you to write the story of Mara and Shem?

When I read the Bible, I'm sometimes left with many questions. In some passages, so much of the story is not told that it seems to beg me to fill in the gaps. The Samaritan woman at the well is one of those. Who was she? What had happened to her and why? And why did Jesus stop on that day, at that particular well, and speak to her? I couldn't resist filling in the details. And when I did, there was the story that I wanted to write.

You include a lot of specific details in your novel, lending authenticity to your settings and characters. How did you conduct the research for this story?

I absolutely love the research part of writing. In fact, I can get so caught up in research that I spend days deep in books. The Internet is useful but I love finding books that are written by historians, archeologists, and anthropologists. There is nothing as thrilling as discovering that little kernel of historical detail that puts the reader right into the story, experiencing it firsthand. Besides, with piles of books all over my desk, I always have a good excuse to avoid laundry and dishes.

The characters of *The Well* travel across the ancient world from Caesarea to Galilee and Sychar. Have your own travels changed your writing? In what ways?

I've traveled since I was a teenager, and it never fails to amaze me that as diverse as people are—in language, clothes, food— we are more alike than we are different. We all search for love, for happiness and security, and ultimately we all search for God. No matter what our cultures or geography, God has given each human a hunger to find him. Like Mara and Shem, we are all on a journey to discover his plan for us, no matter if we live in Minnesota, Sychar, or Timbuktu.

Mara was often outside the community of women, though she longed to be part of it. Do you have a community you rely on, both in life and for your writing?

Absolutely, and I'm blessed that my writing and faith communities intersect so much that sometimes I can't tell them apart. My family is a huge support and always there to lift me up. Friends who have helped me through pregnancies and child rearing are now glad to be my first readers and my biggest fans. In the past few years, many of the talented writers I've met have become instant friends because of our shared love of words, but even more so because of our shared faith. Of course, my larger church community is a huge source of strength and inspiration and is where I go for spiritual rest and peace.

Was it difficult to write Jesus as a character in your novel?

Yes and no. I'm always excited when Jesus enters into the story. He's the only character who is not only real but present—here and now. I love to imagine what it must have been like for my characters to meet the Incarnation face to face. On the other hand, he's not fictional. I can guess what he looked like and imagine what he wore, but I'm not comfortable putting words in his mouth. Surely Jesus said much that wasn't recorded, but I don't want to guess what that might have been and I don't think readers want that either. So I stick to what was actually written down in the Bible.

Not much is known about Stephen the Martyr's conversion to Christianity. Why did you choose to have him encounter Mara and the Samaritan community?

That was one of my most amazing moments as I researched *The Well*. At first, Shem was just a wayward Samaritan, unsure of his faith and sent to Sychar in shame. But as I began to research the Samaritan people, I came upon a debate among scholars (scholars do tend to debate). Some Samaritan and Bible scholars, after examining Stephen's speech against the Jews in Acts, believe that Stephen could have been a hellenized Samaritan—a well-educated Samaritan from a Greek-speaking, cosmopolitan city, such as Caesarea. It fit so well with my mental picture of Shem, I still get goose bumps. We don't know much about Stephen, which is why it was exciting to imagine what he might have been like and what might have inspired a faith so strong that he was willing to be the first to die for Jesus.

Were you tempted to give Mara and Shem their happy ending?

No one wants to see their favorite characters die or be separated, even the author! But sometimes what the world considers a happy ending is different from THE happy ending: eternal life with Jesus. That is the happy ending that I always want—for my family and friends, my readers, and yes, even for my characters.

The different religions and groups portrayed in _The Well_ seem to be at constant odds with each other, from the Jews, to the Samaritans, to the Romans. Did the religious tensions of the modern world affect how you chose to portray this issue?

We've all experienced religious differences—in our communities, among friends, and even within our own families. Since our belief in God is so fundamental to who we are, I think those differences can divide us more deeply than, say, cultural or language divisions. Nava found that believing in Jesus in the midst of disbelief in Sychar required both faith and humility. Humility—not self-righteousness or judgment—is just as important today as we live among differing views of Jesus, God, and religion.

How does your faith influence your writing?

I hope that it influences everything I do, from loving my husband and kids to volunteering at school to battling the daily household mess. And so, when I sit down at my desk to write, my prayer is pretty simple: Here I am, Lord, I come to do your will.

Are you working on another book? Can you tell us anything about it?

Yes, and I'm really excited about it. It's called *Siloam* and is set in Jerusalem. Like *The Well*, it is told from two points of view and one is that of a familiar character: the red-haired Roman, Longinus. *Siloam* is about a Roman centurion looking for peace and a Jewish woman hiding a terrible secret. When a miracle at the Pool of Siloam brings them together, her secret will keep them apart and ultimately lead them both to the foot of a cross on Calvary.